THE SIXTH WORLD OF MEN

Paths of Intimate Contention

Volume 2

(Revised Edition)

THE SIXTH WORLD OF MEN

Paths of Intimate Contention

(Revised Edition)

by Walter E. Mark

Volume 2

Editor
Kurt Conrad

Editor
Marianne Thurmond

Senior Publisher
Steven Lawrence Hill Sr.

Awarded Publishing House
ASA Publishing Company

ASA Publishing Company
Nominated for the 2012 BBB Torch Award
105 E. Front St., Suite. 101, Monroe, Michigan 48161
www.asapublishingcompany.com

Copyrights©2013 Walter E. Mark, All Rights Reserved
Book: The Sixth World of Men *Paths of Intimate Contention*
Date Published: 4.29.2013
Revised Edition - *Trade Paperback*
Book ASAPCID: 2380586
ISBN: 978-1-886528-11-6
Library of Congress Cataloging-in-Publication Data

This book was published in the United States of America.
State of Michigan

A Publisher Trademark Title page

About the Revised Editions

This edition of *Paths of Intimate Contention* is a revision of the original published form of the book. Although the base storyline has not been altered, the revised edition does offer many new insights into the characters and events of the *Sixth World of Men* series. Some new scenes have been incorporated into this edition of the book and the depth of many scenes in the book has been enhanced, providing the reader with a deeper experience within the sixth world of men.

It is my sincere hope as the author that you enjoy the revised edition of this book even more than you enjoyed the original edition.

Walter E. Mark
Author of *The Sixth World of Men* series

Dedication

This book is dedicated generally to fathers everywhere who teach their children to walk in the way of God and good men. It is dedicated specifically to the memory of two fathers: Kenneth W. Mark and Douglas A. Ryburn. First, to the memory of my own father, whose only expectation of me was to live my life with vigor and integrity. Second, to the memory of the father of my wife, whose life was lived in the light of truth. The world would be a far better place if all fathers prepared the path of their children as these two fathers prepared the way for their children.

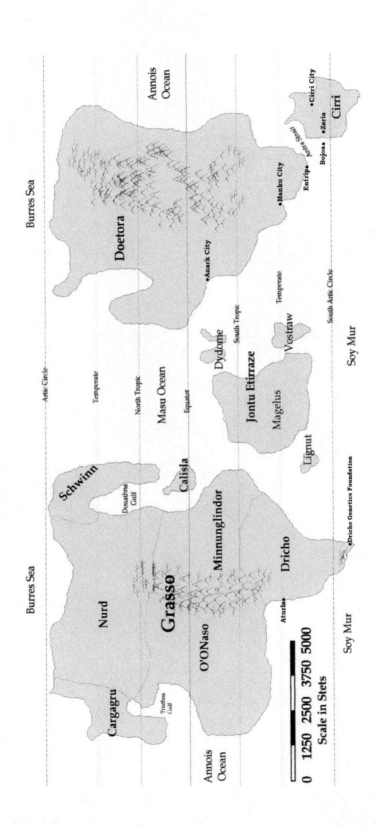

TABLE OF CONTENTS

THE SIXTH WORLD OF MEN

Paths of Intimate Contention

by Walter E. Mark

Volume 1

(Revised Edition)

Chapter One
The Envelope

In the vastness that is the universe, there are innumerable stars. Around these stars, revolve many planets. Of the unfathomable number of planets that exist in the universe, only the rarest contain life. Of the planets where life exists, only seven are planets that mankind has called home. On the sixth of these worlds, a great evil started to grow.

This evil exists only where man exists, but it is not of man. Instead, the evil stalks man wherever he is present in the universe. The power that rules the universe allowed the evil to visit the sixth world of man at its inception; but the evil could not stay, for it had dealings with the other worlds of men. Instead, the evil planted its evil as man plants a seed and waited for the opportunity to revisit the world.

The first five worlds of men suffered under the influence of the evil until mercy overruled and forced the evil to flee. Mercy forbade the evil to enter the last world of man, so evil turned to the sixth world of men to exact revenge. The evil influenced enough men in the sixth world to make war rampant for two thousand years; but then it was forced to relent, giving Kosundo a tenuous peace. But the evil still lurked; the evil still planned.

Times were changing in Kosundo. It was hard to tell what changes were for the best and what changes were for the worst. On a large continent in the east called Doetora, a man was wondering what these changes might have in store for him. His name was Abin, and he was facing destiny in the form of an envelope.

It was Diotiri morning, a moment to face destiny. Abin considered the envelope in his hands, wondering if he dared to open it. Temeos had said that he *could* open it on Diotiri morning as long as he was alone and somewhere safe. He was alone. As far as being safe, that term was relative. He was in the small town of Salu, about two hundred stets northeast of Manku City. He thought he had covered his tracks well. He had rented a flyer with an assumed name. Temeos had taught him that trick. He had flown the flyer to Garad, which was south of Manku City. He had then bought a two-wheeled, hydrogen-fueled ground vehicle called a tsik. He had ridden the tsik to Salu. He knew no one in Salu, so he thought he was as safe from the emperor's reach as he could be.

He had kept the envelope wrapped in a handkerchief in an inner pocket of a case and had never so much as looked at it since Temeos had given it to him—until now. Now he found himself staring at the envelope. Part of him wanted to tear it open to satisfy his curiosity. Another part of him wanted nothing to do with the information that Temeos had called dangerous. Still, Temeos had said it was information that he needed to know.

He sighed and put the note on the table that was in the middle of the hotel room that he had rented. The room's door was on one side of the table and the bed was on the other side. In between there was enough room around the table for a person to walk. That is what he found himself doing right now, walking around the table. He took an occasional glance at the envelope on the table; but most of the time, he was thinking about Temeos and about what might be happening in Manku City this day.

Temeos was the lord director. It was a post created about three hundred years ago by Emperor Tirenos. He had touted it as a way to streamline government. It did in a way, but mostly it just gave a way for the emperor to enforce his policies without having to go through the Edvukaat. The lord director replaced the positions of director of the Edvukaat and chief polichi. He was both the head of the Edvukaat and the enforcer of laws. He was only the head of the Edvukaat when he was present in the Edvukaat, but he would be present when the emperor desired him to be present. As lord director, he could effectively veto any decision made by the Edvukaat. It made him a powerful man, but not too powerful. He could be replaced at the emperor's whim at any moment. Temeos was able to balance skillfully the emperor's wishes with his own judgments and did it all without being replaced. He had managed this for almost all of Tryllos's reign—some eighty years he believed.

Abin had been Temeos's aide since he was just a boy. He had been eighteen when Temeos showed up at his upper school just before graduation and said he was searching for a boy to train as his aide. All of the graduating boys were assembled in lines within the school gym. Temeos walked up and down the lines, gazing intently at each boy. Some boys he dismissed right away. Others, including himself, he examined several times. Eventually, every boy was dismissed from the gym except him. He remembered that Temeos looked him square in the eyes and asked him several questions.

"Boy, are you trustworthy? Boy, are you afraid to work? Boy, can you do what you are told without question?"

He remembered being very intimidated. Yet he must have answered well in Temeos's eyes because Temeos had asked him to come to his office the day after he graduated. It was strange though; he couldn't recall Temeos ever asking him his name during his barrage of questions, although surely he must have asked at some point.

He was beginning to tire himself out by pacing about the table. He stopped and stared once more at the envelope.

After a while, he picked it up and held it up to the light stick that was on the table. The light silhouetted what appeared to be a piece of paper folded inside. He scolded himself for being such a ninny. Of course there was a piece of paper inside. He *was* expecting a note after all. He now realized he was pacing about the table with the envelope in his hand. He let out a long sigh. This was ridiculous. Finally, he made a definite decision to open the envelope as soon as he sat down. He paced for another orbit about the table, and then he pulled out one of the chairs that was neatly tucked under the table and quickly sat down.

He turned the envelope over and studied the seal. It was, of course, Temeos's seal, his official seal. The center of the seal was a beautiful rendering of the Imperial Building of State, where Temeos's office was located. A giant oak tree stood on one side of the imperial building while a huge archer stood on the other side. The oak stood for the enduring power of the empire and the archer represented the fact that Temeos was once an honored member of the armed services. Around the outside of the seal were palm branches. These symbolized prosperity. Embossed under the building were the words *Lord Director*. The white and gold of the building, the green and brown of the tree, and the red uniform of the archer stood out boldly on the silver background of the seal. Slowly, he pulled the seal off of the back of the envelope. The envelope flap rose enough to reveal the paper inside. He carefully removed the paper and unfolded it.

Dearest Abin, the letter began.

> I trust you are safe and alone since you are reading this letter. There are many things that you need to know. The first is that it was my privilege to train you in the workings of my office and the office of the emperor. You have met, and indeed, surpassed all my expectations for you. You have learned both

the roles of a servant and a leader well. I trust both of these lessons will enable you to fulfill your future duties well.

If you are reading this letter on Diotiri, as I had hoped, I will have met with a few select suvatens to discuss the evidence that I have accumulated to support a no-confidence vote in the emperor's reign. If I am successful in winning their support, tomorrow, the Edvukaat will meet in full session; and I will preside briefly until I call for the no-confidence vote. The head suvaten will then preside, and I will be the chief witness against the emperor. If all goes well, the emperor will be held in isolation according to law after discussion on the vote has started. Perhaps by the end of Treti, the emperor will no longer rule. I can only pray that Thaoi wills it.

If I cannot persuade the suvatens to act, I will go to the palace on Treti and assassinate the emperor. I know that this action might seem rash to you, but it is the only way I can hope to save the empire and Kosundo should the Edvukaat fail to act.

I now have a confession to make. I have purposefully hidden the truth from you for all these years that you have served as my aide. I have let you believe that the people who raised you were your biological parents. In fact, I know that they are not. Tryllos had your parents killed over sixty years ago when his paranoia first began to manifest itself. Your mother was Tryllos's sister, Navin. She was killed while she was still carrying you. When you were discovered living in your mother's womb, I arranged with your mother's doctor to take you out of the womb and nurture you to health. Only the doctor and I know who you truly are. You are Abinos, nephew of Tryllos and the only heir to the imperial throne. Not even the people that you know as your parents are aware of this, but in the safe in my residence, I have the papers from the doctor to prove who you are.

On Treti, carefully watch the happenings in Manku City. If you see that the emperor no longer reigns by legal vote, make haste to come to my office in the Imperial Building of State. It is imperative that you be revealed quickly so that no struggles for power are allowed to breed. On Titarti, you will be revealed. On Paraskevi, you will be the Emperor of Doetora.

If you see that I have failed, either by killing Tryllos or by my death or capture, hide yourself well. My safe will be searched, and your existence will be made known. I do not want you to be involved in a power struggle that can only end badly for you.

Please understand that what I have done and what I will do are for the good of the empire. Pray that Thaoi will preserve it.

Your servant,
Temeos

He was dumbfounded. *I am Tryllos's nephew.* That thought alone sent shivers down his back. It was no wonder that Temeos had kept this hidden. If Tryllos knew that an heir to his throne lived, the emperor would surely have had him killed.

He thought further. This meant that it was no accident that Temeos had picked him to be his aide that day in the gym. Temeos had saved his life and then trained him to be an emperor. It was obvious that Temeos always had borne a desire for him to get involved in the government of the empire one day, but he never thought in his wildest imaginings that Temeos was grooming him to be the next emperor.

Then his thoughts shifted to Temeos. Was his plan going forward or was his plan exposed? He had no way of knowing. Since leaving Manku City, he had often thought of what might be happening. Now that he knew why Temeos had made him leave, he found it more urgent to find out what might be transpiring. The news might not tell the story since the Imperial Palace controlled the news. However, no news might indicate good news. It would be hard to keep an arrest of the lord director completely secret. A news story about it might be slanted, but it would have to make the news. *Treti is tomorrow.* Temeos indicated that the vote would take place on Treti if all went well. Tomorrow would let him know about Temeos one way or another.

As far as becoming the next Emperor was concerned, he truly believed that Temeos was out of his mind. Sure, he had taught him quite a bit about the workings of the government; but that was not the same as actually making decisions. He had never had to make an important decision in his life. Temeos had always made the big decisions, although he had to admit that Temeos often explained his decisions to him.

Right now, he couldn't even imagine people calling him by a royal name. Abinos just didn't seem to be his name. He was Abin, just plain old Abin.

A stray thought caused him to wonder what Temeos's name was before he became lord director. It could have been Temen or maybe Temeon or maybe even Temeonu. He doubted it would have been Teme. He couldn't imagine Temeos ever being called Teme.

His thoughts then shifted to this stranger called Abinos. *What about Abinos? What kind of emperor would Abinos make? Is the paranoia that had afflicted so many of the emperors an inherited condition, or is it the pressure of running an empire badly that brings on the paranoia? Would he be wise enough to avoid gross mistakes and thus avoid the paranoia? Most importantly, would he be a good emperor?* He didn't know anything about this Abinos. He only knew about Abin, and Abin had no desire for power. He dreaded the thought of becoming emperor. Abinos might find the power seductive. He hoped that Abinos would not. He hoped that Abinos would still be Abin.

Treti — Treti will reveal much about the future.

Chapter Two

Isolation
And
Alienation

Time was running out; it was nearly four parzes. Degmer mentally went through the list of things that Neaotomo had told her to do. She wanted to be sure that she hadn't left anything undone. He would know if she did because he would undoubtedly probe her mind to make certain. The airlock was just down the hall. The hall was quiet. It usually was. There were no active quarters in this section apart from hers. There were no lab entrances in this hall, except for the airlock which led to the sealed labs. Still, she felt compelled to peer continually up and down the hall as she approached the alcove where the controls for the airlock were located. Once she was absolutely sure that no one was within sight, she ducked into the alcove. She took some deep breaths while leaning against the wall of the alcove, flicked her short red hair a couple times, and held her ID badge up to be scanned. Once the light on the console turned green, she opened the airlock door. The system wouldn't register her access. Neaotomo had shown her how to bypass the system's recording routine, and she had done what he had told her to do to bypass it. No one would know that anyone had activated the airlock of the sealed lab this morning. A chill went up her spine at that thought. It also meant that no one would know to look in the sealed lab for Beltram, Laysa, or her.

She entered the airlock, and a decontamination scan sequence started. That was why the airlock was there, to keep dangerous microbes out of both the sealed labs and the rest of the complex. It was also a security measure. The airlock would not open again if a nonhuman genome was encountered. This security measure was one of the main reasons why Neaotomo couldn't exit the sealed labs without help.

The scan concluded, and the airlock doors opened. Neaotomo was standing in the outer lab next to her old workstation, waiting for her to exit. He patted her down. He was probably searching for a stray medical stick or something similar. "Did you do all the tasks that I assigned you?" he demanded.

"Yes, I did. You've nothing to hold against me or my friends. I did as I was told," she said emphatically.

He smiled. "You need not worry about your friends, Degmer. Both Laysa and Beltram have been quite cooperative."

"They're already awake? Did you reduce the dosage in the lab's medical sticks?" she asked.

"No. You gave them a full dose. I used a mild stimulant to bring them around earlier this morning," said Neaotomo.

"You gave them a stimulant? That could have put them into cardiac arrest. How could you be so reckless?" she said with a gasp.

He shrugged. "The risk was minimal. They had already been under for over eight parzes when I administered the stimulant. Besides, I thought it was a risk worth taking. After all, time is of great importance to me. Their deaths would have been an acceptable loss."

"An acceptable loss? You gave me your word you wouldn't harm them if I cooperated. What gives you the right to determine that a human life is an acceptable loss?" she demanded.

Neaotomo seized her shoulders and lifted her up to his eye level. "Who gave humans the right to manipulate the genome to create a more advanced species and then try to annihilate it? I did not ask to come into being, but I have every right to protect my life by any means I deem necessary. Humans gave up their right to be well treated when they committed genocide here in this very lab," he snarled in his deep booming voice.

She could barely breathe in Neaotomo's squeezing grasp but managed to say, "More humans — were killed — that day — than your kind."

"Is that a fact, Degmer? The ten of us turned over thirty humans into something better than they were, into a species of their own with abilities like our own. This was a great gift. How were we repaid? We were slaughtered, and the humans we turned were slaughtered with us. Only a handful of unturned humans were sacrificed to slaughter us. I do not owe humanity anything but my disdain!" he roared.

"It's not right to judge — all of humanity based — on the actions of a few," she said while laboring to draw her next breath.

Neaotomo glared at her for a moment, and then his appearance softened as he put her down. She felt sure that she showed her relief visibly as her feet felt a solid surface under them again. Neaotomo let his shoulders slump and fixed his gaze on the floor.

"None of what was done in this lab was right, Degmer. They said they wanted to improve humanity — so they played with things they could never fully understand, and they created us. If I am hard on humanity, it is no harder than humanity has been on me," he said determinedly.

She found herself feeling sorry for him. She reached out and touched his hand.

He responded by squeezing her hand slightly and said, "What am I, Degmer? I am not a man, yet I am not an animal. I have consciousness but no conscience. I have this life—this existence—nothing more. I have been in the minds of humans. Humans have something more. My mind has more abilities than a human mind in this existence, but I have seen infinite possibilities in the mind of a human. Humans can exist on a plane where I cannot."

She squeezed his hand in response. She thought she would try to soothe him. "I agree that many wrong things happened here, Neaotomo. Humans did have no right fooling themselves into thinking that they could improve on creation, but it *has happened*. Whatever you are, you are here now. Why not just accept what you are and move on? Perhaps accommodations can be made for you in the human world. You don't have to live your life alone."

Suddenly, his sulk turned into rage again. He took her head in his hands and held it roughly. "I do not need any accommodations from humans, Degmer. I will make humans accommodate me. Now, I need to see if you have done as you have said. Look into my eyes," he snarled deeply.

She let out a faint gasp at the abrupt harshness, but she gazed into Neaotomo's eyes. As she gazed into those empty eyes, she lost herself in blackness. The endlessness of the darkness was terrifying and suffocating. She wanted to scream but couldn't find the breath for it. She felt a whispery touch within her being, although she couldn't comprehend it as a touch. It was a presence that was there but not there. The blackness became more intense around her until she felt that she would break into hysterical soundless crying—for she didn't have the breath to make a sound. Then light, bright

light, engulfed her being. She felt as if she were lost in the
light and searching for something—anything. Then she
sensed something; she could sense the world around her
again.

Her eyes were still focused on Neaotomo's face. His
demeanor was clinical, as if she were a specimen to be
studied. He still had not let go of her head, so his face was all
that her eyes could see.

Abruptly, he let go. She lost her balance and fell,
landing hard on her bottom. A sudden jolt of pain reverberated up her spine and then settled in her bruised posterior.
Neaotomo had turned away when he released her and didn't
so much as glance back when she hit the floor, though she
was sure he was aware that she had fallen. She picked herself
off the floor, carefully rubbing her bottom to try to soothe the
pain.

Neaotomo had gone into the main lab, so she headed
that way. When she entered the lab, she saw him sitting at a
small table on the left hand side of the lab close to a window
that looked out upon another lab.

In the lab to her immediate right were two large
dataterm circles. The terms in each circle were suspended
from the ceiling. Under the circle of terms was a circular
counter that had operating consoles embedded within it.
These circles were standing stations, meaning that the
operators of the stations stood to operate the consoles and
view the terms. She was glad that she hadn't been asked to
work at those consoles. The terms were nearly a det above her
eyelevel. Working there would have given her quite a kink in
the neck. Of course, no one worked constantly at the standing
stations, but she had seen scientists work for nearly a full parz
at a time at those stations.

There used to be a large block of workstations to her
left, but all that remained of them was the large table. The
terms and consoles that had sat upon that table had been

destroyed by hurtling human bodies and parts of bodies as she recalled. The floor by the table was still faintly stained red where Neaotomo must have attempted to clean up the blood. He must have also cleared the smashed terms and bodies from the lab at some point. The bodies were probably piled somewhere in the labs, but she was glad that they were out of sight. She had known most of those people.

Neaotomo impatiently motioned for her to take the seat across from him so she walked as quickly as she could, given the present delicate condition of her bottom.

As she approached him, something she saw through the window caught her attention. It was the bare back of a slender woman with light brown hair. The woman was sitting on some blankets that were spread out on a pedestal made up of overturned storage containers. The woman was Laysa. It had to be. She stopped in her tracks, glared at Neaotomo, pointed through the window, and demanded in a hushed voice, "What are you doing to her? You said you wouldn't harm her!"

Neaotomo was unfazed. He merely motioned again for her to sit down. She took a couple more hobbled steps and then pulled out the chair and sat down across from him, all the while glaring at him accusingly.

Once she was seated, Neaotomo spoke. "I am not doing anything to her. I merely asked her to pose for me. You interrupted our sketching session when you arrived, although I must commend you for being punctual."

She gave Neaotomo a sideways stare. "And what threat did you make against her to cause her to agree to such a session?" she demanded.

Neaotomo smiled and leaned over the table slightly toward her. "I did not make a single threat against her. Laysa and I have an understanding. She understands her place. I asked her to pose, and she agreed." Neaotomo leaned back in his chair again.

"I don't believe you," she said curtly.

"Why would I lie about something so trivial? If I did threaten to end her pathetic life, why would I not tell you? What are *you* going to do about it? But if you do not believe me, why do we not ask Laysa?" he said, getting up and walking toward the lab's door.

She didn't believe that Neaotomo was really going to let her in the same room with Laysa, so she merely watched him. As she watched, he turned and said, "Are you coming, Degmer?"

The invitation surprised her, but she quickly got up to hobble after him into the lab. Once inside, she saw the easel that he was using for his sketching angled slightly to one side in front of the pedestal. Neaotomo walked in front of the pedestal, where Laysa could see him. Laysa was sitting with her knees up in front of her. Her arms were wrapped around her legs and her head rested on her knees.

Degmer circled in back of Neaotomo, stopping where she could see the partially completed sketch. It appeared that Neaotomo was a skilled sketch artist. The sketch was lovely, even if the state of the subject matter was objectionable to her. Laysa's face flushed when she saw her settle in behind Neaotomo, but Laysa held her pose as if transfixed.

Neaotomo spoke. "Degmer has come to ask you some questions. She is afraid that you are being mistreated. You may answer her questions, but I forbid you to engage in idle conversation. Answer her questions, nothing more. Do you understand?"

"I understand," Laysa answered in a near monotone.

Neaotomo stepped back, put his hand in the middle of Degmer's back and pushed her forward slightly. "You may ask your questions now, Degmer," he said coldly.

She gave Neaotomo a worried glance and then paused to think of a good way to word her questions. She spoke to

Laysa in a soft voice. "Why are you posing for Neaotomo in this manner?"

Laysa stared pitifully at her and then glanced toward Neaotomo before she fixed her eyes on her again to answer. "Neaotomo told me to come to the lab this way. He gave me the choice of how to pose. I chose this pose to cover myself as best I could." Her voice sounded as if it were a bit hoarse.

She shook her head. It was not like Laysa to give in to any form of coercion so easily. "Did Neaotomo hurt you in any way?"

Laysa nodded, "Yes, but it was my fault. Neaotomo asked me to look into his eyes when he was doing a mind probe, but I closed my eyes instead. The pain was indescribable." She seemed to be choosing her words carefully, and there was definitely a hoarseness in her voice.

Degmer asked, "Why is your voice hoarse?" She tried to make her question sound nonchalant, but she wasn't sure she accomplished it.

Laysa simply answered, "From the screaming. I screamed a lot during the mind probe because of the pain."

She was getting frustrated. Laysa was answering the question and only the question, just as Neaotomo had told her to do. "What understanding do you have with Neaotomo?"

"Neaotomo tells me what to do, and I do it," was the reply.

"What happens to you if you don't obey?" she demanded, practically yelling now.

"Happens? Nothing happens."

She was almost in tears from frustration. "You are telling me that nothing will happen to you if you do not obey Neaotomo?" She *was* yelling now.

Laysa gazed at her as if she were terribly sorry about something, but she said, "Nothing will happen to *me*, Degmer." It seemed as if Laysa was trying to tell her something with her answer. She noticed that Laysa's eyes were swelling and that she was trying to fight back tears.

She didn't have any time to consider what Laysa's meaning was because Neaotomo immediately stepped between her and Laysa. He turned to her and said, "I think that will be enough questions, Degmer. You are upsetting Laysa. There really is no need to be yelling at her. She has answered your questions. It is time to go now." Neaotomo grabbed her arm and began to escort her forcibly out to the main lab.

She glanced back at Laysa, but Laysa didn't turn her head from her posing position. Once in the main lab, Neaotomo dragged her back to the table in front of the window and threw her roughly into the chair that faced the large window that looked out on the pedestal, where Laysa remained posed. A new round of pain came from her bruised bottom as it hit the seat of the chair. Neaotomo took a seat on the other side of the table.

"There. You have heard it from her own mouth. Laysa and I have an agreement. She is cooperating. You would do well to learn from her example. Are you listening, Degmer?" he demanded.

She heard Neaotomo, but she was not looking at him. She was staring through the window at Laysa, and she was pondering what it was that he had done to her. She seemed to have none of the spunk that she remembered in her. She was just sitting there in that ridiculous pose, dutifully waiting for Neaotomo to come back to finish his sketching. It was enough to make her want to throw up. Finally, she focused her attention on Neaotomo and replied, "I'm listening, Neaotomo. Am I to be another subject for you to sketch then? Shall I take my clothes off as well? Is that what you consider cooperation?" Her voice grew louder and more defiant with every question.

Neaotomo smiled at her and shook his head. "No, Degmer. I have no plans to ask you to take off your clothes. I may ask to sketch you one day, but I think your body would be more artistically pleasing clothed. Your body lacks Laysa's muscle tone, though it would be aesthetically pleasing with the proper attire, perhaps a nice flowing dress. However, I believe the lab has not been supplied with dresses—except for one dress worn by a woman who you left behind to die when you fled the labs," he said accusingly.

She felt a tinge of indignance over Neaotomo's comments about her body. She might not have the muscle tone that Laysa had, but her body still had some pleasing curves. Yet she felt more strongly indignant about being accused of being a coward. "I did not flee. I was ordered out of the lab," she objected.

"Nevertheless, you are alive and she is dead. The result is the same," he said evenly.

She shifted in her chair uncomfortably and gazed out at Laysa again.

Neaotomo continued. "Perhaps we can have you try on the dead woman's dress after you gather what is left of her body together with the others. I believe the trash pulverizer is working. You can gather her and the rest of the dead bodies up as your task for the day. Perhaps all of their clothes can be salvaged. You and Laysa will be needing changes of clothes anyway. Quite a few females perished along with the males. Their bodies decomposed in those clothes, but we may be able to spruce them up enough for them to be wearable."

Her stomach wrenched at the thought of stripping the dead of their clothing and then wearing those clothes. She marveled at how cavalierly Neaotomo could talk of such things. She grasped her blouse with her first finger and thumb and pulled her blouse away from her slightly as she said, "I would rather let these clothes rot until they fall off than to wear such clothes." Her tone was filled with disgust.

Neaotomo rubbed his chin and said, "I see. Well, you will gather the clothes anyway. You might change your mind in time."

"I doubt it," was her reply.

Neaotomo got up and strode over to a console situated on the nearest dataterm circle. The term displayed a map of the sealed lab complex. She turned in her seat to follow him with her eyes. He glanced at her and then back to the map.

"I have marked this map with solid red circles. Each of these forty-eight circles represents a dead body — or in some cases, pieces of dead bodies. The trash pulverizer is marked here by this green square," he said pointing to the location of the trash pulverizer. "You will carry all of the bodies to the pulverizer and destroy them one by one. After you are done, I will show you which quarters are to be yours." He turned to go back into the lab where Laysa was still posed. Just before he reached the door, he turned and said, "I expect all the bodies to be destroyed by the time I finish sketching. Undress the bodies before you destroy them. I put a table and hanging rack by the pulverizer. You can fold the pants and trousers on the table, put leg and foot wear under the table, and use the rack to hang up the tops." He turned again to go and then stopped once more and added, "I have set the alarm on the door to the outer lab. You should not try to open the door. I would hate to have to do something really nasty to you. Now go and get to work. I will not be happy if you have not completed your task before I am done." He then turned and went into the adjacent lab.

She watched as he took his seat behind the easel and again began to sketch. She felt a tinge of resentment that Laysa did not have to do such gruesome work, although posing for Neaotomo the way she was must be embarrassing for her.

She took a deep breath, got up, and studied the map on the term. There were bodies scattered all over the sealed complex. Many of the people who died here were acquaintances of hers, but the bodies were surely unrecognizable by now. Still, she had never seen a dead body in person before, but surely all of the flesh had long since rotted away from these bodies after seventy years. She hoped that would make the job a little less gruesome, although the prospect of having to gather up bones and sweep up the dusty remains did not sound very appealing to her either. She supposed that the best body to start with would be a body near a janitorial closet. She should find brooms and bags there. She found a likely body on the map. It was near a closet in the hall outside lab seventeen. According to the map, this hall could be accessed on the far side of lab four. She considered the labels on the map. Neaotomo was with Laysa in lab three. Lab four was the lab just to the right of lab three. She took a deep breath, as if it might be the last deep breath she would draw for a while, and headed for lab four.

As she walked, she couldn't help but wonder what had happened to Laysa. Neaotomo must have done something — or maybe she had done something to him. He did seem to favor her. No, that was silly. Laysa wouldn't do what she was doing without a reason, a very good reason.

She found the hallway at the other side of lab four. As she entered the hall, she found herself staring at what was left of a victim of the gas. Bones were visible, but a few parts of the body still had rotten flesh remaining on them. There was a great deal of dust on and around the bones that showed and the clothing was covered in dust as well. She was surprised to see that the fabric of the clothing was still intact. Of course, only synthetic fabrics were worn inside the labs at that time, so she guessed it wasn't all that surprising, really. Neaotomo was right. If she could get the clothes to a washing facility, they might be wearable — but the thought still disgusted her.

She carefully stepped over the body and turned down the hall to the right. Lab seventeen would be a few doors down on the right. The janitorial closet would be on the left. She tried to concentrate on the lab numbers on the doors. It was preferable to seeing the rotting bodies that littered the hallway floor every few steps. The numbers were getting higher.

Finally, she saw the lab number she was seeking and saw that the janitorial closet was across from it. That meant that there was a dead body close by. She slowly let her eyes drop. She saw the remains of a man at her feet.

She skirted the body and opened the door of the closet. She turned on the light of the closet revealing a dead body huddled against the far wall. The shock of seeing the body unexpectedly made her let out a short but rather loud scream. This body wasn't on Neaotomo's map. She wondered if he had purposely left it off the map. He most likely had heard her scream, and he was most likely grinning about it. The thought of Neaotomo having fun at her expense steeled her will and steadied her nerves.

A second inspection of the body's clothing revealed that the body belonged to the man who used to be the janitor. He must have taken refuge in the closet. His hiding place might have worked if not for the gas.

She supposed that she might as well start with the janitor's body. A creepy feeling spread over her as she gawked at the body. She remembered what the man had looked like. It wasn't anything like he looked now. Somehow, it seemed wrong to touch the man's remains with her hands. After scanning the closet, she found a broom and used the handle to poke the body in the chest. The chest crumbled in a sudden puff of dust. Out of the dust rolled the remnants of a head. It came to rest at her feet. She let out a quick yelp and jumped back a step.

Her heart nearly had jumped out of her chest so she stood holding her hand over it for a moment. Once she felt like her heart would stay in its place, she put the broom down and found the trash bag boxes. She pulled out a bag, unfolded it, and then shook the bag open. She took a deep breath and held it as she gingerly picked the broom back up and used it to roll the head into the open bag. Once the head was safely in the bag, she dared to breathe again.

She peered toward the rest of the body. The most prominent thing that she saw was the shirt; so with great hesitation, she picked up the shirt using just her forefinger and thumb. Dust and bones poured out of the shirt as she lifted it. She held her nose as the dust reached her nostrils. This was not going to be a pleasant job at all, but she would not let Neaotomo win today. She would get his dirty work done. He was trying to set her up for failure. She decided she would prove him wrong. As she shook the rest of the dust out of the shirt, some of the dust got into her throat, making her cough. The thought of what the dust had once been nauseated her, but she wouldn't let that stop her. She folded the shirt and placed it on the floor of the hall near the wall just outside the closet door. Then the pants were folded and placed by the shirt. She put the socks of the janitor into his shoes.

She found an electric broom in the closet to sweep up the dust and some bags for the bones and pieces of flesh. She also found extra bags for the electric broom; she had a feeling that many more than one would be needed. The work would be disgusting, but she would get it done before Neaotomo finished sketching his new pet. She would show him.

Back at his easel, Neaotomo examined his drawing of Laysa. It was coming along nicely, though he was not sure he would be able to get Laysa's eyes right. Her eyes were strong and bright. *Vibrant is the word for them,* he thought. He did not know if he would be able to find a way to capture the vibrancy in her eyes with just a sketch. He had made Laysa perform the actions he required; but her spirit, as the humans called it, was still undefeated. He could tell that from her eyes.

A squeal from somewhere in the lab behind him made him grin. Apparently, Degmer was having quite a time with her job.

Degmer too had a strong spirit. Still, he believed that he might have found the chink in her pulsating barrier. She was predisposed to think highly of herself. He just might be able to put a few dents in her mind's barrier—her will—by attacking her vanity. Envious thoughts concerning Laysa were also present in Degmer's mind. He would take every opportunity to tear Degmer down and hold Laysa up as her superior. She would eventually break. Even now, she was probably wondering why Laysa did not have to collect bodies and she did. She could even be stewing over the slight about her body. He hoped she was stewing. The more stewing she did, the more she would try to please him, whether or not she was fully conscious of it. Her vanity would spur her will closer to his will.

In a little while, he would finish the sketch and allow Laysa to use the exercise equipment next to her quarters. He would have to apologize to Laysa about not having laundry facilities in the sealed complex. She would not be able to wear her clothes when she exercised. He would insist, of course, that she exercise anyway. She might not even think of disobeying, since she would think that she was exercising in private. He would not tell her that he could watch her every movement in the exercise room through sensors behind the one-way mirrors that lined the room's wall.

Moreover, he would make Degmer aware that Laysa had gotten in the habit of exercising unclothed. Degmer would not know if Laysa was aware of his watching her or not. It would put doubt about Laysa in Degmer's mind. A little doubt could go a long way in the human mind. He would be sure to exploit this doubt. Degmer's barrier would crack. It was only a matter of time.

Chapter Three
Controlling Madness

Temeos had been in the palace many times before; but this evening, it was different. He was alone. He had never been in the great foyer of the palace without a crowd standing about the foyer. The foyer appeared to be so much bigger and grander when it stood empty.

He was sitting on a couch covered in tigru skin. The handmade rug upon which the couch sat was dark blue, matching the stripes of the couch perfectly. The golden yellow background of the couch stood out dramatically. The couch was situated near a wall at the center right of the foyer, as one would look upon the foyer from the large double doors that served as the front entrance to the palace proper.

All of the woodwork in the foyer was darkly varnished, which made the precious metal trimming of the room seem much brighter. There were handmade rugs under all the furnishings which were located around the perimeter of the foyer. The rugs all coordinated with the fabrics, furs, and woodwork of the furnishings that sat on them. It made for a wonderful color display for the eye.

In the middle of the foyer was the great seal of the Emperor. The center of the seal was a golden hawk sitting perched on an oak branch. The hawk was surrounded by other symbols of the empire: torches with eternal flames, crossed swords, and sunbursts encircled with seven stars. The seal itself was encircled with gilded palm branches. The bright colors of the seal were a bold contrast to the gentle blues and whites of the marble that covered the foyer floor. The ceiling of the foyer was a great gilded dome, the center of which was directly above the seal.

Presently, he heard the footsteps of the palace head servant returning. The servant had gone to see if the private dining room was ready to receive him. The man wore the traditional black suit with red trimming around the lapel. His shirt was white, and the man wore a black necktie with thin, red stripes. The suit was in sharp contrast to the white dress uniform that Temeos wore tonight. The man stopped in front of him and said, "All is in readiness, my Lord Director. Please follow me."

He followed the man through the foyer and into a great, gilded hall. It seemed that the hall's length was infinite as he followed. The doors that lined both sides of the hallway were not uniform in color. Each had a unique shade of lacquer or color of paint covering them. The man continued on for nearly the entire length of the hall. Temeos had never been in this part of the palace. The hall led into the emperor's private quarters.

Finally, the man stopped in front of a pair of white doors. He twisted the golden knobs of the doors and pushed them open. The doors opened into a small yet spectacular white room. At the center of the room was an oval table made of a black, shiny substance that he thought to be ebony. A place was set at each end of the table. There were eight chairs made of the same substance around the table. The chairs had white leather seat cushions that had small images of bejeweled golden imperial crowns imprinted on the corners with a large image of the crown in the middle. In the middle of the ceiling overhanging the table, was a large chandelier made of exquisite crystal. There were paintings of selected Doetoran emperors spaced evenly around three walls of the room. The fourth wall, the far wall, was covered by silky white draperies. The room's floor was spectacular white marble, and the corner posts of the room were covered in black marble.

After he entered the room, the man showed him to the seat at the nearer end of the table. "The emperor will be joining you shortly. Do you have a favorite beverage that you would like to be served? The emperor will be drinking che," the man offered.

"Che will be fine—served cold, please. Thank you," he said to the man.

The man gave a slight nod and disappeared through the white double doors which he left open. He could hear his hurried footsteps growing fainter as he traveled down the hall. A feeling of intimidation crept over him as he waited alone in the elaborate room. Suddenly the high collar on his white uniform felt uncomfortably tight. He fingered the inside of the collar nervously.

After a moment, he heard footsteps in the hall again. This time, the footsteps were not hurried but were steady and measured. The footsteps grew closer and closer and then stopped. He had to turn to see who was standing in the doorway. When he turned, he saw Tryllos. He was dressed in his white dress uniform as well. The only difference in the two uniforms was that Tryllos's uniform had more gold trim than did his. It was unusual to see Tryllos without his imperial robes. He stood when he saw the emperor, and the emperor came to him with an outstretched arm. He met Tryllos's arm, and the two locked arms in a gesture of friendship.

"It was good of you to come, Temeos," greeted Tryllos.

"It is my honor, My Lord," he said formally.

"I hope that I have not kept you waiting long. I was only just informed that you had arrived," said Tryllos.

"I have not been waiting long at all, My Lord. Your servants have been quite prompt."

"That is good. It would not do to keep my friend waiting," said the emperor. He then released his arm and said, "Please sit down. The table is not long. We can talk comfortably while seated."

He sat back down, and Tryllos took his seat at the other end of the table.

Just then, the head servant returned with two cups of che. The cups were made of fine porcelain and had gilded hawks lining their rims. The elderly man served a steaming cup to the emperor before placing a cup of cold che in front of him. The servant then exited via the double doors and closed the doors behind him this time.

"Khulul is a good man," Tryllos said and nodded toward the doors that had just been closed. "He's been here at the palace for over a hundred years."

He nodded. "He seems to be a very suitable servant for My Lord," he said.

Tryllos smiled, "Speaking of suitable servants, you have been the empire's suitable servant for many years. In all these years, I wonder how many times my actions have made you want to quit your post. I haven't always been easy on you, Temeos. Yet, I've never heard a complaint from you or even heard rumor of a complaint. Your service to the empire has been impeccable, and I compliment you for it."

"I have never thought of abandoning the empire or my Emperor," he said. "It has always been my pleasure to serve you, My Lord."

Tryllos nodded. "I wouldn't have expected any other answer from you, Temeos. I have always respected you. That is why I have never asked you to do anything that I knew would make you compromise your loyalty to the laws of the empire. You are a man who regards our laws highly. Your devotion is most admirable and has always demanded my respect. I learned early on that you wouldn't compromise your devotion to the empire to satisfy the whims of an emperor. You never told me that you wouldn't do something. You would just say, 'I am sorry, My Lord, but the law forbids it.' You have given me no choice but to make most of my actions lawful, except for the few actions I could accomplish without having to go through you. Although it didn't always make me happy, I have always admired your devotion greatly."

He didn't know exactly what to say, so he just bowed his head toward Tryllos.

A server came into the room from the small door on Temeos's left. He had bread and salads on his tray. He served the emperor and then him. It was considered shameful behavior toward servants to ignore them while they were serving so he politely watched the servant perform his duties and nodded to him when he served him.

After the servant left, Tryllos said, "I invited you here this evening as a sign of that respect. I have a special surprise for you after we eat."

Tryllos's last comment made him feel uneasy. He wasn't fond of surprises and particularly not the surprises that Tryllos tended to spring on him. However, Tryllos was acting civilly for the first time in ages. Perhaps the surprise would be a pleasant one. "I am honored, My Lord," he said formally.

The two men enjoyed the appetizers and some light conversation. Soon, the main dish was served. It was roast shef served with brown menitiri, a rare delicacy in Doetora. It was truly delicious, and the conversation was ordinary and pleasant. Dessert was a rich butter cake topped with phreyol berries. The berries were a rare blue berry that only grew in the spring on certain mountain slopes of Doetora. They were an extraordinarily sweet and juicy berry and complemented the flavor of the buttery cake marvellously.

When the servants cleared away the last dish, Tryllos got up and said, "Now I have something to show you. I haven't seen it yet myself. I was only told about it. It is outside on the patio, behind these drapes." With that, Tryllos turned and pulled the white cord at the side of the drapes. The drapes opened, revealing glass doors that opened upon a patio. On the patio, stood a pedestal. On the pedestal, there was a small item made of a mesh material.

He got up and moved closer. It didn't appear to be much of anything but some mesh material. The material was cut in a circular shape, but it wasn't obvious for what purpose it was cut so he asked, "What is it, My Lord?"

"You will see," was all that Tryllos said. Tryllos drew open the glass doors, went to the pedestal, picked up the item made of mesh, and put it on his head. It covered the top of Tryllos's head but didn't completely cover his hair. "It does look rather ridiculous, does it not?" he asked.

It did look rather ridiculous, but he didn't laugh or even smile. The mesh item was a closefitting cap, and he feared that he knew its purpose. His only reaction was to stare incredulously at Tryllos.

Tryllos turned his face toward the left of the setting sun. He followed Tryllos's gaze. That was when he saw all of them together for the first time. Seven full squadrons of Avengers rose from just over the distant rise and streaked toward them. He had hoped never to see so many Avengers. Each squadron was flying in a dotted diamond formation. They came close and then bobbed and weaved in synchronized flight above them. He came to stand beside Tryllos and gaped at his face. Tryllos wore a huge smile. He appeared to be a boy at play.

"The funny-looking thing on my head is the controlling device for my Avengers," he said. I can choose to see normally, or I can choose between several displays that only I can see in my mind. Some displays show me a view from the lead Avenger in a squadron, while others show me informational data. All I have to do is to think of which display I wish to see and I see it instantly. I can command all of the squadrons at once, as I am doing now, or only one."

As he said the word *one,* six of the squadrons quickly landed on the lawn in front of them while one shot high into the sky and danced about in perfect synchronization.

"Isn't the control that this little device gives me amazing? I can make the Avengers perform any flying maneuver without fear of their crashing. They are so quick and agile it nearly takes my breath away," said Tryllos excitedly.

The sight of the Avengers had taken Temeos's breath away too, but he felt certain he didn't have the same feelings for the Avengers as Tryllos had. Suddenly, the exquisite supper he had just eaten was not settling well on his stomach. He desperately fought to hide his discomfort from the emperor. He had to seem impressed with these monsters of technology, and not reveal that he actually loathed them with all of his being.

The Avengers were unnervingly close, only a few dets away. He had never been this close before. He hadn't even seen an image of the spheres that revealed this much detail. He noticed for the first time that they did not have a smooth surface. Instead, the surface of each Avenger was made up of a multitude of flat angled trapezoids. No doubt, the configuration of the trapezoids on the surface contributed to the crafts' ability to evade detection. The spheres on the ground were small. He thought he might be able to pick one up without too much effort. Yet he had seen what these seemly benign silver spheres could do. He feared and abhorred them.

The remaining squadron came to rest on the lawn in front of them.

Tryllos took off the cap and handed it toward him. "Did you want to give it a try, Temeos?"

He tried hard not to shrink back from the device and said in a somewhat steady voice, "No, My Lord. I don't think that would be prudent."

Tryllos laughed. "Perhaps not, but it wouldn't work for you anyway. This cap is strictly for me and my brainwave pattern. It will not respond to anyone else's. So, you see, it is of no use to anyone but me. Come next Diotiri, I will fly these beauties in real combat. I will become a one-man attack force that the world will learn to fear," he said triumphantly.

He couldn't restrain himself. "My Lord, please don't put these Avengers into combat. I fear they will be more powerful than even you realize. I beg you, My Lord."

Tryllos was astonished at his outburst. "Calm down, my friend. They have no power other than what I give them. All will be well, Temeos—all will be well," Tryllos said soothingly as he patted him on the back. "You will see. Soon, all will see. We have no reason to fear these wonderful flying machines. They are our friends. Very soon, they will fight for us and we will be victorious." Tryllos put the cap back on and put the Avengers into flight once more.

Tryllos went on talking of the Avengers as his friends. He soon seemed to forget that anyone else was there.

Temeos could only watch as Tryllos lost himself in the Avengers. He tried to talk with Tryllos again, but Tryllos was seemingly not able to hear him. Reluctantly, he left his emperor with his new friends and made his way out of the palace alone. He wondered if Tryllos would realize he was gone. He wondered if Tryllos would realize that he was even ever there.

CHAPTER FOUR

MESSAGES

Words are both the foundation of human society and the curse of human existence. They can both build and destroy. When they are used in love, they can heal. When they are used in anger, they can cause mortal wounds. Words are both powerful and powerless. They can convey profound thoughts; they can be inadequate for the simplest thoughts. Words are either tools or weapons; they are either effective or useless; they either enslave or set free. Words are what they are depending on who uses them, the purpose for which they are used and the complexity of what they attempt to describe.

— From the writings of Grephes, a philosopher of ancient Gratonin

He was just one of many minions of the Great Lord, but he had news, important news for the Great Lord. He had never petitioned for a meeting with the Great One before. He nervously waited for an invitation that he hoped would come. It was not every day that an ordinary minion had the extraordinary news that he had right now. He felt that he must be allowed to deliver the news in person.

He tried to go through the D'Yavoly — this was the normal way to get a message to the Great Lord — but he couldn't contact any of them. It was as if they were not in the Labile Mist at all. That was a ridiculous thought, to be sure; but he knew of no other explanation for the lack of response.

Therefore, he had sent a petition to the ears of the Great Lord. He knew it was risky. Others had been banished to the abyss for this very act. Surely, the Great Lord would know that his D'Yavoly were out of communication with his minions. Surely, he would understand.

Just then, a booming voice was heard from somewhere within the Labile Mist. It said, "Come. Speak to me." It was the Great Lord. He was being granted an audience. He was at once thrilled and terrified. He had never been in the Great Lord's very presence before, but he knew how to go to him. He concentrated on the voice and thought about being in the presence of the voice. Immediately, he was there.

The Great Lord sat before him on a huge, albeit ephemeral, throne. The Great Lord himself appeared to be a giant. He prostrated himself before the throne and the Great Lord.

"Speak to me, minion. What is so important that you dare to contact my person directly? Why did you not tell Zlux your message?" thundered Nenavis.

"A thousand pardons, My Great Lord. I did try to contact the D'Yavoly that I knew, but alas, I did not know that Zlux was again one of your D'Yavoly. Please forgive the intrusion by one such as me," groveled the minion.

For what seemed an eternity, the Great Lord did not speak. Each tic seemed to resound in the minion's ears. As the time passed, the minion began to wonder more and more what his fate might be.

Finally, the voice of the Great Lord said, "You are forgiven, minion. Much change is taking place. I understand how you could have been ignorant of these changes."

"Many thanks, My Great Lord," said the trembling minion as he prostrated himself even lower.

"I have forgiven you for one offense. Do not commit another by keeping me waiting. Up with you, and deliver your information," thundered Nenavis.

"Yes, Great One," groveled the minion as he rose to his knees. "I have news concerning your pawn, Tryllos." Nenavis raised an eyebrow to show his interest. "I know that you have great plans concerning him, My Great Lord. He might be about to lose his power."

Nenavis rose from his throne and manifested himself as a gigantic, dark shadow that loomed menacingly over the minion's head. "What did you say, minion? Is he not the Emperor of Doetora? No Doetoran emperor has lost power outside of a military coup or assassination. How is it you believe Tryllos's power is in jeopardy?"

The minion bowed his head, not daring even to glance at the apparition that hovered over him, and answered hurriedly, "I have access to a suvaten, Great One. That suvaten was informed, only moments ago, that the topic of this morning's session was to be a vote for no confidence in the emperor. The suvaten believes that no one would dare bring such a thing to a vote if there was not great support. The session of the Edvukaat will start soon, Great Lord."

Nenavis sat down on his throne with a thud. His apparition popped out of existence. He was taken aback by the unexpectedness of the news and was visibly disturbed. Nenavis said in a somber voice, "Your news is troublesome, minion, but you did well to bring it to me now, while something can still be done. Go back to your suvaten, and keep me apprised of the situation in the Edvukaat. I will keep my mind open to you for communication while I am still in the mist. If I am no longer in the mist, contact Zlux. I will have to take control of Tryllos before I had planned. If I slow time in the mist so that I can prepare properly, I should be able to salvage my investment in him. Now be gone. My takeover must be immediate and complete."

Jahnu had risen early and had awakened Odanoi. It was Treti morning. The two of them sat at the dining room table of their quarters. Last night, he had received a message from the Voice of Thaoi. It was a message that he thought must be significant, but he was unsure exactly what the message might mean in light of next Diotiri. He and Odanoi had been discussing this message for a full parz.

The message itself was simple enough to understand. It just wasn't clear how it tied in with the other messages that the Voice of Thaoi had given to him. He thought about the words of the message once again: "The father of the soulless has begotten a son, and the son is poised to bring freedom to the soulless. Behold, the soulless will leave an icy prison to begin their conquest for the souls of men."

It was obvious to him that the son mentioned was not a physical son but rather someone that the father of the soulless had influenced. He couldn't imagine how, but a hapless human had committed his soul to the father of the soulless. Whoever the son was, he must be a person of some power and influence in order to free the father of the soulless. Of course, this was the first indication that was given that the father of the soulless was not walking free. The icy prison reference indicated that all this was taking place somewhere cold. What the message did not indicate was an exact location. The mention of ice might mean that the climate was currently cold. If that was indeed the case, it limited possible locations to northern Doetora, a country in northern Grasso, southern Dricho, or southern Cirri. He hoped he could exclude southern Cirri from consideration, but he was not sure that he dared to do so just yet.

He and Odanoi were currently discussing the use of the word *prison* in the message.

"Of course, it doesn't have to be an actual prison. It could just mean someplace remote or inaccessible in some way," he offered.

"Yes. I'm not sure what can be determined from the word other than it's an indication that the father of the soulless is currently confined. As you said, the son he fathered must be someone who has the authority or the means to free him. At least we know to search for his appearance in a location that is cold. This means that we can eliminate O'ONaso and Minnunglindor since they don't have any place that could be considered icy," said Odanoi.

"Unless you count the tops of the mountains that separate the countries, although the tops of the mountains are not inhabited. Still, the soulless *could* be there. We are only talking about two of them at present."

"Hmm. I guess that we are back to where we were then," said Odanoi.

He could hear the strain in Odanoi's voice. They had gone over all the messages and the Levra but couldn't come up with a location to search for the soulless. There just wasn't enough information in the message to draw any definite conclusions about the location.

He thought for a moment and then said, "Well, you remember that I told you that I also get impressions along with the actual words?"

Odanoi nodded.

"I got the impression of a place of intense cold for the location of the 'icy prison.'"

Odanoi scratched his chin through his thick beard. "I don't suppose you received an impression of the prison itself."

He shook his head. "No. The message was about leaving the prison. My impression was about the journey away from the prison." His face then brightened as something else occurred to him. "I did get the impression of several, maybe many, travelers, not just two; now that you mention it."

Odanoi stopped scratching his chin. "That might be significant. It means that the prison, whatever it is, must house at least several people. That might just eliminate mountaintops as the location. The intense cold at this time of year would eliminate all but the extreme southern portions of Dricho and the very tip of northern Grasso and Doetora."

"Southern Cirri would still be a possibility," he said softly. Neither of them wanted to think about the possibility of the soulless being on their home island, but it didn't mean that it wasn't possible.

Odanoi sighed. "Yes, it's true that southern Cirri is as cold and inhospitable a place as there is on Kosundo, but Cirri has held true to Thaoi more so than the rest of Kosundo. Is it possible that such a creature could have been conceived on Cirrian soil? Plus, Cirri is so remote. It doesn't seem like the right location for the soulless to emerge with a goal of the conquest of Kosundo. Wouldn't it be much more logical to assume that the soulless would first appear on one of the two continents?"

"It would seem logical," he began, "but so little of what has happened within the last week or so seems very logical to me. Is it logical that a person like me would be chosen to receive messages from Thaoi? Is it logical that you would accept me as the prophet? None of it seems logical."

Odanoi smiled. "I suppose you're right. No place that fits the message should be ignored. I will contact Phrunoi and ask him to put the best technology team available on the task of searching Kosundo for anything that might seem out of the ordinary, like a group of creatures moving in a cold climate. Perhaps he will put Agapoi on the task. Phrunoi seems seems to look upon the man with high regard."

He nodded. "Yes, that would be prudent, but they should search for a new type of technology that could be used as a weapon as well. Remember, that part of the prophecy speaks of man's works turning against man. You should also make it clear that these creatures will probably appear as if they are people. In fact, all but one will have been human before giving their souls away. Perhaps they could still be considered human — perhaps."

"Very well. It's decided then. I will contact Phrunoi right away," said Odanoi.

He nodded. He knew that Odanoi was anxious to do something. It was a powerless feeling, knowing that something awful was going to take place but not knowing exactly what is was or where it would begin. It took great faith just to believe that something was going to happen so soon, since the world of Kosundo was more peaceful now than it had been in a couple of millennia.

Then it occurred to him. Thaoi wanted man to live by faith. The Levra contained several passages concerning faith. The book of A'Othotate contained these words: "But now, righteousness is manifested in those of good conscience, even the righteousness of Thaoi, which is *by faith*." It wasn't enough just to keep a good conscience. Thaoi expected the exercising of faith. Perhaps they should go public with what they knew. It might sound like foolishness to most, but it might save the lives of those who have faith.

That last thought ignited a brightly burning flame of understanding within him. It drove out much of his confusion. With the clarity that the understanding brought, came the realization that he had no right to keep the messages private; so he immediately said, "We should announce what we know. We have no right to keep the messages from Thaoi private."

Odanoi appeared a bit puzzled. "But you said it would be axi to wait until Paraskevi to announce anything."

He bowed his head and said timidly, "I was wrong, Odanoi." He then focused on Odanoi's eyes and said, "There are people in Kosundo who still have faith. They have a right to know, no matter what some skeptics might think. Whether we have details or not, the people should be informed."

Odanoi took a deep breath. "Axi, Jahnu. I will contact Phrunoi and then contact the communications center in Cirri City. The center will need a day to clear a time slot. I will introduce you to Kosundo tomorrow. May Thaoi bless your message."

It was Treti morning, and Beltram was busy. The one predominate thought on his mind was to keep everything about the sealed labs a secret, although he really didn't know why. He had spent the better part of Diotiri spreading a story about where he had been over the weekend to everyone that he knew. He also checked in with the company headquarters to get a feel for whether they knew anything about the seal on the origin genetics project wing being broken. They didn't seem to know anything. Now he was busily combing access logs to make sure that no trace of access to the wing and its sealed labs was in the system. He couldn't find any records of access to the wing. He didn't really know why he couldn't find any records; but somehow, he wasn't surprised that he didn't find any.

Having confirmed that the access records were clean, he thought about how good he felt now. He felt stronger and healthier than he had in years. He remembered that the doctor, Doctor Upfar, had said that he would be a better person. Rather, he had *thought* it to him, which was both eerily strange and rather drus at the same time. As he recalled, he had given the doctor control of his will so that the doctor could help him. He didn't feel any remorse about that. In fact, he felt happy about it. Still, something deep from within him objected to his decision to give up his will; but it was deep in the background, like an old memory that couldn't quite be recalled.

All he had for the doctor was good feelings and an overwhelming drive to introduce other people to him. Nothing in his memory could explain why he had such good feelings toward the doctor, but the compulsion to spread news about the doctor was definitely present. Even now, he found himself finishing an announcement inviting people to come to a meeting. It wouldn't win any prizes but he thought it served the purpose. He read it over.

Is Your Life Out of Control?

> If you are having difficulty with any troublesome issues in your life, there is a new doctor in the complex who can help you. His technique is even more effective than Lidar Tombun's relaxation exercises. Come to conference room C-66 this afternoon at 6:80. You will learn all about a breakthrough procedure that can help no matter your problem. Appointments with the doctor will be scheduled for those who are interested.

It wasn't too bad in his opinion. He signed the announcement and had his secretary send it to everyone in the Dricho Genetics Foundation Complex. With any luck, there would be a good turnout. That would please the doctor. That good feeling about the doctor came to the forefront of his mind again. It was puzzling to him why pleasing the doctor gave him that feeling and why that feeling affected him so.

Many things in his mind puzzled him these days. He remembered having liked sports. Now he found that he couldn't care less about sports. He remembered hating classical music, yet he found himself buying some classical music on the public link last night; and he enjoyed listening to it. Strange contradictions between the past and present were common. Somehow, even those contradictions seemed natural to him now.

Then a question resounded in his mind. *Beltram, what are your plans?* It was a very general question, but he understood its meaning.

He answered in thought. *I hope to have some visitors for you by tomorrow morning. Many don't know how to control their lives. They will be quite open to letting you take control.*

A thought came back. *You are doing fine work, Beltram. Once you have proven yourself, I will show you how to extend my will to others. Then you will be complete.*

He answered the thought. *I am longing for the day. I will see you soon.*

He knew that those thoughts had come from the doctor. The doctor's thoughts were welcome in his mind. Soon, he would be complete. Although he didn't know exactly what being complete meant, he longed for it. He longed for it because the doctor willed it. The doctor's will was his will.

ASA PUBLISHING COMPANY

CHAPTER FIVE

THE FULL SESSION

Sunshine poured into the chamber from the skylights in the domed ceiling overhead, but the sunshine did nothing for his mood. It was a hard day. Today, he intended to end the reign of the man that he had faithfully served for most of both their lives. Knowing it was necessary did little to soften the day for him. Temeos stood. It was half past three parzes on Treti morning, and he was about to start the full session of the Edvukaat.

He was dressed in his formal, high-collared, black dress uniform. His medals, predominantly red and gold, decorated the right side of his chest. The twenty suvatens in the chamber wore their usual black robes trimmed in silver with a silver flying hawk emblazoned on the back. Everyone else in attendance wore business attire. Most of the men were in suits while most of the women wore modest formal dresses. Today had the appearance of business as usual in the Edvukaat, but it was anything but usual business that would be discussed here today.

The main chamber of the Edvukaat was oval-shaped, with the speaker's podium suspended in the center of the room on a elevatable, rotatable platform. The platform could rotate full circle to view any part of the chamber. It was stationary at the moment, but he would soon put it in motion when he began to speak. The chamber furniture, mainly desks and chairs, matched the wall and railings; all were a medium dark brown wood.

All of the seats in the chamber were filled this morning. The roll revealed that all suvatens were in attendance. That was a good sign. It meant two things: the session had the needed suvatens to conduct the vote, and no suvaten had been able to go to the emperor. If someone had gone to the emperor about the session, that person would not have been in attendance for fear of sharing in reprisals against the Edvukaat.

He had made sure that there were news crews in attendance by having the usual people leak that an important session of the Edvukaat would be held today. Although the media had some restrictions placed on them in Doetora, they had the freedom to attend Edvukaat sessions. The media had come out in force, and had even set up a live PT feed. He was glad to see them and the PT sensors. The emperor would think twice about sending any of his guards to disrupt the session while it was being transmitted live to all of Doetora.

The chamber was nervously buzzing. No one knew for sure how this session would end. The tension in the chamber was palpable. There had been only one no-confidence vote taken in the history of the Edvukaat. It had taken place over fourteen hundred years ago. It had failed. The emperor at the time took vengeance on the members of the Edvukaat who had voted to oust him. It wasn't pretty. The tension came from the knowledge of this history. Many suvatens would be literally putting their lives on the line today. If the vote failed, the instigators of the session each would have a tragic accident that wouldn't be so accidental.

He understood that he would surely be among the accident victims. As director, he had a vote in a full session. If they failed to get the necessary fifteen votes, he would cast his vote in favor of ousting the emperor, whether or not it would make the fifteenth vote. Aside from that, he was testifying against the emperor today. That alone would earn him a death warrant, should the vote not carry.

He strode to the podium and started it in motion. He then pushed the alert button. A loud gong resounded in the chamber. The buzzing ceased. All was now quiet. He began.

"All of the suvatens present today know why this full session is being held, but for the sake of the news media and the people viewing this session across Doetora, I will now state the purpose of this session. This session's purpose is to address the many actions taken by the imperial government against the best interests of the Empire of Doetora. These actions were carried out as the result of unsound—even criminal—decisions made at the top of the government. These actions will be enumerated today for the benefit of all present in this chamber. The most recent action in this chain of destructive actions will be discussed at length today. It is this most recent action that has served as the catalyst for this session. Today, we will hold a vote of no confidence in the reign of Emperor Tryllos."

The whole chamber erupted in a mix of murmurs and exclamations. He understood the surprise involved among the many non-suvatens in the chamber—and the fear. Just being present for such a session could be dangerous should the emperor remain in power. He waited patiently for the clamor to settle, but when it seemed the clamor was not going to settle quickly, he pushed the alert button again. The gong again sounded in the chamber. The chamber became quieter but not quiet. He waited a moment longer, but when the murmurs persisted, he said loudly, "Ladies and gentlemen, I must ask you to be silent so that this session might proceed. Anyone who will not comply with this request will be forcibly removed from the chamber."

The last sentence seemed to do the trick. The names of every in the chamber were already recorded, so no one wished to be removed despite of the fear of reprisals. The chamber became quiet almost immediately.

He first needed to secure the emperor to make certain of a peaceful transfer of power in case the vote passed. The emperor hadn't left vicinity of the palace grounds in many years, so he was certain the emperor would be on or near the grounds. He said in his firmest tone, "We are about to begin discussion on the topic of declaring no confidence. Doetoran law directs the captain of the Edvukaat security to confine the emperor to the residential portion of the palace until he is called to testify on his own behalf. Captain, please come forward, take the writ of confinement from the Senior Suvaten Cemyoz, and secure the emperor."

The captain of security came forward to the inner circle of the chamber, where the four most senior suvatens sat, to receive the papers from Cemyoz. The captain wore a dark blue uniform with a billed white cap trimmed in blue and gold. After he received the papers, he strode out of the chamber. The inner security guards promptly shut the doors behind him. More murmuring ensued, but it died down quickly.

Temeos continued. "We have several witnesses that will testify of improper actions taken by the imperial government. For the sake of time and relevance, we will be confining the testimony to actions that happened one year ago or less. Gus Sakrate, please call the first witness."

The gus sakrate was the Edvukaat head clerk responsible for the disposition of all Edvukaat sessions as well as the main keeper of the records transcribed by the writing clerks under him. The gus sakrate swore in the witnesses, and then the witnesses gave an uninterrupted testimony of the events that they had witnessed.

Each of the twenty suvatens then had an opportunity to ask any question relevant to the testimony. It was the acting speaker who determined if the question was appropriate. Today, he was that speaker. The witness was not allowed to answer the question if the speaker deemed the question irrelevant to the testimony.

The witnesses were easy to find, as there were many complaints lodged about abuses of imperial power during the last year, ranging from a simple misuse of imperial power to murder.

Most of the witnesses' testimonies lasted only a few spens; it took only a few spens more for suvatens to ask their questions. In just a little over a half parz, ten of the twenty-four witnesses had already testified. The proceedings were moving along quickly, despite the murmurs that seemed to rise from the gallery after each witness left the stand.

After the tenth witness had completed his testimony and was leaving the stand, the captain of security came into the chamber and stood a few steps inside the door of the chamber. The captain motioned to Temeos asking permission to approach. He granted permission to the captain with a nod of his head. As the captain approached the speaker's podium, he lowered the podium and covered the sound sensor to allow the captain to speak to him quietly. The usual gentle murmur that followed each witness strengthened as the captain spoke to him.

"Lord Director," said the Captain. His voice was soft yet had urgency to it. "The emperor was not found on the palace grounds."

He felt a cold chill roll up his spine. He said rather urgently, "Are you sure? The emperor has not left the palace grounds in years except to visit the Avenger complex next door."

"I'm afraid I am sure, my Lord," said the captain softly. He further explained, "After we could not find him on the grounds, we questioned the palace wait staff. It seems the emperor took an imperial ground transit to the air travel station in the city. The emperor was gone by the time we arrived at the station. The driver told us that the emperor had boarded an air transport headed to Dricho. The air transport is headed to the city of Aturla on the southwestern coast of Dricho. He was traveling in commoner's clothes. And according to all who witnessed his departure, he was alone."

"That's strange," he said to the captain. Various perplexing questions then flooded his mind. How could the emperor have known about the vote? If he did know, why didn't he strike out at the Edvukaat before the session began? It didn't make sense, unless the emperor had learned of the session only as it began. But then how did he manage to make a flight so quickly? *That was a silly thought. He is the emperor; he has contacts.* Yet, why leave the country? Why didn't Tryllos wait in a remote location in Doetora so he could make a move? None of it made sense to him. His mind was racing, but he kept his composure. He thanked the captain and started to return the podium to speaking height when a thought occurred to him.

"Captain," he said, stopping the retreat of the captain, "search the palace grounds for a mesh cap. It is unlike any cap you would have seen before. I must know if it is still in the palace. Also, check in and around the complex with the green and gold buildings near the palace for some spherical objects about ten dets in diameter. Let me know how many you find in the buildings or on the grounds."

The captain seemed a bit puzzled by that order but nodded his head and gave a small, obedient bow before leaving the chamber.

The murmurs in the chamber turned into a buzz. He finished raising the podium platform and then raised his open hands above his head and beckoned for silence. After the chamber calmed, he said, "The captain has just reported to me that the emperor has fled the empire."

The chamber erupted into a chaotic frenzy of conversation that grew louder and louder. People started to stir from their seats, including the suvatens. He had to stop any thought of an exodus right here and now, so he pushed the alert button three times. Three long gongs resounded in the chamber.

The gongs had the intended effect. He spoke loudly, taking control while there was a lull, "Ladies, gentlemen, and suvatens, please find your seats. The fact that the emperor has fled doesn't change what the laws of the empire demand of us. The emperor has chosen not to be available to testify and therefore has waived his right of rebuttal. This body must still address the matter of a formal vote of no confidence. Remember, your attendance here is already a mater of record. We have several more testimonies to hear concerning this matter. In light of the news of the captain, it is even more imperative that a decision be reached today concerning this matter for the sake of the empire. Gus Sakrate, please call the next witness."

The chamber was silent again as the witness was sworn in—it was a hushed silence. It was as if everyone was in deep contemplation.

This general feeling of contemplation prevailed in the chamber as witness after witness testified and answered questions from the suvatens. As director of the Edvukaat, he could have asked each witness questions as well, but he always passed up the opportunity. He felt that it would be best to be a nonentity in the questioning of the witnesses. He only performed the function of moderator by throwing out questions that obviously had nothing to do with the witnesses' testimonies, and he did that only twice. Finally, witness number twenty-three completed his testimony and was taking his seat in the gallery. None of the witnesses' testimonies to this point had offered clinching testimony against Tryllos by themselves, but their cumulative effect was being felt within the chamber. He felt that the next testimony would clinch the vote. It was to be his testimony.

He took a deep breath and began slowly. "I apologize for not taking a break to this point. I realize that it is past lunchtime, but all witnesses must be heard before the suvatens can deliberate the motion of no confidence. At that time, everyone but the suvatens will be dismissed from the chamber. It is now time to swear in the last witness for today's session. I will now give control of the session to Senior Suvaten Cemyoz." As he expected, the fact that he was relinquishing control of the session created a buzz in the chamber breaking the contemplative feel of the procedings. He lowered the podium to the chamber floor, stepped out onto the floor, and waited as Cemyoz entered the podium platform and raised it to speaking height.

Once the podium was raised, Cemyoz said, "Please come to order."

The chamber quieted.

"Gus Sakrate, please call the next witness."

The gus sakrate rose from his seat beside the witness stand and called out, "The Edvukaat calls Lord Director Temeos to the stand."

The chamber's silence gave way to a multitude of hushed voices as he came to the stand. He knew that the people in the chamber might have suspected that he was going to take the stand when he stepped down from the podium, but the significance of the actual call was the reason for the multitude of whispers in the crowd. After he came inside the stand and faced the gus sakrate, the chamber quieted itself again.

The gus sakrate said, "Please state your title and name and any naming history."

"Lord Director Temeos. I was born Temeon Khrebraysh."

"Thank you, Lord Director," said the gus sakrate. "Please prepare yourself to take the witness oath."

Temeos closed his hands into fists and crossed his arms over his chest.

"Do you solemnly swear that the testimony that you are about to give is completely true and will be given in good conscience toward Thaoi?" asked the gus sakrate.

"I do swear that my witness is true," replied Temeos.

"Thank you. Please be seated," said the gus sakrate.

As he sat down in the witness chair, Cemyoz said from the podium, "Lord Director Temeos, please give us your testimony against the defendant, Emperor Tryllos." After he spoke to him, Cemyoz raised the witness stand and put it in motion.

Somehow he just realized the significance of what he was about to do, even though he had thought he fully understood it before. It made his breath catch slightly before he began to speak; but speak he must, so he began. "My testimony is backed up with documents and images of a clandestine project that the emperor is currently conducting. The name of the project is *Avenger*." He picked up the remote clicker that was located in a wooden holder on the railing of the witness stand and pushed a button. "The migoterms on either end of the chamber are displaying various documents that show the emperor's knowledge and approval of the project. There are over two hundred pieces of documentation. Each suvaten has access to these documents through his desk dataterm. As stated before, I also have gathered some still and moving images. The technical staff of the project took these images to document their progress for the emperor. Among the documentation, you will find sworn testimony from the staff, indicating the authenticity of the images as well as testimony indicating the emperor's direct involvement with every aspect of the project."

He pushed the advance button on the remote again. "The document that is currently displayed is the charter authorizing the project. Notice that Emperor Tryllos has signed and sealed the document. In addition, notice that Emperor Tryllos is listed as the sole overseer of the project. Next, please note the stated goal of the project." He then read the goal. "'The goal of this project is to find a military solution that will enable the Emperor of Doetora to gain vengeance upon the enemies of the empire as determined by the emperor.' When I saw the goal of the project for the first time, I made it a point to keep close tabs on the progress of the project. At first, I thought the development of a weapon capable of delivering great destruction and of being controlled by one man would be unattainable. However, I underestimated the resources of the emperor's spy network. Apparently, Emperor Tryllos had a solid idea who to contact for the necessary technology before the project was commissioned and chartered."

He pushed the advance button on the remote. "The image that is now being displayed is what Emperor Tryllos has dubbed an Avenger. The craft is very light, weighing about fifty libs, and is only about ten dets in diameter. Most of you in this chamber would stand taller than the Avenger stands. It doesn't appear to be very menacing, does it? And by itself, it is not menacing. A single Avenger is completely impotent. It takes four or five of these flying craft, flying in formation, to make the Avenger a weapon.

"However, I am about to show you what a squadron of five Avengers can do." He pushed the advance button on the remote. "This was one of our older missile-launching sites. It still functioned at this point but was of no strategic importance. At the moment that this image was taken from a satellite sensor, a squadron of five Avengers was preparing to engage the site from a distance of two hundred twenty-eight stets. The site computer did not detect the Avengers. The Avengers can evade detection from all existing detection matrixes. Even if they were detected, they would effectively be out of range for this site and many sites like it. At this distance and altitude, they are also out of range of all ground-based energy weapons because they have not yet crested the horizon. The Avengers will fire their weapons at the moment they would become visible on the horizon to ground-based weapons.

He pressed the advance button.

Gasps spread across the chamber.

He let the image display for a few moments and then said, "This is the same missile site less than a tic after the Avengers crested the horizon. Ten people died in the devastation that you are seeing. They were the men and women who manned the facility. Their lives weren't important to the emperor. They weren't warned about the test. The emperor wanted the test to be as realistic as possible."

He let his words sink in for just a few tics. Then he continued in a clinical tone. "The first-strike capability of the Avengers is beyond any weapon that has ever existed on Kosundo. Emperor Tryllos has had seven full squadrons of these Avengers built. They are all in working order. The emperor showed them to me last night at the palace. The maneuverability of these crafts is phenomenal. Even if they can be targeted, chances are they would be able to evade any energy weapon simply because the Avengers would have to be targeted at a great distance. Chances are the weapon firing against the Avengers would be destroyed whether the Avenger is destroyed or not."

He hit the advance button. "The project scientists gave Emperor Tryllos this projection of how long it would take for a single squadron of Avengers to destroy all ground and air weapons as well as all tracking facilities. I will read the high-lights. There are estimated to be a little over three thousand ground defense sites in Grasso. One squadron could destroy all of the Grassoan installations within 12.35 parzes, or a little over a day's time. The installations in the Jontu Etirraze could be destroyed within 2.55 parzes. Notice that the emperor also had the project scientists calculate the time to destroy all defensive installations on Doetora. It would take 8.55 parzes, less than a day, to destroy all our installations. Keep in mind that the emperor had seven of these squadrons created, so, dividing the numbers by seven, Grasso's installations could be destroyed in less than two parzes, the Jontu's in about thirty-three spens, and our own installations could be destroyed in just over one parz should all seven squadrons be used against a single country's defenses. I asked the emperor why he had statistics for destroying the empire's defense installations. The emperor told me that he was considering using the destruction of Doetoran targets as a ruse to reduce the chance of counterattacks from Grasso and the Jontu."

That last statement created quite a stir in the chamber—so much so that Cemyoz had to sound the alert four times before order was restored.

Once order was restored, he continued. "I could cite other instances of Emperor Tryllos using questionable judgment in his decision-making, but this Avenger project is the most egregious example. The Avengers were constructed solely for the purpose of meting out the emperor's personal vengeance. The emperor has given no thought to the consequences that would result from using the Avengers. Paranoid delusions fill his mind. Nothing else is real to Emperor Tryllos anymore. The emperor is no longer capable of the rational thought it takes to run the empire. He is willing to sacrifice any number of lives to fulfill his dreams of vengeance against anyone he believes has wronged him personally. What is best for the empire is no longer a concern for Emperor Tryllos. He is willing to use an experimental thought wave interface to control his Avengers. He has been told that the interface has not been thoroughly tested, yet he still intends to use it. I ask you, which is worse, the prospect of the Avengers being unleashed against the world by an unstable personality like Emperor Tryllos, or the prospect of the Avengers being loosed on the world without anyone being able to control them? This is why I believe that Emperor Tryllos's reign must be ended today."

He sat back, indicating that he was finished with his testimony, and awaited questions. Murmurs spread throughout the chamber, but they quickly died down in anticipation of the questions that would be asked of him. He knew that the emperor's pawns would try to undermine his assessment of the emperor's mental state, but he had signed testimony from the emperor's personal physician to counter that strategy. He also had documents that proved the purpose of the *Avenger* project was as he had stated it. He felt confident that he would be able to handle those questions.

As expected, the questions did start off that way. First, Slipar and then Kryse asked if there was any documented proof of the emperor's state of mind. Then Khenzhe attacked Temeos's motives for testifying against the emperor. He was able to point out that he stood nothing to gain since he could not succeed the emperor because he testified against him, and he mentioned that he already held the second most powerful position in the empire. Other questions followed that tried to get him to contradict himself, but he saw through those questions easily. The final attacks became personal in nature, as the emperor's pawns were making a final desperate attempt to discredit his testimony. He felt that he answered all those questions well; and finally, those questions were replaced with questions about the Avengers from concerned suvatens. He answered those questions as best he could with his understanding of the technology, although there were some questions that he felt he was not qualified to answer. He was glad that other questions came about the recruitment of scientists for the project. This allowed him to reveal the horrible butchery of the families of the scientists, done to keep the project secret.

After all the questions were asked, he was dismissed from the witness stand. As a witness, he couldn't be in the chamber while deliberations were being made. He could only hope that his testimony was enough to convince the suvatens who were not pawns of the emperor to act. If not, he had certainly sentenced some good men to death. Cemyoz would be among them, and probably Pitar and Dizkuh too. Failing to end the reign of an emperor would have its consequences.

As for himself, he didn't matter. He would be glad to be executed for doing what he knew was best for the empire. He had counted his life forfeit long ago if he had to choose between himself and the empire.

Eventually, the deliberations would be over and the witnesses would be allowed to reenter the chamber for the vote. He would be in the awkward position of presiding over the vote even though he was a witness. It might very well be necessary for him to vote as well in order for fifteen votes to be mustered against the emperor.

It was ironic that it was the emperor's pride that enabled this vote to happen. The emperor never figured on having one of his pawns turn against him. Shipunke had won his respect and admiration with how he came forward. Cemyoz had told him all about Shipunke's heroics. He supposed that he would have to like him now, but he thought that the best he would be able to do for now was to tolerate him. After all, the man did look like a rodent.

Whatever his feelings toward Shipunke, they were irrelevant at the moment. The vote against the emperor was all that truly mattered. All he could do now was to wait and to hope. His thinking was that ousting the emperor would save the empire, but he was uneasy about Tryllos's sudden departure. He could only wonder what the emperor was thinking. He hoped that the control cap would be found in the palace, but he had a sinking feeling that it wouldn't be found.

It was then that the captain appeared in the hall and came striding toward him. "My Lord Director," he said, "all of the Avengers have been located within the project facility."

He was relieved to hear that, but he asked the captain, "What of the control cap?"

The captain shook his head. "The project staff says that the emperor never returned it. A search of the palace produced only this." The captain held up a mesh cap that certainly appeared to be the control cap that Tryllos wore during his crazed demonstration.

A smile spread across his face when he saw the cap. "But, Captain, that *is* the control cap that Tryllos was wearing," he said. His dread started to melt away. Tryllos was only trying to avoid confinement after all. There was no master plan.

He was about to congratulate the captain, but then he noticed that the captain was not smiling. "Is there something wrong?" he asked.

The captain peered at him intently and then said, "Lord Director, this is not the control cap. According to the project staff, a mockup was produced as a model to show the emperor what the cap would look like. The emperor had both the mockup as well as the real cap. This is only the mockup. We couldn't find the real cap."

He took the cap from the captain and peered inside. There was nothing inside the mesh cap. It was true; the cap was just mesh, nothing more. Tryllos had taken the real cap. His heart sank. Surely Tryllos couldn't control the Avengers from Aturla. Aturla was over ten thousand stets from Manku City. Still, he decided that he couldn't take any chances. He stepped closer to the captain and said softly, "Should the

emperor be deposed today, I want you to lead a team to have
the Avengers dismantled. I will not ask this of you if the vote
goes in favor of the emperor. I will attend to it myself in such
a case. These monstrosities must not be allowed to launch an
assault against any part of Kosundo. This is of the utmost
importance, Captain."

The captain stood back slightly and saluted him. "It
would be my pleasure to carry out this task no matter what
happens in the Edvukaat chamber today. You can count on
me, Lord Director Temeos."

He gave the captain a gratified salute in return. "Thank
you, Captain. By the way, what's your name?"

The captain relaxed his stance and said, "My name is
Varnupud Danosku, My Lord."

He nodded and said, "You have my gratitude, Captain
Danosku. The empire needs more men with your valor."

"That is kind of you to say, my Lord. Do you have any
other orders for me?" asked Captain Danosku.

"No, not at the moment. The best to you, Captain Danosku," said Temeos, offering the captain another salute.

The captain returned the salute, strode down the
hallway to the chamber door, and entered. He wished just
then that he could take the captain's place. He would love to
know what the suvatens were discussing at the moment, but
he would just have to wait until he and the other witnesses
were summoned. The dismissal of witnesses during
deliberation had long been a custom in the empire's judicial
system. It was thought that having the witnesses present
would unduly influence the proceedings. He supposed that it
might be a good custom, but he really didn't care for the
custom at the moment. *What is going on in that chamber?* His
mind groaned in anticipation.

Food had been provided in the witness waiting area.
He supposed that food had been delivered to the chamber as
well. From his experience, a little food in the mouth never

stopped the suvatens from debating an issue, but they might have a little more decorum with the media present. The food didn't tempt him right now, though he supposed he was hungry. There was too much on the line right now to eat. Perhaps some of the suvatens felt that way too—although his friend, Pitar, was probably not among the suvatens who felt that way. Pitar could eat while being attacked in the midst of a battlefield. He smiled as he envisioned that thought, but his smile quickly faded.

He sighed and sat down in one of the chairs in the waiting area. Pacing around was not going to make the deliberations go by any quicker. It was all about waiting now—and hoping while waiting. He could only hope that his hoping was not in vain.

CHAPTER SIX

PLAYING
FAVORITES

It was early afternoon on Treti. Neaotomo sat in the main lab, thinking. This morning, he had given Laysa the run of the inner labs. She had spent the better part of the morning discovering what equipment the labs had to offer. As for Degmer, he had confined her to her room, except for a brief time when he brought her to the main lab for a mind probe. He had made certain that Degmer had seen that Laysa was free to roam the inner labs before he escorted Degmer back into her room and secured the door. For now, he would continue to let Laysa have the run of the inner lab and confine Degmer to her quarters, except when he wanted Degmer to see something. The latest mind probe revealed even more fluctuations in Degmer's mind barrier. Eventually, the barrier would develop a weakness or hole that he could exploit. It was just a matter of time.

He had discovered that the origin genetics lab's computing terms were still tied into the rest of the complex's terms. Since the origin genetics lab was sealed, no one had bothered to physically sever the links. They had merely made it appear as if the networking devices of the labs were severed from the network. The terms were still physically connected to the network. All that had to be done to link the computers to the network was to reestablish the network paths and protocols again. That information was in his memory. He had taken it from Doctor Upfar himself. It was fortunate that the powers that be believed that everyone in the labs was long dead. The thinking that no one would ever again step foot inside the labs was why no one had felt it necessary to sever the network links physically. The network connection had already proven quite helpful. He had been able to access the employee records with Beltram's help. It helped to link a face to the people that Beltram was to bring in tomorrow. He knew that a personal touch would assist him in turning as many as possible.

Of course, it would not do for people to realize that the origin genetics files were part of the network again, so he—with Beltram's help concerning the new codes—set up a firewall to keep people out of the files. After he had tested the firewall from his office, Beltram indicated that the firewall made it seem as though the origin genetic computers were still offline to the rest of the computer terms in the complex. After he had turned enough of the complex's staff, the firewall would no longer be a necessity. Right now, the firewall supported the illusion that the origin genetics labs were still sealed very nicely.

Beltram also said that he thought he found a way to bypass the scanner in the airlock. If that was so, he would be able to leave the sealed labs for little recruiting excursions. First things first though. He must concentrate on breaking Degmer through Laysa.

Laysa had set up a workstation for herself this afternoon. Since she could access her project's workstation in her lab outside the airlock, setting up the workstation had allowed her to continue her research. It also gave her something to do and allowed Beltram to make up some story about Laysa and Degmer working offsite. Besides, being able to work seemed to please Laysa; and that pleased him, although he really did not understand why pleasing Laysa pleased him. It was strange, but he found that he viewed Laysa differently than he viewed any other creature that he had known. Just making Laysa do discomforting things had begun to bother him. It did not affect him enough to change his plans, but he thought it curious that it bothered him at all. He had never been bothered by the fact that he was using someone before.

Nevertheless, in a moment, he would use Laysa against Degmer again, no matter how it made Laysa feel. It would not be that bad for her, but he thought it might well be a very effective ploy in weakening Degmer's barrier even further. Laysa would not even be aware that she was being used, but the key was that Degmer would not know that Laysa was not aware she was hurting Degmer. His goal was to make it seem to Degmer that Laysa was either aware of what was happening to Degmer or that Laysa just did not care what was happening to Degmer. It did not really matter which Degmer believed. Either one would serve to drive her away from Laysa and toward him.

He got up and strolled toward the workstation that Laysa had set up in the main lab. "Are you making any progress?" he asked her nonchalantly.

Laysa glanced up from her work. "Well, I am not on the verge of a breakthrough, if that is what you mean. I am merely studying the sequence of this disease germ's genetics. If I can understand the germ, I might be able to engineer a human resistance to it," she said.

"Perhaps I might be of some assistance in your fight against this pathogen," he offered. "If it is a pathogen to which my body has not already developed a resistance, you might be able to see how my immune defenses react to the pathogen. It might give you some ideas."

Laysa nodded. "That is a generous offer, Neaotomo. Perhaps I might pick up some clues at that. Is this an offer that I can take you up on right now?"

He smiled. "I will let you take some of my blood to analyze today. Perhaps tomorrow you will be ready to expose me to the pathogen. As for right now, it is nearly six parzes. It is time for you to exercise. I expect you to keep your muscles well-toned."

Laysa sighed. "Axi, Neaotomo. If you want me to have an exercise session, I'll do it. I suppose that you haven't found a way to access facilities for washing clothes just yet."

He tried to imitate a sorry expression and said, "No, it just would not seem right to people if they saw either Beltram or Degmer to go to the laundry. Degmer is supposed to be working offsite and Beltram is the administrator. He would not be doing laundry. He has his clothes washed for him. I am afraid you will still have to disrobe for your exercise session. You will not have to be disconcerted about that though. You can disrobe in your room. I will not be present in your room or the adjacent exercise room."

Laysa gave a hint of a shy smile, but then her face became sober. "It doesn't matter to me what you do. I will obey you. After a moment of hesitation, she asked, "Would you consider it disobedience to ask you something about the exercise session?"

"No, you may ask what you will."

Laysa glanced downward for a moment as if trying to think of a way to form her question. "May I keep my short undergarments on for exercising?" She then added in a pleading tone, "I can wash them in the sink afterwards."

He considered the request. A little shock value would be lost if he allowed Laysa this concession, but he did not think enough would be lost to matter. "You have been very obedient; I suppose that I can allow you this request."

"Thank you," she responded simply. Had he not known better, he would have thought that he had just promised Laysa her freedom from the smile that radiated from her face. She had only said, *thank you,* but her countenance conveyed a deeper meaning than her words conveyed.

However, Laysa's smile was soon replaced by a sober expression. "Just remember our bargain about Degmer," she said in an almost threatening tone.

Neaotomo held back a smirk at her tone. "I have not forgotten. As a matter of fact, I have not yet punished Degmer for your disobedience yesterday," he said casually.

"You haven't? What was making her gather up dead bodies yesterday? Was that a reward?" she asked in desperate sarcasm.

His demeanor became stern in return. "No, it was not a reward, but neither was it a punishment. It was a job that I chose for her to do, nothing more."

"And the rough way you treated her?" she asked accusingly.

He shrugged. "She brought that upon herself. I did not damage her with my rough demeanor, other than hurting her feelings a little."

Laysa did not appear satisfied at that answer, but she did not say anything further. She wrapped up her work and turned off her workstation. She then turned and went toward her room.

He watched her as she went. There was something unusual about Laysa, something that he admired. She did not act like a captive. She acted as if she were doing exactly as she wished to do, even though he knew that she was not. A part of him felt emotion for her. It might be pity. It was very interesting to him how Laysa affected him.

ASA PUBLISHING COMPANY

After she disappeared from view, his thoughts shifted. He headed toward Degmer's quarters. It was time to give Degmer something else to stew about.

Degmer, in fact, was stewing in her quarters at that very moment. She was stewing over the treatment she was being given as compared to the treatment accorded to Laysa. She still could not believe that Neaotomo let Laysa set up a workstation this morning. Why should Laysa be allowed to work on her project's research without her? Laysa was titled as a co-lead of the project, but Degmer had been working in the field much longer than Laysa. She considered herself to be the lead scientist, not a co-lead with Laysa. Then last night how did Laysa get out of the disgusting work of picking up dead bodies? It seemed that Neaotomo favored her. She couldn't help wondering what Laysa had done to gain that favor, or perhaps it was what Neaotomo had done to her.

Just then, her door signal sounded, and in walked Neaotomo. He still insisted on wearing that ridiculous lab coat, although today he had casual attire instead of dress attire under it.

She greeted him by demanding, "What have you done to Laysa?"

Neaotomo took on a puzzled demeanor. "I have not done anything to Laysa. What makes you think that I have?"

"Don't play innocent with me." She was practically yelling. "If Laysa has been as cooperative as you say she has been, you must have done something to her. I've known Laysa for a good many years. She is not one to just buckle under."

Neaotomo shrugged his shoulders. "Perhaps you do not know her as well as you think. She has been very reasonable. She is quite the woman though. Do you not think so?"

It was not like Neaotomo to give out compliments of any kind. She wondered why he would compliment Laysa so freely. Then she had a thought. "You've taken a liking to Laysa, haven't you? You haven't taken advantage of her, have you?"

"Taken advantage of her? If I understand what you are asking me, no, I have not. As you should know, I am incapable of doing any such thing. Remember, I am sterile. I do not have the capacity to reproduce physically," said Neaotomo.

"But you can reproduce yourself in the minds of people. Have you been messing with Laysa's mind?" she asked probingly.

Neaotomo appeared as if he were insulted. "No. I have done two mind probes on her, nothing more. I have been civil with her, and she has been civil with me. I do find her body aesthetically pleasing, and I must admit to having gotten pleasure from sketching her. I have found her to have a personality that is nearly as pleasing." Neaotomo stopped and gazed at her with a slight smirk on his face. "Do I detect a hint of jealousy, Degmer? Do you think that I have been neglecting you?" he asked.

"Don't be silly. Why should I be jealous? As far as I'm concerned, you can spend all your time with Laysa. That way I won't have to see your sorry face," she said indignantly.

"Good," replied Neaotomo. "I am glad that you feel that way because I want to spend some time watching Laysa right now. But since you are obviously feeling neglected, I insist that you come along."

"Why should I want to go watch Laysa? I've seen her plenty of times before. I am very content just to stay right here in this room," she said, turning away from Neaotomo.

Neaotomo grabbed her by the shoulder and turned her around roughly. "You seem to have missed the part where I insisted, Degmer. You *will* come with me, even if I have to carry you. It would do you good to see how someone properly takes care of her body."

She fumed inside and gave Neaotomo a hot stare. "What are you saying now, that I'm a slob? I'll have you know that many men find me attractive. At least I don't go flaunting myself around like some kind of slut."

Neaotomo slapped her hard across the face. "Watch what you say, woman. I have no problem being uncivil to you when you are not civil."

She was surprised by the slap and staggered backward. It took a couple of tics for the sting to be felt, but when the feeling came, it felt as if a dozen insects had stung her face. She rubbed her cheek with her left hand. Her cheek felt hot. It most probably was very red as well.

"Now, if you can manage to hold your tongue, we will proceed."

She didn't say anything. She just lowered her head and walked by Neaotomo, out of the room and toward the main lab. Neaotomo caught up to her within a couple steps and took the lead. He led her into the lab where he had sketched Laysa. The platform was still in place where Laysa had sat as if it were a momument to the moment. As her eyes lingered on the platform, he had gone to a door to the left of the room and was opening it by keying in a code.

She wandered over to the door and peered in. The walls inside the room were lined with several terms, each displaying a different part of the sealed lab complex. In the middle of the far wall was one large term that was blank right now. In front of the large term were two chairs. Neaotomo motioned for her to sit in one of the chairs. After she was seated, he sat in the other chair. On the arms of the chairs were several control knobs and buttons, along with a keypad. Neaotomo punched in something on the keypad and pressed a green, triangular button on the armrest. The term in front of them sprang to life. The term was now displaying an exercise room, complete with all kinds of equipment. The view of the room was currently a wide view. In the room, a woman was using the treadmill; but it was impossible to make out much more than that. The woman was to the right of the screen, and her image was out of focus. Neaotomo used a control knob to bring the image to the center of the screen and bring the image closer and into focus.

It was Laysa. She was running furiously on the treadmill, and she was clothed only in her short undergarments. Degmer instinctively averted her eyes, being embarrassed for Laysa.

When Neaotomo saw that she wasn't looking at the screen, he clapped his hands near her ear. She jumped and her head jerked toward him.

Neaotomo leaned over and said, "Why do you look away, Degmer? Do you not think that her form is quite good?" He glanced back at the screen and pointed toward it.

Her eyes followed his finger.

"Nothing bounces about on her body as she moves. Her muscle tone is magnificent."

She turned away again and said disgustedly, "You're a real piece of work, aren't you, Neaotomo? A real pervert." The next thing that Degmer knew, she was flat on her back on the floor behind the chair where she had been sitting a moment before. Her vision was blurred, but finally, Neaotomo came into focus standing over her. Next, she became keenly aware that her right cheek and her bottom lip were both throbbing in pain. She felt a warm liquid on her chin. She used her finger to wipe it away. When she peered at her finger, she saw blood on it. Her lip was bleeding.

Neaotomo appeared to be relieved and said, "I must apologize. I did not mean to strike you quite so hard, but you can be exasperating at times. I was afraid that I may have permanently damaged you."

Neaotomo offered his hand to help her to her feet. She took his hand and pulled herself up to her feet. The sudden move upward made her dizzy, and she leaned against

Neaotomo for balance. She was amazed at how solid Neaotomo's body felt. He was built like a brick building. As she righted herself, Neaotomo put his hand on her back for what she supposed was support. As she watched the term in front of them, she noticed that Laysa was no longer running. She was putting down two barbells as if she just was finishing up some arm curls. That meant that some time must have passed since her last conscious moment.

Neaotomo still had his hand on her back, and she glanced up at him to ask why, but before she could ask, he said, "Laysa will do some work on the chin-up bar next. I have watched her many times, and she always seems to do the same routine. How many do you think she will do?" He spoke without taking his eyes off the screen in front of him.

She shrugged her shoulders. "I don't know. You've watched her before. How many does she do?"

Neaotomo stared down at her. There was something cruel in his look, and it made her shiver.

He must have noticed her shivering because he said, "You do well to be afraid. You have shown no respect for someone you call your friend. Laysa will determine your punishment. You had better hope that Laysa has mercy on you and does only twenty chin-ups. I intend on punishing you each time she completes a chin-up for your transgressions against her today."

She became wide-eyed as she watched Laysa put down the free weights and walk toward the chin-up bar. She felt Neaotomo grasp both of her wrists in one hand and groaned as he lifted her off the floor with that one hand. She could feel Neaotomo's hand on her back tense slightly. Laysa jumped up to the chin-up bar, hung for a moment, and then pulled her chin above the bar. Her breath caught as she felt Neaotomo's hand leave her back. The next thing she felt was pure agony. Neaotomo's hand came back in contact with her back with a vengeance. She swung helplessly in Neaotomo's grasp, not able to catch her breath. The blow to her back rocked her entire body, and then she felt a searing pain spread across her back.

Laysa had gone back down and now was rising up again. All she could do was think, *No, Laysa. Don't do this to me.* However, Laysa did not relent. Instead, she kept rising until her chin was again above the bar. Degmer tried to brace herself for the impact, but it was no use. The next blow came and rocked her. She hadn't had time to find her breath from the blow before, and now her breath was knocked out of her again. The pain on her back intensified. She managed only a grunt at the impact of the blow. The grunt was produced by the residual air in lungs being forced out by the force of Neaotomo's blow. She had no breath to scream, though she wanted to do so with all her might.

Again, Laysa started to rise; and again, she wished her to stop. But Laysa did not heed her. She was rocked with another blow as Laysa completed another chin-up.

This happened time and time again. Each time, she had only enough time to dread the next blow and barely any time to breathe. Each new blow knocked less of her breath out, as she just did not have as much breath left in her. Her grunts became less and less until she could not manage a grunt at all. Her back became a mass of searing pain. She felt pain from deep within her body now. Sweat freely fell down her body from the intense pain.

Laysa had now gone past twenty chin-ups, she was sure, and still, Laysa persisted. She couldn't understand why she didn't stop. The only thought that she could sustain in her mind was, *Why Laysa? Why?*

After what seemed to be an eternity, Laysa dropped from the chin-up bar. Neaotomo released his grip on her wrists, and she fell to the floor. She writhed in agony, trying desperately to breathe. Her back was on fire with pain, her wrists and arms throbbed, and she just couldn't pull a decent breath. Then she felt a need to cough. She started coughing uncontrollably. She put her hand over her mouth and then pulled it away in horror as she realized that she had just coughed up blood.

Neaotomo was standing over her. As she made eye contact with him, he said, "Perhaps you will treat Laysa with more respect now. She is worthy of respect. Her very being demands respect. Be careful, Degmer. She might demand more than you can withstand the next time."

She really didn't understand exactly what Neaotomo meant by what he said, but then she was having a hard time thinking coherently at all. The only meaning she gathered from Neaotomo's words was that Laysa had demanded that she be punished.

She was still writhing in pain and still having difficulty breathing when Neaotomo scooped her off the floor and carried her to her quarters. He stopped about two paces short of her bed and tossed her onto it. Her back hit the bed and responded with renewed pain. Her breath left her completely for a few tics. She watched Neaotomo leave her quarters without even sneaking a peek back—as if she were not worthy of his attention anymore. She was left sprawled on her bed, unable to move and barely able to breathe. The only thought rolled across her mind was, *Why did you do this to me, Laysa? Why? Why?*

Neaotomo smiled as he walked away from Degmer's quarters. He thought that he might have damaged Degmer's lungs while giving her the punishment that Laysa's only disobedience had allowed him to administer. He did not believe the damage to be immediately life-threatening, so he was not concerned about it. The damage might even prove to be beneficial in turning her. He would know after he probed Degmer's mind tomorrow morning what effect the beating had had on her mind.

His thoughts then turned to Laysa. Regret was too strong a word, but Neaotomo did dislike having to use Laysa the way that he felt he must. He disliked the idea of hurting Laysa, although he had no rational reason to dislike the idea. It was unlike him to think irrationally, but somehow, Laysa made him do just that—but only at times, only for a moment. Then his rational thinking returned. Laysa was a remarkable human. She was both vulnerable and strong at the same time. It was an unusual contrast to exist in a single individual.

Unfortunately, his plans for Laysa were only short term. He would use her to help him turn Degmer. He had just used her very successfully, in his estimation. He thought that the little lie about Laysa sometimes stopping at twenty chin-ups was effective. Of course, he knew that Laysa always did thirty chin-ups. Hopefully, planting the idea that Laysa somehow was making Degmer's punishment more severe would go a long way in getting Degmer to doubt Laysa's friendship. Once Degmer thought that Laysa had turned against her, Degmer would feel alone and betrayed; and she would be much easier to turn. If Laysa were aware just how he was using her, she would be quite angry with him. He did not understand why, but he had grown to dislike the idea of her being angry with him; so the less Laysa knew the better. It was too bad that he had no use for Laysa in the long run. His rational thoughts about her labeled her as too big of a risk. It was a risk to let her go and a risk to let her stay. The whole issue of Laysa created a cloud of conflict within his mind. The conflict created interesting feelings within him. The whole Laysa issue engaged and intrigued him.

Meanwhile, the chin-ups had ended Laysa's exercise session, and she had quickly rinsed out her undergarments and hung them to dry on a towel rack. After she had showered and dressed in her long undergarments, she knelt by the bed in her quarters and began to pray.

It was a prayer that she had prayed many times since her capture. The words varied slightly from time to time, but this time, she prayed these words:

"Thaoi, I don't understand why you have allowed a thing like Neaotomo to exist, but I am now at his mercy, as is Degmer. Oh, Thaoi, I don't care what happens to me, but please, please help Degmer. She doesn't know you as I know you. She might be susceptible to Neaotomo's influence. I know I have not been as strong of an influence on her as I should have been in the past, and now I am helpless to be that influence. I am not allowed to speak with Degmer unless Neaotomo allows it. I fear that I might have failed Degmer already. But please, Thaoi, hear my prayer for Degmer now.

"From what I remember of your prophecies in the latter books of the Levra, you predicted the existence of a being such as Neaotomo. I realize that he is not your work but a monstrosity wrought by the work of man. Still, he is too much for Degmer to withstand in her own strength. Please show mercy to my friend. Help her to seek your will and your way before Neaotomo traps her away from all outside reason. Nevertheless, if she will not seek you and does fall under Neaotomo's influence, keep her safe until such a time that a way can be found to free her from his power. May she meet you with a clear conscience. I humbly pray."

Laysa intended to pray for Degmer like this until her life was taken away from her. Even then, she imagined that she would pray for Degmer in the other realm. She had resigned herself to death from the moment she laid eyes on Neaotomo. She couldn't see how her end could be any other way. Neaotomo seemed content to humor her for the time being, but she wouldn't give up her soul, as Neaotomo no doubt would demand. His rational mind would consider her a lost cause eventually, and he would have no more need for her to be alive.

Still, she thought Neaotomo didn't seem to be entirely evil. He seemed nothing worse than a spoiled child at times, and he could be quite civil as long as he was getting his way. However, he didn't seem to have any real good in him either. He seemed to be completely unaffected by morals. All his decisions were based on what was best for him.

Neaotomo had been treating her well today, but she knew that was because it suited his purpose. It was not because he cared anything for her. As far as she could tell, he was incapable of caring for anyone except himself. When he finished with her, he would dispose of her as one would dispose of a piece of scrap paper. She would be dead, and Neaotomo would never think about her again. She fully expected that to be her end.

He could take much away from her, but not even Neaotomo could take away her ability to care. He could make her do things that she didn't want to do, even things that in other circumstances would violate her clear conscience before Thaoi. Yet she would continue to be true to Thaoi and true to Degmer in her innermost being while she lived. She was determined that her end wouldn't be on Neaotomo's terms, but on hers. He couldn't take away anything of importance but her physical life. She would retain all that made her who she was even in death. That was her resolve in the deepest part of her soul.

CHAPTER SEVEN

HISTORY AND INFAMY

Eutay Eneke Aogan was alone in the team's main lab. Axopen, Supeb and Opsil were meeting in a separate room off the lobby and Agapoi might be in his office. The thing that was keeping him in the lab after his shift was the Doetoran broadcast. It wasn't that he had to stay in the lab to watch it. Holon had skillfully pieced together the private broadcast and had given him the protocols for it, and he had set up his nona to receive the transmission. His nona would receive the broadcast no matter where he went in Bojoa so that wasn't keeping him in the lab. It was something that he had seen during the broadcast — particularly during the lord director's testimony — that kept him in the lab.

During the lord director's testimony about something that he had called *Project Avenger*, an image was shown of one of the Avengers. The testimony about the Avenger was startling to be sure, but it was the familiarity of the image that had sparked his interest. He had captured the image on a memory card and inputted the image into the archive storage term as a search value. His initial searches had turned up empty, yet he was sure that he had seen that image before.

He had wanted to show the image to Axopen earlier, but he, Supeb, and Opsil had requested privacy to work on developing the long-range transport array. He wasn't sure if his memory was correct, but he seemed to recall the image being associated with early transport schematics and prototypes. He hadn't thought that interrupting them merely to confirm a hunch was a good idea so he set out to prove his own hunch.

So far, his attempts to find a match in the archive term were proving fruitless. He was about to give up and call it a night when he noticed how the term had saved the criteria about the Avenger image. The image of the Avenger was taken in front of a hangar. The programming of the term had used the hangar as a point of reference to determine the size of the Avenger. It had listed the size as approximately one hundred dets in diameter. Yet, he remembered the lord director saying something about the Avenger being small. One hundred dets for a diameter would not make the Avenger small; it would make it about the height of most passenger aircraft in use today. The programming assumed that the hangar in the background was a huge hangar mainly because it dwarfed the trees to the side of it. But he recognized the trees as being a type of miniature decorative tree. He didn't believe that the hangar was huge at all.

He ran over to the communications term that was recording the broadcast and searched backward in the time index until he found the image being displayed. He listened to the voice of the lord director as he talked about the Avengers. He had mentioned a measurement: ten dets. The diameter of the Avenger was only ten dets.

He walked thoughtfully back to the archive term. He supposed that adjusting the parameters of the search to an object of a smaller size was worth a try. He corrected the diameter of the search image to ten dets and started the search.

He glanced back at his nona that was displaying the live broadcast of the Edvukaat session. The display indicated the time in Manku City was 6:42. It seemed that the suvatens were getting ready to take a vote, as all the witnesses were being shown coming back into the chamber.

Before the witnesses were seated, the archive term gave two fast, even tones that indicated that a search item was successfully found. His eyes fell on the term. Displayed there was his search image, and beside it an identical sphere that the search had found in the archive records. Eutay touched the archive image to reveal the details. The image was dated over three years ago, the twenty-second of Cencam, 4517 MENS. The description of the archive image said that the image was a prototype of the mobile transport array platform.

He thought that the match was too identical to be a coincidence. He quickly saved the archive file to a memory card, and then he immediately went to see if Agapoi was still in his office. He had heard Agapoi tell Holon that he would be working late, so he hoped that Agapoi was still there. If he wasn't still there, he would certainly contact him via a commterm. This discovery could be important. It was very likely, perhaps certain, that the design of the Avengers came from the team's research.

As he neared the meeting area, he could see lights coming from the windows in Agapoi's office. Agapoi had to be there. He never knew Agapoi to leave his lights on after he left for the day. He quickened his pace. This was probably the most important discovery that he had ever made. He just wished it were a technological discovery instead of a discovery of treachery. As he approached the office, he saw Agapoi sitting at his computing term at the far corner of his desk. The migoterm on the far wall of the office was also on. It was tuned to the Edvukaat session. He hurried to the door and knocked vigorously.

Obviously startled by the sudden loud knocking at his door, Agapoi turned around to see who had knocked. His expression turned from surprise to what he thought might be annoyance when Agapoi saw him. Still, Agapoi waved him into his office. He opened the office door and stepped in.

"You had better have something serious to discuss with me. The gus sakrate is about to take a roll call vote. This could be an historic vote, one that could forever change the Empire of Doetora," said Agapoi as he entered the office. Agapoi sounded as annoyed as he looked. Agapoi turned from him back toward the migoterm.

He wasn't surprised at Agapoi's annoyance. He had gained a reputation as a jokester—a well-deserved reputation. Agapoi merely thought he was about to pull a prank or waste his time in some way. He decided that he might as well wait to tell Agapoi what he had discovered until after the vote was over. Agapoi's attention would be divided until then. "I think it's a very serious matter, Agapoi, but it can wait until the vote is over," he said.

Agapoi cast a curious glance toward him, but he shook his head and pointed to the migoterm to tell Agapoi it was all right to watch the vote. He sat down in one of the chairs in front of Agapoi's desk and swiveled it around toward the migoterm.

The gus sakrate was just explaining the voting options. An *aye* vote meant that the suvaten was voting to depose the emperor. If the suvaten voted *no*, the suvaten was voting to keep the emperor in power. The gus sakrate then explained that he would call the suvatens' names in alphabetical order.

He then began. The first name called was Andryo. The vote was *aye*. This vote brought a few murmurs from the chamber gallery, but it didn't appear to have any effect on any of the suvatens. It seemed that this *aye* vote was the expected vote from this suvaten.

The next name was Cemyoz. Cemyoz had helped chair the session so he figured that his vote would be *aye*—and it was.

The next name was Devaranu. Devaranu seemed reluctant to vote, but another suvaten seemed to coax him to stand. Devaranu slowly rose to his feet. He looked to the suvaten that had been talking to him, and then he peered past that suvaten. He seemed to be searching for someone else. After a moment, he focused again on the close by suvaten, and the suvaten nodded. Finally, the vote came. It was *aye*. The whole chamber, including the suvatens, erupted into an electric buzz. The camera went to a wide view of the chamber and then focused on the center podium. The lord director, who was again chairing the session, hit a button in the railing of his platform. A gonglike sound reverberated in the chamber. After the sound had dissipated, the buzz in the chamber was gone as well.

Agapoi moved to the edge of his seat and turned his head toward him. "Now that was interesting. Apparently, that suvaten was a swing vote of some sort. They need fifteen votes to pull this off, you know."

He nodded at Agapoi but did not say anything, as Agapoi's attention immediately went back to the migoterm after his nod. *A swing vote might be an understatement on Agapoi's part,* he thought. The whole vote might have hung on that vote, based on the reaction he saw. The camera had gone to a wide view of the chamber again.

"Do you see those six suvatens on the left side of the chamber? They seem to be huddled for a conference, and they seem to be signaling for the suvaten that sat next to Devaranu to join them," said Agapoi. He sounded as excited as a boy that was playing a favorite game.

He saw what Agapoi had described. "It doesn't appear that he's interested in joining them though," he said as he watched the scene unfold.

"No, it doesn't, does it?" asked Agapoi rhetorically.

The gus sakrate called the next name. The name was Dikurzk. The vote was *aye*. The next was Dizkuh, and the vote was *aye*. The next name was Felshivke. One of the huddled six suvatens stepped out from among the others. He requested a pass. Murmurs again erupted within the chamber.

"Hmm. The plot thickens," said Agapoi. "I believe that those six suvatens want to vote no, but they are not sure that they now have enough votes to stop the vote from succeeding."

He was puzzled. "How do you figure that?" he asked.

"Just watch," was the answer.

Eutay watched as the next name, Khenzhe, and the next name, Kryse, were called. Both suvatens stepped out of the six-man huddle and requested a pass just as Felshivke had done. Again, there were murmurs in the chamber.

"You see? They are not at all sure how to vote now. They want to see how someone else is going to vote. I bet it's that suvaten that they were trying to convince to come over to them," said Agapoi. His eyes still shone with excitement.

He knew that Agapoi always did love a bit of intrigue. "But, Agapoi, there are six of them. I believe there are only twenty suvatens. As you said, they need fifteen votes for the vote to succeed, wouldn't it be more likely that they have someone in their group that is undecided?" he asked.

"You forget, Eutay," said Agapoi. "The lord director is again chairing the session. He can cast a vote if he wishes. Since he testified so brilliantly against the emperor, I don't think it is a stretch to believe that he will use his vote to make the measure succeed if necessary."

"Oh yeah. I see now. They need a seventh no vote to prevent the fifteenth aye vote. But why don't they just vote *no* then?"

The next name was called, and Agapoi held out his hand to indicate he wanted to hear the result. The name was Naomast, and the vote was *aye*.

Agapoi then took another glance toward him and said, "They are worried about what might happen if the vote succeeds and they were the only ones to vote *no*. Who knows what changes in government a new emperor might bring. They fear both reprisals and public opinion."

He nodded. That made sense. Agapoi certainly had an ability to discern things that others might miss. He figured it might have to do with the constant reading that Agapoi did.

The next suvaten, Suvaten Navinuvnu, voted *aye*. Eutay smiled briefly, thinking that he would hate to have to say that name in public. It was kind of a tongue twister.

Next was Nu, and the vote was *aye*.

Now that name is much better, he thought, *short and sweet.*

The next name was Nurmen. The vote was *aye*.

"That makes it ten to nothing in favor so far. Those six have to hope that one of the next five suvatens votes no," said Agapoi. He sounded as if he was a sports analyst describing game strategy.

The next name was Shipunke. The suvaten that had talked with the undecided suvaten stood. He couldn't remember the undecided suvaten's name.

"I think this is the vote the six are waiting to hear," said Agapoi quietly. Even though he nearly whispered, his voice was thick with excitement.

He watched intently. Shipunke did not take as much as a glance at the six. Instead, he peered over at the suvaten who chaired the session while the director was out of the room. He thought he remembered his name was Cemyoz. Shipunke gave a nod to Cemyoz and voted. The vote was *aye*.

The chamber erupted, not in a buzz, but in a roar. The six suvatens who were huddled went back to their seats. A wide shot of the chamber revealed reporters streaming out the door and photographers fighting to take a picture of Shipunke. His was only the eleventh aye vote, but everyone there seemed to believe that the vote was decided on that vote. They were certainly in a better position to know than he was, but maybe not in a better position to know than Agapoi was. He noticed that Agapoi had sat back in his seat. He just seemed to want to take in the moment he was witnessing.

It took several gong sounds for the chamber to be restored to order. When order was restored, the votes came quickly. The next vote was from Slipar. He was one of the six. He voted *aye*. It seemed as if Agapoi was right. Nothing could prevent the vote from passing now. Indeed, it appeared that the vote would be unanimous.

One by one, the remaining suvatens voted. All votes were *aye*, including the votes of those suvatens who had previously passed their turn. The last to vote was Zhulkiy. His vote made it twenty *aye* votes to zero *no* votes. The gus sakrate looked to the director. The director had a smile on his face but shook his head and waved his hand. The gus sakrate then announced the final vote to the chamber.

Loud shouts and celebration erupted in the chamber. It was as if the weight of ten thousand worlds had been taken off the backs of those present. Even the six suvatens who had huddled put smiles on their faces in front of the cameras.

"Remember this date and time, Eutay. History will remember what happened in the Empire of Doetora today. Those in the chamber seem to think that Doetora is better for it. I suppose history will determine that for sure," said Agapoi. He had a huge smile on his face. He closely resembled a child in a ducas store, gawking at all the delectable treats that such a store offered.

He took note of the clock. It was 7:70, 6:70 in Manku City. Today was Treti, the eighth of Setmi. The date and time were worth remembering. Indeed, what they had just witnessed had the earmarks of a monumental event.

Agapoi turned off the migoterm, got up, and walked to the refreshment area in his office. He poured a cup of cefa, and then he turned to him and asked, "Can I get you some cefa or che?"

He shook his head, so Agapoi returned to his chair with his cefa.

"So, Eutay, what is this serious matter you wished to discuss?"

Agapoi was never one for small talk when an issue needed discussing, so it didn't surprise him that Agapoi went straight to the point. He swiveled his seat to face Agapoi and began with a question. "Did you see Lord Director Temeos's testimony about the Avengers?"

Agapoi smiled and said, "It would have been hard to miss it. They replayed portions of it whenever the deliberation discussions reached a lull. Is that what you wanted to discuss with me?"

He shook his head. "Not exactly. I wanted to show you something I found on the team archive term. It's a file of an old mobile transport platform."

Agapoi shook his head and sighed. "I'm afraid I am not following what an archive file has to do with Temeos's testimony. What is your issue, Eutay?" asked Agapoi impatiently.

He thought that Agapoi must be tired because he was usually a little more patient. He just handed Agapoi the memory card and said, "Look at the file, Agapoi."

Agapoi sighed again, reached across the desk, took the card from him, and inserted it into his computing term. He transferred his term display to the migoterm that they had been watching. The memory card was displayed as a small, black square on the bottom, right corner of the migoterm. Agapoi picked up a pointing pen and pointed it toward the migoterm. The pen produced an arrow on the migoterm to indicate where on the screen Agapoi was pointing the pen. He maneuvered the pen over the black square and said, "Open."

The black square converted into a larger white square that listed the different items on the card. "What am I looking for, Eutay?" asked Agapoi.

"It's the only transport file on the card: Transport-m-p-05224517. It has a scroll icon," he said.

"Cute, Eutay. A scroll for an archive file," said Agapoi with a slight smile. Agapoi pointed at the scroll icon and said, "Open." The migoterm filled with the file image and description text. Agapoi stared at the file for a moment and then glanced over at him. He then pointed his pen on the image and said, "Enlarge image to fill screen." The image of the mobile transport platform filled the screen, and the text was no longer visible. "I remember this," said Agapoi in a hushed, musing voice before turning to him and asking, "Do you have an image of the Avenger on this card?"

He nodded. As he suspected, the image of the mobile transport platform got Agapoi's attention. He said, "It is the PT file on the card from today. It has a blue PT icon."

Agapoi said, "Shrink active file to icon." The migoterm displayed only the scroll icon and the white box with the list of files now. Agapoi found the blue PT icon for file PTblue07084520, pointed the pen at it, and said, "Open." The image from Temeos's testimony filled the screen. The Avenger was in the foreground, with a hangar in the background. Agapoi said, "Reduce image fifty percent." The image became smaller, but it was still centered on the migoterm. Agapoi pointed to it and said, "Drag." As he moved the pen, the image moved with it. He moved the image to the left side of the migoterm, revealing the scroll icon. He pointed at it and said, "Enlarge to fifty percent, image only." The migoterm now displayed the two images side by side. He pointed to the Avenger in the testimony image and said, "Select this object only. Enlarge to fifty percent of screen." The image of the Avenger now was on the left side of the migoterm, with the image of the mobile transport platform on the right. The identical nature of the two objects was very apparent. Agapoi peered at him with a mild scowl. "I had forgotten about this prototype. This was, what, three years ago?"

He nodded. "According to Temeos's testimony, the Avengers are exactly the same diameter. He said the Avengers were about ten dets in diameter. The specs on the mobile transport platform call for a diameter of 9.95 dets. Notice the round outline in the front of the Avenger. It is the same on the MTP. I hope you don't mind the acronym." He paused, and Agapoi shook his head to indicate that the MTP acronym was fine to use in place of mobile transport platform. He continued. "On the MTP, that round outline housed the rod for the transport beam. It wouldn't surprise me at all if the round outline on the Avenger housed a similar rod to deploy the weapon beam."

Agapoi nodded and scratched his chin while saying thoughtfully, "No. That wouldn't surprise me either, Eutay. It wouldn't surprise me at all." After a moment of reflection he asked, "Do you remember much about the early transport beam, Eutay?"

He replied, "I remember it was unstable and that it blew more things up than it transported before the confinement beam was perfected."

"Exactly," said Agapoi. "It blew things up. What did the damage to the old missile site that Temeos displayed look like to you?"

"It looked like everything on the site just blew up." He paused as Agapoi's point rammed itself home. "The Avenger weapon could very well be the early transport beam. The early beam also had to be focused from five beam rods to reach full power. We lacked the ability to transmit a beam of that magnitude from one rod. We blew out several rods trying to transmit the full strength beam with one rod. It wasn't until Axopen developed the current confinement beam technology that the five rods could be combined into one array without the beam jumping to another rod and overloading it. That would explain why the Avengers have to have a five-craft formation for the beam to be fully effective. It all fits." He was at the same time exultant and horrified.

"I believe it does indeed. There is still one more thing in Temeos's testimony that troubles me," said Agapoi. "Temeos said that the Emperor used a thought wave interface to control the Avengers. Noso developed such an interface about three years ago. The council didn't approve production of the technology, but I am told that it was tested successfully. It is possible that whoever leaked the transport technology to Doetora also leaked the thought wave technology to them. The really disturbing thing is that whoever leaked the information would have to have level three clearance or higher. If both my team and Noso's team had an information leak at the same time, the leak couldn't have come any one person on either team or any one person on a single manufacturing team---unless..." Agapoi didn't finish that line of reasoning aloud. Instead he continued with a new line of reasoning. "The leak could have come from two or more informants, but lower-level access to such technology is closely regulated. It doesn't make sense that security could have failed on a lower level twice. However, higher-level access is not as closely watched. In the past, such vigilance for the persons more honored in their field was not deemed necessary. Perhaps that should be changed now. This could prove to be an infamous moment for Cirri."

Agapoi's revelations had stunned him quite a bit. Agapoi had come to a conclusion that seemed correct, yet unthinkable. A higher-level person in the technology field was guilty of spying for the Empire of Doetora. Level-three access was granted only to Cirrians who had earned their fourth name. These were highly honored, very respected people. It seemed bad enough to him that any Cirrian would be guilty of spying, but to think that a highly honored Cirrian was guilty of spying for the empire was truly a horrible thought. Yet, Agapoi was right. It would be very hard for a person with level one or level two access to steal technology details and transmit or transport them outside of Cirri or even outside of the facility where the information was stored. Cirri was well-known for their information security measures. These measures were one of the reasons why all of Kosundo entrusted Cirrian institutions with their financial information.

"What can we do, Agapoi?" he asked.

"I will report your findings to the technology council," said Agapoi. "They'll have to launch an investigation. The information is three years old, and so might be the theft. It will take a while to uncover the tracks that are most likely well hidden by now. Still, I trust that the spy can be found before he can do further damage. I will also ask the council to rush the approval of Noso's move to Bojoa. I think the council will want Noso in Bojoa since his team's information might now be considered sensitive. Besides, it would be best if the council can get information from his team directly about this matter."

Eutay listened to the list of things that Agapoi said he would do, but his mind centered on only one sentence. He mumbled a goodbye to Agapoi, left the office and shut down his terms and workstations. He then headed for the LC. All the while, he couldn't get Agapoi's statement out of his head: *I trust that the spy can be found before he can do further damage.* It was a haunting thought that somewhere in Cirri, maybe even somewhere in Bojoa, was a high-level traitor waiting to betray Cirri. Nevertheless, he had come to have great faith in Agapoi's ability to solve mysteries of all sorts. *If no one else can, perhaps Agapoi can unmask the spy.* That thought brought at least some comfort to his troubled mind. He just was glad he didn't have to bring this news to the council. If *his* mind was troubled, he could only imagine what Agapoi's mind was going through right now.

He had earned his fourth name nearly sixty years ago for his achievements in fusion technology. Yet, since that time, his achievements had been overshadowed by some young upstarts who had found a special metal. They had discovered how to make more energy with smaller devices. They had found out how to transport raw ore from an underground vein directly to a refining facility. They had done this. They had done that. It sickened him to see so much come so quickly to someone else. It was he who was supposed to be the next great figure in Cirrian technology, not some young hotshot from some insignificant cave city in southern Cirri. Now his own spy, who called himself Ketesku, had told him that this peon was building a long-range matter transporter. It was too much. He was enraged with jealousy.

It was this jealousy that had driven him to steal information in the first place. Since he had the information, he could see no harm in making a few credits from it by selling it to Doetora. Sure, it was against all he had believed in as a younger man, but it was not really that big of a deal. When he was young, he had fancied himself as serving Thaoi and country. Now he knew the folly in that ideal. It was far more advantageous for him to serve the Great One. The Great One had given him many opportunities to advance toward fortune and power.

Sure, he would have to settle for a position of lower esteem in Cirri for now, but when the Great One took over Kosundo, he would gain more power than Cirri ever could offer him. For now, he would content himself with being a consultant for the Bojoa manufacturing team. He had hoped that he could land a position with a technology team, but it seemed that all technology positions in the dome were filled. A technology team in Cirri City had offered him a nice position, but that position was not in Bojoa so he turned it down. Bojoa was where he needed to stay right now. This was where the action was. This was where he could do the Great One the most service and prove himself worthy of a high position in the Great One's Empire of Kosundo.

A technology position would have been nice, but he could keep tabs on any new developments that came through manufacturing. They would be sure to consult him, a high-ranking technology expert, whenever new technology needed to be manufactured. They would want to know how to produce it more efficiently, and he would advise them well. The better he advised them, the more new technology he would see. The more new technology he saw, the better he would know the happenings in the dome. The better he knew what was going on in the dome, the better information he could give to the Great One. He would redirect his spy to follow the high council chair. He could keep track of the technology of Bojoa on his own now. Yes, this position would do just fine.

Chapter Eight

Thinking About Destiny

Abin turned off the PT. It was early evening, about 6:70 on Treti. He had been watching live coverage of an historic event: the no-confidence vote taking place in the Edvukaat. He had never been so scared in his whole life.

It was not the vote itself that had him shaking in his boots. The vote had turned out fine. The emperor was deposed by a twenty-to-nothing vote. It was what the vote meant for him. Tonight, he must head back to Manku City. Tomorrow, he would be revealed as the only surviving heir to the imperial throne. On Paraskevi, he would take the Oath of Empire. He was not at all sure that this was a good thing for the empire.

It was true that he would have Temeos to rely on for advice, but Temeos could only advise him so far. There were going to be decisions that he would have to make, decisions that only the emperor could make.

One of the things he wanted to do was to empower the Edvukaat again. Though they had just ousted an emperor, the body had no real power to do much of anything else. The session he had just witnessed wouldn't have happened without Temeos. He had been the catalyst. It was his leadership that had spawned the session.

Though the Edvukaat needed to have some say in the everyday running of the empire, restoring its power would have to wait until he restored elections for Edvukaat seats. Since Edvukaat membership had become an inherited position, the Edvukaat had become a noble class. The body didn't have much in the way of real power, but it did have a great deal of privilege for its members. That is what made it so remarkable that a no-confidence vote had even been considered. The suvatens had nothing to gain in a personal way by deposing the emperor and stood to lose quite a bit whether the vote passed or not.

Of course, Temeos's argument was very convincing, and his use of media coverage was a stroke of genius. Once his testimony was out in the public arena, the suvatens had no choice but to take action. Even the most crooked suvaten could not make a case for keeping the emperor in power. The suvatens saw that Emperor Tryllos's fate was sealed when the goals of *Project Avenger* were revealed, although some still tried to discredit Temeos. The attempt was more for show than any substantial attack. Everyone who knew Temeos knew that his character was beyond reproach. In the face of all this, no suvaten dared to mount a serious attempt to defend the emperor. None of them wanted to appear too sympathetic to an emperor who showed total unconcern for the well-being of his people, as the testimony about project Avenger proved to everyone today.

Apparently, even Tryllos knew that his fate was sealed since he had fled the empire. He didn't even care to try to mount a defense for himself. Still, it was unlike Tryllos to give up so easily. He couldn't see how Tryllos could have won if he had stayed. Still, it wasn't like him just to accept defeat meekly. He thought it ironic that Tryllos's last decision as emperor, the decision to flee, might have been the most rational of his recent reign. There certainly wasn't anything about *Project Avenger* that showed any rationality. Temeos had said it best. The Avengers had no place in civilized society.

If Temeos had not done so already, Abin knew that his first act as emperor would have to be to have every last one of the Avengers destroyed. As he understood it, as few as four Avengers could pose a very serious threat to world security. No one in Kosundo would be safe until the Avengers were eliminated.

It suddenly occurred to him that this was the first time that he had thought at any length about what he would do as emperor. He hadn't dared to think on it to any real degree until he knew how Temeos had fared. Now that he knew, he supposed that he should think more about it. The Avengers were a given; they had to be destroyed. But what should be done after that? Through Temeos's guidance, he understood some of the things that needed to be done, but he hadn't a clue how to accomplish those things nor did he know what should be done first.

He knew that he had to find a way to limit the emperor's role. Right now, the emperor was an absolute ruler. The emperor could make laws, and he could decide how laws should be enforced. The emperor appointed all local officials or had people who appointed them in his name. There was only one control on his power, one that had never been used successfully until today, and it took an outrageous display of instability from Tryllos to initiate that control. There had to be more controls put on the emperor's power that would curtail wrongdoing by the emperor before he was allowed to run amuck. Not to do so would eventually bring the empire right back to the same mess that it had faced today. How best to accomplish this he didn't know.

Right now, all of his thinking on what to do came back to Temeos. Temeos would have some ideas, and he would listen to them. He would have to make it official when he took office, but he certainly would retain Temeos's services as lord director. How could he do anything else?

The empire owed its very existence to Temeos. As it happened, he had been the only true control on Emperor Tryllos's power all along. He had caused the emperor to change his plans on numerous occasions. On numerous more occasions, he had limited the damage caused by Tryllos's poor decisions. If anything positive came from Tryllos's reign, it was because of Lord Director Temeos. Temeos was the only person he would trust in the position of lord director.

He glanced over at the clock. It was getting late in the afternoon. He should think about getting some sleep, if that would be possible. Temeos was regularly in his office before three parzes, and he wanted to be at the Imperial Building of State at about the time that Temeos arrived. He thought the trip from Salu to Manku City would take about two parzes on his tsik, so he would need to leave around the first parz of the new day. He could get a full night's sleep if he managed to get to sleep in a half parz or so.

He would need a full night's sleep if he could get it. Tomorrow would be a busy day, to say the least. He didn't know what Temeos meant exactly by "being revealed," but he thought it would mean an appearance before the Edvukaat and the media at the least. What else needed to be done to implement his reign, he didn't know. He would have to rely on Temeos to fill in the blanks for him tomorrow. The reliance he would have on the lord director was very clear; and he was comfortable with that, very comfortable. As he headed for the bedroom, he only hoped that his mind was now comfortable enough to allow him to get some sleep. It wasn't enough just to show up and let Temeos do the work of securing the throne for him. He needed to show that he was a worthy successor, not just an heir. He would need an alert mind to accomplish that.

CHAPTER NINE

THE ESCAPE OF A TROUBLED MIND

Nenavis breathed a sigh of relief. It was obvious that his various sessions, as well as his D'Yavoly's many sessions, with Tryllos had made Tryllos's mind nearly useless as a thinking tool. Tryllos was nearly helpless without his presence now. It was this weak mind that had made it necessary for him to take control and rescue Tryllos from sure imprisonment in Doetora.

Tryllos had been careless. He had left incriminating proof of his illegal and unwise activities where that snoop, Temeos, could find them. Erith! Tryllos had given Temeos the key to his undoing when he gave him a copy of the project Avenger charter. Still, all was well for now. Tryllos's fragile but important mind had now been brought to Dricho, closer to that abomination, that very powerful abomination.

He had managed to get Tryllos to Aturla. The time was so short that he was unable to get Tryllos there without leaving a trail that the Doetoran authorities would surely find and follow.

He knew of a person in Aturla that one his minions had contacted many years ago. Her name was Wissa. A cringe rumbled through him upon thinking of a human's name, but knowing this human's name was an unfortunate necessity. Necessity drove him to stoop to rely on human contacts from time to time. Wissa was a scientist that was working for the Dricho Genetics Foundation in Aturla. She knew about the genetics complex that was located in the remote icy southern tip of Dricho as well as many other secrets of the foundation. He would need Wissa to get Tryllos to the complex without leaving any trail to follow. The minion had already contacted Wissa, and she was to meet Tryllos shortly at a park near the hotel where Tryllos currently had taken a room. He was walking Tryllos to this rendezvous point at this very moment.

It was still early in the morning in Aturla. It was a cool morning—much cooler than recent mornings had been in Manku City. Tryllos thought it odd that he wasn't in Manku City but in Dricho of all places. He hadn't left the vicinity of the palace in years, and he had never left the empire before. Why he was here was a mystery to him.

He was thinking that it was surreal that he had boarded an air transport in Manku City at a little past three parzes, rode the aircraft for over five parzes, and still arrived in Dricho just before it was the third parz in Aturla. *Shouldn't it be later in the day instead of earlier?* He had thought it beneath him to travel to Dricho in the first place. All he knew was that he was supposed to meet someone called Wissa. Something inside him had compelled him to do many things this morning that he didn't understand.

He was walking toward the park now where he was supposed to meet this Wissa even though he had never heard of her before. He knew that there was a white bridge in the park where Wissa would meet him. He didn't really know how he knew that. He just knew it. There was certainly nothing in his memory that told him of the bridge or Wissa.

The park looked to be of decent size. He obeyed the urge he felt to walk down the main path into the park. Somehow he knew that this path would eventually take him to the other side of the park, though he could point to no memories that told him that.

After a couple of spens, he saw the white bridge on the path to his left so he took the path and waited near the railing on the bridge. The bridge spanned a small stream that ran through the park. It was almost cold this morning. He was glad of the heavy jacket that he had felt compelled to put on as he left the hotel. It was late spring, but the sun hadn't had much time to warm the air yet this morning.

After a short time, a black-haired, dark-skinned woman walked onto the bridge and casually stopped next to him. Without turning toward him, she asked, "Are you Tryllos?"

Something inside him told him not to look at the woman, so he continued to peer over the railing. Then something inside him spoke, and his mouth moved. "I am. Are you Wissa?"

"I am," came the reply. "It is an honor to serve you, My Great Lord."

He was flattered that someone in Dricho would call him a great lord, but it also confused him, as did many things about this morning, which felt as if it should be evening by now. The voice inside him asked Wissa, "You have arranged transport then, my child?" *My child? That is a strange thing to call the woman. She appears as if she is about my age.*

"I have, Great Lord," replied Wissa without hesitation. "You will go to the other end of the park, where a hover transport waits. The driver will take you to the complex for a price. I have loaded the necessary amount on this credit monitor. The funds will be drawn from my account, so they cannot be traced back to your host, My Great Lord."

Something inside him told him to stick out his left hand. He felt something cold placed into his hand. Again, obeying the impulse inside him, he put the object into his coat pocket. "You have done well, my child," said the voice inside him.

"Perhaps I can be of further service to My Lord someday," said the woman hopefully.

"Perhaps," said the voice within him.

The woman smiled slightly as she nodded to him before walking off the bridge in the direction she had been heading before she stopped. Some impulse caused him to leave the bridge as well. He took the path that led out of the park and then scanned for a parked hovercraft. He saw one on his right so he walked toward it. A Mugmi man got out of the hovercraft and said, "Are you Tryllos?"

The voice inside him answered again, "I am."

The man then asked, "Do you have the credits?"

The impulse inside him made him hand the man the object that he had received from the woman.

The man said, "Axi then. I will take you to where you wish to go. Get in."

The impulse inside him made him get into the backseat of the hovercraft while the man got into the driver's seat. A voice from within him said, "How long will it take to get there?"

The man turned and answered, "A little over two days. We will arrive sometime late on Paraskevi. I know of a couple of places that will put us up at night along the way, discreetly. I will pay for the rooms for us with the credit monitor you provided, as agreed. And, as agreed, I will keep what is left over for my own use. Why do you want to go to such a place anyway? You don't look like a scientist, and there is nothing else within fifty stets of the place."

The voice inside him said, "It would be best for you if you do not ask any more questions. I hope I make myself clear."

The man appeared a bit shaken. He turned back around quickly and said in a trembling voice, "I un- understand — believe me — p-please. I won't tell anyone anything. I will tell nothing — to anyone. And — and I won't ask any more questions."

"Good. See that you abide by your word or pay the consequences," said the voice inside him.

The man had stared at him with wide eyes. It was as if he were suddenly terrified of him, which seemed very strange to him. The man started the hovercraft hastily and put the craft in motion. All the while he could see the terror in the man's eyes in the driver's mirror. He didn't understand the man's reaction any more than he understood any other part of this morning. He didn't even know where the man was taking him. All he knew was that he was headed south to some remote place where there appeared to be scientists. Judging the distance from the time it would take to get there, he was thinking that his jacket was not going to be nearly warm enough. He only hoped that the place that he was being taken to had a good source of heat because he had no idea how long he would be there.

His mind then wandered to his Avengers. The impulse inside him had made him put the mesh control cap into his jacket pocket this morning. As he fingered the cap, he longed for the time he could talk to his Avengers again. Perhaps the next time he talked to them, he could let them show off to all of Kosundo. That would be a show that all of Kosundo would certainly remember—well—at least those who were left on Kosundo after the show would remember it.

He sat back in the seat and closed his eyes. All of a sudden, the travel today was making him tired. He had no trouble falling asleep; and while he slept, he dreamed of his Avengers and the wonderful show they would put on soon. It made him feel that all the wrongs against him in this world would soon be righted. He dreamed of his glorious victory with a smile on his face.

Chapter Ten

Facing the Council

As Epetaones hung on the gallows, many of the people in the crowd that was gathered in the courtyard of the prison to witness the execution gathered up stones, hurled them at Epetaones's body, and shouted, "Traitor!" and, "Betrayer!" The crowd quickly turned into a mob. It was all that could be done to restrain the crowd from charging the gallows to rip Epetaones's body into pieces.

Such was the end of Epetaones Plauvax Diesam, the only Cirrian citizen ever to be convicted of treason. His whole life had been devoted to the pursuit of money and fame. In the end, he died penniless and stripped of all earthly belongings. His vain search for fame ended only in infamy.

Agap closed the book and put it aside. He had been reading *The Traitor of Cirri*. He peered over at the clock to see if it was time to log into the technology council meeting. It was 3:96 on Titarti morning. It was about time. He was in his office and had closed the vertical shutters on his windows for privacy. The team knew not to disturb him when the shutters were closed. The book seemed appropriate reading for this morning, given the information that he was about to give the council.

He brought up the council meeting console on his desk. The entire technology council was still in Bojoa, but old habits were hard to break. The council members preferred to remote into meetings rather than to meet in person. It was more convenient and took less time. The meeting console consisted of eleven holographic arrays that expanded into a semicircle about the desk. He liked to look people in the eyes when he talked, so he had the console adjusted to follow the height of his holographic headset that was used to produce his image to the other council members via the holographic array. The headset was so tiny that it was barely noticeable, even in close proximity to the wearer.

He had Eutay prepare holographic images of the Avenger and the MTP for the meeting. Upon inspecting the holographs, he found it remarkable that he couldn't tell which image was which. Every detail of the holographic images of the Avenger and MTP were identical right down to the trapezoidal pattern on the surface, which could be seen only when viewing a magnification of the images. The match was undeniable. He was certain that the Avenger was merely a replica of the MTP that was modified to be controlled by thought waves. He readied the images that he would display during the meeting.

It was nearly the fourth parz now, so Agap put his thumb into the scanner port and said, "Agapoi." The console's hololights lit up. He then said, "Meeting TC07092040." The meeting code was simple enough. It simply meant the technology council meeting for today's date, the ninth of Setmi, 2040 MENS.

The console immediately popped up the holographs of ten torsos. The middle array was still uninitiated. Everybody but Phrunoi was logged on. It was customary for the council chair to log in as close to the meeting time as possible. This prevented the other council members from being perceived as late—unless, of course, they really were late. It was within a spen of the announced meeting time. Phrunoi should be logging on at any moment.

The council members were quiet and did not move their heads. This was also customary. It was the sign that you were ready and in a serious mind for the meeting. He hadn't known this custom the first time he logged on and had greeted the other council members upon seeing the holographs. He was promptly reprimanded and told how to conduct himself in a meeting. It was the most difficult part of the meeting for him. That was why he now logged on only tics before the council chair. It was all he could do to stay quiet and still for those few tics.

After what seemed like an eternity to him, Phrunoi logged on and an eleventh holographic torso appeared on his array. The eternity in his mind had only been a few tics of course, but over seventy tics of being still seemed like an eternity to him. Phrunoi scanned the array images as if he were making sure that all council members were present before saying rather robustly, "Good morning, council members."

All the council members said, "Good morning, Chair Phrunoi."

Phrunoi then stated the purpose of the meeting. "We have been called to this meeting at the request of Agapoi, the young council member from Zaria. He says that he has uncovered some disturbing news. It seems that Doetora is in possession of some uncirculated technology that appears to have its origins in Cirrian testing facilities. This is a very serious matter. We will hear Agapoi's presentation, and then we must decide the merit of Agapoi's claims and the course of action to be taken, should his claims appear to be valid. Agapoi, you have the floor."

Agap cleared his throat and began. "Thank you, Chair Phrunoi." He paused for a moment to clear his mind and order his thoughts. He had never been the main speaker at a council session before, and his stomach was churning. First experiences always put a few extra bubbles in his stomach and made his mind race. He quickly thought of a sunrise through the valley opening near Zaria. His mind cleared and his agenda was now clear to him, and he proceeded. "A member of my team, Eutay Eneke Aogan, was watching a broadcast of the proceedings of the Doetoran Edvukaat session yesterday, a session that I am sure you have all heard about this morning." He paused as he looked about the console.

All of the members nodded that they were aware of the session. Indeed, it would have been hard to miss the news of the session since it was the lead story for all major news organizations in Kosundo last night and again this morning. Still, the news reports in Cirri did not mention the Avengers at all. They mentioned only that Emperor Tryllos was deposed. The reports also contained wild speculation about who would be the next Emperor since it was believed that Tryllos did not have an heir. This speculation led the news stories to concentrate on the possibility of an unstable Doetoran government as well as the ramifications that a Doetoran civil war might have on the other countries of Kosundo. Either the Doetoran news ministry did not release information on the Avengers to news agencies outside Doetora or the Avengers simply were not thought to be a story since Tryllos no longer ruled. Either way, he was about to tell the council something that he was sure that they didn't know.

"During the proceedings, Lord Director Temeos gave testimony about a project that Emperor Tryllos had initiated. The project was called *Avenger*." His eyes moved about the council holograms. None of them showed any particular recognition of the project. This was what he had expected.

"The *Project Avenger* developed a very dangerous first-strike weapon. The weapon itself is called Avenger." He paused and displayed the Avenger hologram to the council. "This is the Avenger as shown in Temeos's testimony." He paused to let the council examine the hologram image of the Avenger before continuing. "Eutay discovered that about three years ago my team developed a prototype for a mobile transporter platform. As you know, the transporter beam will not retain effective concentration through the thick, ionized ozone layers that surround Kosundo, so a satellite system was not an option for any future long-distance site-to-site transporter array. The mobile transport platform, or MTP for short, was an option that was considered for such transports. Since then, the transport beam underwent several modifications, and the long distance and mass transport capabilities of the beam were never successfully developed at that time, so the MTP was forgotten. However, the Avenger lit a spark of memory for Eutay, and he dug up this image of the MTP." He displayed the MTP hologram.

The identical nature of the two images was not lost on the council. He could see from the stern demeanor that overtook the council members' faces that they did not think Doetora could have developed such similar technology on their own.

He continued. "Notice that the two images are identical, right down to the circular groove in the outer shell in the front of the craft." He used a pointing pen to make a red dot of light circle the groove in the front of both crafts. "In the MTP, this groove outlined the cover for the beam rod port. The transport beam rod could extend outside the MTP when the covering retracted. I believe the rod inside the port shown here would serve to extend the weapon beam rod of the Avenger."

He took down both images and then continued. "Another striking similarity that exists between the Avenger and the MTP could very well be the beam that is used." He put up a still image of the beginning of a video from a test of the original transport beam. "The image that you are seeing now is the beginning of a test video shot over three years ago. It is a video of one of our first attempts to transport an item. In this case, the item was a large melon. Watch as I run the video." He started the video.

The transport beam flashed, and the melon exploded. This drew a few chuckles from the council.

"As you might have noticed the test was not successful."

That statement drew a few more chuckles.

"But beyond that, look at the debris pattern of the melon. It is nearly a perfect circle. Now observe the damage inflicted in a test of the Avengers' attack capabilities, as testified by Lord Director Temeos."

He put up a still shot of the missile launch site destroyed by the Avengers. There were a few gasps and murmurs from the council as they saw the image.

"There is a lot of devastation there, but let me zoom in where there appears to be debris from only a single item." He zoomed in on an area where it appeared only a single explosion took place. "Notice the debris field. It is a nearly perfect circle."

The council stirred for a moment but quickly quieted to let him continue.

"There is still another similarity in Avenger technology when compared with transporter technology that I would like to point out. I will leave the image of our transporter test up so that I can point out that similarity."

He took down the image of the Avenger test and then reversed the video of the transporter test until he saw the transport flash. He then slowly advanced the video until he found the point at which the transport beam fired and stopped it there.

"Now, if you would look near the top of the image, you will see how our old transporter beam worked. You can see five distinct beams originating from five beam rods. In the middle, where the beams come together, you can just make out a very small, five-sided pyramid. This simulated matter inverted pyramid was used as a focal point to bring the beams together into one beam. This was necessary because we could not get a sufficiently concentrated beam with only one rod without blowing out the rods. It took five beams to get maximum beam concentration. I will now replay part of Temeos's testimony from yesterday's session." He took down the transport test image and put up the testimony video.

The video clip played, and on the clip, Temeos said, "The image that is now being displayed is what Emperor Tryllos has dubbed an Avenger. The craft is very light, weighing about fifty libs and measuring about ten dets in diameter. Most of you in this chamber would stand taller than the Avenger stands. It doesn't appear very menacing, does it? And by itself, it is not menacing. A single Avenger is completely impotent. It takes four or five of these flying craft, flying in formation, to make the Avenger a weapon. However, I am about to show you what a squadron of five Avengers can do."

He stopped the clip. "This is where Temeos showed the devastation of the Avenger test," he said. "I wanted you to notice that he said that it takes four or five Avengers to make the Avengers a weapon, and then he said that there were five Avengers in a squadron. Just like our old transporter beam, the Avengers need five beams to gain full beam concentration. I believe that it takes five Avengers because the Avengers are using our old transporter beam technology as a weapon. I just don't know what they are using as a focal point. We used simulated matter to project our pyramid at a fixed point to focus the five beams. They would not be able to use a fixed point, since the Avengers move in the air. I can only speculate that they are not using a projected focal point. Perhaps they are using the target itself as the focal point. I guess if all you want to do is to blow something up with the beam, the focal point could be the target."

He paused to glance at his notes. He must have paused for longer than he thought because Phrunoi asked, "Is there anything else you wished to present on this issue?"

He answered. "I apologize for the pause, Chair Phrunoi. I just wanted to be sure that I had covered what I wished to cover on the issue of the beam. I did have one more point, if I may be permitted to continue."

"By all means, continue, Agapoi," said Phrunoi.

"Thank you, Chair Phrunoi," he said formally. "The last point I have about the similarity of Avenger technology to our uncirculated technology is the manner in which the Avenger is said to be controlled. Temeos stated that the Emperor could control the Avengers by a thought wave interface. Although Temeos did not elaborate on this control device, I am assuming it is very similar to the neural cap that Noso's team developed just about three years ago. I don't know of any other group that pioneered thought wave technology. I suppose that Doetora could have developed this technology on their own, but there has been no mention of it in any of the technology advisor reports from Doetora. Of course, there was no mention of the entire Avenger project in those reports either. The Doetoran government can be rather clandestine at times. That is the last thought that I wanted to present today on this issue, Chair Phrunoi. I relinquish the floor."

"Thank you for your presentation, Agapoi," said Phrunoi formally. "It was very informative. At this time, the floor is open for discussion."

Radoi started the discussion by saying, "Agapoi, I agree with you that the technology for much, if not all, of the Avengers came from Cirri. My question is concerning the

Avengers themselves. Given the fact that the Doetoran Emperor has been deposed, do you have any information about any possibility that these Avengers could be used in an attack by rival factions or by someone loyal to the emperor?"

He answered, "I am sorry to say that I do not have any inside information other than having seen the session broadcast yesterday. Holon, our communications specialist, found and pieced together the broadcast for my team. The lord director did indicate on the broadcast, however, that only the emperor could control the Avengers. Temeos announced that the emperor had fled Doetora during the session. I can only assume that he would not have access to the Avengers anymore. If that is the case, then indeed my conclusion would be that the Avengers are no longer an imminent threat."

Mageloi was the next council member to add to the discussion. "Agapoi, I too am in agreement that the similarity in design and function of the Avengers to your group's prototype is probably not mere happenstance. That would mean that someone with access to your group's research data is responsible for leaking the information to Doetora. I suggest we start any investigation with people who were members of your team during the time of that research."

"Very well," he said. "If no one knows of any reason to suspect a particular individual, my team is as good a place to start as any. I have full confidence in my team, and I am sure they will give an investigator their full cooperation. But I don't think that the investigation should stop there. Temporary access to a team's information is often granted to heads of other teams and to any other double-honored Cirrians who request it. There are also manufacturing liaisons, designers, and even high-level foremen who see the plans to a prototype that they are fabricating for a technology team. We need to make sure that any investigation that is launched follows all leads to their conclusion. The investigating team should be allowed access to question anyone who ever had the remotest opportunity to access this information."

Phrunoi then spoke. "Agapoi makes two good points. First, is there a particular person of interest that should be questioned? Second, we need to appoint an independent investigator that will report directly to this council and give him the right to question anyone whom he deems of interest. Let's address the first point. Does anyone on this council have a person of interest in mind?"

No council member responded to the question. That did not surprise him. He had not ever considered that someone might actually steal his team's work until last night. He was sure that the other members had the same illusion of security. There would be no suspects that would pop into anyone's mind; he was sure.

"All right then," said Phrunoi after nearly a spen of silence. "Does anyone have a suggestion for an investigator to look into this matter?"

After a moment of silence, Taknikoi suggested, "How about Kenun Pelen Ischor Opuptu? He is well respected in the technology community and was both an ambassador and advisor to Doetora for a time. He's not one to suffer a lot of nonsense either. I think he would make a fine investigator. He might still have contacts in Doetora who may be able to help him discover who might have accepted the information from our informant."

"He might be a good candidate, but I think Mantiru Tawn Zaluto Hedran might be a better discerner of the truth," suggested Awphousoi.

"He too advised in Doetora, and he is also well respected. Plus, he is quite tenacious. That is a good quality for an investigator," added Mageloi.

"Another excellent candidate is Staphen Gren Turin Luorgus," declared Eluthoi. "He has a background in law enforcement and is a skilled diplomat. He is thought of very highly in all circles."

After a few moments of silence, Phrunoi asked, "Are there any other nominations for investigator?" He waited a few tics. When no one suggested anyone else, he said, "Very well. All of the names put forth are well-known by the council, I believe; but is there any discussion on any of the nominees?" He waited a few more tics. When no one spoke up, he said, "Very well. Lock in your votes for investigator. I will approach the nominee with the most votes to be our investigator."

Agap knew all the men that were suggested. As far as he knew, any of them would be a good choice, but Staphen was not in the technology field. He thought it might be best to keep the investigator in house so to speak. That left Kenun and Mantiru. He thought that Kenun was the more open-minded candidate. Kenun also was an active team lead whereas Mantiru hadn't been involved with a team for some time. He thought that meant that Kenun would understand the dynamics of team research better. After just a moment of reflection, he voted for Kenun.

After the votes were locked in, they were revealed to the council. The council had voted Kenun as the investigator. He would have been happy with any of the men as investigator, but he was gratified that Kenun won. He really did think he was the best candidate for the job. He just hoped he would accept, as he was quite involved with a team of his own.

"Very well," said Phrunoi, "I will contact Kenun immediately, after I inform Odanoi of our discovery. He might want to bring the matter to the High Council's attention." He then turned toward him and said, "Agapoi, will you be with your team for the day? Odanoi might want to speak with you about this matter."

"Yes, I will be with my team all day, Chair Phrunoi," he said respectfully.

"Very good. I might be in touch myself. If Kenun accepts the responsibility of investigator, I will have him meet with you first." With that, Phrunoi logged off and the other council members with him.

He took down the meeting console. He couldn't get over how casually Phrunoi had told him to expect a call from High Chair Odanoi today. He had never spoken directly to Odanoi before. *Well, there is a first time for everything,* he told himself. Somehow, the prospect of this first-time conversation seemed to be more monumental than most. He still thought of himself as plain, ordinary Agap Virdod. Now, he was going to have the chance to talk to the highest-ranking Cirrian—the person other countries recognized as the leader of Cirri. Now this could be a conversation to remember—as long as he didn't make a complete fool of himself.

CHAPTER ELEVEN

LOOKING FOR SOMETHING TO SAY

Odanoi was a bit frustrated. It was late Titarti morning. He had scheduled a national PT announcement this evening for the eighth parz, and he really didn't have anything substantial to say. Jahnu would make the announcement about the soulless, but he still didn't know how the twelfth of Setmi fit into that prophecy. He couldn't say with any certainty what crisis might befall Kosundo on that day, but still he wanted to issue a warning of some sort. Yet he felt that he couldn't warn people if he didn't know what was going to happen. He was at a loss as to what he could say about the twelfth that would make any sense at all to mention. He was faced with a conundrum. Either he could say nothing about the twelfth to the national, and eventually worldwide, audience; or he could give a very vague warning that some crisis is coming. Neither of the two options agreed with him very much.

He was sitting at the desk in the bedroom that he had claimed as his, trying to puzzle out if anything he could say would make much of a difference. He had talked to Jahnu earlier this morning, but the prophet couldn't offer any more light on the happenings of the twelfth this morning than he could before.

When he had last seen Jahnu, he was praying in his own bedroom, but he thought he heard someone stirring in the main room now. The time he spent puzzling seemed to be wasted time to him. In reality, the time he had just spent was more like worrying than puzzling. It was high time he did something more constructive. He decided he would go see if Jahnu had any questions about his part of the announcement this evening.

He got up from his chair and started to walk to the door when he heard an old folk tune coming from his commterm. He had left his commterm on the desk so he turned back to the desk, picked up his commterm, and looked at the display. The display indicated that the call was from Phrunoi, a high council member from the technology council. He hit the button on his commterm that connected the incoming call and said, "I am here." As Phrunoi's image filled his commterm display, he added, "Hello, Phrunoi. What can I do for you today?"

The voice of Phrunoi came through the commterm. "I don't want a thing from you, my friend. I actually have some information for you. Now that's a switch, isn't it?"

He chuckled. For someone who was so formal while in a meeting, it was amazing how familiar he could be when talking personally. He answered, "Yes, it is a change of pace, Phrunoi. You're usually after me to help you get funding for some project or another for one of your technology teams. Does this mean that you have another discovery to tell me about?"

"In a manner of speaking," said Phrunoi slowly and somewhat hesitantly as his face became sober.

The smile vanished from his face. "Is there something wrong, Phrunoi?"

"Well, the news I have is not exactly good news, Odanoi. It is rather disturbing, in fact," said Phrunoi somberly.

"That's all I need right now: more disturbing news. All right then, Phrunoi. Out with it."

"Our promising young council member, Agapoi, blessed the technology council with news concerning the testimony of Lord Director Temeos during yesterday's Edvukaat session," began Phrunoi.

He interrupted. "The no-confidence vote session? That was a secure broadcast within Doetora. How did he get access to that testimony?"

Phrunoi smiled and said, "It seems that young Agapoi and his team are a talented bunch. They found a way to get around that little inconvenience. Anyway, in his testimony, Temeos referred to something called *Project Avenger*. This project produced an attack platform called Avenger—"

He interrupted again, "Attack platform! What sort of attack platform?"

Phrunoi seemed a bit flustered at another interruption. He stammered, "Well — it's a small, spherical thing — anything more is only conjecture on my part — Agapoi is good at answering those kinds of questions. I will send you his contact information when we are through."

He felt a flush of warmth cross his face. He was acting as antsy as a schoolboy. He owed Phrunoi an apology. "My sincerest apologies, Phrunoi. It was rude of me to interrupt you. Please go on. I will try to restrain myself."

Phrunoi's smile came back to his face. "That's all right, Odanoi, old man. All of us are a little on edge these days with the talk of the soulless and all. I suppose that you, most of all, have reason to be a bit less than composed. As I was saying, the platform is called Avenger. Agapoi got hold of an image of the thing, and a person on his team matched it up to an old transporter prototype of theirs. It seems the two are identical. It is the consensus of the technology council that the technology for the Avenger was stolen from us. We have decided to appoint an investigator, Kenun Pelen Ischor

Opuptu, in an effort to find who might have leaked the information. I thought you would want to know about the breach in security." After Phrunoi had finished speaking, he gave a slight bow of his head to Odanoi.

"It is appreciated, Phrunoi. It is sad news, indeed. But I know Kenun. He's a good man. I believe he will conduct a thorough but fair investigation. I hope that he will get to the bottom of the issue quickly. I don't like the idea of having a traitor running loose in Cirri." He knew that he was talking fast and was aware that he seemed to be giving a summarized response. But the mention of an attack platform being developed really did get him thinking. He was anxious to see how Agapoi characterized this weapon.

Phrunoi seemed to sense his haste as he quickly said, "Nor do I. That is all I had to tell you, Odanoi. I will talk to you at a later time."

Thinking that Phrunoi was about to end the communication, he hastily added, "Please do send me contact information for Agapoi. It seems that I might have a few questions for him."

"Of course, Odanoi. I thought you might. He is already expecting you to contact him. I will send his information immediately."

He smiled cordially. "Thank you, Phrunoi. I will talk to you again soon." He hit a button on his commterm, and the communication ended. He sat down at his desk and waited for the contact information from Phrunoi. He wondered if this Doetoran Avenger was what would cause the crisis of the twelfth. It might be; but then again, it might very well not be too. Still, he needed to consider any possibility at this point.

His commterm beeped twice, indicating an incoming data transmission. He checked the display. It was from Phrunoi. He opened the transmission and found that it was indeed the contact information for Agapoi. He would contact Agapoi, but only after he talked with Jahnu.

He left the bedroom and went into the main room. Jahnu was reading the Levra in one of the two chairs that were separated by a table. Finding Jahnu reading the Levra surprised him slightly since he knew that one of the signs Jahnu was given was the ability to remember the Levra word for word. Then he considered that Jahnu might just simply enjoy reading the Levra. He went to the other chair and sat down. Jahnu glanced up from his reading.

He took advantage of Jahnu's momentary pause from his reading by saying, "I have just received a communication from Phrunoi. It seems that we might have a security leak."

Jahnu did not change expression but said, "Oh?"

"Yes," he said, "but more importantly, we have a new avenue to search for the cause of the crisis on the twelfth. Doetora has a new attack platform, the technology of which seems to have been stolen from one of our technology teams. I don't know how different it is from other weapons in Kosundo, but if it is significantly different, do you think it would fit the feeling that you have of the crisis on the twelfth?"

Jahnu set the Levra down on the table and peered at him. Though his eyes looked in his direction, they appeared to be focused on something in the distance. "That is hard to say. If you find that the weapon can strike without people seeing it, it just might," said Jahnu.

"You mean you think that whatever causes the crisis on the twelfth is invisible?" he asked incredulously.

"No. Not at all, Odanoi," said Jahnu. "I mean that people are not going to know what is happening. They are not going to know what is causing the destruction that I sense will be all around them."

"And there is nothing that can stop this destruction from happening?" he asked. He really didn't like the feeling of helplessness that was presented by knowing something was going to happen and not being able to prevent it.

"The voice only said that it would happen. I've not been given any sense that it can be prevented," said Jahnu as he shook his head.

He got up and started to pace. "Just because nothing can prevent the destruction doesn't mean that lives can't still be saved," he thought aloud. Then, in a more outward voice, he said to Jahnu, "I will contact someone who Phrunoi says might be able to give us more information on this Doetoran weapon platform. I will contact the young councilman that Phrunoi values so highly. I will contact Agapoi."

Chapter Twelve

Consultation

It was less than a half parz until noon on Titarti. Agap had sat in his office for the last few spens with the shutters closed, thinking about what to tell his team. He had to tell them something before Kenun came around asking questions. He just wanted to be sure that his words were clear. He didn't want to be misconstrued in these circumstances. He had been stewing over what would be the right words to say for nearly twenty-five spens now. He supposed that that was long enough to stew.

He called for the office intercom, and the intercom interface appeared on top of his desk. The intercom interface showed every lab area and workstation area in the team lab complex in a map layout format. He needed to talk to Yotux, and she should be at her workstation working on the chomile interface. He hoped that she and Holon would be done with the interface today. He wanted them to be free tomorrow in case they were needed. Yotux's terminal indeed showed active, so he pressed the button that corresponded with Yotux's workstation and said, "Yotux, I am sorry to interrupt, but could you gather the team for a little impromptu meeting?"

Yotux's voice was heard to say, "Yes, Agapoi. I will gather them immediately."

"Thank you," was all that he said. He would wait a couple spens to allow the team to get assembled before leaving the office, but he thought he might as well open the shutters. "Open shutters," he said loudly into the air. The shutters folded back upon themselves until they could fold no more, and then the shutters simply vanished. The shutters were simulated matter, much like the chomile furniture in the LC.

He loaded the images that he wanted to use in his impromptu meeting onto a memory card. He saved the Avengers and MTP as holograms and decided that the dataterms in the meeting room would be the best place to show the image of the missile site that was devastated by the Avengers. They needed to know what was being done with their hard work without their consent.

He took a glance out his office window and saw Holon and Yotux staring back at him. The girls were standing near his office window. They were probably talking when they saw movement in his office. Eutay was also standing about talking with Kowtsom and Phunex. Axopen, Opsil, and Supeb were still not there. They were probably in the middle of some grand discussion about one detail or another of the new transport site-to-site mass transport array. They would most likely be there soon; so he smiled at Holu, retrieved his memory card from the card slot in his desk, and went out to the meeting area.

As he left the office, he saw Yotux whispering something into Holu's ear. They both started to giggle.

Eutay, who was standing on the other side of the meeting area, shouted, "So you two are the ones who stole my gelinhe feathers. You're not supposed to eat them, you know."

He hid a smirk at that remark, but Phunex and Kowtsom burst out laughing, which made it all the harder for Agap to hide the fact that he also found it humorous. Yotux and Holon were gazing at Eutay indignantly. The statement was funny though. Gelinhe feathers are widely known to be an especially good tickling tool. The picture your mind made of someone who swallowed a tickling feather was quite comical, plus Eutay pulled off a punch line better than anyone he knew. Still, he managed to fight off a chuckle and put on a straight face.

"Honestly, Eutay, I don't know what you are talking about," said Yotux in a stuffy voice. "We are girls of impeccable manners. We do not go about clucking like hens."

"That is quite right," chimed in Holu stiffly. "We have not even laid an egg for days."

The girls kept straight faces until they caught each other's gaze. Then they broke into hysterical laughter. It did his heart good to see that the girls were getting along so well now. But as their laughter continued, he found it contagious. He couldn't hold a straight face any longer and broke out into laughter himself. Eutay joined in. Soon, all six of them were fueling off of each other's laughter.

"Hey, I thought this was supposed to be a team meeting, not an impromptu comic revue," said Axopen as he arrived in the meeting area.

Eutay shrugged his shoulders and said, "A meeting is what you make of it."

Agap thought he had better take control now that Axopen, Opsil, and Supeb had arrived. "And I am about to make it serious," he said in an authoritative tone.

A collective groan went up from the formerly laughing group. But they quickly found their seats in the two-row semicircle and made their consoles ready to receive whatever he might send to them during the meeting. They had come to expect him to use something as an illustration, even in impromptu meetings.

He took his place behind the speaking desk and inserted his memory card into the card slot of the desk. His eyes scanned the faces of his team, and he began slowly. "Eutay has made a rather startling and sobering discovery. I have reported his discovery to the technology council. Before I tell you of this discovery, I want to preface it with a remark." He paused and surveyed each of the faces of the team again before continuing. "I count it a great privilege to lead this team. I personally believe that each one of you is a first-class technician and that each one of you possesses the highest standards of character." He paused again.

By now, the team knew that there was something unpleasant coming their way; they were just not sure what. He didn't want to keep them dangling, so he proceeded at a quicker pace.

"Our team has suffered a security breach," he blurted.

The expression on each one of the faces of his team, except for Eutay, was that of extreme surprise--perhaps shock better described the expressions. He was glad to see that those expressions seemed genuine, although he had no reason to suspect any of them.

"I am sending two holographic images to your console displays," he said as he dragged two files into the team console interface on top of the speaking desk. Immediately, holograms of the Avenger and the MTP were floating in front of each team member. The images rotated slowly to show all angles of the images. "Most of you are probably wondering why I have just displayed two images of the same device. The answer is that these two images are not the same device. The image on your right is a new attack platform in production in Doetora, and the image on your left is our team's mobile transport prototype, which I will refer to as MTP. Our team designed the MTP over three years ago. We never put this prototype into production, and we conducted no follow-ups on this research." He paused for a moment to let the team digest what he had just said. After he scanned the room once again, he continued. "The attack platform is called Avenger. Five Avengers form a complete squadron formation. The Avengers' attacking efficiency is maximized in this squadron formation." He readied the image of the destroyed missile site and said, "I am now putting an image on your dataterms. It is the aftermath of a test attack run made by a full squadron of Avengers." He sent the file to the team console dataterm interfaces.

Gasps filled the room as the team saw the destruction. Phunex let out a long whistle in response to the image. He decided to go ahead and note the obvious about the picture and then point out something that was a little less obvious. "Team, I am sure that you have noticed how small the pieces of debris are in the debris field and also how no part of any building is left standing. This was not an ordinary explosion or chain of explosions. I am going to zoom in to a part of the image where only one thing appeared to have exploded." He marked an area and zoomed in using the desk interface. "Notice the nearly perfect circle of debris. Axopen, this might look familiar to you."

Axopen's face was filled with puzzlement for a moment, but when he studied the image again, his face lit up as he said, "Of course! This is the same debris pattern left by the old transporter beam, the one with the makeshift array. That was before we learned we could use a confinement beam to prevent the dispersion of the matter. Our first few tests all resulted in circular debris fields, and the pieces of debris were sm —." Axopen's voice cut off and the excitement on his face changed instantly to soberness.

He nodded his head. "Yes, the debris pieces were small in those first tests, Axopen, just as we see in this image."

"Someone stole the research!" exclaimed Kowtsom with an expression of disbelief. "But Agapoi, who would do such a thing?" Kowtsom's expression of disbelief transformed into an expression revealing the hurt she felt as she asked her question.

He understood the hurt look. The theft felt personal. His eyes went from face to face. With the exception of Eutya, each member of the team bore some form of a stunned expression. Eutay and he had had their chance for stunned silence last evening. He answered Kowtsom with a slight shake of his head. "I don't know, Kowtsom. I truly don't know." He glanced up toward the ceiling for an instant before he continued without really answering Kowtsom's question. "There is going to be an investigation. It will start with our team."

Murmurs spread across the room, Holu cast an accusing gaze at him as if to say, "How dare you suspect a person on your own team!" Or maybe that was just how he interpreted it.

He held up his hands in front of him and said, "The council wants to start the investigation with our team simply because there is no other logical place to start. I have complete confidence that the investigator will find no evidence that will lead to any of you becoming a suspect, but the information he gleans from us might lead him to the real perpetrator." He had tried to sound reassuring, but he didn't know if he had pulled it off. At least Holu was not glaring at him accusingly anymore.

"Who are they assigning as the investigator?" The question came from Eutay.

"If he accepts, the investigator will be Kenun Pelen Ischor Opuptu."

Eutay nodded. "He seems to be quite tough, by my impression anyway."

"Kenun is tough, but he is fair. He is a good choice for investigator," he said.

Eutay then asked, "Will Kenun also be investigating Noso's team?"

He wished he hadn't asked that question, but it had been asked. "Only if the investigation leads him to do so," he said.

"Why should they investigate Noso's team, Eutay?" asked Yotux of all people.

He wanted to alleviate any concern that his team was being singled out unfairly, so he intercepted the questions by saying, "There is some evidence that one of Noso's team's prototypes might have also been stolen, but the evidence is not as nearly as solid about that as it is that our research was stolen. If the investigator deems it proper to ask Noso and his team some questions, I am sure he will do so."

Just then, an ascending series of tones came from his commterm. That signal indicated that someone was contacting him whose information was not programmed into his commterm. He thought that alert signal appropriate since it sounded like a question to him. He excused himself and walked away from the speaking desk. As he was walking, he read the commterm display. It displayed the name Odanoi. His heart skipped a beat, and he hastily turned to his office and said to the team, "I will need to talk to this person in my office. The meeting is adjourned, and you can get back to what you were doing or take a lunch. Sorry for my hasty departure." He entered his office with a bunch of gaping faces following his movement. He closed the office door behind him and quickly hit the button to accept the contact and said, "I am here." The image of Odanoi, the actual, real Odanoi, appeared. He said a bit more excitedly than he intended, "Hello, High Chair Odanoi. Phrunoi said that you might contact me."

Odanoi lifted an eyebrow, and he thought he saw a brief smirk on his face as he said, "Then I assume that I am indeed talking to Agapoi?"

He felt like an idiot. He had not identified himself to Odanoi. He answered sheepishly, "Yes. I am sorry. I am Agapoi."

"Excellent," said Odanoi, "I need to ask you a few questions. Do you have the time to speak right now?"

"Certainly," he answered perhaps a little too eagerly. "What is it that you wanted to know?" Just about then, he realized that he was still standing with his back toward the door, and he felt eyes on his back. He said, "I'm sorry, High Chair. Could you pardon me just for a moment?"

Odanoi said, "By all means."

He turned off the display and muted the commterm with the push of a button, and then he turned to see eight pairs of eyes straining to see who was on the other end of his commterm. He shook his head and said loudly, "Close shutters." The shutters appeared and unfolded to cover the office windows, much to the dismay of his team. He couldn't help but chuckle to himself. It wasn't like him to end a meeting for a commterm contact, but this was no ordinary contact. The abruptness with which he ended the meeting naturally had made the team curious. He would tell them all about it once he finished talking to Odanoi.

He quickly took a seat at his desk and resumed the communication. "My apologies, High Chair Odanoi. We will not be interrupted again. Please, what is it you wanted to ask?"

"Oh. You were interrupted? I was afraid that I might have caught you in the middle of something. Anyway, what I contacted you about was to find out if you had any information on the new Doetoran attack platform," said Odanoi.

The subject of the call surprised him a bit. He thought Odanoi would be calling about the breach of security, not about the Avengers. "I have a little bit of information about it. Was there anything in particular that you wanted to know?"

"Not really," said Odanoi. "I don't really know enough about it to know what to ask. If you would, just give me an overview of the platform and any capabilities it possesses."

"All right, High Chair," said Agap, slowly trying to think what he actually did know about it. He decided that he would just give Odanoi everything he knew from the broadcast first; and then if he asked questions, he would tell Odanoi what conclusions he had drawn about the Avengers from non-direct means. "The name of the platform is Avenger. The platform is a spherical, flying craft. It is small, measuring only ten dets in diameter, and lightweight. The

Avenger has to fly in a formation of four or five Avengers to have any attack capabilities. The attack capability of a complete squadron of five Avengers is devastating. It is capable of attacking targets from long distance with great efficiency. The Avenger was designed to be controlled by a thought wave interface, effectively giving one person the ability to control the Avengers. That is all that I can be absolutely certain about the Avengers at this time."

"I see," said Odanoi. "You said that the Avengers can attack from long distance. Can you quantify that statement?"

"From what I understood from Temeos's testimony about the Avengers, the Avengers can destroy a target in just a fraction of a tic after they crest the visual horizon," he said.

"So, would it be fair to say that anyone attacked by the Avengers would never see what had attacked them?" asked Odanoi.

He nodded. "If the Avengers are designed as I believe they are, the Avengers wouldn't even show up on an electronic detection grid before the attack. Multitudes could come under attack without ever knowing what had attacked them."

Odanoi had a strange expression on his face. It seemed to be a combination of exhilaration and dread. "That information is quite helpful, Agapoi. Thank you. By the way, you didn't break any international laws in obtaining this information, did you?"

He was puzzled for a tic and then said, "Oh. You are talking about the secure broadcast from Doetora? No, High Chair. Neither I nor any member of my team broke the law in listening to the broadcast. Every broadcast, even a secure broadcast, transmits scattered data in non-secure broadcast bands. If these bands can be picked up close enough to the source of the transmission, it is possible to reintegrate these scattered beams into a coherent pattern if you are skilled enough in communications. The dome is fairly close to

Doetora and has a very powerful communications array, and our team has a very skilled communications expert."

Odanoi smiled. "That is good to hear, Agapoi. One last thing though. Do you believe that the Avengers pose a serious threat against Kosundo?"

He didn't want to give a decisive answer to that question. He was really in no position to know for sure, so he said, "They might, High Chair Odanoi; but I cannot be certain. All of the information that I presume to have about the Avengers came either from Lord Director Temeos's testimony or from the information derived from what we know about our own technology that we believe was stolen and used in the manufacture of the Avengers. It is all speculative at this point. If you are asking if I personally believe that the Avengers pose a serious threat, then the answer is yes, I do. Whether or not the Avengers pose an immediate threat, I am inclined to say no. According to the Lord Director, former Emperor Tryllos is the only person that can control the Avengers, and Tryllos has fled Doetora. If this is true, I am inclined to believe that the Avengers are not an immediate threat unless Tryllos goes back to Doetora, which would seem unlikely."

"So if Temeos was being untruthful or has inaccurate information, anything could be possible," said Odanoi distantly.

"I am sorry I cannot be more precise in my estimation of the threat that the Avengers pose," he said. Then a thought came to him. "You are worried that the Avengers will be the reason for the crisis on the twelfth of Setmi, aren't you?"

Odanoi was silent for a moment. He seemed to be sizing him up through the commterm display. Finally, he said, "Yes, Agapoi. You are quite perceptive and apparently a Levra scholar in your own right. Nothing else but that crisis has been on my mind since I learned of it. It took Jahnu, the prophet, to help me understand that the crisis was not directly related to the soulless. You apparently had concluded that on your own. I must say that you are a very impressive young man. Thank you for your help. I will no doubt be talking to you again soon. Good-bye."

"Good-bye, High Chair Odanoi," he said, and the communication ended. He couldn't help but feel good about hearing praise from the high chair of Cirri; but at the same time, he felt more disturbed by the impending crisis on the twelfth of Setmi. Could the Avengers be the threat that Kosundo would face on the twelfth? He didn't know, but it was certainly possible.

It suddenly dawned on him what it would mean if the Avengers were the cause of the crisis. It would mean that his team's work would be responsible for it. It meant the he would be responsible. That line of thought gave him great anguish in his heart. But what could he do about it if it were true?

He considered contacting Temeos in Doetora to get more information, but with the Doetoran government in flux, as it was right now, that idea might have to wait. He hoped that the lord director was not planning to vie for the throne of Doetora. He seemed to remember that Temeos couldn't take the throne in a lawful manner since he was a witness against Tryllos. Still, as far as he knew, there was no lawful heir to the throne in Doetora so it seemed that Doetora might be in upheaval for quite some time. With Doetora in possession of the Avengers, upheaval in Doetora could prove dangerous for all of Kosundo. Tryllos might even be able to take back the throne if the government was in chaos for any length of time. Yet he couldn't realistically envision a scenario that would allow Tryllos back into Doetora by the twelfth, so he couldn't bring himself actually to think that the Avengers were going to rise up on the twelfth.

He would have to talk to Noso about the thought wave interface when he arrived on eKureaki. Perhaps Noso would be able to put his mind at ease. He had been wishing that

Noso's team could arrive sooner; but after considering what it took to move a team logistically, he decided that he should be content with Noso's scheduled arrival time.

His eyes drifted to the closed shutters causing him to remember his team. He wondered if they had gone to lunch as he had suggested or if they were out there pretending to work, hoping for some news of who had just called. If they had gone to lunch, they might very well be having roast Agapoi right about now. He decided that whatever his team was doing, he might as well open the shutters. He said in a loud voice, "Open shutters," and the shutters opened and then disappeared.

He saw only one person in the meeting area outside his office. It was Holu. He got up from his desk and went into the meeting area. Holu met him just outside his office door. The delicate scent of flower blossoms, her scent, met his nose. She peered at him expectantly after she greeted him. "So, who was the mysterious person who contacted you, or is that a secret?" she asked.

"No. It's not a secret," he said, "but it was kind of exciting." He stopped there, and Holu raised an eyebrow. When he continued to be silent, she put her hands on her hips. He continued to be coyly silent for just a moment longer, until she appeared to have had enough of his teasing. He then told her, "It was High Chair Odanoi."

Holu's eyes got big for a moment; then she tilted her head away slightly and said, "Erith! You're joking, aren't you?"

He thought about playing along with that path of thought for a while, but then Holu *would* have a reason to get angry with him. The little bit of fun it would bring him was not worth the price of having Holu truly angry with him so he said, "No. It really was Odanoi. He wanted to talk with me about the Avengers."

Holu's brow furrowed as she said, "Oh, don't tell me that the High Council is going to be involved in this whole stolen research mess too. I'm sorry, Agapu. I'm sorry that I was curious enough about the news rumors concerning Doetora that I searched for the broadcast signal. I'm sorry that I ever found and put together that stupid Doetoran broadcast. That broadcast has done nothing but give your team grief."

"That's not true, Holu," he said as he took her hand. "The broadcast gave insight into history and revealed a possible threat in the Avengers. Truly, I am glad that we know that technology was stolen. It will help keep us more vigilant about security, not to mention that whoever actually stole the information should be called to account for it. Besides, Holu, Odanoi didn't call about the stolen technology. He wanted to know about the Avengers. He wanted to know if they would pose a threat to Kosundo. He didn't mention anything about stolen technology. You just keep doing your communications magic. I have a feeling that your magic touch will be quite useful in days to come." He pulled Holu's hand up to his mouth and kissed it.

Holu blushed ever so slightly and then put her forehead against Agap's forehead. "I love you," she said as she put her head upright again.

He smiled at her. It was hard not to smile when he was with her. As happened so often when he was alone with Holu, he found himself overwhelmed with impetuousness. He had resisted saying this before, but the thought over-whelmed him this time, and he blurted, "Why don't we just go off and get united now, Holu? Why should we wait over four months to join in union? We know we love each other. Why wait another day?"

Holu got a wide smile on her face. Then it faded to a wry smile, and she said, "Why, Agapu, that is so unlike you. You would be willing to throw away all our plans that we've made for the union ceremony? And what about our parents and relatives and friends? Don't you want them to take part in our union?" Holu playfully broke away from Agap, taking a couple of steps backward.

He strode quickly toward her and took Holu into his arms, gazed down at her passionately, and said, "Holu, I would forsake friends and family for you if that is what it took to win your love."

Holu was trembling in his arms and breathing heavily. She was staring directly into his eyes, and he was staring into hers. Then he saw Holu's slightly open mouth and those wonderful pinkish red lips seemed to invite him nearer. He felt his head moving down toward those lips, seemingly without his willing it to do so; but before his lips could meet their intended target, Holu's hand intervened. Pushing herself away from him, she said breathlessly, "There are many things we can do together as intendeds, but this is not one of them."

He came to himself as he felt his face grow hot. He had nearly let himself do something that he knew was not right. He had nearly sullied not only his name but Holu's too. He peered over at Holu, who was just a couple of steps away from him and still breathing hard. Conflict was written all over her face. Then she started to turn away from him. He grabbed her arm, and Holu stopped and stared directly at him. Her expression now had fear mixed with the multitude of other emotions he had just seen cross his intended's face. He released his hold on her arm and cast his eyes toward the floor. Holu moved closer and touched his hand. He felt tears forming in his eyes. He strained to see Holu through his blurry eyes.

Her hair was pulled back into one long, flowing strand behind her. He thought that it made her appear to be even younger than she already was. She was wearing an ordinary outfit, a blue, one-piece, casual suit. Yet nothing looked ordinary on her. She was as beautiful in her plain outfit as any other woman would be in her best formal dress. But now he saw more than just her outward beauty. He saw her as the very vision of a virtuous woman, and he had no right to take that away from her. When he finally managed to speak, he said only, "Thank you, Holu." He let go of her hand, turned, and moved a couple of steps away.

Holu came up behind him and said, "Soon, Agapu. Soon."

He didn't turn to face her; he was still too ashamed. He answered her by saying, "I hope to Thaoi that it is soon enough."

He heard Holu sigh and said, "The others have gone to lunch at the restaurant in the lower level plaza of this building. They invited us along. Perhaps it is time we joined them."

He wiped his blurry eyes with his handkerchief and then turned to face Holu as he put it back in his suit coat pocket. "Yes. Perhaps that would be best," he said as he managed a smile.

Holu smiled back at him and took his arm. "It won't be that long. You'll see. You'll get busy, and time will just fly by, and before we know it, the Week of Remembrance will be here. I promise that it will be a week that you won't soon forget." Holu squeezed his arm as they made their way to the lift at the other end of the team area.

Before he pushed the call button for the lift, he thought he would try to get both of their minds off his lapse. "Have you seen that man anymore?" he asked casually.

Holu didn't answer him right away. He was just thinking about what a jerk he was for asking that question when she said, "I think I imagined him."

"Oh," was all that came out of his mouth.

He pushed the button and as the lift doors opened she added, "I saw him when I had dinner with Yotux and I saw him when we went for breakfast on my first day of work." She then entered the lift.

He stood in the doorway of the lift. He was puzzled by that last statement. "I don't remember you saying that you saw him then," he said slowly.

"I didn't say anything. I ignored him and he went away," she said plainly. "He is just a figure my mind made up, just like you said."

He remembered implying that. He smiled at her and said, "Minds can be funny things."

Holu gave him a weak smile back as he stepped all the way into the lift and the doors shut behind him.

The ride in the lift was silent. Neither he nor Holu made an effort to look directly at each other. They just rode motionless, arm in arm, as if they were posing for a portrait image. Once the lift door opened, they walked silently across the first floor plaza toward the only restaurant in the building, the Meeting Circuit, which was an appropriate name for a restaurant in a technology building, he supposed.

The first thing that always caught his eye when he stepped into the restaurant was the silver floor with black lines that resembled the circuits of a circuit board. The tables and chairs were similarly etched with lines, but the background and line colors were reversed to provide a contrast with the floor. It was a clever design theme, in his opinion. They found the rest of the team sitting at two small tables toward the left. There was a small table open adjacent to them. He went to the table and held the chair for Holu. As Holu sat down, he scooted the chair under her; then he sat down at the table.

The team members who noticed their arrival acknowledged them with a slight nod. It seemed they didn't want to talk over Phunex—as if that were even possible—who apparently was in the middle of talking about a couple of new technical liaisons that were now working with the Bojoa manufacturing team.

"Both of them seem to understand technical schematics quite well. They should save me quite a bit of time and aggravation. I just wonder what took the manufacturing team so long to get some technical assistants," finished Phunex.

"Who are you talking about, Phunex?" asked Holu.

"Mantiru and Motan. The manufacturing team actually decided that they needed some help with technical drawings and specifications. Mantiru and Motan are the new technical liaisons for the Bojoa manufacturing team," said Phunex.

"So what are they like, Phunex? Is either of them cute?" asked Kowtsom.

Phunex grinned. "Well, neither one will hurt your eyes, if you get my meaning. But Motan can be a bit nosey. I was talking to him about the specifications for the waste disposal units, and he started asking me a bunch of questions about what new things he could expect from our team."

"You didn't tell him anything, did you?" said Axopen.

Axopen was obviously very sensitive about his work's security now. Agap thought he would probably feel the same way if it was his personal work that was stolen. Erith! He nearly did feel the same way. The research was based on his theories after all.

"No, I didn't. I told him that he would have to wait and see what our team develops. I will make sure the security tracker is used on everything the liaisons see. Don't worry, Axopen," said Phunex, trying to reassure Axopen. "Motan seems like a good sort. He's just a bit nosey. That's all."

"Maybe we're all just a little oversensitive right, now," offered Yotux.

A server came to take his and Holu's orders. He ordered a fish lunch, and Holu chose a salad.

"So who contacted you that took you away from the meeting so abruptly, Agapoi?" Supeb asked.

"It was High Chair Odanoi," he said casually.

The team obviously thought he was kidding because laughter rippled through the group.

However, Yotux must have noticed that Holu was not laughing because she asked, "Is it true, Holon?"

Holu nodded. The laughter ceased, and the faces of the team ranged from shock to concern.

Now it was his turn to chuckle. "Don't worry. It wasn't an ominous conversation in the least. The high chair just wanted to know more about the Avengers," he said.

"Speaking of which," said Axopen, "Supeb, do you think we could modify the old MTP to house the new array? That way we won't have to come up with a whole other platform for long-distance transports."

"I don't see why not," said Supeb. "The new array tapers down to the same diameter as the old single rods. We would just have to create a little more space in the rod compartment. If Eutay ever gets the millennium generator shrunk to the size we asked for, it should free up plenty of space in the general housing."

"Axi then. Let's finish up and get cracking on the design," said Axopen as excitedly as he had ever heard him. "This could take months off the project completion time."

Supeb, Axopen, and Opsil all quickly finished what they had left on their plates and got up to go back to the team lab within a few spens.

"Have a good time, guys!" called Kowtsom to the departing trio.

They all turned and waved a quick good-bye.

It wasn't long until Eutay finished his lunch and said that he'd better get back and complete the specifications for the smaller version of the millennium generator before Axopen came looking for him. As Eutay left, he grinned and waved at him.

That left him alone with the four women of the team. The conversation from that point was not directed toward him in the least, so he started thinking about the events of last night and this morning. A lot certainly had happened. He couldn't help but wonder just how those events would affect him in the next few days. He was certain that he would have to answer a lot of questions. He had decided that he would be in the vicinity whenever the investigator, Kenun or not, questioned anyone on his team. That was the least he owed them. At least Holu wouldn't have to be questioned about the theft. She had nothing to do with his team three years ago. She barely had anything to do with him back then. Then he started thinking about Holu again. That was pleasant until his mind drifted to the incident in the meeting area a few spens ago. He needed to get a better handle on his emotions and desires. Holu was too precious to him to mess up their relationship by letting his desires get the better of him.

The girls were now talking about shoes. It was amazing to him how much could be found to talk about concerning shoes to hold such a lengthy conversation. At least they still could talk about less important matters, like shoes, as if they were the most important thing in the world. He hoped that he would still be able to hear them hold such trivial conversations after the twelfth.

CHAPTER THIRTEEN

MISSING

It was early Titarti morning, just before three parzes, and Abin was in the Imperial Building of State, in the reception room of the Imperial Office of the Lord Director to be exact. He was there waiting for Temeos to arrive. It was unusual for Temeos to arrive later than three parzes. In fact, Abin had never known Temeos to arrive later, unless he had an appointment to be somewhere else. Yet, here is was 2:95 and Temeos was not yet in his office.

He got up and wandered over to the secretary's desk again. Temeos's secretary had a pleasing way about her. She had made him feel quite welcome when she found him waiting by the office door this morning. Of course, she knew him well. When Temeos was in his office working and he had nothing else to do, he would visit with her to pass the time. Granted, the idle time he had was limited. Temeos had kept him busy as his aide, but he had spent enough time talking to her to know how pleasant a person she was.

As he lingered by her desk, she peered up at him smiling. "I'm sure Lord Director Temeos will be here any moment now. He had me clear his calendar this morning. Although he didn't say so, I believe he was expecting you this morning."

Her smile and the twinkle in her green eyes took some of his angst away. "Thank you, Nanki. I guess I'm just a bit antsy."

She nodded and began to work at her term again. He stood for a moment admiring her hair. The morning sunlight accentuated the red in her brown hair making her hair even more vibrant than normal. Though he was sure that she was aware of his staring at her, she pretended not to notice and kept working.

After a few more tics, he wandered back to his seat across the room and resumed his anxious thoughts concerning Temeos. He hoped nothing had happened to him. He conjured a vision of some Tryllos-paid assassin waiting in a dark alley to pounce on Temeos. He tried to reassure himself. *No. Nothing has happened. He is just otherwise engaged somewhere.* It really didn't seem to be working. It was now only a spen until the third parz. *Where is Temeos?*

As if bidden by his thoughts, Temeos walked into the waiting area, followed by a man equally as tall as Temeos but thinner, in a blue Edvukaat guard uniform. The uniform bore the rank insignia of captain. The man was Miera by race, having dark skin and jet-black hair. He wondered who the man might be, but his focus quickly returned to Temeos.

He was never so relieved to see his mentor as he was at that moment, but Temeos seemed to be distracted and didn't notice him at first. However, when Temeos finally did catch sight of him, a big smile spread across his mentor's face. Temeos walked over to him and held out both his arms. He responded by grasping both arms near the elbow as Temeos grasped his arms.

The two men stood in the embrace of friendship for a moment, and then Temeos spoke. "Abin, it is so good to see you. To be honest, I didn't know if you would come for sure. I am sure my note gave you more than a bit to ponder. I am extremely glad to see you here. Your presence is the first piece of good news I've had this morning."

"It is good to see you as well, Temeos," he said. "It was getting so close to the third parz that I was beginning to have concerns for your well-being."

Temeos's smile grew wider, and the man with him donned a smile as well. "See. I told you, Varnupud. I am never late to my office, not even today. You know me well, Abin. I hope that does you more good than bad in the coming days." Temeos paused as Abin's eyes glanced over to the man beside him. "Oh. Where are my manners? This is Varnupud Danosku, captain of the Edvukaat guard. He has been more than willing to assist me during and after the full session." He then turned to Varnupud and said, "This is Abin, he was formerly my assistant. Soon his name will be Abinos, when he becomes your next Emperor."

Varnupud's eyes grew wide with surprise, and then he snapped to attention, put his right hand up to cover his heart, and then brought the same hand up near his forehead to form a salute. As he finished, he said, "I give my pledge of loyalty and honor."

He smiled and stuck out his right arm toward Varnupud. "I'm not an emperor yet. I offer the embrace of friendship to you, Varnupud, for your service to Temeos."

Varnupud hesitated to end his salute. He glanced toward Temeos, who gave him a nod. Only then did he relax his stance, grasp his arm with his right hand, and cast his gaze directly upon him. The two men held the grasp for a few tics, and then Varnupud retreated a couple of steps as the grasp was released.

"Abin is Tryllos's nephew, the son of Navin," said Temeos. "He is Tryllos's sole living relative. I hid Abin right under Tryllos's nose, and he was none the wiser. Sometimes that is the most effective place to be hidden."

Varnupud and he politely nodded their agreement as they stood in silence.

"Why are we standing out here?" asked Temeos robustly without expecting an answer. Temeos put his arm around his shoulders and started escorting him toward the office door. "Come, Abin. Let us go into my office, where we can sit and talk. We have much to discuss." Temeos then stopped and turned to Varnupud and said, "Captain, please go to your guard and secure the main hallway and main entrance of the Imperial Building of State and the Edvukaat. I do not fully trust the imperial guard. There might be some sentiment that favors Tryllos among those who were closer to him. I would feel better if your men were stationed on our route to the Edvukaat. I will use my regular personal guards to escort us when the time comes. I have no reason to doubt them."

Varnupud stiffened, gave Temeos a salute, and said, "Yes, sir. It will be done." He then turned crisply and walked away.

As he walked with Temeos toward the office, Temeos shouted to his secretary, who was in the adjoining reception room, "Nanki, hold all calls. We are not to be disturbed."

Nanki's voice came back from the reception room. "Yes, Lord Director."

Temeos opened his office door for him, and both men entered the office. Temeos offered him a chair near a low small table on the near side of his desk. The chair was familiar to him. He had sat many times in that chair while talking to Temeos as his aide.

"Did you want something to drink? I assume you had a long trip this morning. I can have Nanki bring us something," offered Temeos.

He had to smile at the offer. In the past, it was he who would always ask if there was anything the he could get Temeos. Putting that thought aside he said while settling into the chair, "Yes. That would be nice." After he sat back he asked, "Do you have a fruit tonic?" He hadn't had a tonic in quite some time.

"I believe so," said Temeos as he walked to his desk to push a comm button. "Nanki, could you bring us a couple of fruit tonics?" asked Temeos into the comm.

Nanki's voice responded, "Right away, Lord Director."

"It will take her a moment or two to get our tonics. A lot was thrown on her when you left," he said to him as he sat down in the chair on the other side of the table.

"Oh, I hadn't thought about the effect my absence would have on Nanki," he said with a furrowed brow.

Temeos grinned. "Don't fret over Nanki, Abin. She's tougher than both of us. She can handle the extra work."

He donned a grin as well. He knew full well how tough Nanki was despite her meek demeanor.

"How are you faring, knowing that you are related to Tryllos?" asked Temeos increasing his grin.

He gave an inaudible grunt and said, "It was quite a revelation to be sure. Though it did explain a few things, like why you chose me that day in the gym and why you always insisted that I learn things about the imperial procedure."

Temeos nodded thoughtfully and then said, "You were my contingency plan to be used in the event that Tryllos ever went too far. It is only by the hand of Thaoi that Navin came to me before Tryllos launched his paranoid crusade against his own family. She sensed it coming. She said that Thaoi had warned her. I don't know how literally she meant that, but it was certainly a miracle that she was able to keep her pregnancy concealed from Tryllos. Tryllos never knew she was with child." Temeos was lost in thought for a moment before he said, "I tried to save her, Abin. I tried, but I failed. Your mother was a special person." Temeos paused again briefly before continuing. "I arrived too late to save your mother, but I praise Thaoi that I arrived in time to save you.

Navin told me of a doctor she trusted, though I didn't know why she told me at the time. But she knew why. She knew." Temeos's word's drifted to a stop, and his eyes were unfocused, as if recalling something in his past.

The door swung open, and Nanki came in with the tonics. She set both of them on the table and asked with that twinkle in her eyes, "Will there be anything else?"

Temeos seemed to be startled at the words as if waking from sleep, but he recovered to say, "No. No, Nanki. That will be all. Thank you."

He got the feeling that Temeos and his mother were more than just acquaintances. Although he wanted to ask Temeos about her, he realized that there were more pressing issues to discuss this morning. He decided to try to steer the discussion back to the here and now. "You seemed distracted when you walked in this morning. Is there something wrong?"

Temeos picked up his drink and took a sip. Then he said, "Yes. I'm afraid there is." Temeos paused for a moment to put down his glass before turning his focus back upon him. "The Avengers have gone missing."

Those words sent shockwaves through his mind and body. He stared in silence for a moment before finally managing to ask, "How?"

Temeos got up and meandered to the window behind his desk. He was silent for nearly a spen. Finally, while still studying the grounds outside the window, he said, "We don't know. No one knows anything. Everyone we talked to insists that the Avengers were in the hangar yesterday. Five staff members reported doing a routine check on them around six parzes. When Varnupud led his security team to the hangers just a little before the seventh parz, the Avengers were gone." Temeos turned around to face him. "Abin, there were plenty of people on that project who helped me get the documentation to depose Tryllos. None of them had a clue what happened to the Avengers. The guards outside the hangar reported that no one came in or went out of that hangar after six parzes. No one saw or heard anything. It just can't be explained."

He sat as still as death. His mind raced, trying to think of what to do or even say. Finally, he asked, "The Avengers can't become invisible, can they?"

Temeos shook his head and stared out the window again. "If they can, it's news to the scientists who built them," said Temeos quietly.

He thought aloud. "There has to be an explanation. They couldn't just have dissolved into nothingness. Maybe Tryllos is holding something over the workers and the guards. Somebody has to know something."

"That was my first thought too," said Temeos as he turned around and came back to his seat. "But Tryllos has already taken nearly everything away from most of the people on that project. Besides, everyone took a veracity scan when we interviewed them. The scans all said that they were telling the truth."

"Could Tryllos have flown them out?" he asked.

Temeos shook his head. "If he had, someone would have seen or heard something. Everyone that was on duty says that the hangar doors were closed. I saw no place where the Avengers could have flown out with the doors closed." Temeos shifted in his chair. "Erith! I even had a team of soldiers join hands and walk across the hangar bay, just in case the Avengers *had* become invisible. No one came into contact with anything. The bay was empty."

He was at a loss. How could the Avengers just disappear? His mind searched for some explanation, any explanation, but it could find none.

Temeos at last said, "Abin, there seems no explanation for the missing Avengers. I can only hope that they disintegrated each other."

He sighed. "But they don't disintegrate things. They explode them." The joy of seeing Temeos had melted away now. He felt as if someone had punched him in the stomach. He couldn't help but wonder if the worst that Temeos had spoken of the week before had actually happened, and they just didn't know it yet. "Temeos, if the Avengers are let loose on Kosundo, there might be no empire to rule." That thought sounded worse when spoken, but he had just said what he knew the both of them were thinking.

Temeos concentrated his gaze on the floor in front of him. "That thought has crossed my mind many times during the last few parzes. Still, we cannot afford to think that way right now. I will take care of the proof of your identity. You must prepare yourself to think like an emperor. Your name is now Abinos. Abin is no more. Abinos must now take the reins of this empire and steer it on a steady course. No matter what happens, you must lead. You cannot afford to think like Abin anymore. If the Edvukaat sees any weakness in you, there are those who will try to exploit it and undermine your appointment. A civil war is still just a misstep away. You have to think like an emperor in order to become an emperor."

He immediately knew that Temeos was right. The Avengers would have to be dealt with after he secured the throne. Right now, he must concentrate on being the leader the empire needed. *He must do what was necessary before he could do what was needed.* That thought came from an old proverb that Temeos had quoted to him time and time again. Finally, the proverb made sense to him. It was necessary that he secure the throne before he could find the Avengers, which the empire needed. Perhaps Temeos had taught him more than he realized. He couldn't help but wonder what else Temeos had told him that he would come to understand within the next couple of days.

CHAPTER FOURTEEN

CONFIRMATION

Abin watched as Temeos continued his testimony to the Edvukaat. This session was not being broadcast, and only the Doetoran government-run news agency was allowed to have reporters present. The decision to keep the hearing private was the Edvukaat's decision. That was another thing he would have to change, should he become emperor. The people should have the right to know exactly what was going on in the government via a free press, not a government-controlled press.

He had watched as Temeos presented the documentation of his birth. He was born on the day his mother was killed—after she had been killed. Temeos had presented his role in giving him to the people that he remembered as his parents, people that his mother had hand picked before she was killed. He wondered exactly what kind of person his mother had been. She was a mystery to him. When Temeos had spoken of her, he had made her seem like a remarkable woman. He really would have to ask Temeos about her sometime.

Temeos was the last person to testify on his behalf. Earlier, Abin himself had testified about Temeos's letter to him being the first time he knew who his real parents were. He had also told who raised him and how he came to be Temeos's assistant. He also told the Edvukaat how Temeos had prepared him to be emperor. As Temeos had drilled into him, he tried to exude the confidence of an emperor as he testified.

After he had finished his testimony, the people he knew as his parents testified, as did the doctor who had delivered him during a supposed autopsy. As far as he knew, those would be the only witnesses; but they should be enough. The testimonies meshed together accurately, and the documentation that Temeos had in his possession would seal the deal as long as no power play was initiated by someone of influence.

Temeos's testimony was powerful and concise. Most of the suvatens seemed to be suitably impressed with the facts he presented to them, but then reading the faces of suvatens in session wasn't in his training.

After Temeos finished with his testimony, Cemyoz ordered all of the witnesses out of the chamber, and he got up along with the other witnesses and joined Temeos, who was just coming down from the witness stand. The witnesses filed out into the waiting area in the hall.

He had worn his best suit coat. Temeos had retrieved it for him from his closet in his Manku City quarters. It was black. He had trimmed the suit with a red pocket decoration and a red necktie. He had worn a white shirt under the coat. Temeos was wearing a black suit as well, but he had chosen silver pocket trim and a silver necktie. Temeos wore a white shirt under his suit as well. It was the first time that he had seen Temeos in anything but some sort of uniform. That answered a question that he had for a long time; Temeos *did* have clothes other than uniforms in his wardrobe.

His mind wandered to thinking that it had been a few days since he had been in his regular quarters. It would be good to be back in a place he could call home. He had not been there since Temeos had told him to flee the city. Of course, if he was approved as the new emperor, he would be sleeping in the palace tomorrow night. He would have to learn how to call the palace home. It would be quite a change from what he was used to calling home.

"You handled yourself marvelously, Abin," said Temeos with a huge smile on his face. "I didn't see anyone positioning himself to make a run at the throne either. Presenting you so quickly might have spared the empire that headache. I believe that you will soon be known as Abinos."

A weak smile crossed his face at Temeos's comment. "Well, I'm glad that you think I did axi," he said with only a touch of enthusiasm. He then searched for a place to sit down. His nervousness had sapped his energy from him.

Chairs lined the walls of hallway on both sides to the right of the chamber doors. There were only five of them, so he and the rest of the witnesses sat at least a chair apart from each other, except for the people Abin called his parents, who sat next to each other and across the hall from him.

He studied the faces of the man and woman who had raised him. Their faces held some wrinkles now that hadn't been there the last time he saw them. He hadn't seen them since becoming Temeos's aide, though he had corresponded with the woman frequently. It had been a good many years since he laid eyes on them. The man and woman lived in Anark City. That was where he had been raised before he went off to school. He remembered the woman crying when he went away to school in Manku City for the first time, and he remembered her crying again when he went for his last quarter of school. He understood the reason for her crying better now. She must have had an understanding that she might never see the boy she raised again once he graduated from school. He still thought of this man and woman as his parents; but right now, he couldn't seem to bring himself to think of them as Mother and Father. They both had testified how Temeos had brought him to them. They said that they never asked any questions about who he was. Somehow, he felt better knowing that they didn't know who his parents truly were. As far as they were concerned, he was their son. Both of them were beaming at him proudly but at a distance. They admired the man he had become, but they didn't really know Abin the man.

He smiled at them, and they returned the smile. The woman wore quite a big smile, in fact. Still, they didn't speak to him and he didn't speak to them. He really didn't know what to say to them. He wondered if he should invite them to stay in the palace, although he doubted that they would accept if he did invite them. He really didn't know his parents well any more, and his parents barely knew who he had become.

Temeos was sitting a couple of chairs away from him. The doctor was sitting a couple of chairs away from Temeos. The doctor and Temeos were talking about something quietly, but he wasn't really listening to the conversation. It had the tone of being only small talk.

Finally, he got up, crossed the hall, and sat in the chair next to the woman he had formerly called his mother. Both of the people that he thought of as his parents had their eyes glued on him as they anticipated his speaking. He was not sure whether he should call the woman Mother or not, but he did anyway. "Mother, it is good to see you and Father again. Is it axi if I call you Mother? It doesn't seem right to call you by your first name."

The woman smiled and said, "Yes, you may call me Mother if I can call you Abin instead of Abinos."

Now it was his turn to smile. "Yes. Abin is fine. I can't be called Abinos publicly just yet anyway."

"It seems that you will be called Abinos publically very soon. Lord Director Temeos had all of his petus in order," said the woman.

He smiled even wider when he heard his mother's metaphor about petus. Her parents had raised the small, swimming birds to sell to restaurants. He remembered how she used to use metaphors about petus constantly when he was a small child. His smile faded as he thought about how hard it must have been for his parents to let him go, especially since they had no children of their own. He had been the only child they ever had.

"How have you been? You haven't written in a little while," he said in the warmest voice he could muster.

"Your father was laid up with a broken leg and is just now able to get around again. I was busy waitin' on him," said the woman as she gave a loving glance at the man next to her.

"You should have contacted me directly," he said.

The man scooted up in his seat to see him better and said, "It was just a broken leg. Nothin' that bad. Besides, the lord director told us to communicate to you only through letters without addresses. He said it could put us in danger if we talked with you directly. We didn't really know what kind of danger, but the director can be very convincin'. So your mother, she wrote to you. I'm no good at writin'."

The woman frowned at the man and said, "Eruv, You shouldn't have told him that. The lord director told us never to tell Abin that he contacted us."

"Sellia, I don't think it matters anymore. The boy knows he's not ours now anyway," said the man. Then he looked at him sheepishly and said, "I'm sorry, Abin. Didn't mean any disrespect by callin' you a boy."

He couldn't help but laugh inside. "That's axi," he said, deftly hiding his chuckle. "No offense was taken. As I recall, you frequently referred to me as the boy. It's refreshing to hear it again." He meant that. He really did. With everything that had happened to him since he last saw his parents, it was good to be reminded of his roots. He perceived that his mother and father hadn't really changed at all. It was good to see them again.

Then his mother put her hand on his leg and said, "Just look at you, Abin, all grown up. You've turned into quite a handsome young man." Her hand went from his leg to his cheek. He leaned his head into the caress. He remembered his mother caressing him like that when he was a small boy.

"Did you and Father want to come live in Manku City, in the palace with me, if that is to be my destiny?" he blurted.

His mother gazed at him lovingly but shook her head. "No, my son. The palace is not a place for us. But if you want, we can come an' visit from time to time."

He was only a little disappointed. He had figured that they wouldn't come. "I would like that. Please do visit anytime you like," he said as warmly as he had ever said anything.

He thought he heard his name called, but he ignored it. His mind had gone back in time and didn't want to be brought back so soon. But when he heard his name called a second time, he came back to the present.

"Abin, they are almost ready for us." Temeos was standing in front of him now. "I'm sorry to interrupt, but they sent a message that they would be ready for us in a couple of spens. I guess they wanted to give us warning in case we were using the facilities or something. It's good that the deliberations were short. I believe it can only mean good news," said Temeos.

"Yes. Good news is good," he said halfheartedly. All of a sudden, he thought that maybe being approved for coronation was not really such good news after all. His gaining of the throne did mean that Doetora wouldn't face civil war so he supposed that it was good news for Doetora, but he was not so sure it was good news for him. He felt very fearful and overwhelmed at the prospect of being emperor now that it seemed that it was nearly a fact. Before, the idea was just maybes and could-bes. It seemed very different now.

"Having anxious thoughts, my son?" said his mother.

He didn't answer. Instead, he peered steadily into his mother's loving eyes. Comfort was still found there for him.

"Remember who you really are, my son. You have greatness in you. I have seen it."

He stood and then bent over and kissed his mother on her cheek. "Thank you, Mother," he said. Then he turned to his father and stuck out his right arm.

His father stood and grasped his elbow. The two embraced for a moment.

Then he said, "Thank you, Father."

He then heard the chamber door open. A guard appeared and said, "They are ready for the witnesses to re-enter. Please take your places in your former seats."

He stuck out a bent arm to his mother, who embraced Abin in a hug instead of taking the arm. After she had hugged him, she said, "Now you can lead me in."

He stuck out a bent arm again, and his mother took it. Temeos was grinning from ear to ear. It seemed that Temeos was enjoying the moment as much as he was. He then proudly led his mother into the chamber.

After he saw his mother to her seat, he sat down in his seat beside Temeos.

Cemyoz was just elevating the podium platform as he sat. After it reached the proper height, Cemyoz said, "Abin Stigen, please stand."

His heart skipped a beat when he heard his common name. He glanced over at Temeos as he stood. Temeos smiled and nodded. He then straightened the lapel on his coat in preparation and fixed his attention on Cemyoz.

Cemyoz continued. "Abin Stigen, it is the determination of this session of the Edvukaat that your true name is Abinos. By merit of your relationship to former Emperor Tryllos, it has been decided that you are to be crowned Emperor Abinos of Doetora in a ceremony at midday tomorrow. Congratulations, and may Thaoi bless your reign! You may now take the seat of honor reserved today for the future emperor."

He stood, dazed, for a moment. It was really happening. He was going to be emperor. Then a terrible thought occurred to him. He had no idea where the seat of honor was.

His eyes immediately went to Temeos, who stood, smiled, and stuck out his arm.

Abin grasped it and whispered urgently to him, "Where is the seat of honor?"

Temeos nearly laughed out loud but caught his composure and said, "It is the chair to the right and below the huge throne-like chair behind and above the podium."

He peered upward past Cemyoz, who was in the process of lowering the podium. He saw two sections of stairs that led up to a large landing. On the landing were three wide steps leading up to a large, throne-like chair. There were two chairs, one on either side of the steps on the landing, below the throne-like chair.

"My right or the chair's right?"

Temeos smiled. "The chair's right, your left. 'Seat of Honor' is actually engraved on the back of the chair. You will sit on the throne after the coronation ceremony. That is the emperor's seat. You'd better get going if you are going to beat Cemyoz up the stairs."

He released Temeos's arm and made his way to the stairs. He paused to study the stairs for a moment before ascending. He was surprised how tall the landing was once he reached the bottom of the stairs. It must be forty dets up to the landing. He wanted to keep his posture straight as Temeos had taught him, even going up the stairs; so he ascended slowly. He hoped that he appeared to be regal, not unsure of himself. He made each of his steps higher as he had seen Emperor Tryllos do so many times as he ascended steps. It was difficult going up the steps keeping a straight posture. He thought he might fall backward with each step, but he just thought about being confident. Once he was at the top, he walked straight to the back of the landing and turned toward the seat of honor with a crisp turn of his body. Once in front of the seat, he turned crisply, paused, and then sat down. As he sat, the chamber broke into applause. He hoped that was in recognition of the future emperor and not because they were just glad he had made it up to the platform without falling.

After the applause died down, Cemyoz began the climb up the stairs, followed by the rest of the suvatens. He saw Temeos get in line to go up to the steps behind the last suvaten. His mother and father were next, and then the doctor. The other invited guests brought up the rear of the line. It was quite a sight really.

When Cemyoz made his way in front of Abin, he bowed deeply and said, "You bring us new hope, young Abinos. May Thaoi grant you wisdom to deal with all the problems you will inherit."

He nodded to him. He knew of some of those problems and knew that he did need wisdom. Cemyoz then made his way to the steps on the other side of the chair and began to descend.

The next suvaten, a balding man—he believed his name was Pitar—said, "I hope you are able to restore the people's hope in the future of the empire. May you find joy in your office and give joy to your subjects." He then descended down the steps.

One by one, the other suvatens echoed the part about hope as they came in front of him. Some seemed more sincere

than others did, but all said similar words about hope and
gave best wishes of some sort. He did notice that only one
person came on the landing at a time. Everyone else who was
waiting to come before him waited in a line on the steps or on
the chamber floor.

After all the suvatens had come before him, Temeos
came before him next. Like the suvatens, he bowed deeply
before him. Seeing Temeos, his mentor, bow before him was
surreal. Once Temeos had bowed he said, "I have taught you
all that I can. It is you that must lead now. I only hope to be as
good a servant to you as you were to me."

As Temeos walked away, he couldn't help but think
how significant Temeos's words were. Abin the servant was
now Abinos the master. He couldn't help but wonder if he
truly was prepared for what lay ahead. Only time would tell
that tale.

His parents came by and bowed as well. That seemed
odd too. But his parents beamed with pride as they bowed,
which brought a smile to his face. After that, people that he
didn't know at all came and bowed. These were mixed with a
familiar face here and there. All of them muttered some
congratulatory or honorific utterance and moved along.
Finally, the last person in the chamber came by and bowed.

After the last person had left, he was left sitting alone
on the landing. He wasn't quite sure if he should just get up
and go or if something else was coming. Temeos really hadn't
gone over his ceremonial duties very well. He noticed that
people were not leaving the chamber but rather were sitting
back down after they came down from the elevated landing.
He decided to remain sitting there, although he would feel
quite the fool if someone had to come fetch him so he sat there
uncomfortably.

Then, to his relief, Cemyoz raised the podium platform
slightly so that Cemyoz's head was still below his while he sat

behind the podium. Cemyoz announced, "Please rise while the honored Abinos leaves the chamber."

He was glad to take that cue to stand and proceed, as regally as he could, down the stairs, up the main aisle, and out the main doors to the chamber. He was relieved to see Temeos emerge first out the door behind him.

Temeos asked, "How are you holding up? You seemed quite natural for your first ceremony."

He looked at him flatly. "That was all dumb luck. I was scared to death I was doing something wrong."

Temeos laughed briefly but heartily. "You're the emperor, or soon will be. You can't do anything wrong in a ceremony." With that, Temeos started to walk and nodded for him to come along.

He fell into step slightly behind Temeos. Temeos tried to hide a grin while shaking his head and finally stopping. He stopped as well, still slightly behind Temeos. Temeos's grin increased, he repeated the shaking of his head. "Abinos, you are no longer my aide. You should either be walking with me or slightly ahead of me."

He felt a slight flush cover his face and smiled sheepishly. "Sorry. Old habits die hard."

Temeos laughed again. "I see we are going to have to work on this. There is no reason to be so uncomfortable. You should simply tell me to slow down if I go ahead of you. You are the emperor. I am your subject. I was mistaken for taking the lead. You see, old habits die hard with me as well. Let's try this again. You lead back to my office. There are some things that I feel I must go over with you before tomorrow's ceremony."

He wasn't the emperor just yet, but he couldn't resist the temptation to do a little mock impersonation of an emperor. He tilted his head, with his nose up slightly, and said, "Very well, Temeos. You may speak to me." He didn't pull off the feigned haughtiness very well though, as he broke out giggling like a schoolgirl. At least he did take the lead, and Temeos fell beside him, about a quarter step behind his pace.

"That was better. But I'm not sure that the giggling is appropriate," Temeos said.

They both started to break out in full-scale laughter as they exited the Edvukaat. They regained their composure quickly when they caught the glance of a few passersby and the outside guards. The Imperial Building of State was just across the road, but they waited just in front of the Edvukaat steps for the guards to clear a path across the street.

The escort guards then surrounded them, and they continued toward Temeos's office. As they walked, he thought, *This might be the last time I go to Temeos's office*. He would be expected to call for Temeos after he was crowned. This part of his life was nearly over. He was going to miss it.

CHAPTER FIFTEEN

THE ANNOUNCEMENT

Holon sat in one of the middle swivel chairs in Agapu's office. There were four swivel chairs in the office. All of them were situated in front of a massive migoterm that took up the majority of the office's back wall. She had taken the middle chair to the left of center while Agapu was just about to settle into the middle swivel chair to her right. She liked swivel chairs; they were fun to sit in. Of course, she had to make the chair swivel as she sat waiting for Agapu. What would be the point of sitting still?

It was Titarti evening. They had gone out to dinner just before, and Agapu had suggested that they go to his office to watch the announcement. Odanoi and Jahnu were to make a public announcement tonight. At Agapu's request, she had made arrangements for the broadcast to be bounced back to Cirri City before being transmitted freely. Bojoa was still not public knowledge, and Agapu said that Odanoi wanted to keep it that way for now. It was nearly time for the broadcast, which was scheduled for eight parzes this evening.

Agapu had tuned the migoterm to view PT programming. It didn't really matter what Cirrian broadcasting station they tuned into since the broadcast was going to be seen on all of them. He had offered to make the PT images three-dimensional, but she didn't really like watching someone giving a speech when it appeared that he was standing right in front of her. She thought that it was better to view the speaker as one did while in an auditorium. It seemed more natural. The two-dimensional viewing seemed more like an auditorium setting to her.

Agapu finally settled into his chair, glancing in her directions before turning his attention to the migoterm. He had been quiet since he had asked her about the hologram display. She wondered what he was thinking. She knew that he had to be thinking about something. He was never one to leave his mind idle. She fancied that he might be thinking about her, although with the announcement forthcoming, it was probable he had his mind elsewhere now, though his mind had been focused squarely on her earlier in the day.

The unbridled passion that Agapu had displayed just outside this office earlier today had taken her by surprise. It was not like him to lose control in the slightest way. If she hadn't stopped him, well, they both would have been regretting it now. Though even now, she had to admit that she had mixed emotions about stopping him.

It wasn't easy for her to restrain herself around Agapu, but she thought it was easier for her than it was for him. Women were more emotional to be sure, but women tended to react emotionally whereas a man's emotions were fueled by aggressive passion. The more passion a man had, the more worthwhile he was. She wouldn't have given her heart to a man that didn't have passion. It was healthy for a man to exert his passion by taking the lead in a relationship. She had seen unions where the woman had become dominant. Those unions just didn't seem to flourish; the man always seemed miserable, which made the woman just as miserable. Somehow, she didn't believe that a lack of leadership or passion would ever be an issue with Agapu. He was used to taking the lead in everything he did and then doing what he did at full speed.

Despite the incident and the passion that she knew Agapu felt toward her, she didn't feel at all uncomfortable being alone with Agapu. She was sure that it was just the heat of the moment that had brought on the earlier overspilling of heated passion. She was confident that he would contain his passion and behave himself quite gentlemanly tonight. Knowing him, he was probably reluctant to be alone with her in either of their quarters, especially today. She was sure that the reason Agapu suggested his office was the lack of privacy it afforded when the shutters weren't in use. The whole office wall facing the meeting area was windows, except for the doors. Someone could wander into the team lab at any moment and would notice the lights of the office. At least that was the theory she was going with right now. It was most likely true, and even if it weren't, the theory gave her a sense that Agapu would honor her virtue tonight.

About then, a news announcer came onto the screen, saying that they were interrupting their usual programming for an announcement from the chair of the High Council of Cirri. Then the screen displayed Odanoi standing behind a podium. A wider view revealed that Jahnu was standing behind and to the side of Odanoi.

Agapu's eyes were transfixed on the migoterm as soon as the announcer had started to speak. She stopped swiveling so that she wouldn't be a distraction.

The view on the term zoomed to a close-up as Odanoi started to speak. "Not long ago, an all-council meeting was held in which an announcement was made that will be partially repeated tonight. I am here to introduce the person who will be making the announcement. His name is Jahnu

Vija. Some of you may recognize that his name follows the old custom of naming. This fact was one of the signs given to me concerning him. Thaoi used this sign plus many other evidences to reveal to me who Jahnu Vija really was. I believe that Jahnu Vija is the prophet that is prophesied to come in the book of Malluntekas."

Agapu stirred at that statement, and she swiveled slightly toward him. "That was a bold statement. It will make the headlines," he said quietly.

She had to agree with that, but she didn't respond. Instead, she made her chair swivel to fully face the screen again.

Odanoi continued. "This statement might seem extreme to some, but I am thoroughly convinced of this truth. I believe that everyone who was in attendance at the all-council meeting came away knowing that there was something different about this man. I have spent much time with Jahnu since that meeting, and I am more convinced of this truth with every spen that I am with him. When he speaks, he speaks with authority. Not as I do. I speak only with the authority of man. Jahnu, the prophet, speaks with the authority of Thaoi.

"I know that there is a falling away from the Way of Conscious in other nations of Kosundo and even to some extent in Cirri. I know that hearing a message that says that some person fulfills a prophecy of the Levra will raise doubt among many. Yet I also know that Jahnu has a message that needs to be heard, no matter what your personal beliefs may be. I urge you to consider carefully what is heard tonight. It is with this admonition that I introduce to you Jahnu, the prophet of Thaoi."

Odanoi then stepped back, and Jahnu walked up to the podium. Jahnu offered a sharp visual contrast to Odanoi. While Odanoi was wearing a crisp, expensive black suit with a decorated sark and a silk neck scarf, Jahnu was dressed only in a plain tan sark and workmen's trousers. His clothes were clean and neat, but they were certainly not fancy. They were the complete opposite of fancy, in fact. He was a plain-looking man in plain-looking clothes.

She had to agree with Odanoi though; there was definitely something different about Jahnu. It was hard to grasp what that difference was. It was as if he had a different aura, although she didn't know exactly what she meant by *aura*. If she were to be pressed to describe the difference, she would have to say that he emanated a presence that was more than a mere man's presence. She could even sense that difference through the migoterm.

She noticed Agapu glancing over at her with a raised eyebrow. She had been swiveling again without realizing it. She gave Agapu a quick apologetic smile and swiveled her chair to fully face the migoterm again. Hopefully, she would be able to keep it still for a while.

Jahnu took a moment to situate himself, but he spoke strongly as he began. "I wish to start by quoting a passage from the Levra. It will serve as a basis for my other remarks. This is the passage from Malluntekas that is often referred to as the prophecy of the soulless." Jahnu then started to quote the passage from memory. His voice was particularly strong as he quoted.

"The time will come when the works of men will wax great. Barriers of old will be broken down. The heavens will feel the presence of man. The depths will be his abode. Man will think to be the creator, but his work will be empty, waiting to be filled with evil. Only the faithful will remain.

"The time will come when man will think that his work can surpass the work of Thaoi. They will be swallowed up by their own work and bring death and destruction to the whole of

Kosundo. It is Thaoi that gives life, but men, through pride, will think of the one as a work of their own hands. Thaoi is the only giver of life. Man will only make abominations from the life that Thaoi created. For the one who is not a full man will have no soul, and he will hate the ones that took his soul and made him an abomination. His being will yearn for what it does not have and will seek to take captive the souls of men. His hate will cause him to destroy the bodies of those who will not give their souls to him. Only the faithful will remain.

"Beware the soulless. They will offer gifts, but the gifts are not true, for they have a great price. Because the time will come when men will give their souls to the will of the one who is not a full man and the destroyer will laugh. Beware then the soulless. They are destroyers of souls. Only the faithful will remain.

"The time will come when the one who hates will bring destruction. All men will come to fear his works, though few will see the one. The soulless one will demand the will of the proud, and the proud will give it for a gift. Nevertheless, this will not satisfy the one, and his hatred will increase until he will seek to dominate the souls of all who dwell on Kosundo. Then will he know the destroyer. Only the faithful will remain.

"He who hath understanding, listen and take heed. When the destroyer comes, he will cause man to war with man. Man will not be given rest from war save for a season, and then will the soulless be unleashed by the destroyer for the one will be vanquished by the destroyer.

Then the works of men will be turned against man, and the destroyer will destroy men's souls. This is the beginning of sorrows. Only the faithful will remain.

"Nevertheless, Thaoi is faithful. He will raise up a prophet and will appoint a faithful servant who will understand Thaoi's great gift, which is the way of salvation from the destroyer. Heed the words of the prophet, for in the latter days, Thaoi will save a remnant to himself. Only the faithful will remain."

She caught herself swiveling again, so she quickly centered her chair toward the migoterm again. Agapu didn't seemed to notice. His focus was fully on the migoterm.

Jahnu had paused for a moment after he finished quoting the prophecy, but by the time she centered her chair again, he had resumed. "Nine days ago, on the twenty-fourth day of Sismi, I received a visitation from Mechial, High Ongiloi of our Lord Thaoi. His message was simple and plain. Hear now his message: 'The time has come. The father of the soulless is among the people of Kosundo. Only the faithful will remain.'

"This message is Thaoi's warning that we are entering the latter days and the days of the prophecy of the soulless.

"After I received the visitation from the ongiloi, I was compelled to seek out Odanoi. Odanoi was compelled to accept me as the prophet. We both know that Thaoi brought us together.

"Nine days ago, I was a maintenance supervisor—a humble occupation that did not prepare me to speak to you on a national broadcast tonight. Those who knew me knew me as a quiet man who was not at all eloquent. The prospect of speaking to a group of people scared me witless. I would never have believed it possible that I could muster the courage to be able to speak to billions of people on a broadcast such as this. Yet here I am, and I feel calm and confident. This is a sign I give to you. It bears witness that Thaoi has given me the charge of delivering His message. Those who know me will bear me witness of this sign.

"Since I have contacted Odanoi, a presence in the form of a voice has delivered other messages to me. The presence has identified himself in the old tongue. His name is Phunu tu Thaoi. Scholars of the old tongue know that this translates into Kosundo's present-day language, Linuve, as the Voice of Thaoi. The Voice of Thaoi has given me three additional messages. The first two of these messages were only intended to be heard by those who attended the all-council meeting that Odanoi alluded to earlier. The third message I will give to you now: 'The father of the soulless has begotten a son, and the son is poised to bring freedom to the soulless. Behold, the soulless will leave an icy prison to begin their conquest for the souls of men.'

"If there is any doubt that the prophecy of the soulless is a literal prophecy, I believe the visitation message and this third message dispel this doubt. The time of the soulless is at hand. The one who is not a full man has become the father of the soulless. A literal army of the soulless will be revealed shortly. It will be comprised of men and women who have given their souls to the father of the soulless and become his offspring.

"A further impression was given to me that the Spirit of Thaoi put into these words: 'A crisis will face Kosundo in seven days' time.' I was given this impression four days ago, on the fifth of Setmi. I have been given an additional impression that the crisis will involve destruction on a large scale. It is not clear if the crisis, which will occur on the twelfth, will be the direct result of the soulless. But the impression leaves me to believe that the destruction associated with the crisis will come from a source that is unknown to the people who are being attacked.

"Do not think that Thaoi is responsible for the soulless or for whatever destruction the day of crisis brings. Thaoi has warned us through prophecy about these things, but this prophecy would never have been necessary if we had heeded other warnings given to us by Thaoi. We have no one but ourselves to blame for whatever evil might befall us in these days. The destroyer, as the evil one is named in the latter days in the Levra, will use the soulless; but it is mankind who is responsible for the very existence of the soulless. It is also the works of men that will bring destruction on the twelfth of Setmi. This is the beginning of sorrows spoken of in the prophecy of the soulless.

"Thaoi is merciful in giving us this warning."

Jahnu paused, seemingly in deep thought for a moment, and then said, "Thaoi calls for men everywhere to sanctify themselves in their hearts on the twelfth of Setmi. Every man, woman, and child must come apart if they hope to avoid destruction. Leave behind all of man's devices. Come apart from the devices of your dwelling. Flee into the open fields, and do not trust man's works that have their power within themselves. Find those who are faithful and band together with them. In this way, you will have a sure hope of salvation from the events of that day." Jahnu then walked out of sight of the PT audience.

After Jahnu had abruptly left the podium, there was an awkward silence. The silence was broken when Odanoi hurriedly appeared and said, "I am proclaiming the twelfth of Setmi a day of reflection for all of Cirri. All employers are to give their employees the day off. Citizens of Cirri are urged to leave all technological devices behind and make plans to spend the day away from their homes and away from all buildings that contain technology. Use the day to reflect on the goodness of Thaoi and to give thanks. Thank you for your attention. Have a good night." The broadcast then cut away from Odanoi to a couple of news broadcasters who were obviously caught off-guard.

It was an abrupt ending to an engrossing broadcast. She had become so captivated by the prophet's words that she hadn't even swiveled her chair once since the prophet had finished quoting the prophecy of the soulless. But now that the prophet had finished speaking, she swiveled her chair— but only once so that she faced Agapu.

Agapu turned off the migoterm and said, "Well, that was unexpected."

Agapu did have a way of understating things. No doubt, his mind was trying to understand what had been said during the brief but powerful announcement. "Were we told to quit using technology on the twelfth?" she asked in a confused tone.

"It would seem so. That is going to be somewhat difficult for everyone in Bojoa, since the whole dome depends upon technology for survival." Agapu paused for a moment and added, "It would mean the evacuation of not only Bojoa but also every city in Cirri. How can Odanoi expect such a thing to be carried out within a couple of days?" Agapu sat back in his chair and scratched his chin repeatedly.

She knew Agapu well enough to know that he wasn't scratching his chin because it itched. He was thinking. But she had some thoughts of her own, so she asked, "You don't think the announcement to forsake technology on the twelfth was planned, do you, Agapu?"

Agapu smiled at her. "I have always admired your ability to read people, Holu. I was just going to ask if you thought Odanoi seemed unusually flustered to you. He did, didn't he?"

"From what I have seen of Odanoi, yes, I would say his appearance was flustered at the end of the broadcast. He had definitely lost his usual calm demeanor," she replied while first nodding then shaking her head. She focused again on

Agapu. "I suspect that Jahnu had just had another impression from the Spirit of Thaoi during the broadcast."

Agapu was grinning broadly now. "Why, Holu, you do think as I do; don't you?"

She smiled and raised one eyebrow and said, "Isn't it scary?"

Agapu laughed and said, "No. I believe I would choose to call it wonderful. It just confirms to me that you are my true complement. You are truly the one to whom I should be joined — of that I am certain."

Agapu's voice revealed the passion that he felt within, but he stayed seated and made no effort to get closer to her. She was glad of that since Agapu had let his desires briefly take control earlier today. He had nearly fallen into a trap of passion and had nearly pulled her in with him.

She knew that they must be careful not to do anything that they would later regret. Too much of that sort of thing was happening in Kosundo recently. A few of the Grassoan PT programs seemed to encourage physical relationships before marriage. She was determined that such impetuousness would not occur in her relationship with Agapu. Having a pure union meant too much to her to let rash feelings spoil it. She was sure that Agapu felt the same way, which was probably why he was making a point of staying where he was right now.

Still, the moment was tending toward being awkward, and she realized that she was swiveling again. She decided to change the subject back to the broadcast. "Do you think that Jahnu and Odanoi believe that the Avengers could be the cause of the crisis on the twelfth?"

That question seemed to catch Agapu off guard. For the first time, he swiveled his chair a few times. His brow furrowed; and he scratched his head, though his scratching didn't mess his hair. She was always amazed at how he could scratch his head without misplacing one strand of his perfectly combed hair. He then stared at her incredulously for a moment and said, "It is strange that you would ask that question. I asked Odanoi that very question earlier today."

She swivel to face him and sat up straighter. "And what did Odanoi say?"

"He didn't really answer the question directly but rather said that I was very perceptive. It seems as if he has his suspicions about the Avengers, as do I. But as I told Odanoi, I am not sure how the Avengers could play such a role so soon, given the situation in Doetora. I will have to talk to Noso to see what kind of an interface they might be using as a thought wave transmitter," said Agapu.

She was interested in what Agapu was saying, but her relief over successfully changing the subject outweighed her interest in the subject at the moment. She just nodded at what Agapu had said and then started to swivel again.

Agapu sat forward in his chair a bit, turned his chair toward her, and said, "What really has me curious is the fact that Jahnu's impression, supposing that is what is was, focused on technology. It basically was telling us to stay away from technology on the twelfth. It is a curious thing."

She stopped swiveling and pondered what Agapu had just said. *The exhortation to stay away from technology certainly seemed to come out of nowhere. There seemed to be no logical reason for it. After all, hadn't technology made life in Cirri prosper? Wasn't technology responsible for many benefits to mankind? Still, since the advent of technology, people had come to rely on it more than they relied on Thaoi. Perhaps that is why the charge was issued.* "Perhaps that is Thaoi's way of telling us that we are starting to worship our technology," she offered aloud.

Agapu took on a pensive mood after she said that and sat back in his chair again. All he said was, "Maybe you are right, Holu."

She sat farther back in her chair too while taking her feet off the floor and tucking them under her. The past few days had been hard to get a handle on. She thought about what the soulless could be offering. *What did they have that made people give up their very souls to them?* She couldn't understand how anyone could value his or her soul so little to be willing to give it up for anything—unless people didn't truly believe they had a soul. *On the other hand, who would be so ignorant to think such a thing? There are evidences of the human soul everywhere. Even physiological science and mental sciences are aware of something different about humans, something that science cannot quantify. What is that if it is not a soul?*

Her thoughts then shifted to the warning against technology. She and Agapu had devoted their lives to the furtherance of technology in order to benefit the human race. *Could our devotion be in vain?*

Agapu broke his silence. "Perhaps the warning is less general than we dare assume. Perhaps the warning is meant to be a literal warning that somehow technology is going to turn against us. We are used to spiritualizing what we hear in Levra proclamations. Perhaps Jahnu has been given the honor of receiving very specific warnings from Thaoi. Perhaps this warning should be taken quite literally. Perhaps the destruction is a literal destruction. Perhaps the preservation of life that Jahnu spoke of is not only spiritual life but physical life as well." Agapu had risen from his seat at the end of his discourse and was pacing back and forth.

She was astonished. The realization that the destruction could be literally caused by technology overwhelmed her. "But how? We have safeguards on all the technology that we have created. We have limited artificial intelligence in robotics to specific tasks. How could technology turn on us?"

Agapu kept pacing back and forth. Finally he said, "Perhaps it is not technology turning on us but man using technology against man."

Agapu didn't elaborate any further; neither did he have to.

What if some crazed person has found a way to use technology against mankind? She shuddered at the thought. Technology was rooted deeply into every Kosundo society. Even Doetora, which was a full generation behind in technology, still had technology everywhere. Kosundo had technology in nearly every household on the planet. The only exception that she was aware of was a few resort villages in Calisla that offered a vacation experience away from technology. The climate in Calisla was perfect. There would be no need to have technology for survival. Be that as it may, not everywhere on Kosundo was the climate perfect. Many locations needed technology to make life tolerable. Everywhere else, technology was needed to make business possible. *What if some crazed person did use technology against mankind?* The question reverberated a few times in her mind. When her mind finally stopped dwelling on the question, she pondered the results of such a happenstance. *The results would be horrifying.*

CHAPTER SIXTEEN

ANGER

Degmer woke up again. She had been drifting in and out of consciousness. Each time she awoke, the relentless pain in her chest screamed at her. The pain seemed more severe now than ever. She was having extreme difficulty breathing. She feared that her lungs were badly damaged in yesterday's beating. She glanced over at the clock beside her bed. It was still very early in the morning. She was fairly sure it was Titarti morning; but for all she knew, days might have passed. Her body was in bad shape. She found it hard to believe that any blows made only with an open hand could have been so forceful. She cringed as she remembered the blows coming one after the other.

Then she remembered something else. It was Laysa. Every time Laysa had pulled herself up on that floched bar, another floched blow had landed on her back. Laysa had been her friend, and now she was helping Neaotomo hurt her. Laysa was just as responsible as Neaotomo. In fact, she was more responsible. She had Neaotomo wrapped around her little finger. It was Laysa who was flaunting herself in front of Neaotomo like the tramp that she was. Floch on Laysa and floch on Neaotomo. They both could jump into a lake of acid and be floched forever for all she cared. She didn't know how she could get back at Neaotomo; but given the right opportunity, she would show that floched tramp.

Her emotions were causing her to breathe harder. Breathing was difficult as it was, and hard breathing made her body's pain scream at her louder. She tried to calm herself to control the pain. She didn't remember when she had ever resorted to profanity even in her thoughts. Only the vilest of the uneducated used profanity. Still, Laysa deserved vile thoughts directed at her. It made her furious to think that she had had pity on Laysa when she first saw her posing for Neaotomo. The tramp had been playing him all the while. She was manipulating Neaotomo like any skilled whore. More importantly, Laysa was playing *her*. Laysa had made her think that she was being totally embarrassed by Neaotomo when in fact she was setting her up. She was playing Neaotomo like a drum, and he was dancing to the beat.

She began to cough. Each cough felt as if her insides were being flayed. She felt something coming up with the coughs, so she caught it in her hands. It was blood. She was coughing up blood again. Laysa had made her see her own blood. That tramp would pay for this. She would make sure that floched tramp saw her own blood before long. She didn't know how, but it would be soon.

The anger that spawned her thoughts was causing her to breathe too deeply. Her lungs cried out in pain with each deep breath. She tried to think of pleasant thoughts so that her breathing would slow, but pleasantness wouldn't come to her mind. Her mind was filled with hatred and vengeance. She had suffered greatly, and she couldn't wait to make Laysa suffer as well.

Footsteps reverberated in the hall. She knew whose footsteps they were. It could only be Neaotomo. Her hatred turned to fear and dread as she heard the footsteps grow nearer. With Neaotomo under Laysa's influence, today might be the end for her, but not if she could help it. *Laysa is out for blood is she? Well, I will find a way to get back at Laysa. I only have to find a way to survive.*

As Neaotomo approached Degmer's door, he sensed that she was awake. He thought that she might be. He had left her in rather bad shape yesterday. He did not know what was going on in Degmer's mind today, but he soon would. Perhaps today would be the day he would find a weakness in her barrier that he could exploit.

He unsealed the door and entered. Degmer lay on her bed, staring directly at him. She had blood on her hands and all over her multi-colored, patterned blouse. Bloodstains also were smeared on her bedding, where she had attempted to wipe the blood off her hands.

Neaotomo came close to Degmer's face. Her ragged breaths made her chest jerk irregularly. As he neared her face, he said, "Why, Degmer, you look a sight. Why do not we clean you up a bit? Can you walk?"

He then jerked her out of bed by both of her arms and landed her on her feet. Her legs gave way, and she hung limply by her arms as Neaotomo held her arms to keep her body from hitting the floor.

"Well, I guess that answers that question. I guess you cannot walk." He gave a chuckle. He thought his glibness was quite amusing. "I guess I will have to carry you then."

He scooped Degmer up into his arms. She grunted as he put his arm under her back to support her. Her head hung backward because she did not have the strength to support her head's weight. Neaotomo was impressed by the outline of Degmer's bosom while she was in this position. Her body did have some attractive qualities, to be sure; but he could not tell her that. That would ruin everything.

He carried her to the bathroom, bent over, and started some water running in the bathtub. He could have stood in the shower with her and got her just as clean, probably cleaner, but that would not be as fun as immersing her in water. Besides, the tub water could be used as an extra motivation for her. He tested the water to make sure it was not too cold or too hot. It would not do to shock her body too much with her being as weak as she was. It felt adequate. He let the bathtub fill until it was nearly up to the top. Her head was still dangling backward. He knew that she could see the tub.

"How does that look to you, Degmer? Feel like jumping in?"

She grunted something that not even his ears could understand. He slid his hand from Degmer's back to the back of her head. Degmer grimaced in pain as her back was allowed to sag. Her breaths became even more ragged. "I suppose that I underestimated the damage that I caused. It seems as though you might be dying, Degmer. That would be too bad. But—." He stopped his speech short as he tossed her into the tub.

Water splashed everywhere, but the tub was still full up to the rim after Degmer's body sank to the bottom of the tub. Her problems catching her breath made her take in water almost immediately. She became frantic and struggled to move her weak body so that her head was above water.

He bent over and gawked down at her as he sent a thought to her mind, *Do you want me to let you drown, or would you prefer a quick mind probe?*

Her mind was fading fast, but a weak thought came through: *Mind probe.*

He smiled and pulled her head above water. She was not breathing at all now. He pulled her farther up out of the water and pushed forcefully upward on her abdomen, just below the diaphragm. Immediately, water and blood came spewing out of her nose and mouth. He released the pressure that he had held on her diaphragm and then pushed hard again. More water and blood came out of her mouth and nose.

He repeated this twice more until no more water came from her lungs. Then he pinched her nose, covered her mouth with his mouth, and breathed out hard. Her damaged lungs partially filled with air, and she took a ragged breath and then coughed furiously. No blood came with the coughing. He supposed that most of the loose blood in her lungs had come out with the water.

"Well, at least your heart never stopped," he remarked to her. "But it was a good thing you made your decision quickly. You had already taken in a lot of water. You know, I never get tired of the feeling of having someone's life entirely relying on me. It is a whole lot of fun. Care to do it again?" He asked only half-jokingly.

She managed a very faint, "No."

"No sense of adventure, eh? Oh well. We have a mind probe to perform anyway," he said lightly. Then in a very serious, very deep voice he said, "Look into my eyes."

Degmer struggled to keep her eyes open, but she managed. The longer she gazed deeply into his eyes, the more clearly he could see into her mind. When he felt the presence of her mind strongly enough, he began to probe the barrier of her mind. He could still sense the other presence in her mind, but that presence was still sealed off. He could just ignore the presence since she would not be aware it was still there anyway. He felt for her barrier, and to his delight, he found what he was hoping to find: a tear in the barrier. The tear was linked to thoughts of hatred toward Laysa. His plan had worked marvelously. With the right prodding, he should be able to turn her right now.

He thought for a moment and then projected thoughts into her mind. *Degmer, I am afraid your body might be dying. Your lungs are still bleeding, and your body is very weak from the loss of blood. It is very hard to take a breath now, is it not?* He did not care if she answered, in fact, he did not expect an answer. He paused only for the briefest of moments before projecting again. *I do not wish your body to die, Degmer. I want you to join me, to become one with me. Think of it as a union proposal. I know I am responsible for putting your body into this condition, but it will not happen once we are of the same mind. I only did what I did because of Laysa. It was her idea.* He would not ordinarily tell a blatant lie like that when in someone's mind for fear the person might be able to perceive he was lying. However, her mind was in such a weakened state right now that he thought it reasonable that she might not be able to perceive much past her hatred of Laysa—especially if he poked at it a bit. It was akin to poking the embers of a fire to stoke a flame. Once a negative emotion like hate filled a person's mind, the mind did not have much chance of perceiving thoughts that were not directly associated with the fiery emotion. He continued. *I am sorry about the beating I gave you. Laysa just affects me as no other person has ever affected me before. I did not know how to resist her wiles. Still, it is you whom I really want to be one with, Degmer. It has always been you, not Laysa. She is merely a side attraction, a passing fancy. You are the one with the deeper thoughts, the more complex mind.*

Thoughts came to him from Degmer's mind: *I wish I could believe you, Neaotomo. Let me die in peace. Don't trouble me anymore.*

The thoughts surprised him slightly. Her mind must be stronger than he had anticipated. This did not discourage him one bit, but rather it encouraged him. He loved a challenge. He sent this thought back: *You can believe me, Degmer. I can prove that it is you with whom I want to be one. I can grant you the one thing that your mind truly desires. What do you really want most of all right now, Degmer?*

He paused for a moment to see if there would be a response. As he expected, a response came: *I want to hurt Laysa. I want to see Laysa bleed.*

He smiled. He had her now. All he had to do was close the trap. *I can make that happen for you, Degmer. I can let you*

*hurt Laysa as often as you wish. As long as you leave her alive,
together, we can heal her again. Think of it, Degmer. You can have
vengeance against Laysa as many times as you want. You can hurt
her until she is about to die over and over again. You can make her
cringe every time she sees you. Is that not what you want?*

Degmer's mind responded thunderously. *Yes! That is
what I want. I want to hurt Laysa time after time!*

He then sent one final thought. *If that is what you want,
you must let me in. I can then heal your body. You can have a body
that is far more powerful than Laysa's. You can have a mind that is
stronger and far more complex than it is already. You can have
vengeance, Degmer. Vengeance.*

That was it. That series of thoughts pushed Degmer to
the point that all she desired was vengeance on Laysa. He had
prodded her anger to such an extent that she would give
anything to gain vengeance on Laysa. For this reason, she
gave up her will, the thing that humans often call the soul.
She handed it to him gladly. With a great *pop*, her mind's
barrier was gone.

He quickly and smoothly imprinted his mind and will
on the floor of her mind. That's all that needed to be done.
The barrier would come back, but her mind was now his. He
broke off contact with Degmer's mind and he was aware of
his surroundings again.

Degmer's body was convulsing wildly, and she was
again coughing up blood. He hoped that he had not taken too
long to convert her. It would be a sad irony if her body died
after he had won such a victory in her mind. He lifted her out
of the bathtub and wrapped dry towels about her. Then he
carried her back to her sleeping quarters. He folded down the
bloodstained blankets and sheets on the bed and laid her on
the bed facedown. Next, he tucked Degmer's body under the
coverings. She was still convulsing, but the coughing had
stopped. In the place of the coughing was a rattling sound
coming from her throat. Her body was dying. He would have

to act quickly. He placed both of his hands on the bedding about her back since this was the part of her body he had beaten. He then concentrated on her back. Neaotomo did not fully understand how he was able to do it, but by concentrating on a certain area of the body, he could sense what was wrong with the cells of that part of the body—both the surface cells and the cells of the organs underneath. Once he knew what was wrong, he could repair the damage. He sensed broken cells in the skin but ignored those for now. He sensed damaged cells in the muscles but ignored them as well. He concentrated on going deeper into her body until he got to the lungs. The lungs were full of blood. Many of the air sac cells in Degmer's lungs were completely destroyed while others were severely damaged. He must repair the damaged cells first and then help her body rebuild the destroyed cells. He found a healthy air sac to use as a pattern. Then he sent energy and instructions to her damaged cells. Immediately, the cells started to repair themselves. The cells of Degmer's body now knew how to heal themselves quickly because her mind was able to tell them how since her mind and body now were like his. Degmer's mind had the same abilities as his mind had now. With Degmer now working on healing damaged air sacs, he moved on to replace destroyed sacs. He sent instructions to the healthy cells to divide to create new cells so that new air sacs could be formed. The instructions included exactly where and how to create the new cells. He then went to surrounding tissues and did the same thing. He decided that the muscle and skins cells would heal themselves in short order since he had given her mind healing properties like his own mind when he had imprinted his will in her mind. He could not imprint a person without imparting his own body's characteristics to that person's body as well. It was part of his makeup, a part of his pattern. He did not know how to imprint a mind without giving the mind his powers as well. It might be possible, but he had not yet discovered how. Truthfully, he really did not see a need to discover how to do it anyway. Since he controlled the person's will, that person's enhanced abilities could only benefit him. Giving the physical and mental gifts of his body to those whose minds he had conquered was like giving gifts to himself.

In less than a spen after he had placed his hands on her back, the lung cells and the surrounding tissues were repaired. Degmer's new imprint on her mind and subsequently on her body had made her rapid healing possible. Without the help of her mind, he would not have been able to save her. Her convulsions had now stopped and were replaced by coughing. She coughed up a huge amount of blood within tics, and then the coughing stopped.

Degmer rolled over toward him. "That was a bit intense," she said clearly.

There was no trace of the labored breathing and Degmer's energy level was quickly surpassing her former healthy energy level. Although he could sense that her body was healed, he asked, "How do you feel?"

"I feel like a little vengeance," was the reply. "I want to do it now. I want to do it *slowly*."

He nodded slowly twice to indicate that he fully understood. "You will find a scalpel in the main laboratory."

Degmer raised an eyebrow at that revelation.

He smiled as he said, "I put it under the seat cushion of the chair nearest Laysa's quarters. I believe that this instrument should make the process as slow as you desire."

Degmer smiled a vicious smile as she started toward the main lab.

As she left, he sent Degmer this thought: *Remember, Degmer. You can only do this again if you leave Laysa alive.*

A reply thought came back: *She will be alive after I am done. She will only wish that she was dead.*

He found that he actually regretted letting Degmer have her vengeance on Laysa. Regret was an interesting emotion. He had never experienced it before. Yet he disregarded the feeling since it was necessary to let Degmer have her fun. If Laysa was to remain alive, she would have to fulfill a purpose. Currently, her purpose was to fulfill his promise to Degmer. It certainly would not be a pleasant experience for Laysa, but she would be alive. Perhaps he could find another use for her before too long, a use that might be less painful for her. He only hoped that Laysa was as emotionally strong as she seemed to be or her fate might end up being worse than death. He did not want that for Laysa. If she started to lose herself, he would kill her himself—a quick, painless death. It was the least he could do for her.

As Degmer reached the lab, she was delighting in the anticipation of the pain that she would inflict on Laysa. Laysa would not get off easily. Degmer's pain was now only a memory, but her hate was fresh and unsatiated.

She found the scalpel under the seat cushion, right where Neaotomo had said it would be. She tested the blade with the tip of her finger. The blade sliced into her skin easily causing a trickle of blood to ooze down her finger. A renewed smile spread across her face as she felt the pain that the blade had inflicted on her finger. A multitude of much deeper cuts would cause Laysa great discomfort. As she gazed at her finger, the bleeding stopped. She wiped the blood off her finger on her wet clothes and found that the cut had vanished and the pain had ceased. Her finger had healed on its own. That was sort of drus. For just a moment, she wondered what else her new body could do before remembering her anger.

With scalpel in hand, she headed for Laysa's quarters. She nearly stopped before she reached Laysa's quarters because she briefly thought that she didn't know the unlock code for her quarters. Then she discovered that she did know it. The code must have been a gift from Neaotomo. Apparently, her mind also had unique abilities now. She continued on her way, thinking near-murderous thoughts all the while.

Laysa was at the desk in her quarters, reading a journal on genetics that one of the origin genetic scientist's had written while working in the lab. Neaotomo had discovered it and given it to her to read. While she was thoroughly impressed with the science involved in the work of the lab, she was horrified at its application—particularly how the subjects, as the journal called them, were spawned using parts of animal and synthesized genes. Especially horrifying were the callous accounts of how the subjects were treated. They were not treated humanely. They were treated like lab rats—or worse. The particular entry that she was currently reading mentioned no less than twenty injury tests conducted on a single subject. The purpose of the tests was to measure the healing rate of the subject. However, purposely injuring someone—a test subject or not—twenty times in one day bordered on insanity. It could not have been a pleasant life for any test subject of the lab.

Just then, Laysa heard the door open behind her. She didn't bother to turn to see who it was. It could only be one person. "What is it this time, Neaotomo? I thought you said you were going to be off bothering Degmer for a while," she said casually.

She was surprised to hear a woman's voice answer— and it wasn't just any woman's voice—it was Degmer's voice. "Neaotomo has finished *bothering* me. I think your choice of words is much too kind for the treatment that I have been subjected to."

It was Degmer's voice, but it sounded different. It sounded very rough. Extreme anger — almost to the point of madness — resounded in her voice. She turned around. It *was* Degmer. Her short dark red hair seemed nearly black because it was wet, as were her clothes; and her blouse was stained with blood.

She exclaimed, "What happened to you, Degmer?"

"You know what happened to me, Laysa. Don't act so coy," growled Degmer.

She was perplexed as she got up and faced Degmer while standing at the foot of her bed. Though her voice was intense, Degmer's posture was relaxed. She was favoring her left foot and had her right hand in her pants pocket. But something about her was different. It was her eyes. Her eyes were wild. "How can I know what had happened to you, Degmer? I have been forbidden from seeing you or talking to you. Degmer, you need to get out of here. If Neaotomo finds you here, something bad will happen to you."

Degmer smiled. "Oh, you don't have to worry yourself about that. Neaotomo knows that I am here."

"He knows?" she asked with surprise.

Degmer nodded.

"Then he is probably watching. Oh, Degmer, I am so sorry. He has set you and me up again. Degmer, you must leave. Maybe if you leave now your punishment will not be so bad."

Degmer's smile left her face. "So you admit that you are responsible for my punishment."

Her voice was so full of hate that it took Laysa by surprise. She took a couple of steps backward, and said, "Yes, Degmer, I am, but — ."

Degmer cut her off. "I know, I know. You were going to say that if I don't leave, your beloved Neaotomo will come to your rescue. Well, my *friend*, he will not come to save you."

"Save me? Why would he come — ?"

That is all that she was able to say. Degmer had closed that gap between them, and she made contact with her before she could finish her question. Degmer had taken her hand out of her pocket and had thrust it into Laysa's midsection with such force that it knocked all the air out of her lungs. She managed to keep her feet as Degmer finished the thrust and pulled back her hand, but confusion filled her mind as she saw Degmer's withdrawn hand. It was covered in fresh blood. Then confusion turned to horror as she peered down to see her bloody midsection. Soon, a sharp pain shot from her abdomen. She staggered backward. She didn't understand what had just happened. Degmer now dominated her attention. She hoped to see something of her old friend in her, but Degmer was glaring at her in pure hatred and her eyes not only looked wild, they looked incredibly empty. Degmer's right hand caught her attention. It was bloody, but there was something else; she saw something that she had missed the first time. The blade of a scalpel was sticking out from Degmer's closed fist. She staggered backward again until her back hit the wall behind her. The pain in her abdomen was intense. Obviously, Degmer had cut deeply with her thrust.

"Aw. What's the matter, you floched tramp? Do you have a boo-boo?" mocked Degmer.

She labored to answer. "It's strange. As soon as I saw — Neaotomo I knew — that I would die soon — I just never thought — it would be you who killed me — I thought—."

Degmer, who had moved very close to her face, interrupted. "You thought nothing of the sort. You thought you would turn against your old pal, Degmer. That is what you thought. You thought you would save your sorry skin by flaunting that body of yours in front of Neaotomo. Well, it backfired on you. That's all. Your plan didn't work. You can't seduce someone who doesn't have a sexual organ in his body. You were just a stupid, floched whore to think that you could manipulate someone like Neaotomo."

Her breathing was labored now because of the pain. She took a deep breath, and her abdomen screamed at her. She then said with the limited force that she could muster, "Is that what you think? It is you who has been deceived. I never stopped caring about you, Degmer."

Degmer stopped her ears with her hands, leaving blood on her right ear and on the hair surrounding it. "Liar!" she shouted at the top of her lungs.

The shout was so loud that it caused Laysa to cringe.

Degmer then added, "You never cared a thing for me. You were just after my research. I saw you working on *my* research. You didn't know I saw that, did you? Well, I did. I saw you, and I saw your disgusting performance for Neaotomo in the exercise room too."

"You saw me as I was exercising?" Only now did she understand Neaotomo's insistence about having frequent exercise sessions.

"Don't act all innocent. You will only infuriate me more. I suffered greatly because of you." Degmer was now wielding the scalpel threateningly about Laysa's face.

She realized now that Neaotomo had been using her to get to Degmer all the while. She forced herself to look closely at Degmer's eyes. Her eyes *were* empty, just like Neaotomo's eyes. "He has turned you, hasn't he?"

"Thanks to you, yes," answered Degmer. "I guess I should thank you for that, but I am not in a thankful mood right now."

"I am so sorry, Degmer. I am so sorry," she lamented and began to cry.

"Don't think that tears are going to save you, tramp. I've got no patience for your theatrics," growled Degmer.

"The tears are not for me," was all that she said. She tried to hold them back, but she was failing miserably. She had failed Degmer again, despite her best intentions. She deserved whatever death Degmer had planned for her. "Axi,

Degmer. I can see that there is no stopping you. Do what you want with me. Just know that I still love you no matter what."

"Don't talk to me of love. You never knew what that word meant," hissed Degmer. "And by the way, I don't need your permission. I will do whatever I want with you no matter what. You *need* to understand that," Degmer screamed.

Degmer then turned from her and shouted something that sounded like a war cry. When she turned back, there was a terrible resolve in her face. "I think now that I have your attention, I will go slowly." Degmer approached her menacingly and very slowly.

She tried not to show fear, but it was no use. She felt terror as she had never known before. Her breathing became fast and deep, despite the pain it brought.

"First, I think I will cut up that pretty face of yours." Degmer raised the scalpel up to her face, held it close to her eye for a moment, and then dug it into her cheek, cutting downward and nicking her jawbone.

She screamed. She couldn't help it. The pain was unreal. Degmer continued with her face for a few more strokes of the scalpel. Laysa's screams intensified with each cut as Degmer's smile became broader. Soon, blood was streaming into her mouth and eyes. She felt her strength fading with every new cut. She was losing a great deal of blood. She felt her back slide down the wall until she was sitting on the floor against the wall.

The cuts kept coming. The next cuts came on her arms and then her legs. Each new cut brought its own torture and brought her closer to unconsciousness. Then she felt her blouse being cut, as were both of her top undergarments. She felt the scalpel dig into her flesh after breaching her clothing. Those cuts made her body jerk wildly, but she was no longer in control. She had no strength left. Then the scalpel was slicing down her sides. She started to lose consciousness. *So this is what it is like to die.* She vaguely felt her head hit the floor, and then blackness covered her mind.

Neaotomo, who had made his way to the door of Laysa's quarters, watched as Laysa lost consciousness. He sent a thought to Degmer. *All right. You have had your fun for today. It is time to heal her now or you will not be able to torture her again.*

A thought came back: *Her heart still beats strongly. She can take more torture.*

He then said audibly, "What good will torturing her more do you now? She is beyond feeling anything."

Reluctantly, Degmer put the scalpel on the floor. "Axi, Neaotomo. Show me how to heal her. I think we should leave some nice scars on her face, something to remember me by."

He shook his head. "If you do that, it will lessen the horror the next time you torture her. She will already feel that she had lost something. No. I think she will not soon forget any of her tortures. I am sure she will tremble every time she sees you."

Degmer smiled as she thought of Laysa cringing and shaking every time that Laysa saw her, and she said, "Now that would be a welcome sight."

He knelt beside Laysa. Then he looked at Degmer and said, "I think we should start with the internal injuries you inflicted with your first thrust. Follow my lead, and I will walk you through the healing procedure."

Degmer seemed to enjoy the healing almost as much as she had enjoyed the injuring. She was someone who had studied how to heal for most of her life. She seemed very triumphant now that she discovered how easily it could be done.

For his part, he had found no pleasure in watching Laysa being tortured. A strange feeling was emerging within him. There was part of him that had wanted to stop Degmer from torturing Laysa, but that was not his rational mind. It was something else. He tried to dismiss it, but there was no denying this curious new part of him. This part of him did not seem to belong within him. It seemed as though there were something new growing within him. Nevertheless, he would not let it stop him from his own vengeance. He would just have to control it and let his rational mind have the final say. It was an intriguing feeling though. Perhaps it was just a natural part of his progression toward final perfection. Yet it was just strange that this new feeling made him feel a little less perfect than he had felt before.

ASA PUBLISHING COMPANY

CHAPTER SEVENTEEN

DOCTOR UPFAR

Neaotomo had stayed in Laysa's quarters after Degmer had had her fun. He and Degmer had tucked Laysa into her bed after the healing. Her body was not like Degmer's; it could not heal itself so rapidly. They had healed all of Laysa's damaged cells. Not even a scratch remained on Laysa's skin. Still, she had lost a fair amount of blood, so it would take some time for her body to recover. She did not have the regenerative powers that he had gifted to Degmer. But she would be fine in time; she was sleeping comfortably at the moment.

Degmer had cut all of Laysa's clothes. They were no longer fit to wear; and unfortunately, the only female that had worn clothes that were remotely Laysa's size had been torn to bits by some of his compatriots during their final stets of existence. Her clothes were torn apart as well during her annihilation. There was a one-piece undergarment that had survived, probably because it did not cover the limbs at all. It had been the woman's limbs that were torn asunder. The garment had terrible blood and body matter stains on it, but he could take care of those by the same technique that he used to heal. It was just a simple matter of separating the stain from the strands of fabric. But that would have to wait for a bit. He did not have much time to think about cleaning garments and presenting them as gifts right now—though Laysa would be quite fetching in the abbreviated garment.

He would send Degmer or Beltram out to get new clothes for Laysa some time today if he could. After thinking about which one to send, he decided that Beltram would be the better choice. Degmer might cut up Laysa's whole wardrobe just for spite in her current state of mind. Eventually, Degmer's anger would cool. Her anger was anger that he had purposely provoked and amplified in her. Laysa had been a good friend to her. That had all changed now, at least as far as Degmer was concerned. He wondered if Laysa still had the capacity to call Degmer her friend after this morning's encounter. It would be interesting to see if she did.

The clock on the wall said that he had only ten spens until he would start receiving company. Beltram had said that he would be bringing in the first of his patients—that is, Doctor Upfar's new patients—at 4:20, blindfolded; they all would be blindfolded. A lab among the auxiliary labs had already been transformed to resemble a psychiatrist's office. At least Laysa had thought it looked like a psychiatrist's office. She had helped him set it up yesterday. She thought that it was just going to be part of his cover when he emerged from the sealed labs. If she knew that it would really be his recruitment office, he seriously doubted if she would have been so helpful. She did not approve of his recruitment of humans to become one with him. Rationally, he did not really understand why. He was improving their bodies after all. There was the incidental matter of the recruits losing their own will to his will, but it was a conscious decision that they made—every one of them. Degmer's decision had taken a bit of prodding to be sure; but in the end, it had been her decision.

Well, time was wasting. He now had less than ten spens to get ready to meet his first new patient. He sent a thought to Degmer. *Did you find the nurse's outfit?*

Yes, but it's a little tight in the bust.

He smiled as he sent his next thoughts. *That is good. You will draw much interest from our male recruits if it is tight. The more they are distracted when they first come in the better. Did you print out the list of patient names and appointments?*

Yes. The thought from Degmer had mild irritation attached to it. Degmer still had a bit of a chip on her shoulder.

How is the waiting room outside the sealed labs? Does it resemble a psychiatrist's waiting room?

It is nicely furnished. It makes you seem like a successful psychiatrist.

Excellent. I am going to get dressed as Doctor Upfar now. I will be in my office shortly. Wait until precisely 4:20 to bring in the first patient.

Axi. I understand. Good hunting.

Good hunting? The phrase was unfamiliar. He knew that humans often hunted animals—sometimes for food, but most times for sport. He supposed that the phrase was probably a wish for success, so he sent, *Thank you. I will see you in a few spens.*

He took another glance toward Laysa before he left. She was still resting comfortably. She would be surprised when she woke up. Whether it would be surprise at being alive or surprise to find that she had not a scratch on her, he was not sure. *Who knows? She might think she dreamed the whole thing. Perhaps she will think her encounter with Degmer was just a nightmare.* On the other hand, Laysa would wake up to find herself without any clothes on and find that her clothes were not in the room for that matter. That might make her conclude it was not a dream after all.

He sighed and moved toward the door of Laysa's quarters. It was time to play doctor. He hoped that Beltram's recruits were as ready to be turned as Beltram had indicated. Beltram had been easy to turn. Perhaps he would have special insight that would help find more people like him.

He looked back one more time at the sleeping Laysa. No matter what happened with his recruiting, the problem of Laysa would persist. Degmer would eventually tire of tormenting her and want to end it. He would have a hard time giving a good reason why she should not when that happened. The rationality of his mind said just to use her until she could be used no more, but there was a growing part of him that did not see Laysa in that light. He wished he had more time to dwell on this contradiction within his mind, but he needed to go. Reluctantly, he stepped into the hall letting the door to Laysa's quarters close behind him. He stole one last glance back at the closed door, and then he headed down the hall to his "office" to await the arrival of his "patients."

Degmer did indeed bring the first patient in at 4:20. The patient was a male. He was delighted to find that, just like Beltram, the man had weak spots in his mind barrier that were easy to exploit. His mind barrier was breached easily, and he wove his will and pattern into the man's mind.

Patient after patient came in, and he found it easy to turn each one either by tearing apart weak spots or exploiting an existing tear in the mind's barriers. Most of the patients were males, but some were females. He gave each one of them a small task to perform. That task was to tell Beltram of someone who would be interested in receiving treatment from Doctor Upfar. All of the recruits left thinking of him as Doctor Upfar, just as Beltram did. He would reveal himself in time. It took the entire day to see all of the patients on Beltram's list. He finished with the last of the patients at 7:44, just about suppertime.

He had instructed Beltram to make the appointments ten spens apart, but it did not take nearly that long to turn most of his patients. He had turned thirty-two humans into his kind during his day as the doctor. Counting Degmer's conversion early this morning, he had turned thirty-three in one day. Even with the stamina that his body gave him, Neaotomo was tired. Thirty-three conversions in one day was quite a day's work.

He could not help but wonder how much time he really had to play doctor though. Eventually, someone would notice a change in the complex's population. His recruits had not changed in appearance other than an occasional subtle change in their eyes, but if they displayed feats of unusual strength or self-healing abilities, they would be noticed. He needed a way to pull all of the probable recruits in at the same time to speed things along. He would have to discuss this with Beltram. He had never tried a group conversion before, but if they were all as easy to turn as this lot had been, it should be possible. He could just about have them turn themselves through general probing commands such as, "Think of the one thing that would make you happy," or "Think of the one thing in your life that you would change if you could." Desires and regrets were his best tools to turn a human mind. He just was not sure how many minds he could probe at the same time.

Then a thought came to him. He would not really have to probe them at the same time. He could use his new recruits to probe for him. He sent a message to Beltram. *Have you discovered a way to disable the airlock scanner?*

The answer came back, *I have already disabled it.*

He then sent another message to Beltram. *Good. There has been a change of plans. Bring everyone who shows interest into a large room out in the main complex instead of the waiting room outside the airlock. I will come to them instead of having them come to me. I will meet them at midday tomorrow. Find a suitable room. Communicate with me once you have decided on a location. I am going to convert all of them at once. I will be free of the sealed labs once and for all if you find sufficient recruits for me.*

The response came: *It will be done, Doctor.* Then another thought message came from Beltram. *Odanoi of Cirri made an announcement at four parzes this morning, our time, along with someone named Jahnu. Odanoi called him the prophet. This prophet told of something called the prophecy of the soulless from the Levra. He also said that there would be a crisis on Diotiri for all of Kosundo. Odanoi proclaimed Diotiri a day of reflection. He said he wanted all of Cirri to stop using technology that day for whatever reason. Everyone is talking about it, but no one seems to be taking it too seriously. I just thought you might want to know what is happening in the world.*

Thank you for the information, Beltram. That is interesting. He thought about what Beltram had sent to him. The phrase "prophecy of the soulless" interested him. Beltram had indicated that the prophecy was in the Levra. The Levra was a religious book of some sort. He thought that maybe Laysa might know something about it. He would have to ask her. The name soulless did have a certain ring to it. By some people's estimation, his little band of converts might be considered soulless. *Soulless* would be a catchy name for them.

Be that as it may, it was of little concern to him now. He had to achieve his freedom from the sealed lab before he could pursue his freedom from the lab complex. He would need more than just a handful of *soulless* before he could possibly think of leaving this icy region of Dricho. He did not really have the information he needed to formulate a plan past taking over the genetics complex, but he would get it. In time, his recruits would furnish him with the information he needed. If not, he would think of something.

He thought about the name *soulless* once again. In a way, his recruits had given him a part of themselves, but they retained a good bit of themselves. Perhaps the name was not the name that he wanted for his little band. It was better that they think of themselves as a family. *Yes, they are my family.*

CHAPTER EIGHTEEN

PLOTTING AGAINST A PLOTTER

It was late in the evening on Titarti. The driver had stopped at a motel that he knew of for the night. The driver had been true to his word; he had not asked another nosey question since the journey had first started. Nenavis supposed that he had been a little over the top with the man, but appearing as a dark apparition was always a good way to make sure people listened to you.

Tryllos was fast asleep. He decided to take the opportunity to let a part of his consciousness leave Tryllos's body. He wanted to see what was going on in the Labile Mist, and he couldn't do so when he was fully in Tryllos. He could communicate with other entities that were fully in someone else, but he had to know who that someone else was first. When he was partially in a body, he could use the Labile Mist to communicate with the D'Yavoly and other entities that were free spirits or only partially in a body.

As soon as Nenavis freed part of his consciousness from Tryllos, he had a presence in the Labile Mist. He went to his familiar place in the mist, the place where he had constructed his ethereal throne. The throne was large and impressive, but it wasn't real. It was constructed from the ever changing mist that made up this sphere. It was only his will that held the throne together. It wasn't always a part of the mist; it only existed when he was present in the mist. He chose to make the throne his home in the mist. He didn't bother making a throne room. The throne was the only thing that existed in this place other than the drifting mist that was everywhere a mind wasn't present to form it. The unshaped mist was the perfect setting for this throne in his opinion. It gave an unsettling air, which was most helpful in instilling the proper fear in his D'Yavoly and their minions.

Other D'Yavoly shaped entire rooms and some entire buildings as their dwelling places in the mist. He didn't need the solace that a stable room free of drifting mist provided. That was for entities with weaker minds than his. His mind thrived in the uncertainty that the free mist provided. Where the free mist caused other minds to falter, his mind was strong. It was a distinct advantage for him to keep the free floating mist around his throne.

The mist felt empty. Most of the D'Yavoly were completely in bodies now — or at least should be. The only D'Yavoly that he knew would be available in the mist was Zlux. Zlux was partially trapped in Degmer's body. He had no influence there, being sealed off from Degmer's mind by Neaotomo, the abomination. He had known that was likely to happen; of course, but he could spare Zlux. He still didn't trust him anyway. Zlux was right where he wanted him to be. He was close enough to see what was going on with Neaotomo but unable to meddle. It was a perfect situation as far as he was concerned.

He summoned Zlux; and before long, Zlux appeared before him. "I had not heard from you for a while, my master. I was beginning to think that you had forgotten about me."

"I would never forget about you, Zlux. I have been otherwise occupied, but that is no matter to you. Tell me what news you have of the abomination." he demanded.

Zlux practically squealed with enthusiasm over what he had seen. "My master, the abomination is strong. He is gifted both physically and mentally. He has schemed successfully to take over the soul of the redhead where he has trapped me. His work was magnificent and pales only in comparison to your work, most evil one. He let the redhead torture another female human whom he had used to gain access to the redhead's soul. Then he helped the redhead heal her. The redhead believes that the woman was healed only so that she can be tortured again. It is truly a stroke of evil genius, my most evil master."

He was growing impatient with Zlux's praise fest for the abomination, so he demanded, "Enough of this incessant praising of the abomination. Just tell me what other progress he might have made."

"Yes, most excellent master," groveled Zlux. "He had previously taken over the soul of a human named Beltram, who is of some importance in the complex. Today, after claiming the soul of the redhead, he took thirty-two other souls individually without taking so much as a break. He is using the guise of a mental doctor. His power is as you had hoped, my master. I believe he will be a fitting vessel for you."

"That is excellent news, Zlux," he said. "I have taken Tryllos to Dricho. He was nearly arrested in Doetora. His broken mind still holds the key to my plan. I will be arriving in Tryllos's body sometime tomorrow evening. Are there other D'Yavoly who have successfully taken bodies in the complex?"

"I am aware of three D'Yavoly who have taken up a presence in humans in the complex. I have no way of knowing who else might have taken full control of someone since the redhead has been confined to a sealed portion of the complex until just today, and then she only went a few dets outside of the sealed area to escort victims to the abomination," said Zlux.

"All right. Contact the ones that you can, and warn them to stay away from the abomination. I will deal with him after I arrive. I don't want any more of my D'Yavoly trapped inside a body. See if you can get the ones who are partially in a body to warn those who are wholly in. When will Sarditu arrive?"

"The last I heard, he will arrive early on eKureaki," said Zlux.

"That is good," he said with a slight nod. "Sarditu has made quite a name for the human he possesses, Lidar Tombun. He will be able to provide credibility for us. I will make my move after he arrives. Spread the word. I do not dare leave the imbecile Tryllos for very long. He might wake up and do damage to himself in some way. If we don't do this correctly, we could see the whole prospect of dominating Kosundo through the abomination slip through our fingers. I am depending on you to convey my messages. You know what your fate will be, should you fail to obey me."

"I am fully aware, my master. I do not wish to spend any more time in the abyss. Your messages will be delivered," said Zlux smoothly.

He growled. "See that you do. I have informed the other D'Yavoly that you are to be my contact. They might very well contact you. Be accurate in your information, Zlux, no ad-libbing. If some do not contact you, do your best to contact them."

"It will be done, my master. What else is there for me to do? I am wholly at your mercy," groveled Zlux.

He smiled a sinister smile. "Yes, you are. Keep that in remembrance." He ended the contact with Zlux.

Zlux was in no position to do any mischief. He knew where he could be found. He was in complete control of Zlux. Soon, he would also control the abomination. He looked forward to using him to marshal an army of the soulless. *Given the abilities that he can pass on to the physical bodies of the soulless, the army will be invincible once the technology of men is taken away from them.* An eerie smile made its way across his face as he thought. *The very streets will be paved with the bodies of anyone who dares oppose the army of the soulless. Then I will rule in the physical world as I have in the nether regions. It is my destiny. It is my right. Then the Other One will be vanquished in this world just as the Other One has vanquished me in the other worlds before.*

Chapter Nineteen

Admitting the Truth

True answers take time and effort to give. There are many more answers that are untrue. They are more convenient and easier to find than the truth. This is how false history is made. It is much easier to report a false news story than a true one. Truth requires the weight of proof; it requires one to care enough to find it. On any given day, it is likely that truth never is seen in conversation; it is much too hard to prove, and few care enough for truth to care if they speak it.

Just as certain, it is easy to deceive oneself. What each man wishes, he also wants to believe to be true. It is easy to care about one's own wishes, but self-centered wishes do not lead to truth. One might wish that a koh's large tail be called a leg, but a koh still has just four legs. Wishing the tail to be a leg does not make it a leg.

Every society can easily succumb to self-deceit; and if the society has universally deceived itself, telling the truth becomes a revolutionary act. Truth can be considered a threat to those who have lost the ability to receive it as a blessing.

Truth is more than accuracy of fact. It is the correct interpretation of fact. If an image is taken of a man chasing a woman, the image is accurate. All the details can be considered fact; but unless one knows why the man is chasing the woman, the truth of the image cannot be known. Insanity can be caused by overstating accuracy and fact without regard to the context of those facts.

So then how is it one can find truth? First, one must face the truth about oneself. Without facing the truth about oneself, one can never know the truth about others. Not being truthful about oneself creates hatred and prejudice. When others are viewed in the light of truth without prejudice, then truth can exist with love.

In the end, truth combined with unconditional love will have the final say about what is reality. This is why right, even temporarily defeated, is stronger than evil, which appears to be triumphant.

Agap closed the book and put it aside. He had been reading *Can Truth Exist without Love?* written by Elathay Upus, a philosopher of the ancient Grattoan Empire. The Grattoan Empire was the first great Kosundoan empire. It existed for over a millennium before the breaking. The passage that he had read was a summary passage in which the philosopher summed up what he was about to write. In ancient writing, it was common to set up premises before details were given. Even though it was only a summary of thoughts, he found the words he had just read to be profound, especially the part about facing the truth. With Kenun set to begin his investigation today, he must remember to face the truth about himself so that he could aid Kenun in understanding the truth about the stolen technology. Otherwise, he would just be in the way of truth.

He wasn't at all happy about the truth. The truth about himself was that he had somehow allowed an untrustworthy person to have access to his team's data. He must admit to that truth first, and then the truth might have a chance of being known.

It was early on Paraskevi. Kenun was to visit him here in his office at 3:20, just a couple of spens from now. Agap had brought the philosophy book to his office to remind himself of his responsibility in the affair. If anyone on his team bore the responsibility for the stolen data, it first and foremost would be him. Oh, he had followed all the existing protocols for handling and storing information; but somewhere, somehow, he had allowed a viper into his house. A snake had slithered among his team and stolen valuable information.

He couldn't get Odanoi's question out of his mind: "Were the Avengers a threat?" He could only hope that they did not prove to be so. If they did prove to be a threat, he would be responsible. He had let down his guard and let a snake slither away with information, and that information could end up bringing harm to people. He would not soon forgive himself if the Avengers harmed just one innocent person.

He was still pondering the issue when he saw Kenun through his office window. Kenun was a shorter man, but he had broad shoulders. Although Agap had never seen Kenun in anything but a suit and a long-sleeved sark, he had the impression that his arms were powerful. Kenun was built much like a speedball midfielder: powerful and low to the ground. Playing the midfield in the sport of speedball demanded a physical approach. A midfielder's job was to advance the ball through the hotly contested midfield into the offensive zone where a quick forward took over the ball in hopes of scoring. He could imagine Kenun being able to power his way through the midfield and into the offensive zone quite effectively. Kenun had very yellow blonde hair and steely blue eyes. Kenun also had a thin, neatly trimmed beard. Cirrian males generally did grow beards, but only after their one hundredth birthday. He hadn't realized that Kenun had already turned one hundred.

As Kenun approached, he caught Kenun's eye and waved him into his office. He greeted Kenun with a deep bow as he came in. Kenun returned the bow, and he gestured toward a seat in the sitting area of his office. It was hard to read Kenun; he always seemed to have the same stoic expression on his face. Once Kenun sat down, he took a seat across from him and watched for any hint of a change in Kenun's expression. As Kenun put his case on the table between them, no change in expression was apparent. He assumed that the case contained information about the stolen data so he took his eye off Kenun for a moment to eye it.

After Kenun was situated, he donned a pleasant smile and said, "Good morning, Agapoi. It is good to see you again. I only wish our meeting were under more pleasant circumstances."

"Good morning, Kenun. Don't let the circumstances worry you. I understand the job you have been handed. It is not a pleasant one, but I believe, as does the council, that you are the person for the job. If anyone can learn the truth about the stolen information, it will be you." His words were sincere, but they sounded as if he were trying to flatter the man. He hoped that Kenun didn't take his words that way.

Kenun sat back in his chair and crossed his legs. "I appreciate the confidence and the niceties, Agapoi, but I will need to ask you some rather pointed questions to begin the interview. I hope that the questions will not offend you." Kenun's countenance had returned to its normal impassiveness.

"I will not take offense, Kenun," he said while settling back in his seat. Trying to read Kenun was not going to be easy.

"Very well," said Kenun. He uncrossed his legs and leaned forward slightly in his chair. It looked as though

Kenun had just a hint of red in his yellow blonde hair in this light. He wore his hair cut close to his scalp. His steely blue eyes fixed themselves on him. Finally he bent forward, reached inside his case and pulled out a nona. It was a writing nona. "I dislike the first question that I have to ask, but it is necessary to set my line of questioning. Did you benefit from the disclosure of the data in question?"

He gave a sarcastic smile. "You mean did I steal the information?"

"Or arrange for it to be stolen or purposely ignore violations of data security," added Kenun. His tone sounded clinical.

"No. I did not," he said plainly trying his best not to sound offended.

"Very well," said Kenun. "Has anyone on your team experienced a financial windfall within the last three years as far as your knowledge is concerned?"

"Nothing that I didn't apply for them to receive. My team has had several notable accomplishments that have recompensed them well. But I know of no mystery money for anyone on my team," he said matter-of-factly.

"I see. Very well," said Kenun.

Kenun's tone had not changed. The clinical tone mixed with the constant placid look made getting a read on Kenun very difficult. This combination of mannerisms made him more apprehensive than any question that Kenun would ask. *Yet, his manner does make him a good investigator,* he conceded in thought.

With that same tone, Kenun asked, "Have you checked the security records for the data in question; and if so, what security was used?"

He shifted in his seat slightly. This time it was the question that made him feel uncomfortable. If he had set higher security on the records, the information most likely couldn't have been stolen. He answered defensively. "I have checked the security records for the data. Axopen put level-three encryption on the data when stored. I put a level four seal on the data, ensuring that only the twice-honored could download the encrypted files. This was all that was required of this information since it was not being used and was not deemed sensitive."

"So no tracking numbers or attachments were used in connection with this data?" asked Kenun. His steely blue eyes seemed to try to burn a hole in him.

"No. No tracking was required for storage due to the nature of the information. The research was thought to be a dead end at the time," he said, again defensively.

"Yet some of this information is being revised for use in a current project, is it not?" asked Kenun.

"Yes," he began slowly. "It has just recently been included. I see you have done your homework. This use only started—."

"Yesterday," broke in Kenun. "I now have access to all your team's research and logs by Phrunoi's order. I must commend you on the depth of your team's analysis. The analysis makes things so clear that nearly anyone could understand the complex research that you are doing. Of course, that is a two-edged sword, isn't it? The easier it is to understand the research, the easier for a foreign power to implement, don't you think?"

"Yes, I suppose, but—."

"But you encourage this level of detail so that the team can take up each other's work if need be," interrupted Kenun again. "I do understand, Agapoi. I am just pointing out some alternate possibilities."

Kenun's tone was still as clinical as ever. It was beginning to annoy him.

"It is not my job to approve or disapprove of your team's practices. My job is to find out how the data was stolen and try to ensure that a similar occurrence does not happen again. It very well could be that this investigation could change the way Cirri handles data storage in the future. Part of my job is to report anything that could impact the security of Cirri's technology designs," said Kenun, completely without emotion.

Kenun certainly knew how to get down to it, and he didn't give away anything in his voice. *He will make a good investigator,* he reiterated in his thinking. "Is that all the questions that you have for me then, Kenun?"

"Actually, I have one more. I have all the team's personnel records and meeting logs as well as access to your team's research, but the one thing I don't have is a personal understanding of your team's personalities. Could you outline the personality types that you have on your team? You can leave out Opsil and Holon. They were not part of your team during the time frame when the data was most likely stolen." Kenun paused for an answer without any further explanation.

"All right," he began slowly. He was not quite certain what Kenun was expecting, so he decided to give him just general traits. "I will start with the men on my team. Axopen tends to be quiet, unless he is discussing his work with a colleague. His interests are work, work, and more work while he is at work. He will engage in limited social talk at times, but he dislikes rehashing an old subject, especially if he has discussed it before or has written a report on it. He does like to poke fun at what he sees as the stupid actions of others. He tends to carry a chip on his shoulder.

"Supeb is a lot like Axopen, except he is even more serious-minded. I think I have seen Supeb laugh twice since I have known him. If he has a social life, I don't know anything about it. I haven't seen Supeb display ego of any kind, which is also different from Axopen.

"Eutay is a good worker, but he loves to have fun. He tries to find humor in nearly any situation, and sometimes he is successful in finding it. He is very outgoing and talks of his social life quite a bit. He says he is currently between girlfriends. The truth is, like the rest of the team, he is so busy that he has not made time to look for one. I don't know if you're wanting this kind of personal information; but I believe he might have taken a liking to a female member of the team, but I don't believe the feelings are mutual — yet.

"Now for the ladies on the team. Yotux is my associate team lead, and I trust her implicitly. She also looks out for the emotional needs of the team. She is an encourager. I haven't heard much about her social life other than I know she has a sister in Cirri City. I believe that they are close.

"Phunex is a take-charge personality. She will get the job done, even if she has to bully people to get it done. She is instrumental in transforming our designs into physical product. Her personality is useful in getting the product right.

"Kowtsom is a likeable person, though she is our team gossip. She is very social, which leads to her getting a lot of news. She likes to spread the news to anyone who will listen with her own unique conclusions included. She is only a social gossip though, not a security risk. I have never heard her having loose lips about work-related matters. She barely talks about work-related matters outside of work that I have observed. Besides, the team spends most of their off-time with each other," he finished.

"Most, but not all," said Kenun in that clinical tone.

"No—of course not all—I am aware that each team member does have friends and acquaintances outside of the team. Still, the team is very close. They do spend the majority of their free time with each other," he reasserted.

"I see. Very well," intoned Kenun mechanically.

During the meeting, Kenun was busily making notes. Agap would like to have seen what he wrote on his nona; but he knew that that would be improper, so he did not even think about asking. Kenun shifted in his seat and then looked up from his nona and asked, "What of Psawton?"

Psawton was the only person ever to leave his team. He still wasn't sure why, other than Psawton saying that he was leaving for personal reasons. Any personal reason that he might have had was a mystery to him—the entirety of Psawton's personal life was a mystery to him. Supeb had given him a glowing recommendation when he left. Part of the reason that Supeb had liked him so much might have been because he was so quiet. He couldn't remember Psawton stringing together three sentences when he had talked to him. He decided just to give Kenun what he knew of Psawton on a professional level. "He became chief designer on Noso's team. He was only with us for a short while, maybe five months. He was a very good designer, and Supeb actually recommended that Psawton be given a chief designer role. Psawton was assistant designer for several teams before he came to us. He is a very private person, so I really don't know anything of his private life."

"Very well," Kenun said in a near monotone. He wrote on his nona again, and then he looked up and asked, "What about the transport beam? Isn't the present beam technology still utilizing a form of the original beam?"

He thought for a moment. Kenun was right—sort of— but they had gone a different direction in transport beam technology since the early days. He answered, "In a very rudimentary sense, yes. The original beam as it was constituted was basically useless. It's like saying that the first displacement field used in a flying craft that flew for only a few fets is still being utilized in today's supersonic flying crafts. The principles are the same, but the design is totally different. We used the basic principles of disintegration in both beams, but we use many refinements now that the first beam taught us. The beam has been drastically modified and combined with confinement streams. It is not the same technology."

"I see," was all that Kenun said as he busily took notes. "What about the destructive nature of the original beam? Shouldn't that have been considered when deciding what security classification to assign to the technology files associated with this project?"

He thought about his reading this morning. He knew that he needed to admit the truth about himself so that the truth could be uncovered. "Yes," he admitted. "In retrospect, I believe that the destructive nature of the beam, which we considered a failure for what we were trying to accomplish, should have been considered. The security designation should have been higher. That decision was mine to make. I didn't consider what other uses the beam could serve when I designated the security level. I suppose that I was overly naïve."

"Very well, Agapoi. That is all the questions that I have for you. If it's axi with you, I'll be moving on to your team members now. Thank you for your time and your honesty," said Kenun heartily.

He was surprised at the sudden change to a friendly tone, but it was a welcome change. "Of course, that's fine," he said to answer Kenun's apparent request for approval to interview his team. Then he got up and bowed to Kenun.

Kenun bowed in response more deeply than he had bowed to him. Kenun then left the office, and he watched him go toward the work areas. When Kenun was out of direct sight, he shifted his focus to the surveillance terms in the meeting area, which showed Kenun heading toward Axopen's workstation.

Once his curiosity about who would be the first to be interviewed was satisfied, he went to his desk to get back to work. But before he started working, he thought about the last question that Kenun had asked. He did slip up by not assigning tracking to the files. Kenun was right. He should have considered the destructive nature of the beam when assigning the security level. He just didn't think of the beam being used as a weapon. Cirri had never created weapons. The thought of using the beam as a weapon just never entered his mind. That had changed now. He wondered how much more change would take place in his thinking over the next few days.

Axopen looked up in time to see a bearded man approaching his workstation. Agapoi had warned the team this morning to expect an interview from Kenun. He also said that he might ask some tough questions. The approaching man looked tough. That much was sure. He knew that he had nothing to hide, but the sight of an investigator approaching did give him a funny feeling in his stomach.

The man arrived at his workstation, greeted him with a slight bow and asked, "Are you Axopen?"

He returned the bow a bit more deeply than had been offered him and said, "Yes. I assume that your name is Kenun and that you want to ask me about some stolen research."

"That is correct. Did you want to conduct the interview here at your workstation or in the meeting area?" asked Kenun politely.

"We would have more privacy in the meeting area. We can close the sliding doors and draw the shutters," he suggested. "Agapoi would still be able to see us if he doesn't close his shutters, but I don't suppose that would be a problem."

"No. It wouldn't be a problem," said Kenun. "The meeting area sounds like a good place to conduct all of the interviews." Kenun turned and started walking back toward the meeting area.

He gave a nervous touch to his dark blonde hair as he got up and ended up having to wipe his hand on his trousers. His hair was sticky with hair gel. He was of the opinion that the more hair gel he put on his hair, the less time he had to spend fussing over his hair during the day. He then followed Kenun into the meeting area. On his way into the meeting area, he hit the black button that was on the inner part of the longer of the two glass walls that separated this area from the work area. A large glass door slid down into place between the glass walls. He then hit the blue button, and closed shutters appeared inside the glass walls and door, effectively sealing the meeting area off from the rest of the technology labs and workstations. Kenun had moved to the back of the meeting area to the tables and chairs in front of the refreshment bar. He drew out a seat and sat across from Kenun.

Kenun was staring down at a nona that he was holding above the table. He had a stylus in his hand, indicating that he either had just written something or was about to write something. After a moment, he raised his head and said, "I would like to start by having you give a synopsis of the research you led in regard to the transporter array during the period of time the stolen files were being actively used. Please include the reasoning why this particular avenue of research was abandoned."

He wrinkled his forehead and protested, "The reasoning behind the abandonment of the original beam and mobile platform are contained within the file reports. Surely you have read them."

Kenun gave a slight smile, muttered something about Agapoi being right, and said, "Humor me, Axopen. Perhaps it will reveal some things that the written report failed to reveal. Plus, I can't see your facial expressions or body language in a written report."

"Is there some question about the accuracy of my report?" he asked.

"Accuracy, no. I am sure all the facts are quite accurate. I just need to learn the truth about the reasons behind abandoning your research. Were there biases that affected your judgment? Was there a rush to judgment on the viability of the research? Were there other applications that were not considered for the research? I am just trying to find out why this team abandoned research that a foreign power thought to be quite useful," said Kenun in a clinical tone. Kenun's countenance revealed irritation for just a moment as he spoke his next words. "Now, if you please, could you give me a synopsis of your research and the reasons that you had for abandoning the research?"

He frowned. He didn't like having his work questioned. He always took pride in his work. He blurted, "We were not trying to create a weapon. The beam just didn't work, and we thought that the platform was not going to be of use when we determined we needed multiple beams for a transporter array. Since then, we have reduced the size of the array back to a comparable size of the original beam. At the time, I had no way of knowing the platform could be useful for the transporter technology."

"I see," said Kenun in a clinical tone. "So, you never saw past the uses for your current project when suggesting a security level to Agapoi."

"Well," he said. He knew where this question was leading, but he didn't know how to avoid admitting that he might have had narrow vision on the data. After pausing, he said, "I didn't actually suggest a security level. Agapoi usually just asked what value the information had."

Kenun eyed him closely, expecting something more.

Finally, he admitted, "I told Agapoi that the data was useless."

"I see," said Kenun in that same clinical tone. "Given the current circumstances, was that statement true?" he asked.

"I thought it to be true at the time," he protested.

Kenun just continued to stare at him. He felt as though he were staring through him, not at him. At last, he added, "But, given the circumstances that we now face, I can see that my point of view affected my objectivity on the data. It is now obvious that the data in the files was not useless for certain purposes."

He felt a hot flush come across his face. He felt angry and humiliated at the same time. He was angry with himself for being so short-sighted in his assessment to Agapoi, and he felt humiliated that he hadn't realized it until Kenun had pointed it out. He had always had problems accepting that he was not always perfect in certain aspects of his work, but he had to accept that fact on this occasion. He had done something that was not only wrong but also rather foolish. He really didn't like that someone outside the team had made him realize it. It would have been better if Agapoi had noticed. At least Agapoi was clearly his superior.

"Very well," said Kenun. "Was there any contact with other teams concerning this research?"

He almost protested that the contact information would have been contained in the reports, but he thought better of it. Instead, he said, "Yes. The manufacturing team made some prototypes for us, but all data that the manufacturing team used to create the prototypes was returned."

"Did all the data have copy prevention in place?" asked Kenun.

He sighed impatiently. "Yes. All data is uploaded on copy-protected devices when given to the manufacturing team."

"Still, manual copying of pertinent facts would still be possible," said Kenun quietly.

He wasn't sure if he was talking to him or just talking to himself so he remained silent. Kenun spent some time entering notes into his nona, but finally asked, "Have you ever shown research data to unauthorized personnel?"

"No," he said indignantly.

"I am sorry for the bluntness of some of the questions that I have to ask. Please don't take personal offense to them. Do you have any reason, no matter how slight, to believe that a team member has violated security protocol with respect to research data?"

"A member of *our* team? No. Certainly not. I have no reason to believe any member of our team has violated security protocol." He surprised himself with the strength of his voice as he answered.

Kenun smiled. "Very well," he said. The clinical quality of his voice had dissipated. It now sounded more human. "I see that Agapoi has assembled a very loyal team. That is to his credit. Thank you, Axopen. That is all for now. I might have more questions later, depending on what is uncovered in the other interviews. I think I will use this area for the rest of my interviews. Could you send Supeb out to me on your way back to your workstation?"

He was surprised at the abrupt completion of the interview, but he managed to say, "Sure. I will send Supeb."

As he got up and turned to go back to his workstation, he noticed that Agapoi had closed his shutters. The meeting room was completely shut off from peering eyes. He decided that the area was a good place to hold the interviews. No one could see the embarrassment that Kenun brought upon the interviewee. He hit the black button, and the large door slid up out of sight. As he exited the meeting area, he became aware of seven sets of eyes fixed upon him. He self-consciously ran his hand through his hair, getting hair grease on his hand, and then wiped his hand on his trousers. He went to Supeb's workstation and said to him, "Kenun wants to interview you next in the team meeting area."

Supeb peered at him anxiously. "How did it go? You weren't in there that long."

He shrugged his shoulders. "Not bad. Kenun will ask some rather blunt questions though. At least he asked blunt questions of me."

Supeb got up and started toward the meeting area. He took a glance over his shoulder back at him as he walked. Axopen nodded at him in reassurance. Supeb then strode into the meeting area and lowered the door behind him.

As Axopen went to his workstation, he was greeted by Phunex and Kowtsom. "So, what did he ask you?" asked Kowtsom.

"He just asked about the security on the files and whether I knew anything about the theft," he said nonchalantly. He really didn't want to talk about how Kenun had made him feel ashamed that he didn't think about how else the research could have been used.

"Do you think he will ask me about my manufacturing contacts?" asked Phunex.

He shrugged his shoulders. "Perhaps. He asked me if the research was made available to any other team. Since you coordinate with manufacturing, I am sure the subject will come up. Why? Do you suspect someone in manufacturing?"

Phunex shrugged. "Not really. I mean, I don't know that anything happened."

Kowtsom crinkled her forehead and asked, "Out with it, Phunex. What do you know?"

Phunex paused as if reluctant to answer but then said, "The manufacturing team in Cirri City sometimes delayed in getting the data card back to me." Both he and Kowtsom looked at her curiously. "It wasn't a long delay. I just figured they were unorganized. There were just a few times that they didn't get the card back to me on time. It was sometimes as much as a day late," Phunex explained.

"And you didn't tell anyone this?" he asked.

"Well, no," said Phunex sheepishly. "But until this theft was made known, no one thought much about things like that. We got the card back after all, and it's not as if they were keeping it for a *long* period of time. I brought it to the manufacturing team lead's attention. He said he would deal with it, and that was the last of it. They stopped getting the cards back to me late after that."

"It could be that someone on the team was just being lax," reasoned Kowtsom.

Yes," he said, "but it could also be that someone was taking a closer look at our research too." He wasn't really trying to make Phunex feel bad, though he knew that his statement couldn't have made her feel anything but bad. Everybody had been too lax with the security of their research, including him. He was just making the point that the team needed to change the way they regarded the security of their research, though he didn't see any need to explain himself to Phunex.

Phunex had tears in her eyes as she made her way back to her workstation. Kowtsom gave him an accusing stare. He gave Kowtsom a gesture as if to say, "What did I do?" Kowtsom intensified her stare before shaking her head and turning her attention toward Phunex.

So maybe he had made Phunex feel bad. Or perhaps Phunex was just concerned with how she would be perceived after her interview. He guessed that his last comment didn't help Phunex's mental state any, but what of it? "She shouldn't have been so careless," he heard himself say quietly.

His words lingered in his ears. The longer they lingered, the more the words sickened him. He had worked with Phunex for a long time, but his words indicated a callousness toward her that appalled him. Thoughts of equally callous moments started to pour into his mind. Then the words of His warning that Jahnu had given in the all-council meeting filled his thoughts. He couldn't remember His blessing, and now he was beginning to understand why.

Kenun had made him admit that he wasn't perfect. It was the first time that he had been forced to come to terms with that truth. Oh, he knew that he had made mistakes in the past, but he viewed those mistakes as being trivial. He thought that he was perfect in the important things — until now. Now he understood just how wrong he had been about many important things.

Oh, Thaoi! What a wretched man I am! He was as distressed within himself as he had ever been. He felt tears in his eyes and he turned away so that no one would see. He felt a dark cloud over him, just as he had after Jahnu's all-council message. *Oh, please forgive me, Thaoi. I've not kept a clear conscience toward you or my fellow man. I've not loved anyone but myself. Help me to care about you and others. Help me to trust in you. Help me to remember your blessing!* He only thought the words, but they were sincere. They couldn't have been more sincere if he had shouted them. He searched his memory for His blessing over and over, but he found no peace there.

Then a very quiet thought came to him. *Make things right with Phunex, just as if you were making things right with me.* He had heard a similar quiet thought before, but he had brushed it aside every time he had heard it before, not being willing to humiliate himself in front of others. However, this time he was only too glad to obey. He had had enough. He wiped his eyes and got up.

As he started over to Phunex's workstation, Opsil gave him a quick glance. He wasn't sure if Opsil had overheard the conversation or not, but his glance said that perhaps he did. He dropped his eyes to the floor and continued on to Phunex's workstation. He nervously ran his fingers through the front of his hair again and instinctively wiped the hair grease on his pants. He didn't always realize when he wiped his hands, but he realized it after the fact this time. He inspected his trousers to see if the wipe had left a noticeable stain. His trousers didn't appear to have anything noticeable on them. That was why he always wore dark trousers; they didn't show the hair grease too much. He shook his head. He was thinking about himself again. He cleared his thoughts of himself and concentrated on how to make things right with Phunex.

Kowtsom was trying to soothe Phunex as he arrived at her workstation. "There is nothing to worry about, Phunex. It was probably as you had assumed," she said soothingly.

He cleared his throat, as neither of the two women had noticed his approach. Phunex had her head down. Her crossed arms upon her desk supported her forehead. Kowtsom, who was standing behind her, caught a glimpse of him approaching as she was attending to the weeping Phunex.

"What do you want?" said Kowtsom roughly to him.

Phunex lifted her head to see who had approached. When she saw that it was him, she tried hastily to wipe her eyes on her sleeve. He figured that she didn't want to give him the satisfaction of seeing her cry.

As Kowtsom stared a hole into him and Phunex tried to regain her composure, he blurted, "Look, Phunex. I'm sorry about what I said about the manufacturing team issue." He became antsy as he spoke. He didn't have much practice in the art of apologizing.

Phunex trained her eyes on him unsteadily. Her eyes were red from crying. "No. No, it's not what you said, Axopen. I just realized that my lack of action might have allowed our research to be stolen."

He knew better than to think that his words did not affect Phunex, so he said, "Sure it's what I said. You were wanting support; and I failed to provide any, and I am sorry. Look, Phunex, I would have probably made the same assumption as you. It's not you that is to blame. It's the whole Cirrian security culture that is to blame. We've grown to trust fellow Cirrians too much. That's all." When those words left his mouth, the dark cloud lifted and he could remember. He remembered every word of His blessing as if Jahnu had just spoken it. What he couldn't remember was ever feeling such joy as he did at that moment.

Phunex's face lit up in a small smile. "Thank you, Axopen. That may be the kindest thing I've ever heard you say, delivered as only you can."

He realized that Phunex just gave him a compliment and a criticism at the same time, but he chose to hear only the compliment, and he returned a smile to Phunex. Phunex then got up and gave him a hug, which made him rather uncomfortable, but only for a moment.

Before she released the hug, she whispered in his ear, "By the way, your hair is sticking up again."

Immediately after he was released from the hug, he felt above his hair with his fingers. Eventually, his fingers ran into the wayward strands and patted them back down to his scalp. He gave a sheepish smile to Phunex and strode back to his seat.

As he left, he heard the girls giggling behind him. They could be giggling about him, but he didn't care if they were because his heart felt better for making things right with Phunex. His heart felt truly at peace for the first time ever because he hadn't just made things right with Phunex, he had made things right with Thaoi.

Nearly as soon as he arrived at his workstation, he heard the large door to the meeting area go up. Supeb emerged and motioned to Phunex. She was to be the next to be interviewed. He watched as Phunex slowly went toward the meeting room. When she looked his way, he gave her an encouraging nod. Phunex gave a slight smile and a nod back.

She will be fine, he told himself.

As the door closed behind Phunex, he found himself reflecting on his own interview. He had learned something about being aware of security today. He had also learned that he was not as perfect as he hoped he was. Yet, he was axi with that realization because he had also learned that it's axi to show vulnerability to others. He had realized that no human could ever truly be perfect. It was an important revelation. He couldn't be perfect, but he could certainly make the goal of his life to please Thaoi and others. Just as Thaoi's blessing was now at the front of his mind, so was the thought of pleasing Thaoi and others. The thought of pleasing himself was relegated to the back of his mind.

The interviews went on. Phunex appeared a little shaken when she left her interview, but Kenun could have that effect on people. After Phunex, Yotux was interviewed. She seemed to come out of the interview in good shape. Then Eutay had his interview. He wasn't directly involved with the stolen technology, but he was sure that Kenun was just being thorough. Finally, the last member of the team to be interviewed was Kowtsom. Like Eutay, she was not directly involved with the stolen research, but she seemed very relieved to have the interview over anyway.

The team tried to concentrate on work, but it was difficult. Yotux and Holon did manage to finish the new chomile interface. He was glad about that just so that he could finish furnishing his room more quickly. He hadn't talked to anyone who had managed to completely finish creating a room with the old interface. The old interface made creating walls and furnishings rather laborious. And who had the energy after work to bother with it? No one wanted to mess with it on the weekend either. He thought that the changes would make the use of the chomile much faster so he was all for it.

As for himself, he tried to concentrate on the transport relay he was working on today, but he had to admit that he didn't make much progress. No one talked about the interviews after his incident with Phunex earlier today. He was glad that everyone pretended to work. He had acted like a jerk. He supposed that he had done that many times in the past without realizing it, but even that embarrassing thought couldn't diminish the joy he felt.

A little while after Kowtsom finished her interview, the shutters on the meeting area windows were withdrawn and Kenun and Agapoi emerged from the meeting area. They were talking quietly while they walked. Agapoi walked Kenun all the way to the translift. After Agapoi saw Kenun onto the translift, he talked with Yotux for a moment and then headed back to his office.

Soon, an alert sounded on his workstation. He looked at the bottom left corner of his display. There was to be a team meeting now. He scanned the room and saw everyone else closing out their work and readying themselves for the team meeting. He did likewise, and soon, the whole team was heading for the meeting area. The area seemed to be far less ominous than it had seemed earlier today. Still, there was a bit of leftover apprehension in the room. He didn't think it was because of the interviews themselves but rather because of the realizations that they had caused among the team. No one was really sure how Agapoi was going to handle these realizations either.

The team gathered in the meeting room in what seemed to be record time to Axopen. No one was talking. Everyone just came and sat down—except for Yotux, who was busy readying Agapoi's speaking desk for the meeting. He took his seat in the second row on Agapoi's left.

Yotux was the last to take her seat, and as she did, Agapoi emerged from his office. It was customary for the whole team to be in their seats before the team lead took his place. As Agapoi approached the speaking desk, it was hard to tell what might be going through his mind. That wasn't unusual, as he always had that same serious cast about him before a meeting. Kenun no doubt had given him a copy of today's interviews—at least a shortened version of the interviews anyway. He wondered if Agapoi would want to talk to him later or if he would just address any issues discovered by the interviews in a general manner. He was confident that Agapoi wouldn't mention any names in the meeting. He never did, unless he was bestowing praise. Somehow, he didn't think that much praise would be forthcoming in this meeting. He knew he didn't deserve any praise anyway.

Agapoi had his eyes on his desk, probably scanning some notes, before his head came up to scan each face on the team. "Thank you for your prompt attendance at this rather impromptu meeting," he began. "As you have probably guessed, I have gathered you here to discuss today's interviews with the council appointed investigator, Kenun Pelen Ischor Opuptu. As his beard suggests, he is an experienced man. He is also very well respected. I am certain that he will find who is responsible for illegally delivering Cirrian research to Doetora. Not only do I want to briefly discuss the interviews, but I also want to give you some reminders of the tasks at hand.

"Kenun told me that each of you who were interviewed acquitted yourselves well today. He expressed his appreciation for the cooperation given. I also believe that many of us learned something from the interviews with Kenun. He has a unique way of making a person think about past actions in a way that was not previously thought. I know that I learned that our research should not be thought of only in the light of our team's endeavors but also in the light of other applications. Going forward, I am requiring each canceled research project report to include a synopsis of all possible uses of the researched technology. This synopsis will require each of us to think outside of our areas of expertise, but I believe that it's not anything that will burden us unduly. I am only asking you to explore a few possible alternative uses for technology that we will not be continuing to research ourselves. This will allow me to determine more accurately the security options that should be placed on each research item. It will also allow me to flag items that might be of interest to another Cirrian technology team.

"Don't assign blame to yourselves for any shortsightedness of past actions. The culture of the technology community has been too trusting. This culture is not of your doing. It is the result of over two thousand years of exemplary behavior of Cirrian citizens. It has been over two thousand years since Epetaones Plauvax Diesam was executed for his treason. Since then, Cirri has not had to deal with a treasonous act until now. It is commendable that such naïveté has had the chance to permeate our culture.

"However, as the latter days are upon us now, we are behooved to throw off our naïveté and become vigilant. As I have said before, I believe that our team will be called on to assist Kosundo as it has never been called on before. It is good that the work on the chomile is complete so that all of us can be free to devote our talents to other endeavors that might have a more global significance.

"Don't dwell on the past. No one can undo a whit of the past. Instead, pray that Thaoi would grant us His favor to accomplish what is needed in the future."

He and the rest of the team responded reverently and in a rather subdued tone, "Thaoi grant it so. May Thaoi be praised." That phrase was the traditional response when a call to prayer was announced publicly in Cirri, but it meant more than that to him now. It affirmed that the call to prayer was understood and accepted. Faith in Thaoi was always encouraged publicly in Cirri. He just wondered how many times he had just said the phrase out of habit. He shook himself. He shouldn't be thinking that way today. Do away with the past, and get on with the future. He would just have to make sure that he truly meant it when he said that phrase from this point forward.

Agapoi continued. "As you have done many times in the past, your cooperation today makes me very proud to be called your team lead."

Yotux stood and offered a crisp open hand salute. He and the others stood and joined her in putting their right hands to their hearts, then straightening their right arms as they turned their palms outward while shooting their open hands up over their heads. The gesture was a way of showing gratitude to Agapoi. As he finished the salute he thought, *I was wrong. Agapoi did find a way to praise his team today.*

The salute brought a smile to Agapoi's face. "You have all worked very hard this week," he said, "and there may be very little chance for rest in the future. I would like each of you to take the rest of the day off." Then, in an unusual gesture for a team lead, Agapoi returned the team's gratitude with a very crisp openhanded salute of his own. Agapoi then turned and went into his office.

The team was left in a state of partial disbelief.

"Did he just tell us to go home?" asked a bewildered-sounding Eutay.

He turned to him and said, "That's what it sounded like to me."

The whole team gravitated toward the conversation. Opsil said, "But it's only fifteen spens after the fifth parz."

Kowtsom said, "Who am I to argue with the team lead? I say let's go eat. It's past lunchtime anyway."

Phunex said, "That sounds like a great idea. Let's go to that Doetoran restaurant. I just love their meat dishes."

Eutay said, "I'm not sure I want to think about Doetora any more today."

Everyone chuckled about that, but no one disputed.

Yotux then said, "Ah. Let's just go to the diner just outside the technology complex, The Good Eating Diner."

Holon asked, "That's really its name?"

Yotux replied, "Oh, you haven't been to The G-E-D yet, have you?"

Holon shook her head.

"We must remedy that immediately," said Phunex. "There is only one G-E-D!"

"Yes, an experience of a lifetime," added Eutay.

"Actually, it's a grease pit," he said.

The other team members looked disgustedly at him.

He then added, "But it's a likeable grease pit."

The team resumed their previous smiles at his last remark.

"It was the first restaurant of any kind that opened in Bojoa. It does have a sentimental place in our hearts," he said by way of explanation to Holon.

"I see," said Holon. "The G-E-D it is, then. Just give me a moment to see what Agapoi is going to do."

"Axi. We'll wait for you over by the lift," said Yotux. With those words, she started toward her workstation, and Holon started toward Agapoi's office door. Then Yotux called back, "I'll go ahead and shut down your workstation too if it's axi."

"Thanks, Yotux. That'll be fine," was Holon's reply.

The rest of the team went to shut down their workstations as well before continuing toward the translift as Holon continued to Agapoi's office.

When Axopen reached his workstation, he noticed that he hadn't completed a thought on his relay research so he began to finish his thought.

"Come on, Axopen," called out Phunex. "We're supposed to be done for the day."

"I just need to finish a thought. We won't be working tomorrow or Diotiri, and I won't remember it by the time Treti comes; and who really knows if we will be working on Treti. We might be evacuating Bojoa for all we know," he retorted.

He had to reference the numbers of his relay reflection tests to complete his incomplete note, so he pulled up the numbers for the series of beam reflections he had tested. It was then that he noticed something in the numbers of the data that he had compiled for the transporter relay. The numbers were showing that the energy stream carrying the matter information was actually strengthened slightly with each reflection. Kowtsom's tests had shown no loss of energy intensity for the iri-silver alloy reflecting plate, but futher testing with the transport energy beam actually showed an increase in the intensity of the beam, which should be impossible. The series of reflections he did showed a five percent increase in intensity of the beam. Axopen could not believe the numbers, so he double-checked the original test logs. The numbers were accurate. He hadn't examined the numbers closely until now.

Meanwhile, Holon had returned from Agapoi's office and had just joined the rest of the team, except for him, at the translift.

"Come on, Axopen," called Phunex again. "We are ready to go. How long does it take to finish a thought?"

He looked over at the group and then back at his work-station. These numbers could mean that items could be transported through at least one of the thick, ionized ozone layers of Kosundo. If the transport beam could penetrate the ozone completely intact, then they could be relayed high enough to overcome the curvature of Kosundo via relatively few relay drones. The relay drones could be stationed out of normal air space synchronized with the rotation of Kosundo making it easier to transport items instantaneously anywhere on Kosundo. It would simplify the whole relay process. This was a major breakthrough in their research. It could streamline the whole long-range teleporting technology.

He couldn't decide if he should stay now or go. If he stayed, he could have the relay specifications worked out by the end of the day and he could claim the idea completely as his own. If he went, he would have to wait until Treti; but he could discuss it with the rest of the team. The team's input on this could prove to be important. Besides, it would certainly be an encouragement to the team.

He stopped his rush of thoughts to dwell on the last one that had just passed through his mind. It was strange to him that the thought of encouraging the team seemed like a better idea to him than being able to claim full credit for the idea. It was new to him to think of others first, but the more he thought about it, the more he found that he liked the change.

After milling those thoughts over for a few tics, he reached down and turned off his workstation. He didn't see Agapoi with the team. Apparently, Agapoi had some work he had to finish up. As he turned and walked toward the translift, he said loudly, "It's too bad that Agapoi is not coming to lunch with us. I've just noticed something that could allow us to make long-range transport a reality before any of us thought possible."

As he arrived at the translift, the members of the team stared curiously at him, expecting him to tell them what he had found. Instead, he said, "Drus. I'm hungry! Let's not just stand here. Let's go eat!"

"You're not going to tell us what you have found?" asked a dumbfounded Supeb.

"Yeah. You can't go making a statement like that and leave us hanging," said Eutay.

He eyed Eutay squarely and tried to be as serious as he could. "Why not? You do that sort of thing all the time."

"Oh, I never have anything as dramatic to talk about as that," said Eutay with a wry smile on his face.

Multiple protests from the team ensued.

He thought about telling them right then, but he thought better of it. "It will take a little time to explain. It's

already a little past lunchtime. Let's go to lunch," he said as
he reached over to press the triangular call button. He felt
seven sets of eyes trying to pierce through him as the lift door
opened. "Don't worry. I'll tell you when we get seated at the
G-E-D — discretely, of course."

The piercing eyes turned softer.

He thought he heard Eutay muffle a snicker. He found
that he was trying to suppress a snicker himself.

As he entered the translift with the rest of the team, he
thought about the range of emotions that he had just experienced today. Before the interview, he had experienced fear.
During it, he had been angry. After it, he was contrite —
especially so after he made Phunex cry. He really didn't know
Phunex could be made to cry before today. He was full of a
joy he had never experienced before, then he was
apprehensive about the team meeting. Now, he felt exultant.
*It's funny how one's outlook can change so dramatically in just a
little bit of time.*

The lift came to a stop, and the doors opened. Just to
the left was the G-E-D. The team was energized as they
entered the restaurant which made the greasy old diner
radiate energy. He was sure that the rest of the team also had
experienced an emotional rollercoaster today. He felt his news
would give them a much-needed lift. Of course, he would
have to be sure he told them quietly and away from other
people in the diner.

He was actually more excited that he could provide a
lift for the team than he was about the discovery itself. As a
matter of fact, the more he thought about how the team
would be encouraged the more exhilarated he felt. He
couldn't remember when he had felt such euphoria. His
imagination never envisioned his feeling the way he felt now.
Just yesterday, he wouldn't have been able to feel this way.
Before today, his mind could only conceive of being excited
over the accomplishment of some great technological feat. For

the first time in his life, he felt that it was more important to lift the spirits of others than to gloat over a discovery. Too much of his life had been spent thinking about himself. He realized that now. Doing something for the benefit of others was infinitely more satisfying than just thinking of himself. This new way of thinking brought new feelings to him. *Perhaps the discovery of putting others before myself is more important than any technology discovery that I could ever make.* That thought came unbidden, and quite frankly, surprised him. He had long valued his work over just about everything else. Oh, it was still important to him; sure, but for the first time, he realized that it just wasn't as important as his friends were.

Then a peaceful feeling came over him. He understood then the true source of his euphoric joy. It wasn't just a good feeling; it was much more than that. It was as if Thaoi himself were putting His stamp of approval upon him. The peace was proof.

The idea of putting others first was no longer just good moral practice to him. He thought of it as a way of life now. His life would be pleasing Thaoi — that was important to him now. And he had joy. He never knew that pleasing Thaoi could make him so full of joy. The thought of pleasing Thaoi had always seemed an onerous burden to him before. He remembered viewing it as a dreary duty. Now, he knew better. It wasn't a duty at all; it was an exciting privilege.

Kenun and Thaoi had made him see the truth about himself. Thaoi had transformed that awful truth into a feeling of freedom the likes of which he had never before experienced.

Chapter Twenty
A Change of Plans

As Odanoi stroked his beard, he noticed that it was getting a bit thicker under his chin than he liked, but he wasn't concerned about his beard at the moment. He was trying to make some sense of the message that Jahnu had received from Thaoi during the national broadcast last night. He understood that the message was linked to the previous impression of the crisis on the twelfth of Setmi, but he couldn't understand exactly how. Jahnu had struggled to put the impression that he received with the message into words last night. It was apparent that even Jahnu did not grasp exactly what the significance of the impression was. The only thing that seemed certain in Jahnu's mind was that it was imperative to heed the warning.

It was still early, and Jahnu had not emerged from his bedroom yet. He thought he had heard stirring in Jahnu's room earlier so he hoped it wouldn't be long before Jahnu came out to the main room. Some decisions had to be made today concerning how to proceed with the day of reflection that Jahnu had called for on the twelfth, and he was hopeful that Jahnu might have more insight this morning regarding his latest impression. If not, he supposed that he would have to take the message literally and exercise a little faith by evacuating Cirrian cities. Evacuations on this scale were going to be a logistical nightmare, especially with so little time to prepare and execute a plan.

As he was pondering how multiple evacuations could be accomplished, Jahnu emerged from the bedroom. He was fully dressed in his usual plain sark and tough trousers and was carrying his traveling cases. He glanced over at Odanoi as he put down his cases. "Do you want to go out for breakfast?" he asked.

"Are you going somewhere?" he asked as he eyed Jahnu's cases.

"Yes. I'm going back to Cirri City. I'm hoping that you and the High Council will join me. It's time that we shared our burden with the rest of the council, but we must do so in Cirri City."

He was perplexed by the sudden wish to leave Bojoa. They hadn't discussed going anywhere. This decision seemed to come out of nowhere. "Axi. We can certainly go, but may I ask why we are going to Cirri City?"

"That is where the council and I belong," Jahnu said matter-of-factly.

"But I thought we came to Bojoa to keep the councils safe. I was under the impression that we were going be here for quite some time," he said bewilderedly.

"I never said that," said Jahnu. "We came to Bojoa to hold the all-council meeting, nothing more. There were personal messages to deliver to the leaders of Cirri. Thaoi wanted to encourage the faithful and warn the unfaithful. Cirri's devotion, as a whole, merited this favor from Thaoi. We came here because the message was not meant for the whole of Kosundo, only the people who were present here were to hear that message. Bojoa was a private location for a private message. We have stayed here this long only because I hadn't been told to go anywhere else until now."

He just stared at Jahnu for a moment, fingering his beard. Jahnu certainly had changed since he first met him. When he first met Jahnu on that fateful night, he appeared very ordinary and acted like a completely ordinary, even timid, man. There was the fact that he was wearing his nightclothes on that night, but he had been expecting that. Now when he observed Jahnu, he no longer saw an ordinary man. He saw the prophet. His countenance and actions had changed so dramatically that if Odanoi didn't know better, he would swear that this man was not the same man that he met on that first night.

He finally realized that Jahnu must be beginning to wonder why he was just sitting there staring at him so he cleared his throat and said, "So, Thaoi has told you to go back to Cirri City; but why today? I mean; did Thaoi give you a reason that you and the council belong in Cirri City?"

Jahnu came to a nearby chair and sat down in it. Jahnu peered at him for just a moment before saying, "As a matter of fact, He did." Instead of continuing, Jahnu cast his eyes down to the floor as if meditating. This lasted for a moment or two. Then just as suddenly as he had fallen silent, Jahnu began to speak again. There was a deeply earnest quality about his voice. "A time of great trial is coming to Kosundo, even to Cirri. The twelfth of Setmi is only the beginning of this time. I must be a visible presence during this time of trial. The council should also be visible to the people. Today is the tenth. It's time to be a beacon of hope to the people, even if the personal costs are great. It's time to show the people visible leadership with all the faith that we can muster because these times will try all of us greatly."

He remained still for a time after Jahnu spoke. Finally, he said softly, "Was that you or the Voice of Thaoi speaking?"

Jahnu smiled broadly. "It was me, but the message was Thaoi's. It must be difficult for you to come to terms with the idea of Thaoi speaking directly to and through me. I know it was difficult for me to come to terms with it at first. It must be harder for you though. You don't have the experience of Thaoi's presence as I do. You have to accept what Thaoi is doing purely by faith. I admire you for that, Odanoi. Don't think that your faith has gone unnoticed."

"Those are kind and comforting words, Jahnu. I will make the preparations for the council and us to leave. But what am I to do about the proclaimed day of remembrance?"

"Nothing," Jahnu said. "That proclamation was of your own doing."

He gaped at Jahnu doubtfully.

"Don't worry, Odanoi. You didn't do anything wrong by proclaiming the day of rest. The proclamation was a good signal to send to the people. It's up to each individual to heed the warning. There is no reason to force evacuations. The people who believe will heed the message. Yet you should perform one act before leaving Bojoa. I told you directly after my announcement that I had the strong impression that the works of man in the Voice of Thaoi's message was technology. Bojoa cannot exist without technology. You should inform all the people residing in Bojoa that the twelfth will not bring any harm to Bojoa. They are in the unique position of not being able to get away from the works of man. Thaoi has a purpose for this place. He will not allow harm to come to Bojoa on the twelfth."

He smiled. He had been wondering what to tell Bojoa. It was almost as though Jahnu was reading his mind. Of course, Thaoi could read his mind, and Thaoi did speak through Jahnu. He was not sure if he was talking to Jahnu or Thaoi anymore. "Thank you for your wisdom," he said. Odanoi thought that that statement should be appropriate for either one.

Jahnu hesitated before saying, "I am not sure if you truly meant to thank me or not, but I can only say what I do because of the Voice of Thaoi. It is not my wisdom, so I cannot accept the thanks. If you mean to thank Thaoi, it would be best to do so with a quiet prayer of thanks. However, I will accept your thanks for the relaying of Thaoi's message. I just cannot accept thanks for wisdom that is not my own."

He felt his face flush. "I am sorry, Jahnu. I didn't mean to put you in such a position. It's just that many times when you speak I feel that I am indeed speaking to Thaoi. I thought it might be that I was saying thanks to Thaoi by saying thanks to you. I know now that I erred in forgetting that you are only a vessel of Thaoi, as I am. Please pardon my error. It was born out of my thoughtless ignorance."

"I can see where the mental slip can happen, especially for you, being in such close contact with me," said Jahnu. "I realize that my words and thoughts sometimes closely follow or precede the words and thoughts of Thaoi. It's enough to confuse anyone. I will try to indicate when Thaoi is talking not me, although I do not know when Thaoi might speak through me next."

"That won't be necessary. I think I can pretty much tell when Thaoi is speaking. I only need to remember that you do not become Thaoi. I think I'll go send the announcement for Bojoa now and then arrange for transport," he said. He thought that the less he said right now the better off he would be.

"No breakfast then?" asked Jahnu.

"Do we have time?"

"We have time. As long as we make arrangements to leave for Cirri City sometime today, I will be in obedience to Thaoi," assured Jahnu.

He got up from his chair. "Axi. Let me go spruce up a bit, and we will get some breakfast."

"That sounds good. I'm sort of hungry."

Odanoi nodded and went to his bedroom to clean up and change. As he was readying himself, he thought how much he had assumed wrongly already this morning. He now realized that he would have to quit thinking ahead of what he knew. It would take an adjustment. He had always been one to anticipate his next action. It was not going to be easy to rely solely on faith. He was just realizing how little he had exercised faith in his daily living up to this point. Times were changing for the worse. He would have to rely on the wisdom of Thaoi during the upcoming time. Kosundo's time of great trial was at hand.

CHAPTER TWENTY-ONE
THE CORONATION

Abin stood outside the Edvukaat chamber with Temeos and Varnupud on either side. He was dressed in a blue robe trimmed with the blue-striped yellow fur of the Doetoran tigru around the neck. The robe had gold trim about the hem and bore the imperial seal. The background of the seal was the same dark blue as the robe. In the center of the seal was a golden hawk perched on a fully colored oak branch. The hawk was surrounded by other symbols of the empire: golden torches with yellow and red eternal flames, crossed silver swords, and a golden sunburst encircled with seven white stars. The seal itself was encircled with golden palm branches. The hawk on the seal stood for the vigilance and awareness that an emperor should have. The oak branch symbolized the continuing strength of the empire. The torches symbolized the longevity of the current imperial dynasty. The swords symbolized the authoritative power of the emperor. The sunburst symbolized the glory of the emperor, and the seven stars were the seven districts that made up the empire. The current line of emperors had ruled for over twelve hundred years now, which was quite an accomplishment, seeing that Doetora had only been an empire for a little over sixteen hundred years. The palms that surrounded the seal represented the life-sustaining power that the emperor was supposed to wield for the people of the empire. The palms had been an empty symbol for too long. It was an emptiness that he hoped his reign would soon fill.

He was waiting for the coronation ceremony to begin. After this short ceremony, he would no longer be known as Abin; he would be known as Abinos, the twelfth Emperor of Doetora. The people around him had already been calling him Abinos, but this ceremony would make it official.

The ceremony was full of pomp. There would be an orchestra playing the imperial theme, gold and silver ceremonial decorations, and everyone would be wearing formal clothing. The suvatens were in their ceremonial robes which were red trimmed in black with a golden symbol of the flying hawk embossed on the back of the robe. The invited guests wore their formal suits and formal dresses. Even Temeos was dressed in his ceremonial uniform, which was black and trimmed in gold, complete with his formal ehri cap which was also black and trimmed in gold. The tall ehri cap made Temeos appear even taller than his height of twelve dets.

He heard the orchestra playing the imperial theme. He glanced to his right at Temeos, who gave him an encouraging smile and nodded toward him. The Edvukaat guard opened the tall doors to the chamber, and two imperial guards dressed in ceremonial blue and holding blue and gold imperial banners led him into the chamber. Closely following him was Temeos and Varnupud. They were followed by a squad of fully armed imperial guards.

The procession headed down the main chamber aisle. Tall, slender poles decorated in fine gems, silver and gold, lined the aisle. The speaker's podium was elevated nearly to the vaulted ceiling of the chamber. The podium wouldn't be used today so it was raised to make way for the procession and to make the sight lines better in the chamber. The stairs that usually led to the podium were also removed for the ceremony. The result was a large clearing in the middle of the chamber. Both Edvukaat and imperial guards surrounded the clearing on two sides to be sure that no one approached the procession. In the clearing, Cemyoz in his red robe joined the procession and replaced Varnupud, who fell out of the procession at the same time. Beyond the clearing, the main aisle continued toward the stairs that he had ascended yesterday.

Once the procession reached the stairs, the two ceremonial imperial guards stood on either side of the stairs and crossed their banners, making an archway for him to pass under before ascending the stairs. He started up the stairs slowly. He tried to keep his back straight so that he looked regal. It was difficult to ascend the rather steep stairs in a robe. Thankfully, each step was only about three-fourths of a det high; otherwise, he was sure he would have had a misstep. He also saw why the robe only came down to the top of his ankle in front, though it touched the ground in back. He counted the steps to keep concentration. He discovered that there were forty-eight steps as he reached the landing. On the landing stood a leading Levra scholar from the Manku City Proclamation Center. He was to give the oath of office. An imperial guard was on the scholar's left, and an Edvukaat guard was on the scholar's right. Behind the scholar was a slender pedestal placed on the first large step going toward the throne. On the pedestal was the imperial crown. It was blue like his robe and had the same yellow tigru fur as trim. The crown rose to a peak in the front with a large golden sunburst at the top of the peak.

As he arrived in front of the Levra scholar, he felt a person passing behind him. He knew it was Temeos. He was going to stand in front of the seat of honor. He also knew that Cemyoz should now be standing in front of the other seat on the landing, the suvaten seat. He didn't look at either one of them, but they were supposed to be there, so he assumed that they were there. He kept his focus on the Levra scholar in front of him, who was holding a Levra in his right hand.

The orchestra ended the imperial theme with a flourish. This was the sign for everyone—except the guards, the Levra scholar, and him—to sit down. The rustling of a couple thousand people sitting down in unison filled his ears and then silence.

The Levra scholar then said, "It is my honor to offer the oath of empire to Abin Stigen, raised by Eruv and Sellia Stigen, the son of Navin, who was the sister of the former Emperor Tryllos. Abin, do you choose to accept this oath of empire and rule Doetora as its Emperor?"

He said in his loudest voice, "I do."

The scholar then said, "Please place your right hand on the Levra."

He did so.

"Will you solemnly promise to govern the peoples of the Empire of Doetora according to the empire's laws and customs?" asked the scholar.

He said clearly, "I solemnly promise so to do."

"Will you use the power of the empire to cause law and justice, in mercy, to be executed in all your judgments?" asked the scholar.

He answered, "To the best of my ability, I will do so."

Then the scholar asked, "Will you, to the utmost of your power, maintain the laws of Thaoi and the true spirit of the Way of Conscience? Will you, to the utmost of your power, maintain in the empire the free assembling of Levra proclamations? Will you, to the utmost of your power, maintain and preserve inviolably the settlement of the faith of Thaoi and the doctrine, worship, and discipline thereof? And will you, to the utmost of your powers, preserve unto the scholars and to the assemblies committed to their charge all such rights and privileges, as by law, do or shall appertain to them?"

He answered plainly, "All this, to the utmost of my power, I promise to do."

The scholar then stepped toward him and extended the Levra toward him while bowing.

He took the Levra from the scholar, turned to face the chamber, and knelt with the open Levra in front of him while saying, "The things which I have here before promised I will perform and keep. So I promise you and Thaoi." He then kissed the Levra and stood motionless, facing the chamber. The scholar and the guards went two steps back and knelt down, facing Abin's back. Simultaneously, Temeos and Cemyoz arose and went to the pedestal that held the imperial crown. Together, they lifted the crown from the pedestal, came, and stood behind him.

Temeos began the crowning discourse. "As Lord Director—"

Cemyoz continued the discourse with his part. "And as appointed suvaten—"

Both of them then finished the discourse together. "We now crown thee Emperor Abinos, ruler of the Empire of Doetora."

Abin tucked the Levra under his arm and knelt down, and together, Temeos and Cemyoz placed the imperial crown on his head. At that moment, Abin ceased to be and Abinos was. When he rose to his feet, he did so as Emperor Abinos. Temeos and Cemyoz knelt on either side behind him.

Applause and cheers erupted in the chamber. It was a noise of celebration that had not been heard in the chamber since the coronation of the beloved Emperor Yumal at the very beginning of the empire. It was to this sweet noise of jubilation that Abinos ascended to the throne and sat, facing his subjects. The applause and cheers lasted for over ten spens and probably would have lasted longer, except Abinos stood and beckoned for silence.

Once the noise of jubilation subsided, Abinos said, "I am overwhelmed today by your enthusiasm and the faith that you have expressed in me. I only hope that I am able to earn the adulation that you have bestowed on me today. I must remind you, however, that I am only a man. As a man, I have my shortcomings and faults, but there is one thing that I promise to you today. I will never put my interests over the interests of the empire or the good of its people. May Thaoi bless your lives with His joy." After he finished and sat again on the throne, the cheering resumed even louder than before.

Once the cheering finally died to scattered cheers, Abinos rose, handed the Levra to the scholar, and started to descend the steps to the landing. Mass cheering once again arose from the chamber as he reached the edge of the landing. He paused just for a moment to make a slight bow of appreciation. He then proceeded down the forty-eight steps to the chamber floor as applause joined the cheering. As his foot hit the last step, the ceremonial guards resumed their lead of the procession. If everything went according to plan, Temeos and Cemyoz were right behind him, followed by the Levra scholar and the landing guards. Cemyoz would drop out at the clearing in the middle of the chamber, and Varnupud would rejoin the procession there, along with the armed squad of guards.

The cheers intensified as he passed through the chamber, acknowledging the cheers as he went. Only after the entire procession had left the chamber did the cheering subside. He appreciated the cheers, but he knew that the cheers would only matter if he ruled wisely; otherwise, all the cheers may have just as well as been jeers for all the good they would do.

The suvatens had wanted to arrange a festive ball in honor of his coronation, but he had politely declined their offer. There was too much to do, and enough time had already been spent in celebration yesterday.

He turned and found that Temeos was indeed behind him, along with Varnupud. "Temeos, would you and Varnupud accompany me to the palace office?" he asked.

"Certainly, Your Imperial Highness," replied Temeos.

He found it strange to be addressed in that manner. This whole thing of being an emperor was strange. He didn't really feel any different, but after that ceremony, he had just become the most powerful man in Doetora. It was really a rather staggering realization. Nevertheless, he just nodded and turned down the hall that led toward the palace. The ceremonial guard had been replaced by a dozen of the emperor's personal guard, which Temeos had handpicked himself. The personal guard surrounded them as they walked. He thought that if he sneezed, he would have twelve hands handing him a handkerchief.

As they reached the end of the hall and approached the door, the captain of the guard stepped directly in front of him and stopped. Abinos practically ran into him.

"Sorry, Your Highness, but we must check to make sure it is safe before I allow you to proceed," said the captain.

Six of the guards went out of the doors as he spoke.

"Of course—forgive me. I am not accustomed to the security," he said.

The captain glanced at him curiously before turning and scanning outside the doors, no doubt searching for the signal that it was all right to bring him outside. He guessed that the captain's curiosity was because he had said, "Forgive me." No doubt, Tryllos had not said those two words very often, especially not to the guards.

They waited behind the guard for what felt like a full spen before the guard finally went to the door and opened it for him and his party. As soon as he stepped outside, there were six bodies around him. The rest of the guard surrounded them as well as they continued. The party walked the rest of the short distance to the palace in this manner. He guessed that he would just have to get used to the security. He had a feeling it was bound to feel intrusive at first.

Apart from the guards, there were mobs of cheering people, held back by both Edvukaat and imperial guards, lining the way. Abinos nodded and waved to as many people as he could see from behind his protective guard. In just a few spens, they entered the palace grounds through a great gilded gate that bore the imperial seal. The crowds could not follow inside the grounds, but the guards still kept their protective formation around him.

As they approached the palace, he was struck by how magnificent the building really was. He had been to the palace with Temeos before, but not enough to feel comfortable going inside yet. The palace staff had come to pick up his belongings at his house, but this would be the first time he had stepped inside the palace since his return. It felt very different knowing that he had not come just for a visit this time. The palace was now his home.

Once inside the palace, they stopped; and the captain of the personal guard asked if he would like to be escorted to his office.

He answered, "If I were here by myself, I might accept your offer, but I believe that the lord director knows his way to the office, so I should be able to find it."

The captain gave a hint of a smirk and then recovered and saluted. He then led his men to a door that led toward what he guessed was their barracks or maybe a resting room.

Temeos and Varnupud came and stood on either side of him after the personal guard left. It was Temeos who spoke first.

"I would never think to correct you in front of the guard, Your Imperial Highness, but I am no longer lord director," he said.

The statement surprised him. "You are not? Then why are you still wearing the uniform?"

"I was lord director right up until I helped coronate you. Since you are now emperor, it is your right to choose your lord director. I must put off this uniform as soon as I return home," said Temeos.

He looked at Temeos incredulously. "I don't remember that you ever told me that I had to reappoint you. I thought it was just a formality that I had to approve you. I didn't think the office would be vacant."

Temeos looked down at the floor. "No. I didn't tell you the office would be vacant," he said in a low voice.

"Well, you must have had a good reason," he said, willing to change the subject. "Which way to my office?"

Temeos smiled, pointed ahead of them and said, "The door directly ahead leads to the main hall. At the end of the main hall is your office."

The three of them stood in the palace's large foyer for a moment, no one moving.

"As emperor, it is your privilege to lead," said Temeos finally.

"Oh. You are waiting for me. I must get used to that. I'm still used to following you," he said sheepishly.

With that statement, he strode toward the door. As he approached the door, the palace guards stationed at the door opened it for him and his party. As he walked down the main hall with his party, he noticed that each door had one guard, except for two of them. The door directly ahead at the end of the hall had two guards, as did the last door on the hall's right.

Abinos increased his pace as he walked toward the doors at the end of the hall. The guards on the doors opened both just in time for Abinos to walk through. He couldn't help but softly say, "Nice job," to the guards, although he didn't know if they heard him or not. Once his party cleared the doorway and the doors had closed behind them, he came to an abrupt stop. There were three more doors inside the double doors. At least there were no guards in this hall to see his indecision. He looked at the doors and said, "Let me guess. The door in front of me is my office. The door to the right is the reception area, and the door on the left is a meeting room."

"Nice guess, Your Imperial Highness," said Temeos flatly.

He smiled. "You caught me. It wasn't a guess," he admitted "I remember your talking about the imperial office from time to time when you came back from seeing Tryllos. You would say, 'It is better to stay in the right room than go to the room dead ahead, and pray you never get called to the room on the left for a meeting filled with worry and dread.' You said that little ditty several times over the years."

Temeos smiled broadly as Varnupud tried vainly to hide a snicker. "I have always been a creature of habit, Your Imperial Highness," said Temeos, obviously somewhat embarrassed by the mention of the little rhyme in front of Varnupud.

He wasn't sorry. Temeos had embarrassed him enough times when he was his aide, but he thought at least he could change the subject for Temeos's sake. "And why do you keep calling me that? Call me Abinos."

"I call you what every common man calls his emperor; but if you wish, I will call you Abinos," said Temeos.

"Axi. If you wish to continue this farce, I might as well call you by your common name. What is it?"

"It is Temeon, *Abinos*," said Temeos.

Very well. You shall be Temeon from now until I name you my lord director, which will be soon. Believe me," he said, feigning disgust.

All three men shared grins among themselves as he led them into his office. Once inside, he stopped short again. The office was huge. "I could fit ten of my old offices in this office!" he exclaimed. "I can't believe the size of this room. It even has a refreshment area, and look at the desk! It's bigger than my old office by itself. How many terms does it have? I can see six from here."

"I believe it has eight. Ten if you count the two commterms," said Temeos. "But I don't believe you brought us here to discover your office with you. What is it that you wanted to discuss, *Abinos?*"

"Oh yes. I have forgotten myself again. Sor—."

He cut himself off. He was about to tell Temeos he was sorry, but as Temeos had told him, an emperor could be wrong but he could never afford to be sorry so he continued by asking, "Would you and Varnupud be seated?"

He gestured toward the table in the center of the room that was big enough for eight chairs to be arranged around it, yet had only seven chairs. There was a chair only at one end of the table, the end closest to the desk. The other end didn't have a chair. He guessed this was Tryllos's way of making sure that he was the only one seated at the head of the table. Temeos and Varnupud each went to a chair on either side of the end chair but didn't sit down. He slowly realized they were waiting for him to sit down, so he quickly sat in the end chair once his realization was complete. After he sat down, they both sat down in their chairs. He wasn't sure how long it would take him to get used to having no one do anything before he did it. As an aide, he was used to being the last one to do things, like sitting or entering a room. Putting himself in the lead for such things would take some getting used to.

Once they were all seated, he asked, "Did you see last night's Cirrian broadcast?"

Both men nodded, and Temeos audibly answered, "Yes."

He turned to Temeos and asked, "What did you make of it, *Temeon?*" He was repaying Temeos for the way he had been saying his name.

Temeos grunted with a slight grin at the use of his common name, but his face became serious as he answered. "It was surprising, to say the least. I have great respect and admiration for Odanoi, but I don't know what to think about Jahnu. He seems an ordinary man to look at him. Yet, there is something different about him that I can't quite grasp. He speaks with so much self-assurance that you seem to be forced to listen to him." Temeos's voice trailed off as if his mind was suddenly far away.

"And you, Varnupud?"

"I didn't know what to make of any of it," said Varnupud softly. He then continued in a stronger yet still soft voice. "Although I've strived to walk in the old way, I'm afraid I am not as familiar with the Levra as I should be; so I didn't even know that there was a prophecy of the soulless. But if you are asking me if I believe Jahnu, I'm not sure. But it almost seems as if I have to believe him."

He nodded. "I understand what both of you are saying. There is a quality about Jahnu that exceeds my ability to understand completely. What of the message, especially the part of the message that alludes to staying away from technology?"

"It worries me," said Temeos.

Varnupud nodded his agreement.

"Do you have any suggestions for a course of action?" he asked, fixing his gaze directly at Temeos.

"Part of me screams to tell you to make an announcement warning Kosundo about the Avengers. Part of me, the cautious side, tells me that we shouldn't put ourselves in a position to be blamed for a crisis that we don't even know will involve the Avengers," said Temeos.

"Has there been any progress in locating Tryllos?"

Temeos shook his head. "It is as if he has vanished from the face of Kosundo. He can be traced to a hotel room in Aturla, but there is no sign of him at the hotel. No one can recall seeing him leave the hotel either. Wherever he went, he didn't take public transportation to get there. I believe he must have arranged to have help disappearing. I wouldn't have believed that Tryllos was capable of planning for his escape. I thought that his arrogance would prevent him from ever imagining that he would need such an escape plan. Neither we nor the Drichoan authorities have had any success in locating him."

"Do you believe he is capable of launching the Avengers on the twelfth of Setmi?" he asked, staring intently at Temeos.

Temeos peered down at the table as if he was trying to stare a hole into it. After a moment, he raised his head bearing a grim expression on his face and said, "I believe he has the desire to do just that. I also believe that he might very well have the ability to launch as well."

"Temeos," he said, dropping the game of names that he had been playing, "I am going to the Edvukaat to announce you as my lord director right after our meeting is over. After I do so, get in touch with the Cirrians. I want to talk to Odanoi as soon as possible. Also, make preparations for a national broadcast tomorrow evening. I want the broadcast to be open to the rest of Kosundo. Do whatever it takes to make it so."

He stood up, and Temeos and Varnupud stood as well.

"Gentlemen, we haven't much time. We have got to do what is right and forget about the consequences."

"It will be as you command, Abinos," said Temeos as he bowed deeply.

Varnupud bowed as well, imitating Temeos.

He fixed his eyes on Varnupud. "Varnupud, I am going to request that a new position be given you. You will be the new Chief Inspector General of Doetora. You will answer only to the lord director and me. However, you will make all of your reports available to the Edvukaat. Your operations are to be open and honest." He paused to make sure that Varnupud understood.

When Varnupud nodded, he continued.

"I want you to put all the effort you can muster into finding Tryllos. If he is not found, there might be little hope for preventing destruction on a massive scale."

Varnupud bowed deeply as he said, "He will be found soon."

"Temeos, you may leave. I will have your appointment secured within the parz. Plan how to accomplish your orders in the meantime," he said with an authority that he did not know he had within him.

"If you'll forgive me, Abinos, there is one more matter that needs your immediate attention," said Temeos while holding a bow.

"What is it?"

Temeos straightened and said, "I highly recommend that you dismiss all members of the imperial guard immediately. The personal and palace guards that I've hand-picked can fill in for the moment. Many of the imperial guard have been close to Tryllos for many years. I have made a list of men who would be good candidates to become the officers of your new imperial guard. I trust these men. They can be trusted to fill out the remainder of the imperial guard." Temeos pulled out a folded paper from his coat pocket and handed it to him.

He took the paper and put it down on the table as he said, "Very well. I can see where that would be prudent."

"Thank you, Your Imperial Highness," said Temeos with a bow.

"You may now take your leave to accomplish your orders," he said rather firmly. The firmness that was in his voice surprised even him, but he concentrated on keeping a stern exterior to hide the surprise.

Temeos bowed again with a smile on his face and then immediately left the room.

He turned to Varnupud and put his hand on his shoulder. He then said to him softly, "Varnupud, I appreciate your enthusiasm, but I think it would be wise if you don't promise me anything that you cannot know that you can deliver. I have confidence that you will make every effort to find Tryllos, but there is always a possibility that you will not find him, especially not soon. I would prefer if you told me that you are going to do your best to find him instead of telling me that you will find him as if it is a normal or easy task. This task will be difficult, but I need you to try."

Varnupud nodded, indicating that he understood.

"I will have your appointment secured within the parz as well. Do what you can with your present authority until then."

Varnupud bowed even lower this time and said, "I will do my best not to disappoint you, Your Highness." He then turned and left the room with a determined gait.

After Varnupud had left, he shook his head as he realized that Temeos had called him "Your Imperial Highness" again. He would have to talk to him at length about that privately — but at a later time. Now it was time to go to the Edvukaat before they quit celebrating and dispersed for the day. He imagined that the celebration would still be going strong. He would find Cemyoz and make him bring the Edvukaat into session. Well, *make* was too strong a word. He would *persuade* Cemyoz to bring the Edvukaat into session. He planned to be very persuasive.

Chapter Twenty-two

Realization

Laysa awoke. She felt a bit tired, or maybe weak was a better word. She checked the clock in the room and saw that it was fairly early in the morning but a little past her usual wake up time of three parzes. It was strange that the alarm on the clock hadn't sounded. She thought for sure that she had set it last night. It was also strange that the lights in her quarters were on. She thought she remembered turning them off.

She remembered having a very vivid dream last night. It was a terrifying nightmare actually, and she still remembered it clearly. She had been reading at her desk when Degmer had come into her quarters. Degmer had started accusing her of conspiring with Neaotomo, and she was using profanity. Degmer never used profanity. Only the vilest of the uneducated used profanity. Then Degmer attacked her with a scalpel and there was blood all over the place. It was surely a dream, yet it seemed so real. She remembered pain, intense pain, during the dream. It was surely a dream, because she remembered thinking that this was what it was like to die, yet here she was living and breathing. It had to be a dream, yet it was all so vivid. Still, she didn't feel any pain now though she remembered feeling excruciating pain. It had to have been a dream. If it weren't a dream, she would certainly have scars.

She lifted the covers of the bed and immediately became confused. She didn't see any scars on her body, but she didn't see any clothes on her body either. Since she didn't have any nightclothes available in the sealed labs, she had worn underclothes to bed. She always wore something to bed.

She peered over at the hook on the wall. There was nothing there. She had put her outer clothes on that hook both nights that she had these quarters. She had to jump to put her clothes there, so it was easy to remember doing it.

She sat up on the side of the bed, took a sheet from the bed, and wrapped it around her. She then got up and searched the dresser that was on the wall opposite the hook. Her clothes were not in there either. There was a closet by the bathroom door. She went to the closet, but it was completely empty. Her clothes were nowhere to be found in her quarters.

In her dream, there was blood all over. She surveyed the wall beside the desk and below the hook since she was attacked there in her dream. She didn't find any blood there or anywhere in the room. The contradictions between her memory and what her eyes told her could only mean that Neaotomo was up to something. She suspected that he had planted thoughts in her head and then had taken her clothes while she was sleeping to make her wonder whether Degmer had attacked her or not. It made sense that Neaotomo would try to create doubt in her mind about Degmer. But it was also unusual for him not to come to her quarters by this time in the morning, although she knew that he was planning something for today. She had helped him set up a room to look like a psychiatrist's office yesterday — or was that a planted memory as well?

She sat down at her desk while still scanning the room. When her eyes finally fell on the desk, she noticed a genetics journal. She recognized it as a journal that Neaotomo had given her. But according to her memory, he had given her that on the same day that she remembered Degmer attacking her. If the gift of the journal really happened, then did the attack also actually happen?

In her dream or in her memory—she was undecided which it was—Neaotomo had given her a journal to read. She opened the journal. It was *this* journal; she was sure of it. She leafed through the pages and saw something that made her stop leafing immediately. She stared incredulously at the open pages. The pages had blood stains spattered on them.

Her mind raced wildly, trying to reconcile what she saw. She ran to the bathroom mirror, letting the sheet fall to the floor as she ran. She examined her face, and then she searched all over the front of her body. She found no wounds or scars, not even a scratch. Her mind was still trying to come to terms with what she knew as she wandered back into the main room of her quarters, picking the sheet back up on her way. Wrapping the sheet around her again, she sat on the side of her bed wondering what the truth actually was. Either Neaotomo had made her dream about the attack or the attack had actually happened. *Which is more logical? That Neatomo put the attack in my mind, and then planted the journal – complete with blood splatters on my desk, or that Degmer did come in and attack me? Yet, somehow I have no wounds.* As she mulled over her thoughts, she decided that neither scenario made much sense to her.

Neaotomo had boasted about his longevity to her, but he didn't say what else he was capable of doing. She knew from experience that he had great mental abilities. She had also noticed that when he picked her up, he did it without any effort at all—not that she was that heavy, but she was tall for a woman. He had also managed to survive poisonous gas and then survive in a sealed lab with no airflow for seventy years. He also said that he could heal rapidly. *What else might he be capable of doing?* She didn't have an answer for that.

She was about to conclude that Neaotomo was just playing with her mind when she remembered his promise. He had promised her that he would not probe her mind again as long as she was obedient. Placing thoughts in her mind would definitely require him to be in her mind. She didn't believe he would break his word; he seemed to value it greatly. Then she noticed the small numbers on the clock. The time of the all the clocks in the complex were set via a wireless connection to central servers. Each clock displayed a small numeric date at the top right hand corner. The date readout was 07–10–2040. The day that she had thought must have been yesterday was the eighth of Setmi, but today wasn't the ninth; it was the tenth. Somehow, she had lost a day. It was not Titarti, as she had thought it was. It was Paraskevi. If Neaotomo didn't mess with her mind and she had lost a day, then the attack must have been real. The events she had dismissed as a dream or an altered memory were real. That meant the attack was real. If the attack was real, she must have been healed somehow. If the attack had happened, then Neaotomo had succeeded in turning Degmer. Yet, if that was the case, what reason would he have to keep her alive? It didn't make any sense. He would have to have concocted a rational reason of some sort to heal her. Degmer certainly didn't seem to have any compassion left in her from what she remembered of the attack so it wouldn't have been her idea.

Finally, an understanding of the recent events hit her. She started to weep, but not for herself. She was weeping for Degmer. She had known her for over twenty years and had called Degmer her friend, but she had let Degmer down in the most important matter of all: the safeguarding of her soul. She again prayed that Thaoi would help Degmer. As long as Degmer was still alive, there was hope for her soul. At least that is what she told herself as she prayed. She prayed that Thaoi would keep Degmer alive so that one day she might recover her soul. She prayed that Thaoi might still use her to help Degmer. In addition, since Degmer was now controlled by Neaotomo, she prayed that she might somehow be a good influence on Neaotomo and that Thaoi, in His mercy, might grant him a soul of his own.

CHAPTER TWENTY-THREE

PLANES AND BARRIERS

Beltram entered the sealed labs burdened with four large traveling cases. He handled them easily, as if the cases were empty, but the cases weren't empty; they contained most of Laysa's wardrobe. Beltram had gone to Laysa's quarters in the main complex last night and packed most of the contents of her closet and dresser into the four cases. He no longer thought it remarkable that he could handle such weight so easily. He had discovered the ability to lift and move heavy objects with ease after his first encounter with Doctor Upfar. At first, the discovery amazed him; but now it just seemed natural.

He had grown accustomed to many things that he would have thought very strange before his visit to Doctor Upfar. He was now accustomed to the doctor communicating to him in his mind. He was now accustomed to spawning thoughts that were unfamiliar to him yet seemed quite natural to him. He was now accustomed to obeying whatever the doctor wished. That is why he had packed up Laysa's wardrobe and brought it into the sealed labs. The doctor wanted him to do it so he did it; it really was as simple as that.

He had made his way into the main inner lab. Doctor Upfar was not there so he put the cases down by a table, sat down in one of the chairs by the table and waited. Doctor Upfar had taught him how to project his thoughts to others, but he had told him to use this ability very sparingly. He thought that the doctor might have meant to be careful using it outside the lab, but he wasn't going to take the chance that the doctor didn't want to be bothered at the moment. He wasn't waiting long when he saw the doctor come into an adjoining lab and then into the main lab, where he was.

The doctor, dressed in a white lab coat, came toward him and said, "I see that you have brought Laysa's clothes. She will be happy to have them; I am sure."

"It is my pleasure to be of service," he said. Those words caught him a little off guard. It wasn't like the old Beltram to express deference to anyone, and the old Beltram certainly never sounded like a Doetoran servant. Yet, somehow, he felt it quite natural to give deference to the doctor.

The doctor sat down at the table with him and asked, "Is everything ready for today's session?"

"I have set up the C-1 conference room for the session. It's the largest meeting room we have in the complex. The session is scheduled for 6:50. I chose that time because it is a half parz before the end of the workweek. I thought it would attract more people if it meant getting out of work a little early," he said.

"That sounds excellent, Beltram. And how many people are going to be there?" asked the doctor.

"I had received feelers about the meeting as early as last night," he began. "The meeting is open to anyone so it is hard to say for sure. Yesterday's patients have been promoting the meeting and offering to come with people just as you suggested. If I had to guess, I'd be pretty comfortable in guessing that over a hundred new people will attend."

The doctor smiled and said, "Good. How many people currently reside in the genetics complex?"

"Three hundred forty-two."

"Hmm. That means almost half of the people in the complex will have been exposed to my — expertise," said the doctor softly.

"Yes. I'd say that very nearly half will have had that opportunity after today," he replied cheerfully.

"That should do quite nicely indeed. Go and make the final preparations for the meeting. I will arrive about ten spens early," commanded the doctor.

"Yes, Doctor Upfar. Everything will be ready when you arrive," he answered eagerly.

"Oh, and Beltram, I will teach you and the others there how to extend my will to others in this meeting. It will be a wonderful experience for you." The doctor got up, and he rose with him. "I do not want to take up any more of your time. You probably have a lot to do between now and the meeting," said the doctor.

"Yes. I should go," he said. He really didn't have that much to do today, but he sensed that the doctor wanted him to leave so he immediately went toward the airlock. It was a strange compulsion that made him want to please the doctor even in the slightest things, yet it seemed as if that were as things should be.

As he entered the airlock, a great euphoria filled him as his thoughts centered on the session. The doctor promised to show him how to extend the doctor's will to others. He would be very happy when he knew how because then he would be complete. Though he hadn't the slightest notion what it meant to be complete, it sounded much better than being incomplete; and his heart yearned for it.

The day went by slowly because of his anticipation, but eventually it was time to go to the conference room. True to his word, Doctor Upfar, along with Degmer, arrived in the C-

1 conference room at 6:40. He had finished the room's setup long ago, and people were just starting to arrive in the conference room when the doctor arrived.

According to the doctor's instructions, he had set up the room with rows of long tables fit end to end. The doctor wanted a person to be able to walk between the rows, so Beltram had left ample space between the rows. He had managed to fit five rows of tables in the conference room, with each row able to seat thirty-two people. He had some of the doctor's previous patients acting as ushers. They were escorting people to seats as they arrived, filling the front most row first.

The doctor sought him out immediately upon his arrival. "Tell all our current patients in the room to be expecting some instructions in the form of sent thought soon. I trust you know all their names so that you can project into their minds smoothly," said the doctor in a quiet voice.

"Yes, I do know their names, Doctor," he said as quietly as the doctor had spoken to him.

"All right. Go ahead and tell each of them individually," said the doctor. "We will be projecting a thought to all of them in just a few moments. I wish them to be expecting it so that we do not catch them unaware and startle them. That could be bad for our guests."

"Very well. I will tell them now."

Immediately, he concentrated on contacting each of the current patients as he saw or thought of them. He projected to a name in thought, and immediately, a thought from the named mind answered. He gave the named mind the doctor's message and then went to the next name. Everyone's face bore some form of confusion or surprise on it when they were first contacted, but their faces returned to normal after just a moment. Like him, they quickly came to accept the communication in thought as if it were a natural, everyday occurrence. He managed to contact all of the patients giving them the doctor's message within just a couple of spens. Besides him, there were thirty-two patients in attendance. All of the doctor's clients were in attendance. They must have felt that attending the meeting would please the doctor. Each one of them probably wanted to please the doctor just as he did.

By the time he had finished with his contacts, it was close to time to begin, and the doors to the room were being closed. He thought about contacting the doctor in thought, but he decided not to when he found that the doctor was talking with Degmer at the front of the conference room. Degmer was wearing that tight-fitting nurse's outfit that she had worn yesterday. He wondered where she might have obtained it. It certainly had its allure. Putting that thought aside, he went to the front of the room so that he could tell the doctor that all of the patients had been given the message when he got through talking with Degmer. When he got there, he found that the doctor was not talking to Degmer at all. The two were standing motionless, staring into each other's eyes. He was not sure what was happening exactly, but he assumed that the doctor was in Degmer's mind. Just as he was about to turn away, a thought came into his mind that was not his own thought. It seemed to be a thought belonging to both the doctor and Degmer. *Join us, Beltram.*

He turned around to see both the doctor and Degmer gazing at him. He projected a thought addressed to the Doctor. *Was that thought from both of you?*

Both the doctor and Degmer visibly nodded. *We have joined minds. Our minds are one. Join us. Look into Degmer's eyes.*

He now understood why the doctor used the word *we* when he told him of the thought that was going to be projected. Excitement filled him at the thought of being part of such an amazing thing. The joining of minds was just another one of those things that he had assumed to be impossible that was now a reality. Was there to be no end to new and astonishing things that he would experience?

With great anticipation, he drew closer to Degmer until he could clearly see her eyes, and then he fixed his gaze into them. At first, her eyes seemed empty, but then he saw what could best be described as a level surface of thought. He visibly saw thoughts being formed in this plane and other thoughts pop out of existence. This view lasted for only a moment, and then he was looking at Degmer's eyes again. His body moved to the side of Degmer, although he did not command it to do so. It was as if he were being controlled by remote control. It was exhilarating.

He watched as the other people who had been given the doctor's will and pattern came up to the front of the room. He projected a thought to the one named Stetle. Although he did not originate the thought, it seemed to be his mind that projected it. *Look into Beltram's eyes,* stated the thought. Stetle came and stared into his eyes. For a moment, he saw the thought plane again with thoughts popping in and out of existence, and then he saw Stetle's eyes. Stetle moved into line. The next thought was sent to another person, who began to gaze into Stetle's eyes. This same thing happened repeatedly until all of the doctor's patients had linked their minds together. He now understood why the doctor had had him warn the others about the thought they were to receive. The linked thought that was sent out could have caused confusion if the others hadn't been expecting it.

He found that while linked, he could think his own thoughts but he was also aware of the thoughts of those around him. If he concentrated on one of the other's thoughts, he could listen in on it. It was all quite fascinating. Yet, the thoughts that overrode all other thoughts came from the doctor. His mind was definitely the dominant mind in the link. He didn't have to concentrate to understand the doctor's thoughts.

After the mind links were complete, his body moved to the first table in the first row and came to stand facing the table. His body was positioned between the second and third person in the row. Degmer was positioned next, between the sixth and seventh person in the row. Each of the others was positioned so that they would be reasonably close to three or four of the new people that were attending the session.

When he heard the doctor begin to speak in the front of the room, he thought about turning to see him, but his body would not respond; so he remained as he was as Doctor Upfar began to welcome the new people.

"Hello. I am Doctor Upfar. You are here by invitation because you have expressed a desire to better yourself. You have realized that your life is not headed in the direction that you desire it to go. You have decided that you need to find a new direction, a new purpose for your life. I am here to offer you that new purpose.

"My mental technique will relieve any guilt that you might feel about your past actions. It will also dispel any need of guilt for your future actions. This is because my technique will make each of you something more than you are now. Not only will it help you with your state of mind, but it will also make you better physically. All you must do is to place your trust in me by surrendering yourself to me. If you do not feel you can do that, you are free to leave now."

The doctor waited for a moment; but no one left, so he continued. "My assistants are standing in front of your tables. Each assistant will be assisting three or four of you to communicate with me. Assistants, please point to the people you will be assisting."

Without his command — as if by instinct — his finger pointed out the first four people in the first row. The other assistants also pointed to the people to whom they were assigned.

The doctor continued. "Look at the assistant who pointed to you. The assistants will kneel down to be at eye level with you."

Without his command, his body crouched down, closely achieving eye level with each of the four people seated in front of him.

The doctor went on. "In a moment, I will ask you to look into the eyes of my assistant closest to you; but do not do it yet. Once you look into the eyes of my assistant, you will cease to hear my voice. Instead, you will feel our thoughts. These thoughts will encourage you to seek out the things in your mind that are preventing you from fulfilling a worthwhile purpose in life and to give those things up to us. I will warn you that the procedure is intense, but it *will* change your life. Again, if there is anyone who would rather not go through with the procedure, you may leave now."

Again, no one moved. The doctor then said, "Look deeply into the eyes of my assistant."

When the four people peered into Beltram's eyes, he immediately saw a plane of thoughts and something more. It could only be described as a barrier. He could see that there were weak spots and tears in the barrier and that certain thoughts were linked to the weak spots and tears. These emanated from the plane, but a trail of thought led back to these points on the barrier. Then the weak spots and tears changed. The thoughts that linked to these points were different. In just a moment, he saw the plane and barrier change again. Again, it was a different barrier with different weak spots and tears along with different thoughts. Then another change took place to still another plane and barrier. It seemed to him that the changes occurred about once every spen or so. Finally, the plane and barrier changed again, this time to the original plane and barrier that he had seen.

Without his telling it to do so, his mind examined the thoughts of one particular tear. All of the thoughts involved envy in one form or another. His mind then projected the word *envy* to the thought plane. Each new thought created now concerned envy in some way. When the plane and barrier switched again, his mind again involuntarily searched the thoughts of the biggest tear. This time, the thoughts originating from the weak spots centered on dishonesty. His mind projected *dishonesty* as a thought, and again, the plane started to produce thoughts about the projected thought. The plane and barrier switched twice more until all four of the minds that he was probing had a thought projected onto it.

Then he became aware of a single massive thought that came into and then out of his mind and seemed to spill into the minds that he was probing. *You are now thinking about your major weakness. Give that weakness to us. Give yourself over to us. You need help with this weakness. Let us make it your strength. You cannot do this yourself. You need our help. Let us help you. Let us in. Give your will to us. We will make your will strong. You want to give us your will. You are tired. You want to give in. Give us your will.*

The projected thought was so strong that he couldn't concentrate on any other thought, even though the thought was not projected to him, only through him. There was only that thought. It was all that existed.

Beltram's mind then acted again of its own accord as soon as the projected thought faded. His mind seemed to push against the tear in the barrier of the mind he was currently probing. The barrier went out of existence with what seemed like a mighty explosion. His mind immediately switched over to the next mind's barrier. Again, only a little pressure on the targeted tear and the mind's barrier burst out of existence. The third and fourth barriers followed suit. He had done it. He had broken the will of the minds he was probing, and thus, he had broken the barriers of all four minds. It seemed very easy, but then he was linked to many other minds with a powerful mind at the head of the link. He was sure it wouldn't be so easy by himself.

After the barriers were down, a change took place on each person's mind plane that was visible to him. It was as if a new pattern were superimposed over the original pattern. Then, gradually, he saw a new barrier start to appear in each mind.

He became aware of another massive thought.

Welcome to our family. Think of your experience as a rebirth. You are now a child in a new family. You are now one of the Peydie. You will soon learn your father's name. But for now, do not tell anyone of your experience here today or inquire after your father. All will be revealed when we meet in this room in the morning. You shall be here at 2:45.

Then the doctor severed the link, and at the same time, his mind released the four people in front of him. He immediately became aware of his surroundings, but the people in front of him still had blank expressions on their faces. He stood up from his half-kneeling position, and was surprised that his legs didn't feel any discomfort at all. If he had tried to stay in that crouched position for any length of time in the past, his legs would have ached. As he scanned the room, he saw that all of the seated people had the same blank stare.

"Do not be concerned," said the doctor's voice behind him. "They will regain control of their bodies in just a moment. Right now, their minds are trying to adjust to what has happened to them. Once your Peydie have recovered, treat them kindly and dismiss them. I will see all of you at forty-five spens after the second parz tomorrow morning." The term *Peydie* was strange to him, but if the doctor said that he and the people in the room were Peydie, it must be so.

Degmer joined the doctor, and the two of them left the room. Although the doctor didn't say it, he knew that it was his responsibility to see to Degmer's Peydie as well, though he wasn't sure how he knew that.

He glanced at the clock in the room. It was now 6:59. It had taken less than ten spens to change over one hundred twenty people into Peydie. It had felt like much more time than that had passed to him. Time must flow differently inside a person's mind.

As he waited for the Peydie in front of him to recover, he thought about the new identity he had been given. He was glad to be one of the Doctor's Peydie. The term already came naturally to him. The people in front of him started to recover and stir.

"So, how do you feel now?" he asked his group of Peydie.

Each one of the Peydie remarked how wonderful they felt. Then, one by one, they indicated that they would see him in the morning and left.

Beltram remembered the feeling that he had after his first meeting with the doctor. It was a mixture of euphoria and wonder. That was what the new Peydie were feeling now. Their euphoria would fade slightly over time, but their sense of wonder would increase once they discovered what they had become.

As the last of the new Peydie were leaving, a young woman that Beltram recognized but couldn't quite place came through the door. "Oh. Have I missed it?" she asked with a disappointed mien about her.

"You came for the session with Doctor Upfar?" he asked.

"Yes, but I see that I am too late. I'm surprised it ended so early. I didn't think I would miss that much if I were a little late, but it appears that I missed the whole thing," said the woman with surprise in her voice. Her eyes lingered upon the last people leaving. "They certainly seem happy," remarked the woman.

"I am sure they are. Doctor Upfar has a wonderful effect on people," he said. "Did you still want help? Doctor Upfar has made me one of his assistants. Perhaps I can be of some help."

"Aren't you Beltram Chaf, the site administrator?" asked the woman.

"Yes, I am. But I have studied with the doctor, and I might be able to think of a way to help you," he offered.

"Well ... " The woman hesitated and then said, "Axi. If it's not too much of a bother."

"It won't be a problem at all," he said. "I am sorry, but I'm afraid I have forgotten your name."

"Oh. That's not a surprise," said the woman. "I've only been here for a month, and we only met once. My name is Varspeta, but people just call me Peta."

"It is good to meet you again, Peta. Please have a seat," he said, gesturing toward the end chair in the first row of tables.

Peta glanced back at the door as it closed behind the last person, leaving her alone in the room with him. She appeared to be undecided whether to stay or not, but she eventually headed toward the chair and sat down.

Peta was a petite young woman with dark brown hair and light gray eyes. She reminded him of his mother when she was younger, although his mother was not as petite. It would be nice to have her in the family, but he wasn't sure if the doctor would be available.

"Pardon me for a moment. I have to try to ready myself," he said. He closed his eyes to concentrate and sent a thought out to the Doctor. *Doctor, I have a woman who came in late who wants our help. Can you help now?*

The thought that came back surprised him. *You do not need my help. You know how to help this woman. You are complete.*

The thought that he was complete filled him with gratification. He didn't feel any different; but if the doctor said he was complete, it must be so. While he was very happy that he was now complete, he wasn't sure he knew how to help Peta. Still, the doctor thought that he could help her so he would try.

He took a seat beside Peta and said, "We help people by searching for the specific weaknesses that are preventing people from realizing their goals in life. We do this by inducing a hypnotic state of mind on the subject and then isolating and addressing these weaknesses. There are no questions for you to answer. Nothing relies on you. I do all the work. All you have to do is let go of yourself and let me have control. Are you willing to do that?"

"Well, it sounds easy. Oh sure. What do I have to lose?" asked Peta.

He smiled and said, "It's really not what you lose. It's what you gain that's important. You can't be afraid to lose something." He stared at Peta intently and then said, "Are you ready to proceed?"

Peta took a deep breath and said with a quick nod, "I am ready."

"Very well," he said, trying to sound clinical. He focused his mind on Peta. He could feel her mind, but he couldn't see it. He then leaned toward Peta and said, "Look into my eyes."

When Peta obeyed and gazed deeply into his eyes, it was as if a door opened into Peta's mind. His mind could now visualize the plane and the barrier. He examined the barrier. It had many weak spots and some tears. He briefly wondered if all mind barriers had tears. As he wondered, the barrier began to fade into darkness. He quickly regained his concentration, and the barrier came back clearly. He had nearly lost contact with Peta's mind.

Understanding now that he had to keep his focus, he intently investigated each thought linked to the largest weakness on the barrier. All of the thoughts had something to do with procrastination. Many of the thoughts were regrets. Others were bad memories of the results of her procrastination. He didn't have the power of a link while he was in this mind so he thought he would approach the weakness as the doctor had approached his weakness: with a series of thoughts.

He thought for a moment and then projected these thoughts. *Peta, you have procrastinated many times. Each time you procrastinate, something happens to prevent you from reaching your goals. Give your procrastination to me. I can help you. You cannot help yourself. You must rely on me. Give your will to me. I can help you. I can make you better than you are now. You no longer have to procrastinate. I can take that away forever.* He tried to push against the tear in the barrier. The barrier wavered, but it didn't break. He would have to search deeper. He hadn't pushed her to the point where his mind's strength could break her barrier.

He sifted through the thought linked to the tear again. There was something else that he had missed earlier: a lost love. She felt that she lost her opportunity for true love by putting off a decision. It was a decision to move to a different country: Nurd. Her boyfriend, Pracho, had wanted her to move because he had taken a job there. She had put off the decision. Eventually, Pracho had given up on her, and he had left without her. To make matters worse, she had put off contacting him once he was in Nurd; and when she finally did contact him, Pracho had met someone else.

He thought for a moment and then sent these thoughts. *Peta, your procrastination cost you Pracho. Why do you want to hang on to a habit that will cost you again and again? You will never find happiness if you continue to procrastinate. Let go. Let me help you. Let me in. Peta, let me in. You will have new abilities that will attract boyfriends much better than Pracho if you let me in. You deserve better, Peta. Let me help you. Let go. Let me in.*

Suddenly, Peta's barrier burst out of existence without Beltram's pushing against it at all. He guessed that he had hit on the right thought and no coercion was necessary. An instinct of some kind then took over. His mind instinctively wove a new pattern for Peta's mind plane and put it into place. He was amazed that he could remember the pattern that had appeared in the four minds that he previously probed, and he was doubly amazed that he knew how to weave the pattern. Then he sent some instructions for Peta. *You will not tell anyone of our session. You will meet with your new father, the doctor, at 2:45 tomorrow morning in this very room. Welcome. You are one of the doctor's Peydie now.*

He let himself come out of Peta's mind. She had an astonished blank stare on her face. He understood that she would eventually recover just as the others had. He would wait for her to recover so that he could reassure her that everything was normal. She would accept it and would become another faithful Peydie.

As he waited, exhilaration filled his very being. Without any help from the doctor, he had made a Peydie for him. If he wasn't complete before, he certainly was complete now.

He wanted to contact the doctor at that very moment to tell him of his success, but he knew that wouldn't please the doctor at this time, though he wasn't at all sure how he knew that. Right now he had to be satisfied with one thought: *The doctor was going to be pleased.* It was the compulsion to please the doctor that drove his whole being.

CHAPTER TWENTY-FOUR

AN EVENING'S ENTERTAINMENT

The first part of Degmer's evening had been interesting. After leaving the conference room session, Neaotomo had mentioned how tired he was of eating food reconstituted from powder so she volunteered to make dinner for the two of them since her quarters were on the way. She had prepared corni, a very common dish made from koh, but Neaotomo ate it as if it were a fine cut of towrus. She had to admit that her corni wasn't bad, but all Neaotomo had been eating since he had awakened from his deep sleep was reconstituted food so his culinary opinion was dubious at best. Still, his praise had put her in a good mood.

Neaotomo had since gone back to the sealed labs. He too was in a good mood when he left. He seemed much more at ease outside of the sealed labs after the big meeting in C-1. She was sure that that was because he had just succeeded in changing nearly half of the complex's population into Peydie. After all, nearly every other person he would likely meet in the main complex would know him as the doctor and think fondly of him. She could see where it would be easy for him to feel at ease since the odds were now greatly in his favor. Yet, thoughts about Neaotomo were not part of her main train of thought since he left. Despite her good humor, her thoughts had been focused on the best way to make Laysa's night miserable and to entertain herself.

Right now, she was thinking hard on how best to go about it. She had thought of several possibilities, but each would make a mess. Neaotomo told her that he wouldn't clean up after her fun with Laysa again, and she didn't feel like spending a lot of time on cleanup tonight. She wanted to think of something that would exact great pain from Laysa but not make a big mess. Then it hit her. She had the perfect idea for tonight's entertainment.

She had a large array of belts, most of which she no longer used since the vast majority of current clothing styles didn't include belts. She gathered all of her unused belts together and threw out the flimsy ones. The belts that she was interested in would have to be made of leather or something just as strong. The sorting continued until there were nine belts left — nine belts strong enough to use.

She went into her bathroom and found a razor that she used to shave her legs when she traveled and didn't have the leg-manicuring equipment that she had in her quarters. She used the blade to cut one end of each of the belts into multiple thin strands. Then she took the metal buckles off each of the belts.

In her utility closet, she found some leather binding and some adhesive. The leather binding wasn't actually leather, but everyone called it leather. It was a synthetic material that mimicked leather. Combined with adhesive, it was widely used as a multipurpose binding solution — especially in Grasso.

She bound the nine uncut ends of the belts together, using the binding with the adhesive. The adhesive took just a moment to dry. When it had, she picked up the belts by the bound end. It was a good imitation of a whip. She swung her makeshift whip over her head and then lashed out at a small figurine she had on a table as decoration. The whip knocked the figurine off the table, but something was wrong. The whip felt too light to do much damage or inflict much pain so she took both the large and small parts of the metal buckles that she had taken off the belts and attached those to about half of the thin cords of the whip. Then she broke apart an old necklace that had small, colored, solid pirru balls as beads. Each metal ball had a decent weight. She tied the beads into the ends of each strap. She again tested her whip and found that the weight of the metal buckles and metal beads on the end gave the whip much more power. The straps with the metal buckles would deliver blunt force while the thin straps with only metal beads would deliver a cutting, stinging effect that should maximize Laysa's discomfort nicely.

After taking a few more practice swings with the whip and breaking a couple of figurines in the process, she decided that the whip could be capable of breaking Laysa's skin and splattering blood; so she decided she would use some of the covering sheets she saw in the sealed labs storage area to catch any splatter that might occur. The sheets should make cleanup quite a bit easier. All that would have to be done after she was finished with Laysa would be to take up the sheets. Satisfied that she had planned a good evening of enter-tainment without much chance of making a mess, she left her quarters whip in hand and crossed the hall to the sealed labs.

Neaotomo met her in the outer lab. He glanced at the whip and said, "I see you have made a new toy. May I see it?"

She handed the whip to Neaotomo without hesitation. After all, she was rather proud of her handiwork and wanted it to be admired.

Neaotomo tested the whip on a nearby swivel chair. The ends of the whip hit the side of the chair back squarely, and the chair whirled around a few rotations. "It has a nice weight to it. It appears that it is made out of belts. You just threw it together this evening?"

"Yep. It's my entertainment toy. Where's Laysa?" she said with a mean smile as she took the whip back from Neaotomo.

"She has been in her quarters all day and seemed quite content to stay there when I talked to her earlier," he said. "She seems to be in a contemplative mood. I suppose that she is trying to understand what happened to her yesterday. Of course, the fact that she has no clothes to wear might be hindering her desire to venture out as well. She has had a bed sheet around her all day. I was about to take her clothes into her. Beltram brought them this morning."

"No need to bother with the clothes right now," she said roughly. "I came to pay her a little visit. She won't be needing her clothes. They would just get in the way."

"I see," he said slowly. "I guess I could wait for a while to bring in her clothes since I have waited this long." He picked up a white garment that he had put down on the counter when he took the whip. "Since you are going to go play with Laysa, why do not you give her this to wear? It should not interfere with your entertainment. I was going to give this to her as a special present, but it now seems fitting to me that you give it to her." He then added with a smile, "It will leave almost her entire back exposed."

She gave a wry smile, took the undergarment, and then turned and headed for Laysa's quarters.

Meanwhile, Laysa was lying on her bed, thinking about how Neaotomo might fit into the prophecy of the soulless. He certainly would fit in somewhere, but she was beginning to realize that trying to figure out his place was pointless because she just couldn't remember enough of the prophecy. She wished she had her Levra, but it was in her quarters in the main complex. It would help her puzzle some things out—not just Neaotomo's place in prophecy—but a great many things.

The opening of the door to her quarters interrupted her thoughts. She turned toward the door and saw Degmer step into her room with a makeshift whip in her hands. Until that moment, she had still held a slim hope that she had only dreamed that Degmer had attacked her. "So it wasn't a nightmare after all," she said quietly.

"Oh, I don't know about that," said Degmer with a wry smile. "I *am* your worst nightmare." As the door closed behind her, the smile vanished from Degmer's face and she shouted, "Now, get out of that bed!" Degmer grabbed the bed coverings with one hand and yanked on them fiercely, throwing the coverings up against the door.

The suddenness and ferocity of Degmer's actions shocked her. Trembling with fear, she held tightly to the thin sheet that she had wrapped herself in this morning. She instinctively sat up and pulled her legs up close to her body.

"Do my actions frighten you, Laysa? Where is that bravado you showed while you were parading around naked in front of Neaotomo?"

She could see that nothing she could say would make any difference to Degmer. She had already chosen what to believe, and her obvious anger and hatred made reasoning with her out of the question. So she said nothing.

"What's the matter, Laysa?" mocked Degmer as she made threatening movements with her whip. "Nothing to say to your old pal, Degmer?" Degmer circled the foot of the bed and came to the other side.

She turned her head to follow Degmer's movements and tried to keep her distance from Degmer without moving off the bed. Degmer's last visit was still vivid in her mind, and intense fear mingled with awful dread filled her mind without warning. Her breathing became fast as her heart raced faster and faster.

Degmer turned away from the bed for a couple of steps and then said, "But what can you say? You betrayed me,

Laysa. You betrayed me and laughed at me behind my back. It's not so funny now; is it, Laysa?"

Degmer turned back toward the bed and made a gesture as if she were going to strike her with the whip. She cringed and instinctively put her head between her legs and covered her head with her hands.

Instead of striking her, however, Degmer laid the whip beside her on the bed and said, "I am going to fetch some things. But don't worry. I'll be back soon. Take a good look at the whip that I made especially for you. Think of what it will do to you when I use it on you," she said as she headed toward the door. Then she paused, threw a white undergarment on the bed, and said, "Now take that ridiculous sheet off and put that on." She turned and then paused again and said, "Oh, and don't think about running away and hiding. I am locking the door when I leave." As Degmer headed out the door, she glanced back at her, feigned a friendly grin, and said in a cheerful tone, "'Bye. See you when I get back."

Only when she heard the door open did Laysa uncover her head to peer toward Degmer. She couldn't believe the cruelty that she felt in Degmer's feigned grin. The tones indicating that the door lock had been activated sounded immediately after the door closed. Her eyes were fixed on the door even after it closed. Her mind tried to picture Degmer standing at the door differently than her eyes had just seen her, but her mind failed the task she had assigned it. All her mind saw was that horrible grin.

She took her gaze off the door and slowly brought her eyes to the whip that lay beside her. Her breathing was still fast, though she had tried to calm herself. She observed the many beaded strands that made up the business end of the whip and saw the pieces of metal that had been embedded within some of the strands. The metal pieces seem to have been parts of belt buckles from a woman's belt. No doubt the rest of the whip was made from several belts, and no doubt the belts were Degmer's belts. The thought of being beaten with the whip sent new trembling throughout her body, which she futilely tried to control.

She took her eyes off the hand-fashioned whip and stared straight ahead at the wall on the opposite side of the room without really seeing it. Degmer would be back soon. Part of her wanted to take the whip in her hands and use it on Degmer as soon as she came through the door or perhaps tear the whip apart if she could. However, she knew that either choice was not a wise course of action.

Degmer's actions obviously had Neaotomo's blessing. In fact, it was very probable that Neaotomo had instigated Degmer's hatred. It was also obvious that Degmer had been changed. She was not the same person anymore. She had spewed profanity yesterday. At least Degmer used no profanity today. Yet, it was probable that Neaotomo had changed her into one of his kind. Assuming all that was true, she probably had some or all of Neaotomo's abilities, at least to a degree. It would be foolish to anger her any more than she already was. The best thing to do would be to take whatever abuse Degmer wanted to give as bravely as possible.

Bravery wasn't possible in her current condition. She needed to calm down quickly. The fear that had welled up within her was instinctive, but she needed to control it. She had to show Degmer that she had strength of spirit, for Degmer's sake. She had to accept whatever Degmer did and still show as much love for her as possible. If she showed cringing fear, Degmer would only loathe her. She couldn't expect to have any useful influence if Degmer didn't at least respect her. She had to be brave for her sake.

She took a deep breath that was made ragged by her trembling body and closed her eyes. There was no courage within her, but she knew who could help her find the courage she needed. She called upon Thaoi putting every bit of faith that she could muster into her prayer. "Thaoi, please give me courage to face this trial. My friend Degmer needs me. I can't find the courage in my own strength. Please, Thaoi, give me the strength to be courageous." As she finished her prayer, she noticed that her body had stopped trembling. Her pulse was slower and her breathing less ragged.

As calmness settled over her, she ignored the whip to fix her sight on the other object that lay with her on her bed. The white undergarment that Degmer had thrown on the bed had no back to it. She clearly understood the reason for that. Still, she put the undergarment on after laying the sheet aside. Then she took the whip into her arms, rose up from the bed, and stood at its foot. Her arms were positioned as if holding a bundle in front of her; the whip was draped over her arms. She stood there motionless, gazing at the door in anticipation of Degmer's return.

The door soon opened, but it wasn't Degmer standing in the doorway; it was Neaotomo. In his hands, he held four traveling cases. They appeared to be her cases. "Oh," he said, appearing to be surprised. "Am I interrupting something?"

She remained motionless and said nothing.

Neaotomo paused for a moment before turning and putting the cases down against the wall beside the door. "I have brought you some of your clothes, probably most of them by the look of it. Beltram was kind enough to bring them by for you."

Beltram—she had forgotten about him. It appeared that Beltram was under Neaotomo's control as well. She had considered from the start that he might have fallen under Neaotomo's influence, and now it seemed very likely. Though thoughts of all sorts began to swirl within her head, she remained motionless and said nothing.

"Oh, I see," he said while walking toward her. "You are giving me the silent treatment. I have heard that women are prone to do that sort of thing, but it has not been tried on me before. I can see where men would find it frustrating. Are you not at least going to thank me for bringing you some clothes?"

She turned her head slightly to gaze squarely at him. "Thank you," she said curtly and then promptly turned her face back toward the door.

"That undergarment looks very good you," commented Neotomo.

Neaotomo had probably had a hand in providing the skimpy undergarment. It was undoubtedly another ploy meant to humiliate her. She responded to the remark with a hot glance toward Neatomo, but then realized that her anger wouldn't help Degmer. She closed her eyes and took a deep breath. She could feel an inner peace settle over her. When she opened her eyes again, she calmly set her sight on the door.

"You know," he said, "you are a bright young woman. I know that you must have figured out that I let Degmer believe things about you that are not true."

Her expression remained neutral. She remained motionless with the whip draped across her arms.

He came closer and peered down at the whip. "Most people in a position like yours would not be so accepting of their circumstance," he said deliberately. "Why are you so willing to accept such circumstance when you and I both know that you did nothing against Degmer?"

She took her gaze off the door long enough to glance at him once again. Then she reaffixed her eyes on the doors and said, "Degmer believes I wronged her, and there is nothing I can say to convince her otherwise. I still care very much for Degmer. All I can do for her now is to cooperate with her wish for vengeance." She looked past him to fix her eyes on the door again.

He raised an eyebrow and stood before her just as motionless as she was for a moment. He then backed up a step. Her eyes couldn't help but follow him to her desk where he drew out the chair, positioned it by the wall opposite the bed, and sat down. He had a look of deep reflection on his face. As she stared at him, she wondered if perhaps he was thinking about her actions. It would be a step in the right direction for him if he were. But Neaotomo was not her primary interest at the moment. She again focused her attention back on the door and waited.

Before long, the door opened to reveal Degmer in the hall with what appeared to be furniture coverings and a couple of cloth strips, perhaps torn from the coverings in her hands. Degmer started to come into the room; but when she saw her, she stopped and gazed curiously at her.

She was still standing motionless, whip over her arms.

Degmer then noticed Neaotomo sitting by the wall and said, "What brings you here? Wanting a front-row seat for tonight's entertainment?"

He shook his head and said in a cheerful tone, "I just came to bring by Laysa's clothes. But if there is to be entertainment, I might as well stay."

Degmer looked at him askance and then came fully into the room so that the door closed behind her. "I wondered how the door came to be unlocked," she said to him. Then she turned to Laysa and said, "I thought you would be cowering in your bed like I left you. Do you think that Neaotomo has come to your rescue? Is that why you are so calm?"

She said nothing. Surprisingly, Neaotomo was silent as well.

Degmer stared at Neaotomo as if she thought that he just *might* be there to rescue her and said, "Do you have any objections to tonight's entertainment?"

"Not at all," he said. "I am just observing. Proceed as if I were not here."

Degmer peered doubtfully at him for another moment but then focused her attention on her. "I have brought the coverings in case you decide to make another mess with your blood. Neaotomo is making me clean up after you now, so I thought these would make the cleanup faster," Degmer said callously.

As Degmer passed by her, she turned so that she continually faced Degmer, keeping the whip in front of Degmer, keeping the whip readily available for use.

Degmer ignored the presentation of the whip and proceeded to place some of the coverings on the floor under the clothes hook. Then she fixed the other coverings on the wall under the hook, using some sort of adhesive. "There," she said. "That should catch most of it. What it doesn't catch, you can clean up, Laysa. Is that acceptable, Neaotomo?"

He said nothing, but Degmer nodded as if he had assented.

She kept her eyes only on Degmer.

"Good. Then it's settled," said Degmer. Degmer took a small tube of adhesive from her pants pocket and approached Laysa. Degmer glared into her eyes for what seemed like a terribly long time and then defiantly took the whip from her and threw it on the bed. Degmer said roughly, "Hold your hands out, and spread your fingers."

She extended her arms fully with her hands palms up and spread her fingers wide.

Degmer put adhesive on both sides of Laysa's middle finger on both of her hands. After she finished, she commanded, "Now, interlock your fingers," said Degmer, demonstrating what she wanted by putting her hands in front of her with her fingers interlocked.

She dutifully complied. As she put her fingers together, Degmer reached out, squeezed her fingers together and held them tightly, all the while glaring angrily into her eyes.

After a few moments, Degmer let go of her fingers and barked, "Pull your hands apart."

She tried to do so, but the adhesive held four of her fingers together, and she couldn't separate her hands. Degmer smirked, and then a darker expression covered her face. Degmer grabbed both of her arms and tried to force her hands apart. The pressure on her four fingers made them partially dislocate, but her fingers remained interlocked. She grimaced and let out a muffled grunt.

"Good," said Degmer coldly. "Put your hands behind your head."

She complied obediently.

Degmer then used the two cloth strips to bind Laysa's elbows as close together in front of her head as they could be bound. Degmer drew a deep breath and again glared intently at her. Her eyes were full of hate, yet surprisingly empty at the same time. Degmer then drew back and let out a wild grunt as she delivered a powerful punch into her stomach. The blow sent her sprawling and took her breath away. Before she could get her breath, Degmer pulled her roughly up to her feet.

She tried to stay standing, but her body betrayed her and she buckled back down to the floor.

Degmer stood, glowering over her menacingly, and said, "You're not as strong as you think you are, are you?"

She struggled to get to her feet. It was difficult with her hands behind her head and the pain in her midsection. Degmer backed off as she finally made it up from the floor. She stood facing Degmer, trying to bring her head up far enough to look Degmer in her eyes. She was breathing hard, but it wasn't from fear; it was because she was still trying to catch her breath from the blow to her stomach. Finally, she managed to catch her breath and stood motionless in front of Degmer. Degmer gave her a grudging look of respect before a scowl returned to her face.

"Turn around!" Degmer shouted roughly.

She turned so that her back was toward Degmer. Then she felt Degmer's hands grab her roughly by the waist, hoisting her up into the air. Degmer strained just a bit but managed to turn with her hoisted in the air. With some effort, Degmer was able to place the cloth that tied her elbows together over the large clothes hook on the wall.

Laysa hung motionless, her face pointed up to the ceiling and her back arched, with her feet about a three and a half dets off the floor. Her fingers immediately shot protests of pain into her mind as she hung, but she dared not let her hands slip from the back of her head. Such a move would infuriate Degmer even further and send either a message of defiance or a message of weakness. She was determined to stay strong yet meek for Degmer's sake. Therefore, she let her head be cradled by her injured fingers, which were bearing a great deal of pressure. She tried to take some of the strain off her fingers by contracting her biceps. All in all, it was proving to be a terrible ordeal just to keep herself hanging motionless.

Degmer let her hang there for quite some time. She couldn't hear any movement, but she heard what she thought was whispering between Degmer and Neaotomo. After the whispering stopped, she was still left to hang. She could hear nothing at all in the room, though she could sense that someone was still in the room. Her arms and neck began to fatigue and cry out in pain. Still, she heard nothing. Her injured fingers screamed with pain. Sweat started to bead up and drip down Laysa's head and body because of the heat generated in her arms, shoulders, and neck by the tension of her muscles. Still, she heard nothing. She was tempted to try to turn her body to see what was happening behind her, but she did not want to appear to be struggling to free herself. She just hung there motionless. Groans started to come unbidden with her breathing. The fatigue in her arms and shoulders was becoming unbearable, and her neck was cramping. The pain from her fingers was becoming extremely intense.

After what seemed a long time, she heard more whispering between Degmer and Neaotomo. Finally, she heard Degmer say aloud, "I hope I haven't made you too uncomfortable hanging there like that. You do seem to be under a little stress though. I think you need to release some of that stress with a little vocalization."

The sound of the whip cutting through the air meet her ears just before the whip hit her back. Her mouth involuntarily let out a loud grunt as the whip struck. Her back, which was already wet with perspiration, stung from the effect of each empty strand of the whip. Bones and muscles groaned in agony from the blow of each embedded piece of metal on the whip. The combined effect of the whip on her bare back created an excruciating chaos of pain. She found that she had to struggle to catch her breath after just one blow. Still, she kept her head cradled in her tortured fingers as she hung.

"Well, that made some nice welts on your back and I imagine some bruising in the muscles and bones of your back," crowed Degmer. "What do you think of my little toy, Laysa? Not a bad whip for my first one, is it? I think it lacks a little elasticity though. It could have a little more sting if the leather were suppler I think. What do you think, Laysa?"

"It seems — to be — very effective — as it is," she said haltingly. It was hard to draw enough breath to speak.

"Oh, so you can speak. I thought maybe someone had cut out your tongue," said Degmer tauntingly. "Let me see if I can't make each blow even more effective." Degmer grunted as she executed the next blow.

The result of the force exerted was devastating. She gasped in pain. The pain so seared her body that she lost consciousness for the briefest of moments. She fought to keep consciousness in order to keep her head cradled in her fingers. She was determined to do everything she could to show her cooperation—for Degmer's sake. Once her mind returned to full consciousness, she wished she hadn't. Her body delivered the agony of excruciating pain to her mind.

"Hmm. That sounded as if that hurt," taunted Degmer. "Oh, I see some blood escaping your lovely little back. Well, your back used to be lovely anyway," she said with a sneer in her voice.

The next thing she said seemed to be directed toward Neaotomo. "I'm afraid that Laysa's gotten blood all over her new undergarment," Degmer said in a mocking tone of remorse.

Degmer came beside her, while she was gasping to catch her breath, and said, "Enough chit-chat now. It's time to get to work. Let me see if I can create some real damage now." Degmer let out a cruel laugh. She could actually feel the cruelty of it.

She closed her eyes and tried to prepare herself for unspeakable pain. Yet, as the next blow came, she realized that there was nothing that could have been done to prepare for it. The force of the blow overwhelmed her senses with pain. Her breath caught, and she thought she would not be able to draw another. Sweat poured down her face, stinging her eyes. Sweat poured into the open wounds in her back, making her body rock in pain long after the blow had landed. Just as she was just starting to recover from the previous blow, another came that overwhelmed her still more. Her body trembled in pain. Groans came with each exhale that she did not have the breath to finish. Sobs came during both inhales and exhales as other blows came. Her mouth hung open, trying to snatch some air, but her lungs remained unsatisfied. Then another blow came, then another blow and still another. Her eyes were wide open, but she found her eyes could focus on nothing. Still, she had the presence of mind to concentrate on keeping her head cradled on her ever more tortured fingers.

More blows came, each one racking her body with extreme pain. Her vision was just a white blur. But she relentlessly held her fingers behind her head.

As more blows landed, her unfocused vision began to dim. She felt her arm muscles involuntarily relax and her hands came away from the back of her head. Her body went limp. Finally, she saw nothing. All faded to black.

After the beating, Degmer picked up the coverings that she had placed in the room and Neaotomo carefully placed Laysa on her bed. He thought about having Degmer heal Laysa, but using reasoning that he did not at all understand, he decided to do it himself this time. He healed her internal injuries first. They were many, but not life-threatening if healed properly. He then healed the skin on her back. Not a welt remained after he was done. Finally, he attended to her mangled fingers. The skin of her fingers had torn away during the whipping because of the adhesive that Degmer had applied, making them raw and bloody as well as dislocated. It took time to sort out the mangled masses of skin, muscle and bone, but when he finally finished with her hands, they were completely undamaged. He even removed the bloodstains from her undergarment and bedding.

He remained sitting on Laysa's bed for a long time after he had healed her. His eyes were on Laysa, but his mind was not focusing on her body anymore. His mind was busy thinking of how Laysa had behaved tonight, especially how she had remained devoted to Degmer. He was trying to conceive how Laysa could still regard Degmer as her friend. He could not understand why she fully submitted to Degmer's beating without as much as one protest of innocence.

She was innocent. He had tricked her into the only disobedience that she committed, giving him the excuse to beat Degmer and plant the thought in Degmer's mind that the beating was Laysa's idea. It was the tremendous beating that he had given Degmer that propelled Degmer to spiral out of control with rage against Laysa. In truth, Laysa had done everything she could to try to protect Degmer. She had bargained for Degmer, and she had borne shame for Degmer. Now, she appeared to be enduring great pain for Degmer. He had even observed her weeping while speaking of her concern for Degmer. Via the terms on which he viewed Laysa periodically, he observed her sincere demeanor when she addressed her concerns for Degmer to an entity called Thaoi. This was done while she was waiting for Degmer to return to beat her with the whip. His studies of Kosundo had revealed that some people believed in a great spirit called Thaoi. Talking to the Great Spirit was called prayer. He thought that what Laysa was doing was praying for Degmer. Even earlier today, Laysa had wept and prayed for Degmer. He could not understand the devotion Laysa had for someone who had turned against her so violently. Still, he found he had to admire it, even if he could not understand it.

As he thought, a feeling that he had never experienced to this degree before began to swell up within him. He had read about the power of this feeling. The feeling was called regret. It was not the partial regret that he had felt before. It was regret in its most profound form. He found himself desperately wishing that he could let Laysa go. He found himself wishing that he had placed Laysa back in her quarters when she was rendered unconscious by Degmer's medical stick on the day that she had first stepped foot in the sealed labs. Laysa would never have had to endure any of the punishment, any of the shame, or any of the sorrow if he had just let her wake up in her quarters.

His logical mind told him that he could not let Laysa go now, as it told him that he could not have put Laysa in her quarters on that first day. It told him that he would not survive if he did such illogical things. He would not have won his freedom if he had freed Laysa. He knew that his logical mind was right. The part of him that wanted to free Laysa was foreign to him. That part of him did not fully exist before tonight, and now that part of him was in conflict with all he knew before. His mind no longer felt as focused, and he was experiencing something else that he had never felt before: confusion.

His primary goal of freedom was still clear in his mind. He was less clear that he wanted revenge on the human race. Before, both goals were equally important to him. Now he did not know if he needed revenge or even wanted it. Still, he knew that some humans would have to be sacrificed if he was to win his freedom permanently. It was strange that that thought now seemed to bother him, if only slightly.

He came out of his mental trance to let his eyes again focus on Laysa. She was resting comfortably.

Degmer had left Laysa's body in far worse shape by using her whip than she had when she used the scalpel. It seemed that Laysa's lack of resistance had actually fueled her fury, and it had showed in the way she had wielded her whip. She had put every oggi of strength into each stroke. Each stroke had exacted a heavy toll on Laysa's back, especially since Laysa's back had been forced to arch because of the way Laysa had been suspended. She had shown good ingenuity in determining how to extract as much pain as she could from Laysa.

That thought caused him to remember his puzzlement as to why Degmer had struggled a bit to raise Laysa's body to the hook. If she had gained as much strength as he expected, she would not have struggled. She was not an especially muscular person to start with, but her strength should have increased sevenfold. Laysa could not weigh more than seventy libs. Laysa's weight should have felt like ten libs to Degmer. Five of the lab's journals would weigh a bit more than ten libs. Degmer should have been able to lift her easily. Instead, she had struggled to lift Laysa above her head. He guessed that she might have as much as three times the strength that she had before, but certainly no more than that and maybe not that. However, he had turned only one female before Degmer, and that was just before the gas had killed her. He did not know if her strength had increased as nominally as Degmer's had or not. All of the males that he had converted and then observed had gained about seven times their original strength. Their strength had become comparable to his strength, though their strength never equaled his strength. He wondered if all the females whose barriers he overcame would gain less strength than their male counterparts.

Laysa was the main puzzle though. Where did she find the courage to face such torture so calmly? Degmer had whispered to him after she had hung Laysa on the hook that she would wait until Laysa cried out before beating her with the whip. She never did cry out, and Degmer eventually tired of waiting. This calmness in the face of pain was not part of her normal emotional makeup. He had seen her scream hysterically when he forced his way into her mind just a couple of days ago. The pain was real to be sure, but she faced a far more extended session with pain tonight and did not scream at all. Her body made her gasp and groan, but there was no screaming. Laysa had held her fear within her tonight. It was almost as if she had used someone else's strength. He had been searching for an excuse to keep Laysa alive. Perhaps studying her to find her source of courage was enough to let his rational mind keep her alive.

Still, even with her newfound strength of courage, it would be hard for Laysa, emotionally and mentally, to endure too many more beatings like the one she had endured tonight. He must find a way to make the beatings stop.

The easiest way to do that was to tell Degmer the truth about Laysa. Yet, he was not sure how that would affect Degmer, seeing that her anger toward Laysa was the tool he had used to overcome her barrier. His pattern was already imprinted on Degmer, so he knew that she could not disobey him, but it certainly would make for a great amount of inner turmoil in Degmer's mind. It might awaken her old self to the point that she would be crying against herself within her mind. She would become more aware that many of her actions were not her own; but even so, she would be able to do nothing about it.

As he thought about that possibility, he had to smile. He would not have realized that such a struggle could even be possible if it were not for the struggle that he was feeling inside his mind right now. Perhaps his mind's new part was just a part of his growth as a person after all.

Chapter Twenty-Five

Stepping Out

Finally, he understood why he was here. During the trip to the south, it had occurred to him that he would be better off without being hampered by an empire. It also occurred to him that a few loyal followers would be better than billions of subjects, any one of whom might want to stop his quest for vengeance. The plan called for him to meet with people who understood his goals. It was a plan that had been in the back of his mind for a while. It only took the right moment to bring it to the front of his mind.

Tryllos commanded the hovercraft driver to stop. In the distance, he could see his destination: the Dricho Genetics Foundation complex. It was unusual to see the sun so low in the sky behind the hovercraft at this time of the afternoon. It was only close to the sixth parz of the day, but the sun stayed low this far south. The driver said that the sun wouldn't set at night at certain times of the year here. That would be something new for him to see, but he would have to wait until the peak of summer to see that. He had commanded the driver to stop for a reason that he didn't understand. All he knew was that he felt an urgent need to be alone. He leaned forward toward the driver and something inside him said, "Turn off the craft, get out, and secure the vehicle. Walk toward the sun for three spens, and then come back. Don't look back at the hovercraft while you are walking away."

The driver showed surprise. He made an appeal by way of his rearview mirror by saying, "It's below freezing out there, my instruments read -2^0 K, and I don't have a coat on."

He gave the driver a determined gaze, and the driver soon relented and left him alone in the craft.

Once he was alone, he received a message: *It is time.* The message was a delight to his ears. It was time, and he knew exactly what to do.

Nenavis waited a moment to verify that Tryllos had understood his command. The former emperor's mind whirred with activity. Tryllos was responding as he had hoped. Though the mind of the former emperor was a cacophony of disoriented thought, the mind was still perfectly clear concerning the overriding directive that had controlled Tryllos's life for the last few years. While Tryllos busied himself with the task he was assigned, Nenavis transferred part of his consciousness. Soon his form was standing in the Labile Mist, near his ephemeral throne. The randomness of the mist around the throne gave him a sense of belonging. It was here that he controlled the powerful spiritual world that encircled the sixth world of men. It was here that his D'Yavoly groveled before him. It was good to be here again. But he had grander ideas for a throne now. Soon, the D'Yavoly and their minions would be joined in their groveling by the humans that the Other One cared for so much. The influence of the Other One was coming to an end. It was he who would be the preeminent power in this world of men. He sat down on his ephemeral throne and called for Zlux.

When Zlux appeared, he said in a demanding tone, "We are in sight of the complex. Is everything ready for my arrival?"

"Yes. All is ready, my master," cooed Zlux. "You will be met by a man called Kuntru Liartas. He is a scientist of some note in the complex, and he has some friends within the security staff, although security is light here anyway. By the way, it is Vrasku that controls Kuntru."

"It is fitting that he meet us," he said. "Without Vrasku's work, Tryllos would not be nearly as important. It is he who convinced Tryllos to pursue the creation of the Avengers. It will be good to feel his presence again. I just hope he remembers his place. Like you, he sometimes oversteps his bounds."

Then he sensed something. It was just a hint; maybe just a glimmer, but it was there. "I feel him, Zlux. I didn't think that it was possible, but I feel him. The feeling is not strong, but I feel his presence near our world."

"I too sense it, my master," said Zlux. "The redhead was with him earlier, but I did not sense him then. He is currently with that follower of the Other One that the redhead has been tormenting." Zlux smiled wickedly and continued. "I cannot influence the redhead, but she is doing a splendid job of tormenting that decrepit brown-haired woman." Zlux then paused, and the smile disappeared from his face. "You don't suppose that the Other One is interfering in the affairs of the abomination, do you, master?"

"Unfortunately, that is always a possibility, Zlux. Yet the abomination's presence in our realm is so weak that he is not a threat to us regardless. It merely allows me to locate him more easily," he said with a satisfied smile on his face. "This only makes my invasion of the abomination's physical mind easier. I will have influence over the abomination by tomorrow."

"Yes, my master," said Zlux.

"You have done well, Zlux. I might just release you from the redhead after all," he said with an amused smile on his face. Then his countenance grew more serious, and he said, "Make sure you remind Vrasku to be sure to keep Emperor Tryllos's presence a secret. He does have an unfortunate habit of neglecting his duties at times. We don't want to raise the abomination's curiosity. I will be arriving in just a few spens."

"I will remind him, my master. I delight in the prospect of my release," cooed Zlux.

"I think I just might let you control my first conquest through the abomination's mind. I think you have earned the right to be a part of my conquest of Kosundo, that is, if I stay in a generous mood," he said coyly. He then exhibited an aura of evil exhilaration while saying, "Soon, all of Kosundo will know and fear my name and the names of my D'Yavoly. Man's time is at an end. The time of the soulless is at hand!"

CHAPTER TWENTY-SIX

MEETING A FRIEND

Although it had started out as a derisive name for Yumal, the symbol of the hawk grew to become to be a large part of his legend. It wasn't long before his army replaced the sunburst banner with the hawk banner. The banner bore the image of a large, flying hawk with talons extended on a yellow background. It wasn't long after, that Yumal's soldiers began to wear the now-famous flying hawk image on their uniforms. To this very day, Doetoran army troops wear the flying hawk as part of their uniforms in the form of a right shoulder patch.

Yumal's personal guard picked up the theme of the hawk some time later. Instead of a flying hawk, the image chosen for imperial guard uniforms was a perching hawk. The perching hawk symbolizes vigilance, a commodity that the imperial guard of Doetora has proven that it possesses in abundance. The emperor's imperial guard today wears the perching hawk patch on each shoulder of their uniforms.

The imperial seal of Doetora also bears the perching hawk symbol. The hawk is golden and is perched on an oak tree branch symbolizing the emperor's vigi-

lant watch over the empire. Yumal commissioned the
seal once he had solidified the empire.

When asked why he chose the perching hawk over
his banner's flying hawk, Yumal said, "The time for
war is past. Now is the time to be quietly vigilant.
But lest the empire's enemies be emboldened, they
should know that a perching hawk can become a fly-
ing hawk in an instant."

Agap glanced over at the clock. It was now just after
midnight — seven spens after the tenth parz — the first
moments of eKureaki, Cirri City time. He had been reading a
passage from the book *The Legend of Yumal.* Yumal was the
founding emperor of the Empire of Doetora and was as great
a legend that existed in Kosundo. It was amazing how one
man united the scattered tribes of Doetora into a single great
empire. Yet Yumal had never intended to forge an empire.
His biography revealed that he had laid plans for a republic
before he ever embarked on his campaign to unite Doetora. It
was the trust and admiration that the Doetoran people had for
Yumal that caused the formation of an empire rather than a
republic. The people of Doetora wanted Yumal to rule
forever, yet his family lost the throne after only two
successions. The Mikeveos dynasty had ruled Doetora ever
since.

The symbol of the hawk was interesting. Yumal's
enemies called him the gawking hawk because his nose
resembled a bird's beak. It was ironic how the name of
mockery had become an enduring symbol of greatness.

Agap yawned as he tore himself away from his
musings about Doetora. He was tired, but Noso's sub was due
to dock in just a few spens. It was about time to go to the dock
to greet him.

He had two motives for staying up to greet Noso: Noso
was a good friend, and he wanted to talk with him about his

thought wave interface as soon as he could. He had to admit that the latter motive was the overriding reason that he was sacrificing most of his night's sleep.

He got up, put the book back up on its shelf, and went to his bedroom to put on his shoes. He had used the new chomile interface to create a closet in his bedroom. That was where he had put his shoes so he retrieved them from the closet, sat on his bed, and commenced to put his shoes on his feet. The new mobile interface had made the creation process much more convenient. It was great to have all the controls at his fingertips. He had finally put a wall around the other washroom as well. One of these days, the room might actually be ready to entertain a large group, if he chose to do so. He didn't really enjoy parties that much. He would rather sit and read a book.

Having succeeded in putting on his shoes, he started to look for his coat in his newly formed closet, but then he remembered that he hadn't worn a coat since he had arrived in Bojoa. Coats weren't necessary in Bojoa where the temperature was a constant 37° K outside of the buildings at night and a constant 42°K during the day. He had spent his time before he came to Bojoa in his hometown of Zaria, where a coat was seldom not needed when venturing outside. Habits died hard with him, but then many habits were good to have, such as cleaning one's teeth before going to bed.

He stopped off in the washroom to check his yellow white hair. This also was a habit. Being satisfied that his hair was sufficiently presentable, he left his quarters and headed for the translift down the hall. Once there, he pushed the triangular call button. The translift door opened immediately, and he walked in and punched in the code for the lobby of the LC building—LCL1—since the translift didn't run to the sub dock. The L1 referred to the lobby translift junction one. The number one junction was closest to the outside doors that he wanted to use to leave the LC. Once the code was entered, the lift jumped into motion. It wasn't long before the doors opened and he exited the lift into the lobby.

It was the first time that he had seen the lobby when the dome was in night mode. The gentle glow of the simulated moonlight complemented the lobby's soft lighting. With the greenery all around, it gave the feel of walking on a torch lit path, though there weren't nearly so many dark shadows in the lobby.

The nearest double doors led him outside and on the path that led toward the dock. He hadn't walked through this part of the dome since his arrival. He smiled as his eyes came across the beach. It was quite a tranquil scene under the dome's moonlight. His mind reminisced about the commotion that Holu and he had caused there. Oh, it wasn't a commotion exactly, but it had been amusing to see all the people who had piled on the beach because of Holu's lead. The beach was empty now, of course. Nearly everyone in the dome had long been asleep. A wave of tiredness came over him that made him wonder why he hadn't joined them.

He shook off the feeling and continued his pseudo-moonlit stroll down to the sub bay dock. The reflections of the amber lights that surrounded the bay danced with the ripples of the water. The ripples indicated that a sub was in the tunnel.

As he passed the bay, he could clearly see the many bright lights of commercial sector one. This sector contained the first shops to set up business in Bojoa. The sector was in a good place for shops and restaurants. It was near enough to the docks to be the first thing travelers saw when they exited a sub. Since subs arrived all the time, the businesses in commercial sector one stayed open all the time. He could have taken the lift to the commercial sector, but he had felt like walking, and it really didn't take any longer to walk since the lift junction was toward the middle of the commercial sector.

When he reached the dock, the sub was just breaking the surface of the bay. The hull of the massive sub appeared darker than normal in the moonlight. It appeared to be dingy grey, though he knew that the yellow of the iri present in the sub would show in better light. Within a few spens, the passenger door opened and people began to exit the sub. Noso must have been seated near one of the ends of the sub away from the main hatch, since he was nearly the last to exit the sub. When he saw Noso, he darted through the crowd and met him just as he stepped off the dock ramp.

Noso was about his height, but that was about the end of the physical similarity between them. Noso's hair was a much darker blonde than his own hair and Noso was of a stockier build than he was, though he certainly wasn't fat.

He placed himself in front of Noso and extended a partially open fist. Noso dropped his carrying cases and reached out to hook his fingers around Agap's fingers. The two men then pulled themselves closer to each other using their intertwined fists for leverage.

By the time Noso had completed grasping fists, he had a bright smile on his face that contrasted sharply with his dull, grey eyes. He said, "Agapoi, you didn't have to meet me. It's the middle of the night after all."

"What's the point of sleeping when I know that you are arriving?" he asked. "Besides, I have an ulterior motive. Can I help you with your bags?"

"Sure," said Noso, picking up a large bag and holding it out. "Here. Take this one. It's the heaviest."

He shook his head, but couldn't help but grin as he took the bag. Noso had always been a bit of a rascal, but he was a likeable rascal. As they were heading out of the dock area, he pointed to a café about a hundred dets away and said, "There's a little café over there. Would you like to get a cup of che?"

Noso glanced toward the café, then back at him and said, "Make it a cup of cefa and you're on."

"Done," he said; and he and Noso headed over to the café.

The name of the café was simply *The Bojoa Café*. It was a small place, having about ten small, round tables for its customers. A couple sat at one of the tables on the right, so he chose a table to the left of the door. They sat down, putting their bags on the floor under the table. The server came and took their order: a hot cup of che for him and a steaming cup of cefa for Noso.

As the server left, he asked, "So, what do you think of Bojoa?"

"It's huge," Noso gushed enthusiastically, making even his dull, gray eyes sparkle. "Erith. Even the sub that brought us here is huge. The simulated moonlight is a nice touch too. I can't wait to see the rest of the place."

He chuckled and said, "I haven't even seen all of Bojoa, and I helped design the place."

Noso laughed. "Well, what are you waiting for? How do you know the place is any good?" he teased good-naturedly as he ran his fingers across his forehead to put a stray strand of his wavy, dark blonde hair back into place.

The server brought their drinks and left. She was an attractive young lady; and Noso, who always had an eye for the ladies, distracted himself by gawking at her until she rounded a corner out of sight. He finally took a sip of his cefa and then asked, "So, what's your ulterior motive that brought you out to meet me tonight?"

"I wanted to ask you about your research on thought wave technology."

"Now that's something to stay up for," said Noso sarcastically while letting his gray eyes grow wide to feign surprise.

He mused how Noso's dull eye color belied his gregarious personality. "Well, there are circumstances that make your knowledge of the technology important," he said in an exaggeratedly defensive tone.

"If by that you mean that there is suspicion that my team had some information stolen, I know all about that," said Noso more seriously. "An investigator by the name of Kenun wants to talk to Psawton and me about it later on today."

The mention of Psawton made him curious. "Where is Psawton?" he asked. "I didn't see him come off the sub."

"He was lucky enough to catch an earlier sub, so he's probably asleep," answered Noso as if he wished that were what he was doing.

A slight grin crossed his face, but it quickly faded as his thoughts returned to the investigation. "It is true that Kenun is investigating the theft of technology research," he began, "but it might or might not be your team's research that he wants to talk to you about."

Noso cut off a sip, spilling a little bit of cefa on the table in front of him. "Now look what you've made me do, Agapoi. I can't even drink around you." He grabbed a paper napkin and blotted at the spill. Once he had the spillage contained, he turned his attention back to the conversation. "What do you mean it might not be my team's research that he wants to talk about? Why would he ask me about some other team's research?"

"Psawton worked on my team before he worked on yours."

Noso put his cup down and studied him for a moment. "Is your team being investigated?" he asked.

"It is."

Noso said nothing, which was unusual for him, but he knew by his demeanor that he was expecting more.

"There is a very good chance that some dead transporter research was stolen from my team between two and a half and three years ago."

Noso shook his head and gave an exaggerated shrug while lifting his hands and said, "But if it was dead research, who would want to steal it?"

"It wasn't stolen to use as transporter technology. The thief saw another use for it."

Noso made a continuing motion with one hand and said, "And that use was?"

"A weapon," he said bluntly.

Noso sat back in his seat. "Then we're not talking about a rival Cirrian team ending up with this research, are we?"

He shook his head and said in a semi-whisper, "Doetora. One of our prototypes is identical to a new weapon platform they built."

"Our security systems have never been breached. That's why all the banks in Kosundo are based in Cirri," said Noso softly. Then, after he was silent a moment, he exclaimed in a slightly louder tone, "Kenun believes that it was an inside job!"

"It's really the only viable course of reasoning," he said, casting his blue eyes down to peer into his cup. "Since we labeled the research dead, it was only given level three encryption and level four security internally."

"Which means that any twice-honored Cirrian could gain access to the information without causing any security logs to be created," Noso said.

He nodded.

Noso was silent for a moment and then said, "You said that Kenun might or might not want to talk to me about my team's research." Noso paused, and Agap again nodded as he took a sip of che. Noso stared at his cefa for a while before picking it up, but then he put it down again almost immediately. His dull eyes became remarkably sharp as he gazed directly at him. "You wanted to talk with me about thought wave research. Do you have reason to believe this research was stolen as well?"

"There is some evidence that the weapon platform might be using thought wave technology to control it," he said softly just before taking another sip of his che.

Noso closed his eyes and said, "A little over two and a half years ago, our team classified the neural cap as dead technology due to a refusal of funding by council." He opened his eyes and fixed his eyes on him. "There can be only one use for the neural cap," he said slowly. "To allow one-person control—*of a weapon platform*? That's madness."

He slowly nodded and said, "Apparently, the Edvukaat agreed with you."

"The Edvukaat?" said Noso incredulously. "Tryllos?"

He bobbed his head vigorously this time as he said, "The platform is called Avenger. It is a weapon of mass destruction."

Noso wore a grin as he bounced his head vigorously imitating him exaggeratively as he said, "Axi, axi." After his head stopped moving, his visage became very serious. "I guess it was important enough to stay up for after all."

"I don't really know if I should have told you all of this, so do me a favor and act surprised if Kenun asks you about it," he said softly.

Noso raised an eyebrow at him, doubting the motive for the request.

"I am not under orders of silence, Noso. I just would rather Kenun not know I spoiled his surprise. He can get a little put-out about that sort of thing."

Noso smirked and resumed drinking his cefa. "So what do you want to know about the neural cap?" he asked.

"Just one thing really," he said. "What's its range?"

"As far as I know, the cap has infinite range," said Noso.

That wasn't what he had wanted to hear. He slumped down in his seat. "Infinite?" he asked incredulously.

Noso picked up on his mood and answered in detail. "The neural cap transmits thought waves the same way the mind produces them. It just concentrates them so that a receiver can easily pick them up. Thought waves are not like sound or energy waves. They do not fully travel in the physical dimension. They skim along the surface of the physical dimension, and I presume that they also travel in another dimension—call it the spiritual dimension for a lack of a better term. Thought waves are not subject to the same limitations that purely physical waves are. If our physical brains could better transmit and receive thought waves, we could communicate to anyone, anywhere. Certain scientists have had limited success with this kind of communication in the human mind, but it takes an extremely disciplined mind to be able to communicate this way. They believe that our physical brains actually block the mind's telepathic ability, whereas our actual minds can naturally communicate telepathically in the spiritual dimension."

Noso had said a mouthful. He hadn't considered that the thought waves would not be a purely physical wave. "So how does the neural cap know where to send the thought waves?"

"You're still thinking in the physical dimension," said Noso. "Thought waves are sent everywhere at the same time. The receiver of the thought waves is determined by the mind. The cap just interprets the mind's message into a coded impulse which the intended receiver will be able to interpret into machine code. The code that we used was based on minute pattern differences. It was the only way. Conventional coding would become too complex to communicate a rudimentary thought instantly, let alone a complex thought, like a command."

"I see," he said thoughtfully. "And how can the user of the cap know where the receiver is if he can't see it?"

"A mind display. We created a mind display to let the cap wearer know the relative position of the receiver or the location of anything else that can be scanned by the receiver or other sensor arrays in the area. It can be overlaid on a map or on radar readout or any number of other position-relative displays. The person who wears the neural interface can command and access the sensor information as well as the displays mentally." Noso sat back before saying, "The user of the interface has more data available to him about the receiver's surroundings than he would if he were physically with the receiver."

"That would make it possible to control something like Avengers quite easily then," he said numbly.

Noso nodded absently and the two of them sat silently for a time.

As he beheld his old friend, he saw him in a different light than before. He had always known that Noso was brilliant, but he had no idea just how brilliant he was before now. He just hoped that some of his brilliance wouldn't be coming back to haunt them soon.

He brought himself out of his thoughts to glance at his watch. It was getting quite late. He could stay up all night talking with Noso, but that wouldn't be fair to him. He had to talk to Kenun today. He should let Noso get to his quarters. "Well, it's getting late, Noso, and you have an important interview to attend today. May I walk you to the LC?"

"Oh great," said Noso in mock disgust, "Another acronym. What's up with us technical guys that we can't call anything by its full name?"

"Axi. May I walk you to the living complex then?" he said with a chuckle.

"Certainly. I guess I should get to bed before too long. Besides, I am looking forward to riding one of your newfangled lifts that I've heard so much about," said Noso lightly.

"You mean you're not going to set up your room tonight?" he kidded.

"I was told a bed would be in the room. That's all I am going to think about tonight," said Noso with a wave of his hand.

"At least yours has that much set up," he said. "Mine was completely bare."

"Well, I am glad that that is no longer the case," said Noso, smiling. "I'm not sure I could figure out that chomile thing this late at night."

"Oh. Well, you know we made that change just for you," said a grinning Agap. "I hope you appreciate it."

Noso gave him a deadpan expression; and with that, the two men retreived Noso's bags and headed toward the living complex. As they walked, he couldn't help but think that his greatest fear seemed to be coming true. Technology stolen from his team could very well hurt people, and not just a few. He could only hope that Doetora had all of the Avenger technology secured by now. If they didn't, there would be little to stop Tryllos from wreaking havoc on Kosundo.

CHAPTER
TWENTY-SEVEN
THE FLYING HAWK

It was just a little after the ninth parz, Manku City time, on the tenth of Setmi. The day had brought a whirlwind of activity from the newly crowned Emperor Abinos. He had successfully reappointed Temeon Lord Director Temeos and had created a new office for Varnupud. By creating the office of chief inspector general, he had streamlined a rather antiquated and unnecessarily complicated investigatory system. Now one man could coordinate all efforts as all investigators ultimately reported to only one person. It was a brilliant move. Temeos hoped it was a brilliant enough move to find Tryllos.

Temeos had been busy himself. He had arranged for Abinos's broadcast to be aired in the open. That took some doing. It had been over two hundred years since any government broadcast had aired openly in Doetora. He couldn't count how many people he had to talk to before he found anyone who had the slightest idea how to unscramble an encrypted channel for the broadcast.

Unfortunately, he didn't have the same success in contacting Odanoi for Abinos. It seemed that Odanoi was in transit and could not be contacted. At least that was what he was told. The person at the Cirrian state department said that he would leave a message for Odanoi to contact Abinos once he was available. He wasn't completely sure the offer was sincere though. The man had seemed cordial, but sounded suspicious. He wondered if someone in Cirri had found out that Tryllos had stolen some research data from Cirri. Or maybe the suspicion he sensed was all in his mind. In any case, he had told Abinos the message he received. Abinos simply told him to try again tomorrow, and he would do so.

But that job was for tomorrow. Right now, Tryllos and the Avengers dominated his thoughts. He was currently combing the Avenger project reports, hoping to find anything that he might have missed before that would help him find the Avengers. He had been going through the reports for nearly a parz now; but so far, he had found nothing in any of the reports that could point to a time the Avengers could have left the hangar.

He was growing desperate. After having taken statements from the project staff yesterday, Varnupud had learned that the cap that Tryllos possessed was theoretically capable of controlling the Avengers from anywhere in Kosundo.

He had reviewed the statements taken just after the Avengers went missing as well as the order of events from security and compared them with the most recent staments from the staff. The recent statements told the same story. The project staff finished their routine maintenance checks at six parzes on Titarti. Security followed up with routine checks a few spens later. But when Varnupud showed up around the seventh parz, the Avengers were missing. What could have happened in less than a parz?

He found the interview reports with the two guards assigned to the hangar. The guards said that they didn't hear or see anything during that time. The only thing they reported was a feeling of disorientation. Apparently, both of them had felt it. It was strange that both would have a brief moment of disorientation at about the same time. It could be that someone had drugged the guards, but their scans didn't reveal any drugs in their system. Still, the simple drugging of two guards wouldn't explain how no one else saw or heard anything. The Avengers weren't overly noisy, but they did make a distinct humming noise that someone should have heard if Tryllos or anyone else had activated them. If a large vehicle was used to carry them out, someone would definitely have noticed. The project complex had only one gate with two checkpoints. No vehicles were checked out between the sixth and seventh parz on Titarti, and no flying crafts were observed.

He sighed and put aside the investigation reports. All the reports just led to the conclusion that the Avengers still had to be in their hangar. Yet they were not in their hangar. He had thoroughly verified that fact. Maybe the answer lay somewhere in the project history.

He got up from his chair at his dining room table where he had all the reports scattered about and went to his dataterm at his desk in the main room. He had asked that all files pertinent to the Avenger storage and maintenance be forwarded to his dataterm. He sat down at the dataterm station and touched the dataterm screen. The dataterm came to life and displayed a message that he had hoped to see. He had received the download. He brought up the download with his pointing instrument and saw that there were five hundred thirty-two files in the download. On the screen before him, the entire history of records concerning the storage and maintenance of the Avengers was displayed.

He rubbed his forehead. It would take him the better part of two days to go through these files if he sat at his dataterm all day. He just didn't have that much time. He decided to do a search on files pertaining to the construction of the hangar. The display listed only a dozen results. That number was a little more manageable. He sifted through reports and images on the construction of the hangar. Not surprisingly, the images of the outside of the newly constructed hangar appeared to be identical to the current hangar. He searched on images of the construction of the interior of the hangar to see if perhaps Tryllos had put in a secret area of some sort. He was disappointed to see that the images of the designs for the hangar didn't reveal any hidden rooms or passageways. There was only the main hangar bay and the service bay, separated by a half wall, just as he had seen when he had entered the hangar on Titarti.

Then he saw a panoramic image of the completed interior of the hangar. As the image panned around the interior of the hangar, he saw a flying hawk painted on the west wall. He didn't remember seeing anything painted on the west wall of the hangar when he had been in the hangar on Titarti. As he recalled, the wall was just painted white. The hawk symbol could have been painted over with white. Still, the hawk symbol was the symbol of the Emperor, and this was the Emperor's project. Why would the Emperor approve painting over his symbol?

He turned back to his search on the screen. It showed still more images. As he searched through them, it appeared just to be more shots of the same hangar, but as he came to the last one, it showed a completed hangar's interior with a white west wall without a hawk. It looked identical to the other image except for the hawk. He quickly referenced the text accompanying the image. The text indicated that the image was of the completed interior of the auxiliary Avenger hangar. *Auxiliary Avenger hangar? I thought there was only one Avenger hangar.* He quickly brought up the text for the other image, the one with a hawk on the wall. The text indicated that it was an image for the completed interior of the main Avenger hangar.

There were two hangars. Why did he think that there was only one hangar? Why did the project staff and guards not say anything about another hangar?

Immediately, he contacted Varnupud on his commterm. After Varnupud answered, he said, "Get some men together and get over to the Avenger complex. There is a second Avenger hangar."

"But we asked everyone if there was another place that the Avengers could be stored, and they all said that there wasn't," protested Varnupud.

"I realize that," he said "but I am staring at the image of a second hangar with the symbol of the flying hawk on the west wall."

"A flying hawk?" asked Varnupud. There was a pause for just a tic and then Varnupud said, "I am on my way, Lord Director."

"Good. I will meet you there once I inform Abinos," he said, and he ended the conversation.

Immediately, he activated the contact icon for Abinos.

Momentarily, Abinos answered, "Temeos, I am surprised to hear from you at this time of night. Is there something wrong?"

"No, My Lord," he said with enthusiasm. "There just might be something right." That answer caused Abinos to look curiously at him through the commterm, so he explained. "I was searching through the construction records of the Avenger complex. I found that there were two hangars constructed."

"Two?" asked Abinos with a confused cast to his face. "You've been to the Avenger complex on a couple of occasions while Tryllos was still in office. How could you not know that there were two hangars?"

"I think I did know," he said slowly. "I just didn't recall until now for whatever the reason."

Abinos really appeared to be perplexed now. "How could you not recall the fact that there is a second hangar?"

"I am not sure, Abinos," he said, "but I think it's the same reason the staff didn't recall it and the guards felt disoriented and then ended up guarding an empty hangar. Something isn't right here, and I am going down to the complex to find out exactly what it is."

"Axi, Temeos," said Abinos. "I will meet you there."

"With all due respect, My Lord," he said urgently. "I would prefer that you stay at the palace. If something is amiss, the complex might be a dangerous place to be. Your position demands that you don't put yourself in harm's way unnecessarily, Abinos."

"Axi, Temeos. I will bow to your judgment, but let me know what you find as soon as you can," said Abinos.

"I will be in immediate contact, My Lord. I am on my way now," he said as he hustled out the door putting his commterm away as he went.

He took his personal hovercraft to the complex, disobeying numerous speed regulations. There was an urgency to get to the site that he couldn't rationally justify. Even at precariously high speed, it seemed to take forever to get there. But he finally got to the complex and once he did, he found Varnupud accompanied by thirty of his men, talking to the project lead, a man by the name of Zhartve. Zhartve was a shorter man. He wasn't fat but he was certainly stout. He sported a thick, dark mustache below a slightly crooked nose. The two men were talking when Temeos approached and he listened in on the conversation.

"A flying hawk?" said Zhartve, thoughtfully scratching his mustache. He was an Ispra man with a ruddy complexion. "Well, now that you mention it, I do seem to recall that there was a flying hawk symbol on the hangar wall, but it's not there now … " Zhartve let his speech drift off into thought.

"Glad to see that you could make it," said Varnupud with a slight grin.

"Yeah, I always thought having quarters a little bit away from the palace was a good idea — before tonight.

Zhartve finally broke from his thought to say, "Come with me." The man then went into a fast hobble toward the control building in the middle of the complex. They had no choice but to follow him.

Zhartve's gait was noticeably halted. Temeos knew from previous conversations with the man that his limp was the result of a beating that Tryllos had ordered. Zhartve called his limp a "gift" from Emperor Tryllos.

As he caught up with Zhartve, Zhartve glanced toward him as he said, "There is a map of the complex stored on the backup dataterm server in the control building. The other maps of the complex show only one hangar. I now believe that someone changed those maps, but they might not have thought to change the map on the backup server."

That sounded like it was worth a shot so he nodded, and Zhartve increased his pace with a grimace on his face. It was painful for him to watch Zhartve's halted gait, but he still had to walk faster than normal to keep up with him.

Once they were inside the control building, they hurried through the halls until they came to the main control room. Zhartve shooed a technician aside and sat down at the main dataterm to access the backup server. It took him only tics to connect to the server; and in a few more tics, he displayed a map of the complex on the main migoterm in the room.

He went in front of the migoterm to view the map when he saw it there. Zhartve and Varnupud joined him. He looked at the southern part of the complex. That is where the empty hangar was. He found the hangar. It was marked Auxiliary Avenger Hangar. "They didn't change it," he said excitedly. "See? The empty hangar is marked as the auxiliary. But where is the main hangar?"

"In the northern part of the complex, there!" exclaimed Zhartve while pointing to a building marked Avenger Hangar on the map. "It is on the north side of the complex, a couple of buildings away from the living quarters," finished Zhartve. Then he scratched his head and said, "I remember it now, but how could I have forgotten it? I was thinking that the hangar seemed to be further from the living quarters than it used to be, but I never remembered a second hangar."

"Don't worry about your memory, Zhartve," reassured Temeos. "It appears that everyone around here had forgotten it. I don't know how, but someone managed to cloud every mind in the complex concerning this hangar. If I hadn't seen that image of the flying hawk in the construction records, I wouldn't have remembered it either."

"Thanks for the reassurance, Lord Director, but somehow, it doesn't make me feel any more settled," said Zhartve.

"I know what you are feeling, Zhartve," he said, "but right now, let's get out to that hangar." He quickly made his way to the door of the control room, navigated the halls and broke into a trot as he headed for the place where the map indicated that the Avenger hangar was. He could hear the others following close behind.

Being in the center of the complex, he had to go around several buildings before the hangar would be in sight. As he rounded the last building, he came to a sudden halt. In front of him was—nothing. There was a row of miniature trees to his right, but there was no building. There was just empty ground in front of him.

"It's not here!" he exclaimed.

As the rest of the group caught up and stopped behind him, collective disbelief registered on their faces as they stared at the empty ground in front of them.

"Zhartve," he said, "this is the right place, isn't it? I mean, this is where the hangar should be, isn't it?"

Zhartve slowly shook his head but said, "Yes. It should be here. Who could have managed to take a whole building?"

He went closer to the site. "Maybe," he said slowly, "no one took it at all."

Varnupud moved next to him, staring at the empty ground. The chief inspector said quietly to him, "But, Lord Director, the hangar is not here."

"Yes, Varnupud," he said in a normal tone. "The hangar is not here, but something else is not here either."

Both Varnupud and Zhartve, who had moved beside him, looked at him quizzically.

"Don't you see?" he said glancing in turn at both men and then pointing at the ground in front of him. "There are no holes—no disturbed ground. The footing and weight of the hangar would have left holes or at least signs that a building had been here. Instead, all we see is undisturbed ground."

Realization showed on Varnupud's and Zhartve's faces at the same time.

Varnupud shouted to his men who were behind them, "All of you, fan out and walk ahead of us. Stop if you run into something that you can't see."

Varnupud's men appeared confused, but they obeyed. They fanned out and walked forward slowly, with their hands in front of them.

He watched as they walked. Soon, one of them stopped and shouted, "I just ran into something!"

Soon another one stopped, and then another. Eight men had stopped altogether, but the others continued to walk on either side of the eight.

A huge smile came across Varnupud's face and he gave him a delighted glance before he shouted, "All of you who are still walking, stop. Look where the others have stopped, and form a line perpendicular to them on both sides."

His men stopped and slowly made the lines on either side of the eight men.

"Now," shouted Varnupud, "walk forward and stop when you hit something." The men walked slowly forward.

Each of them stopped in a line that was perpendicular to the first eight men.

Varnupud had excitement all over his face. He nodded to him and said, "There, Zhartve. There is your missing hangar. It is not missing at all. We just couldn't see it."

"Amazing," was all that Zhartve said before he started limping toward Varnupud's men. Then he turned back and said, "Come. I think I know where the hangar door is."

Temeos and Varnupud followed a short distance behind Zhartve. He went toward the line of men who were perpendicular and to the right of the first eight. He felt between the second and third man. "Here!" he said. "I can feel the door. Now, if I can just find the security pad. There it is!" He heard some beeps as Zhartve's fingers seemingly wriggled about in the air. Then he heard a lower tone. "I've unsealed the door," said Zhartve excitedly. "Help me open it."

He sprang ahead of Varnupud and went to where Zhartve was standing. He felt and found what felt like a flat surface sticking out from the rest of the surface. He and Zhartve then gave a mighty shove. They nearly fell down as the surface moved; but as it moved, the interior of a hangar appeared where nothing was seen before. Soon, the exterior became visible too. It was as if someone had taken blinders from their eyes. From their reactions, it seemed that everyone there could now see the hangar. Varnupud's men stepped back in disbelief as the hanger appeared right before their eyes.

He shoved the door farther open and peered inside. Before him were all thirty-five Avengers. They were arranged in formations and glistened under lights that had automatically activated shortly after the door was opened. He stepped inside and looked toward the west wall. There on the wall was the image of the flying hawk. He was nearly beside himself with relief so much so that tears began to form in his eyes. He stepped back and gazed at the Avengers fearing they might disappear if he took his eyes off them. Once his mind fully accepted what his eyes told him, he was able to consider his next move. It was then that he rememebered his promise to his emperor. He immediately pulled out his commterm and contacted Abinos.

Abinos answered right away. "Temeos, what have you found?"

He was still fighting back tears of joy and relief, but he still managed to say, "We have found them, Abinos. We have found them." He then turned his commterm around to show Abinos the Avengers.

When he turned the commterm back around, a smiling Abinos said, "Well done, Temeos. So, there was a second hangar. Well done indeed."

A now-recovered Temeos asked, "How do you want the Avengers secured, My Lord?"

Abinos's face became serious, and he said, "I do not want them secured, Lord Director."

He felt his heart drop. Thoughts raced through his mind. *Could it be that Abinos was just as mad as his uncle Tryllos was? Why would he not want the Avengers secured?* But all he said was, "My Lord?"

Abinos's countenance grew even more serious as he said, "I want the Avengers destroyed, Lord Director. Wipe them off the face of Kosundo."

He drew a quick sigh of relief and said, "Yes, My Lord. I will have Varnupud see to it immediately."

"Good. Let me know when they are destroyed," said Abinos.

"I will, My Lord," he said gladly.

He then turned to Varnupud and told him, "Emperor Abinos wants the Avengers destroyed." He then turned to Zhartve and asked, "What can be used to destroy the Avengers?"

Zhartve looked at Temeos as if in shock, and tears began streaming down his cheek.

Temeos felt for the man. He had spent years on this project and endured many sorrows in the name of the Avengers. It was no wonder he would get emotional to think of destroying them. So he said softly, "Zhartve, I know it's hard to think of destroying something that has cost you so much, but they must be destroyed. You can see that, can't you?"

Zhartve shook his head, but he saw a smile on his face, "No," said Zhartve. "You've misread my tears. I want the Avengers destroyed. If I had an oggi of courage, I would have destroyed them as soon as I saw them tested the first time. These tears—they are for joy."

He couldn't help but smile as he said, "So you will tell us how to destroy them then?"

"I will do you one better than that, Lord Director," said Zhartve, wiping his eyes on his sleeve. "I have secretly collected some explosives along with a remote detonator just in case I ever got up the nerve to destroy these monstrosities. I will show your men the explosives. Have them put the charges just above the weapon rod arm. You can tell where the weapon arm is by the round grooves you see in the outer hull of the Avenger. Set the charge to discharge inwardly. The charge will take out the Avenger's power supply as well as its weapon arm, effectively destroying their attacking capabilities. We should hurry; Tryllos could activate the Avengers at any time through his control interface." Zhartve started to limp away toward his secret stash.

"Well," he said, clapping his hands together, "you heard the man. Go with him. Let's see if we can destroy these little monsters before midnight."

Varnupud smiled and said, "My pleasure, sir." He then called, "You four men, come with me. The rest of you, watch these things. If they make the slightest noise, start shooting. Maybe you'll get lucky and destroy a few of them."

He watched as Varnupud and his men followed Zhartve. If his men's weapons could do anything against the Avengers, he was sure that Zhartve would have just told him that. Varnupud was just trying to put a little bravado into his men. He didn't know if it worked too well though. He noticed the nervous faces on the men Varnupud left behind. If hand weapons were not effective, he thought it best to have a contingency plan; so he took out his commterm and contacted Abinos.

"Did you manage to destroy them so quickly, Temeos?" asked Abinos.

"No, My Lord, but Varnupud is obtaining some explosives to take care of them now," he said quickly. "I need to ask your permission to get some attack aircraft off the ground to take out the Avengers, should any of them suddenly activate. The aircraft would be attacking targets in Doetoran territory, so I need your approval before giving the order."

"Certainly. You may order the aircraft. Are you sure I shouldn't be down there with you?" asked Abinos.

"I am certain, My Lord. I have learned that Tryllos could activate his Avengers at anytime from anywhere. You need to keep your distance, in case he should do so," said Temeos.

"Axi, Temeos. I will stay where I am. Good luck," said Abinos, and the communication ended.

He pressed the aircraft icon on his commterm display. That put him in touch with Manku Air Command and he ordered the aircraft. Command told him that five squadrons would be airborne within eight spens. He glanced at the time. It was 9:89. He grumbled over the length of time to get airborne, but it was late at night. Men would, no doubt, have to be rousted from bed to make up five complete squadrons so he decided that eight spens was not that slow after all. They were not at war, after all, and that was the way he wanted it to stay.

He paced impatiently, waiting for Varnupud and his men to return. His anxiety was palpable. He had envisioned a moment like this on the day he first heard of project Avenger over seven years ago. He was now moments away from stopping the most horrific machines ever conceived by man from unleashing terror against all of Kosundo.

Time passed. It was now 9:92. Finally, he saw Varnupud and Zhartve followed by four men carrying four decent-sized wooden crates.

As they approached, Varnupud said apologetically, "I am sorry we took so long. The explosives were well-hidden, and it took time to get to them."

He nodded his head and said, "All is well. Let me help you get the explosives unboxed." He had the habit of carrying a small but handy tool in his pocket since he was a boy. It could be used to cut things and to open all sorts of things. It was called an ubche. It resembled a retracting knife in shape, but it could do some amazing things. He took out his ubche and opened up a part of the ubche that was used for prying. It had a flat edge that could be put between two surfaces. He put the prying edge under one of the crate lids. He continually pushed a button, and the ubche moved the lid upward as his hand rose with the lid. In no time, the lid was opened. He had all four boxes opened nearly before they were all put on the ground.

"Handy little thing," said Zhartve to him.

"Yes, I like it," he said and put the ubche back in his pocket. He really didn't know how it worked, but it was said to be mechanical; there was no electronic technology involved. It worked, which was all he really needed to know about it.

Varnupud barked out commands, and soon his men were unpacking the explosives.

He peered down at his watch. It was now 9:93. Temeos leaned over and whispered to Varnupud, "Have the men arm the detonators as soon as the explosives are attached to the hull of each Avenger."

Varnupud gave him a curious look, but he ordered the arming of the explosives on the fly, which meant to arm them immediately after setting the charge. It wasn't the safest way to arm, but it was better to have some of the Avengers set to explode than getting useless explosives on all of them. He just had a gnawing feeling that they wouldn't get the job completed in time.

The explosives were inert in the box, so each charge had to be fitted with its detonator fuse before it could be attached. It took about a spen to attach the fuses; but only three of Varnupud's men knew how to work with these types of explosives so only those three could fit the fuses. Three other men attached the explosives to the hulls of the Avengers, but most of Varnupud's men could only stand by and watch. It was a slow process—painfully slow from his perspective. Thankfully, the charges could be remotely detonated so no timer had to be set, which saved a little bit of time.

He too could only watch as Varnupud's men worked. He nervously looked down at his watch to see when the aircraft were due to be airborne. It was 9:95 now. Another two spens and he would have aircraft as a backup. Another ten spens and Varnupud's men would have the charges set. He paced and watched and watched and paced.

As he turned during his pacing, he noticed Zhartve's face grow pale. He stopped pacing immediately as he watched him. A moment later, he saw Zhartve's mouth move. It appeared that he said, "Oh no." Then dread filled his mind as he became aware of a sound emanating from the Avengers. The sound was a subdued humming noise.

He turned to find Varnupud. Once he saw him, he shouted, "Varnupud, get your men out of the hangar!" He watched as Varnupud barked the command and the men scrambled to clear the hangar. He took a frantic glance at his watch. It was 9:97. The attack aircraft should now be airborne. He should hear from them any tic now.

Zhartve ran haltingly toward him, pointing and shouting, "Don't let them shoot at them!"

His eyes went to where Zhartve was pointing. He saw a couple of Varnupud's men taking aim at the Avengers. "Don't shoot at them!" he cried, running toward the men. "Don't shoot! Everyone, hold your fire!" he shouted again.

Varnupud joined in shouting, "Hold your fire! Hold! Hold!"

The men held their fire but stood close by the Avengers. They were too close to the Avengers. He shouted at Varnupud again, "Get your men away from the Avengers so we can detonate." There were explosives on only a few of the Avengers. He desperately wanted to set off the explosives while the Avengers were still close together in an enclosed area.

Varnupud vehemently shouted out orders to his men to come away from the Avengers. However, by the time the men started to comply, the Avengers began to rise up, coming to a stationary hover about six dets off the hangar floor. Then, in unison, they moved out of the hangar, hovered again for just a moment, and then moved upward at a steep angle at full speed. He watched intently as they settled into a southwest course.

Although his commterm gave no alert signal, he heard a voice on his commterm. It had to be the flight leader of the attack aircraft. Only the military could break onto a commterm without an alert signal. He held up his commterm to see the flight leader in his cockpit. "This is Lord Director Temeos," he said.

"This is Flight Leader Khurshilut. I am leading the attack aircraft group you ordered up," said the flight leader.

"How long until you are over the Avenger complex?"

"Two spens, sir," said the flight leader.

"Axi. Proceed to the complex," he said. "I will contact you shortly with your orders. Keep the channel open."

"Yes, sir. Proceeding to complex coordinates. Will stay on line," said the flight leader.

He put his commterm on mute and turned to Zhartve, who was still staring upward, although the Avengers could no longer be seen in the nighttime sky. He tapped him on the shoulder, startling him. "How much range do we have on the remote detonator?" he asked.

"Oh — one hundred stets," said Zhartve once he regained his bearings.

"Good. Then we still have some time," he said half to himself.

"We have about eight spens before they are out of range, Lord Director," volunteered Zhartve.

He nodded to indicate that he understood and then said, "They aren't attacking."

Zhartve shook his head. "No, it is as I thought. Tryllos is just bringing the Avengers to him. They won't attack unless they are being attacked."

Perhaps he should just let them fly away. He shook his head at the thought. They might not be attacking now, but they surely would soon after they reached Tryllos. "How can they best be attacked by the aircraft?" he asked Zhartve.

"Your best bet is to detonate the explosives that some of the Avengers have on their hulls," explained Zhartve. "Each charge that explodes will trigger a secondary explosion from the Avenger itself. If we are lucky, other Avengers will be close enough to be caught up in the secondary explosions, and then they too will explode. The explosions will allow your attack aircraft the opportunity to target the Avengers. The catch is that the aircraft must fire very soon after the explosions. The proximity of the explosions will temporarily hinder the other Avengers' sensors, but not for long—maybe five or six tics. The aircraft must fire within five tics or they risk being destroyed. The Avengers will slow to attack speed and defend themselves when they are attacked while in transit. It is an automatic feature. Also, the Avengers cannot be detected by tracking systems. They are small and have tracking avoidance features. The pilots will have to aim manually. It will be a difficult task at night. They should shoot using the light from the explosions."

"Understood," said Temeos.

He took the mute off his commterm and said, "Flight Leader Khurshilut."

"I hear you, sir," said Khurshilut.

"I need you to attack a group of Avengers. They are spherical and very small. You will not see them on your tracking terms. Do you understand so far?"

"Understood, Lord Director," said Khurshilut.

"We have managed to attach explosives to some of the Avengers in the group. I will detonate on your mark; but be advised, we have only seven spens until targets are out of remote range. The Avengers are headed on a southwest course from the complex." He paused and asked Zhartve, "Altitude, distance and speed?"

"Altitude is six point five zero stets. Position is estimated at twenty-four stets directly to the southwest of the complex. Cruising speed is twelve hundred stets per parz," shouted Zhartve as the screams of the attack aircraft engines were heard overhead.

He continued with Khurshilut. "Altitude is six point five zero stets. Estimated distance to target is twenty-four stets. Speed is twelve hundred stets per parz. Again, direction is directly southwest of the complex. It is imperative that you manually target and destroy the Avengers within five tics of the explosions caused by the onboard explosives. Targets have lethal counterattack. Do you understand?"

"Understood, sir. Climbing to six point five zero stets, using closing speed of two thousand stets per parz to intercept in three spens and then slowing to twelve hundred stets per parz for attack. Manual targeting upon sighting. Is this a go?" asked Khurshilut.

"It is a go, Flight Leader Khurshilut. Give ten-tic countdown when you desire detonation. Good hunting."

"Ten-tic countdown confirmed. Flight leader out until countdown," said Khurshilut, and the communication ended.

He turned to Varnupud and said, "Be ready to detonate on Flight Leader Khurshilut's mark."

"I stand ready, Lord Director," said Varnupud.

He nodded and then turned to Zhartve and asked, "We have forty aircraft up there. What do you think our chances are of getting all of the Avengers?"

Zhartve's eyes were fixed downward as he said softly, "It is true that we have the advantage of surprise and numbers. But the Avengers have a large targeting and maneuverability advantage. To get some of the Avengers after the explosions, we have a fifty-fifty chance. To get them all — to get them all, I'd say we have a one in a million chance."

He had expected that answer, but he had to ask. *Eight more spens,* he thought, *and we would have had all of the Avengers destroyed — Eight lousy spens.*

He must have said that last phrase aloud because Varnupud turned toward him and asked, "What about eight spens, sir?"

He sighed and said, "If we'd had eight more spens, we would have destroyed the Avengers on the ground."

Varnupud bowed his head. "I have failed you, Lord Director."

He shook his head and said, "Look at me, Varnupud."

Varnupud slowly lifted his eyes to meet Temeos's eyes.

"You have not failed me. Your men did not fail me. You and your men performed admirably. The game was stacked against us. That's all. There is nothing that you could have done better tonight. Do you understand me?"

Varnupud nodded that he understood, but his eyes went back to the ground immediately. He understood where Varnupud's mind was though. He felt much the same and wondered, *What if I had gone over the construction records earlier?* Then a multitude of other what-if's crossed his mind. Yet these thoughts served no purpose. He had to come up with a plan going forward. He just didn't know what that might be should they fail to destroy all the Avengers tonight.

His commterm alert sounded. It was Abinos's tone. He answered by saying, "Abinos, you contacted me just in time. We failed to destroy the Avengers on the ground. The Avengers took off to the southwest. We managed to get explosives onboard some of the Avengers, but we are waiting to detonate in order to coordinate the explosion with the aircraft group's attack on the Avengers. The flight leader will break through on my commterm at any moment to commence a countdown. We will detonate on his mark, and the aircraft will attack using the detonation to help locate their targets."

"That was quite a mouthful, Temeos. What are our chances of success?" asked Abinos.

"We are hopeful, but—." He let his voice cut off, unwilling to finish that last sentence.

"I understand, Temeos. I will stay connected to learn the outcome," said Abinos soberly.

He simply said, "Yes, My Lord."

He waited along with Abinos, Zhartve, Varnupud, and his men for the flight leader's countdown. They didn't have long to wait; in just a couple of moments, the flight leader broke through on the commterm.

"This is Flight Leader Khurshilut. We are in position to begin countdown. Requesting permission to commence attack."

He answered, "We stand ready, Flight Leader. You may commence countdown." Everyone's attention was on his commterm and every word of the flight commander.

"Very well, Lord Director. Commencing countdown for detonation on my mark. Air group, prepare to attack when explosions light your targets. Ten, nine, eight, seven, six, five, four, three, two, one, mark."

Varnupud hit the button on the remote. Explosions could be heard in the flight leader's cockpit over the commterm and then in the distance from the sky. "We have explosions dead ahead. Move in and attack," said the flight leader.

In the background over the commterm, chatter could be heard from the other pilots as they moved in for the attack.

"Targets sighted. I repeat, targets sighted. Shots fired. Shots fired — targets are evading multiple weapon beams — shots fired, sho—," was the last broadcast from the flight leader.

A moment later, multiple explosions were heard seemingly all at once in the sky at a distance. Then there was silence.

He and the rest of his group bowed their heads. It was obvious that the attack was not successful. It couldn't be known that all aircraft were lost at the moment, but he felt it unreasonable to think that any of the aircraft could have survived. As he bowed his head in despair, his eyes caught a glimpse of the commterm in his hand. On the commterm was Abinos's active image. He quickly uttered words of explanation to the emperor. "We failed to destroy the Avengers, My Lord. The number of surviving Avengers is unknown. It is doubtful that any of the attack aircraft survived."

Abinos said, "Thank you, Lord Director. I know you did your best." Abinos's countenance was somber.

Before he could reply to Abinos, Varnupud was tapping him on the shoulder. "One moment, Emperor. Varnupud wants to tell me something," he said. He put the commterm on mute and asked Varnupud, "What is it?"

"The emperor — er—former Emperor Tryllos has been sighted by a contact in Dricho just tics ago. He's at a remote genetics research facility in extreme southern Dricho," Varnupud said breathlessly.

He took off the mute on his commterm. "Varnupud tells me that Tryllos had been spotted just tics ago in a remote facility in extreme southern Dricho," he blurted to Abinos.

"You don't have to ask, Temeos," began Abinos. "Go with Varnupud and his men to the imperial air station immediately. I will make arrangements with the air station for a large, fast craft. Send me the coordinates of the facility. I will make arrangements with the Jontu and Dricho for you to fly in their airspace. You might beat them to Tryllos, if he took the Avengers around the Jontu islands; but be watchful. I will try to get Drichoan authorities out to meet you at the facility, but don't wait for them if you don't see them when you get there. Be quick and decisive. Good hunting, and may Thaoi go with you."

"Thank you, My Lord," he said. As he ended the communication, he couldn't help thinking that Abinos had sure grown into his job in a hurry.

His focus quickly turned to Varnupud. "Varnupud, we are going to Dricho. I hope your men wore some warm underclothing. We are going after Tryllos," he said with a satisfied smile.

Varnupud immediately began barking commands to his men, and soon everyone was on board the large ground transport and on their way to the air station.

The ground transport's ride felt rough. He had grown accustomed to his hovercraft's gliding ride. But there was hope at the end of this ride. He turned to Varnupud and said, "We now have another opportunity, Varnupud. We didn't get the Avengers, but maybe we can capture Tryllos. Without Tryllos, the Avengers are just a ball that can't even fly."

Varnupud smiled at that analogy but said nothing.

He thought about their destination. He didn't know anything existed at the icy tip of southern Dricho. "How is it our contact came to be in such a remote location?" he asked Varnupud.

Varnupud smiled coyly and said, "He was told to follow anything that he thought unusual. I guess he found something unusual that led him there." Varnupud noticed that he didn't smile so his face became sober as he added, "I guess we will have to ask him for details once we get there."

He thought about Varnupud's explanation. Even though it was partially in jest, there was an interesting element to it. The contact found something unusual. He wondered what that something unusual was. They would find out soon enough if Thaoi willed. He just hoped right now that they beat the Avengers to Tryllos. He figured that it would take at least six parzes for them to reach Dricho once they made it into the air. The attack aircraft had overtaken the Avengers, although it had done them little good. Perhaps they would beat them to Dricho. That should make capturing Tryllos easy. With that thought, he settled back to rest his eyes. If no other surprises waited for them, all of this would just be a memory soon—a memory that he would like to forget.

As Tryllos entered his room at the Dricho Genetics Foundation complex, Nenavis felt a shudder go through Tryllos's body. Tryllos had on the black control cap for the Avengers. The shudder had come in response to Tryllos's interaction with the cap. Nenavis had left himself only partially in Tryllos's mind since leaving it earlier to talk to Zlux, so he was not sure what had transpired that caused the shuddering.

Nenavis went fully into Tryllos and decided to address Tryllos directly to see if he could find out what had caused the shudder. *Tryllos, why do you shudder?*

An answer came from Tryllos's mind. *Some of my Avengers were destroyed while I controlled them.*

Nenavis was alarmed at the answer. How could anyone have found the Avengers? He had sent a delusion to everyone who knew about the Avengers. He had made them believe that the auxiliary hangar was the only hangar. He had made them unable to see the main hangar. Who would be clever enough to figure out where the Avengers were? The answer to those questions came unbidden from Tryllos's mind.

Temeos. Temeos has always been there to limit my power, and now he has done it again.

GLOSSARY

AIRCRAFT
a transport vehicle of any size or purpose that becomes airborne using a combination of displacement fields

AXI
a shortened universally accepted colloquialism of the old tongue word antexai, which means all right; common uses of the word include: an affirmative response, a statement of agreement or of a satisfactory condition; sometimes used to indicate an endorsement

CECEO BEANS
the fruit of a tropical plant used widely to make cefa and a particular type of duca called cecolo

CEFA
a drink that is usually served hot made from ground ceceo beans with a smooth taste; considered by some to be an aphrodisiac while others consider it a stimulant.

CHE
a hot or cold drink made from hutale leaves

CHOMILE
a device unique to Bojoa using concentrated energy fields to simulate matter.

CIRRIAN
a person of the nation of Cirri or a person of a race of people with blonde hair and very pale skin

COMM
a visual or non-visual communications device often capable of functions other than communications.

COMMTERM
any kind of communication device that displays images

COMPUTING TERM
a display or computing device with multifunctional capabilities

CORNI
a common meat dish made up of spiced koh meat

DATATERM
a display or computing device used primarily for displaying data with only limited computing functions

DIOTIRI
the first day of the week

DISPLACEMENT FIELD
a field that replaces normal air with lighter than air gases and excited energy contained in several energy fields around a vehicle making the vehicle lighter than air

DRUS
slang indicating excitement, agreement or approval

DUCA
any kind of a sweet treat or candy

EKUREAKI
the last day of the week; also called the weekend

ERITH
a negative exclamation indicating frustration, disappointment or anger; in some cases a neutral exclamation indicating surprise

FLYER
a small two-person aircraft capable of flying at low altitudes

ASA PUBLISHING COMPANY

GELINHE

> a flightless bird about twice the size of a chicken indigenous to northern Grasso; eggs are highly coveted

GROUND TRANSPORT

> a vehicle that moves along the ground, usually employing wheels for locomotion

GUS SAKRATE

> formal title of the Edvukaat secretary

HOVERCRAFT

> any kind of transportation vehicle that is capable of suspended travel above any kind of surface moving faster than ground transports but slower than aircraft

ISPRA

> a person of a race that is characterized by pale skin, but their skin is generally darker than Cirrians

KOH

> very large herbivores that run in very large herds in warmer climates; domesticated widely because of the ease of care and high rate of reproduction; used for meat and leather products; perceived as a lower quality meat, but it is the common meat for most Kosundoans

LEVRA

> a collection of books believed by many to be supernatural words of wisdom and prophecy written by many authors

MIERA

> a person of a race that is characterized by dark brown or black skin

MIGOTERM

> a very large display of any kind of communications or computing device

MUGMI
a person that bears the traits of multiple races

NONATERM
a small display device sometimes capable of computing or communications; widely used for viewing reading material or taking notes; the name is often shortened to nona

PARASKEVI
the fourth day of the week

PETU
a duck-like bird smaller than an earth duck and much quicker in flight

PIRRU
a common metal alloy used in manufacturing and building

POLICHI
old Doetoran word meaning law enforcer

PT
an abbreviation for a personal term used to receive visual programming ranging from news to entertainment; some are capable of three dimensional displays

PUBLIC LINK
a network of computing devices similar to earth's internet

SARK
a simple pull-over shirt common in Cirri

SHEF
a grazing animal with a very thick hairy coat larger than a molare but smaller than a viah; meat is very tender and expensive; the coat makes a versatile fabric

TERM
a general word that referrs to amonitor or an electronic display or an entire computing or data storage device

THAOI
> *a spiritual being believed to be the creator of Kosundo and the universe*

THOUGHT WAVES
> *the radiated energy of active thought whether biological or artificial; the exact nature of the energy is still under debate but it is believed that thought waves are able to bridge dimensions as they travel*

TIGRU
> *a large cat-like animal that has yellow fur with dark blue stripes; does not rely on stealth when hunting, but boldly charges its prey; it is a very fast and agile hunter that relies on speed and brute force to capture its prey*

TITARTI
> *the third day of the week*

TOWRUS
> *a large two-horned grazing animal a little larger than an earth buffalo; towrus is both the singular and plural form of the word*

TRANSLIFT
> *elevator unique to Bojoa capable of multi-directional movement through tubes and on suspension wires*

TRANSPORT
> *a general term for any vehicle used to move people and/or cargo*

TRANSPORTER
> *a device used to instantly transport matter from one place to another*

TRETI
> *the second day of the week*

TSIK
> *a two-wheeled transport powered by a hydrogen fuel*

UBCHE
a multipurpose tool used for cutting, opening and pryin

ASA PUBLISHING COMPANY

CPSIA information can be obtained
at www.ICGtesting.com
Printed in the USA
LVHW01s1601111217
559406LV00014B/2271/P